SILVERTIP SHIFTERS

BOOKS 1 - 4

J.K. HARPER

HUNTER'S MOON | MOUNTAIN BEAR'S BABY | TAMING HER BEAR | RESCUE BEAR

Hunter's Moon | Mountain Bear's Baby | Taming Her Bear | Rescue Bear

---

HUNTER'S MOON: QUENTIN
a crossover story in the Silvertip Shifters and Black Mesa Wolves worlds

A wolf shifter fighting her heart's desire...
Abby Kenyon belongs to Quentin Walker heart, body, and soul. But she's a wolf shifter from the pure Black Mesa Wolves Pack, and he's one big brute of a bear shifter from the mixed Silvertip Shifters clan. She can't have a bear as a mate.

Or can she?

A bear shifter determined to claim his mate...
Quentin Walker knows down to his bones that Abby is his mate. But she's never seen a mated wolf/bear pair and is certain it can't work. The autumn full moon mating run is Quentin's last chance to prove that only he can win the hunt for his mate's heart...

MOUNTAIN BEAR'S BABY: SHANE

A bear shifter who found a fresh start in life...
Rough, tough grizzly bear shifter Shane Walker left behind his gritty fighting past in the city for a fresh start. Living with his extended family at the shifter-only Silvertip Lodge in the beautiful, soothing mountains of Colorado changed him for the better. Now it's almost Christmas, everything is jingly and bright, and his life is pretty much perfect.

A woman seeking a safe haven for her bear shifter son...
Until Jessie McMillan, the passionate three-night stand he also left behind without saying good-bye, unexpectedly shows up in town with a shocking bombshell: her cute little baby boy is Shane's son.

And a little sprinkle of holiday magic to create some lasting joy.
Stunned at the news, Shane first runs like hell from the huge reveal that he is a father. But he must rein in his wild bear so he doesn't ruin what might turn out to be the most joyous holiday he's ever had: one with his precious son and the amazing woman who just might be his mate.

TAMING HER BEAR: BECKETT

.

A dragon shifter who fled her past...

Pix Camden hails from a powerful line of dragon shifters, but she left their controlling ways behind long ago. Now she lives by her wits, footloose and fancy-free. Yet something big is still missing—until she meets wild bear shifter Beckett and he tempts her restless heart.

A bear shifter out of control...

Beckett North can hardly contain his unruly bear on the best of days. Then he meets the captivating Pix. Even though she soothes his savage beast, he can tell she's hiding something from him, and it threatens to drive his bear mad. Yet the fiery vixen is his mate—and he'll do whatever it takes to spend the rest of his life with her.

RESCUE BEAR: CORTEZ

A woman on the run...

After Haley's life disastrously imploded, trusting a man again is out of the question. Seeking a new life, she lands in the mountain shifter town of Deep Hollow, home to the Silvertip grizzly bear clan. When she meets rowdy bear shifter Cortez, her life might change again—if she can allow herself to trust him.

A bear shifter on the edge...
Thrill seeker Cortez lived life on a risky edge—until a terrible accident changed everything. Tormented by his failure to protect his friends, he now struggles to control his troubled inner bear. Then he meets Haley and faces the biggest risk of all: opening his heart to claim the fascinating woman as his mate.

A shifter town about to join together to battle unknown enemies.
But when Haley's ugly past catches up to her, it will take more than Cortez's protective instincts and her own untapped inner strength to face it. It will take an entire town of wild shifter magic to unleash the fierce courage needed to protect everyone's safety—and to bring together two hearts destined to belong to one another.

HUNTER'S MOON: QUENTIN

*Q*uentin Walker watched as the gorgeous woman in his bed stretched her arms overhead, shamelessly exposing to him the stunning bounty of her breasts. He leaned down again to taste the taut, peaked nipple closest to him, but she playfully swatted his head away.

"Quentin." Abby Kenyon's sweet, sexy voice trembled with laughter as well as the aftereffects of her several mind-blowing orgasms just moments before. "I have to leave. If you start touching me again, I won't be able to."

His inner bear uttered a possessive rumble as Quentin ignored her. He bent his head back down to feast on her sweetness. Abby's soft groan as his tongue slipped around the tight nipple was enough to bring life roaring back into his cock, which had found its release in her sweet depths not just once but already twice this morning.

"Quentin..." Her voice took on the breathy quality he loved to hear. The tone that said she was letting go, that she was focusing only on him and his touch.

The tone of the woman he knew was his mate, no matter the fact that she still denied that truth with every ounce of saucy determination she possessed.

He huffed to himself even as he tasted her sweet curves, one of his hands traveling over the silken slide of skin across her hip and thigh. Abby Kenyon was his mate. He knew it, his bear knew it, every shifter in town knew it. The only one who didn't seem to know it, the only one who could look it right in the face and call it impossible, was the sweet, soft woman dissolving beneath his touch right now. The gorgeous wolf shifter who had been brought up to believe she could only ever mate another wolf, a pack wolf like herself.

Never a big brute of a guy like a bear shifter.

His possessiveness rising stronger at the thought of Abby giving herself to anyone but him, Quentin lightly bit her nipple even as his fingers quested toward that sweet, creamy vee between her legs again. Abby gasped, the sound filled with desire. Yet when she spoke, despite the somewhat ragged tone, he heard the firmness in her voice even as her hands reached down and once again pulled his head away.

"I don't want you to stop. Ever," she added with a low, emphatic growling to her voice that he knew was her wolf. Her wolf, at least, seem to understand that Quentin was her mate. "But I have to get back. I have a lot to do today for—uh, I just have things to take care of," she stumbled a bit.

Shuddering with pure frustration, Quentin eased himself up Abby's sweet body until he covered her with his immense bulk, resting his forearms alongside her shoulders so he could look directly into the dark blue-green of her eyes. Heaving out a sigh as he saw the determination on her face, even though he also was pleased by the increased pulse he could see beating in her neck, Quentin just half smiled, nodding as he bent his head slightly forward to claim her lips with his. One long, almost timeless moment later filled with the sweet taste of her lips and the familiar, always arousing touch of her fingers as she gently moved them along his back, he pulled away with enormous reluctance.

He wouldn't be that guy. The kind who demanded his woman do his bidding, stay locked up in some gilded cage just for him. Ever.

Not even if it meant losing her.

"I know. I'd never stand in your way," he rumbled, equal parts conviction and turmoil boiling under his voice. "You just taste so damn good, woman." He mock growled as he suddenly buried his face into her neck, nipping and licking, making her giggle as she playfully strained away from the tickle of his mouth. "You're my ambrosia, Abby. I can't get enough of you. These moments just aren't enough for me."

The breeze picked up outside the open windows of Quentin's bedroom in his snug little mountain cabin, carrying to both their sensitive noses the scents of the mountain in autumn. Quentin inhaled long and hard, mingling the delicate spice of aspen bark, the promising tang of crisper days yet to come, and the endless fascination of Abby's own wild scent.

Mixing all the scents together, just as they should be. Abby, here in his home, tucked into the mountain high above the town that belonged to him and his clan. All he had to figure out was how to link the scent of his mate with the scent of his home. Together.

With a regretful sigh, Abby eased herself out from beneath him to sit up, giving him that sexy little half smile she always did, the one that she didn't mean to be sexy but managed to slay him every single time anyway. She swung her legs around to slide off his enormous four-poster bed, her bare feet thumping to the floor. His bear willfully grumping at him as he let his mate leave the soft coziness of their den, Quentin propped himself up on the bed on one arm. Feeling slightly deflated and still frustrated, he watched as she searched for her clothes scattered across the room.

"I'm really sorry I have to run," Abby said. Her tone was a tiny notch firmer than it had been earlier. "You know I love coming here." She sighed a bit as she moved around his room. "This side of the mountain is so quiet and peaceful."

Quentin was positive he caught the sound of a struggle beneath her words as well. Yeah. He damn well knew her wolf side felt one way, yet Abby's stubborn human brain side thought it felt differently. She didn't know a single cross-species mated pair. In her pack, all matings were between wolves. But even though she was a wolf, and acted like one, she also seemed more attuned to the bear shifter way of life than she'd seemed to think she would be. At least, she was a hell of a lot more attuned to it than any other wolf shifter from a pure pack like the Black Mesa wolves on the other side of the mountain.

He frowned to himself. Convincing his sexy, sweet she-wolf that he really and truly was her mate was the hardest challenge of his life. It was fast becoming the most infuriating, as well.

"That's how we like it. Peaceful." Quentin watched as she found her shirt, her cute little pants he'd practically torn off her a few hours ago. Her tousled blond hair rippled over her neck and shoulders, teased at him from between her legs as she took a few long strides across the room to where her pink underwear dangled from the arm of a chair. "Peaceful and private. Just like it should be."

She turned back to him, her eyes softening as she pulled the hem of her shirt down over her hips. "It's probably the most beautiful place I've ever seen. You have the most amazing views of anyone in the state, I'd bet." Her throaty laugh quivered in her voice as

Quentin swung himself off the bed as well, facing her with his own smile as he stood.

He took a step, casually leaning his shoulders against one of the sturdy oak posters of his bed, crossing his arms in front of him as his feet stayed planted solidly on the floor. When Abby's glance took a leisurely trip over his naked body, down to his still half-hard dick, then back up to what he knew was a really well-defined chest and arms from the hard work that was a deliberate part of his life, he let his mouth curve up into a slow, gratified smile.

"Hmmm," Quentin said. He opened his arms as she eagerly moved toward him, enveloping her in a giant, well, bear hug. She snuggled right up to him, melting against his body like it was meant to be.

Which it was. Quentin's bear hummed in approval as his mate molded herself to him.

Tucking her in close, he kept his head down so he could inhale the citrusy scent of her hair. "I know. After all, it's why I decided to build this cabin right here. Total chick magnet with these views."

Abby snorted with laughter against his chest, her hands reaching down behind him to slap his ass. Hell, yeah. It was this saucy little side of her that both revved him up and twanged his heart strings. Every time. "Agreed," she said, turning her head so she could look out the window on the front side of the small cabin. "Your views aren't too bad."

This time, Quentin was the one to snort as he

followed her gaze. The main town of Deep Hollow nestled at the bottom of the valley that meandered below them through these mountains, just at the north-western edge of the range before the wildest depths of the San Juan Mountains opened up. All the businesses and most of the locals lived down there, in town. Quentin, most of his brothers, and several other bear shifters all lived up here, though. Far above town, outside the actual town limits, in a sweet little spot known as Silvertip Ridge. Where they had a view, and privacy from a sometimes intrusive world.

Best of all, it was a shifter-only playground. Silvertip Lodge advertised only to shifters, with any emails or phone calls coming from the occasional human being gently yet firmly directed elsewhere. A smorgasbord of different shifter types were to be found on the private grounds at any time of year, wandering the well-guarded premises in their animal forms at will. Quentin still hoped Abby might take inspiration from some of the cross-species mated pairs who often roamed around, but so far she hadn't seemed to have taken the hint.

Quentin's family, his tight band of parents, broth-ers, cousins, and friends, all called Silvertip Ridge their home. Decades ago, his parents had decided to take over an abandoned old mining camp nestled on the side of the mountain, well above town, and make it into a small resort. The years they'd spent building cabins, figuring out how to get water and electricity up here, and how to survive during the epic summer storms as well as the deep winter snows had been an exciting time, according to their oft-told stories. Now, Silvertip Lodge boasted the best views of Deep Hollow, the envy of anyone who ever visited or even stayed for a summer, as some guests did.

Especially Quentin's cabin, which he'd built years ago when it became apparent that managing the lodge was the ideal job for him. His wide front deck extended out from the front of his cabin, from which the edge of the world seemed to drop off as the spectacular views of the San Juans and beyond spread out in every direction. It had taken him a good amount of time to get the trees blocking the view taken down, but it had been well worth it since he used the wood for his cabin and storage shed, not to mention that their removal opened up the views that anyone could feast on every day for the rest of their lives and never get tired of. It seemed like an endless procession of mountaintops, ridges, and hillside folds staggered off in three directions. It was pretty much a postcard of wild and scenic Colorado. And it was Quentin's.

He vowed to himself that one day sooner than later it would be Abby's, too.

After another long, appreciative moment gazing out at the stunning vista, Abby squeezed him, turning her head up to his for one more kiss. He was pretty sure he saw the usual snap of conflict and regret in her eyes when she finally pulled away. Even so, she collected her keys, her purse, pulled on the sexy cowboy boots she usually liked to wear, and headed for the door.

As she opened it, Quentin took a deep breath. Time to throw down the gambit. In a low voice, he called out after her, "Have a good weekend, Abby. Wish you'd reconsider and let me spend it with you."

Her shoulders stiffened slightly under the pretty blue blouse that sadly now hid her even prettier breasts from him. Turning back, she looked at him with a quizzical expression. "I can't see you this weekend." She looked down at her feet for a second before looking back up at him. Uncertainty framed her features. "Aren't you and the boys working, anyway?"

"The boys have to work, yes." Even though it drove his brothers nuts sometimes, they'd resigned themselves to being called "the boys" as they labored on occasion under Quentin's watch at the lodge. "Being the boss, though, means I get certain perks. Such as being able to take some time off. Like on special weekends such as this one."

He gave her a deliberately pointed, searching stare. Abby swallowed again, now looking slightly uneasy. "What—what's so special about this weekend?"

Damn, she was such a sexy little thing, standing there framed in his doorway with the beautiful backdrop of the mountains behind her. She belonged here, dammit. She belonged with him. He just had to prove it to her.

"Well, sweetheart," he said slowly, "it's the full

moon this weekend. A hunter's moon, I think the elders in certain native tribes used to call it. Am I right?"

Gotcha, beautiful, he thought as her eyes darted around as if in search of an escape hatch.

"Um... Yes?" Her voice was hesitant, her tone awkward. She was utterly incapable of lying with any degree of believability. She was an honest, genuine person. It was part of why he just couldn't understand why she refused to see that they were meant for each other.

"Hunter's moon. Right. When all the wolf packs gather for a big run." Quentin gave her a long look. "And your Black Mesa pack has the biggest one in this part of the country. Doesn't it?"

Abby inhaled, her beautiful eyes widening a bit. "Quentin, you know that's a wolf thing—"

Normally, he would take the bait and argue that sort of point with her. But then he'd found out what the real truth behind the hunter's moons were.

It was a time when many wolves found their true mates. And mated with them. Under the full moon.

The thought of it was slowly killing him. But she wasn't ready for him to come to her pack. She wasn't ready to let them know she'd found her mate, and it was a bear shifter. He didn't want to fight with her over it. If he made her mad enough, she might decide being with a temperamental, possessive bear shifter was the wrong thing after all.

So he played it cool instead, much to the chagrin of his utterly enamored bear.

"Yeah, babe, I know that." He shrugged with seeming nonchalance. "It's a big run this weekend, and it's important to your pack. I do listen to you, you know." Hung on her every word was more like it, but he wasn't about to admit that out loud. He dropped his guard with Abby more than with anyone else in the entire world. He just wasn't quite ready to let her know that she pretty much had him totally whipped.

Not yet, at least.

He shrugged again, still trying to look as unconcerned as possible. "I'm just saying, have a great weekend, babe. Since I knew you'd be busy, I made some plans other than working myself."

At that, Abby looked surprised. As if he didn't notice, he went on. "You'd better be getting over the mountain to your pack. You'll be late. Call me, I—"

Damn. He'd almost said the word out loud. The word that seemed too fragile for either one of them to say out loud.

Lover. *Love.*

Catching himself quickly, he said instead, "Later."

It took everything he had to just jerk his chin goodbye at her, then casually turn away and head over to his closet like he meant to get dressed. After a long beat, Abby replied, slight confusion still edging her words. "Okay. Bye. I'll talk to you later."

Hearing the puzzlement in her voice squeezed his

heart. He held firm, despite the distressed grunting of his bear. There was only one way he was going to win this amazing, perfect she-wolf for himself. Wait for her to come to him. Reining himself in so he didn't turn around to run out the door after her to grab her up in his arms again, Quentin just listened as his stubborn, sexy, sweet little mate got in her car and drove down the mountain, away from him. Like she did every time, no matter how many arguments he'd presented to her during the past half a year since he'd first clapped eyes on her.

"You're taking a big gamble on this one, Quentin Walker." His voice muttered out savagely to himself, echoing in the suddenly empty cabin.

Because if she decided not to come back to him, he'd be alone for the rest of his life.

2

"So then he said—oh!" Abby interrupted herself with a soft exclamation. "The trees are turning more every day." A delicate, bright yellow aspen leaf fluttered through the air above Abby's head, landing in her lap as she looked up at the canopy of leaves overhead.

Megan, Abby's closest friend, looked up as well. "I love fall." Megan's voice went dreamy for a second. Then she turned back to Abby, interest sharpening her tone again. "But don't stop there. So then he said what?"

Abby resettled herself against the silvery white bark of the aspen tree trunk she leaned against. She and Megan were tucked beneath it in a far corner of the Black Mesa Wolf Pack den property. Abby wanted to talk to her best friend about Quentin. Her favorite topic of conversation, bar none. Every time she brought him up, she just felt—happy. Settled.

But that didn't matter. Not when he was just an awesome guy to spend time with for now. An awesome guy, but a bear shifter. Wolves didn't hang out with bears. Or mate with them. Not any wolves that she knew, at least.

Inside, her wolf howled and smacked her mind. Somewhat startled, Abby blinked. With a small frown, she went on. "Well, then he said he's already got plans this weekend. I thought he was working. They work really hard, him and his brothers. It's really impressive."

"They're all pretty impressive," Megan agreed, smiling. "I can totally understand why you find him attractive. If it weren't for Sean, I'd probably think they're pretty hot, too." Sean was Megan's mate. Abby knew perfectly well that Megan had eyes for no one else. Even so, it was nice of her to acknowledge that Quentin's bear shifter clan mates were also appealing.

"Right? I mean, even though they're a different species. I mean, they're still people, too. I mean," Abby frowned again as she stumbled over herself. It had been happening a lot lately. "I don't know what I'm saying. He's an awesome guy. They all are. He's just like—the most awesome. Even though he's not a wolf," she ended, bolstering her argument.

Bolstering it with what exactly, she still wasn't quite sure.

This time, the glance Megan gave Abby was more speculative. Idly playing with the stalk from a pretty pink and white mountain laurel, she asked with what seemed like genuine curiosity, "Do you really see them as being that different?"

Startled again, Abby looked at her best friend. Slowly, trying to understand her own thoughts as they spun and darted around in her mind, she said, "Well, no. But—I mean, it's just that we never really hang out much with them. With any other shifters besides wolves."

It was true. Different types of shifters lived all over the world, and even right here in Durango, but the Black Mesa Pack tended to mingle mostly with other wolf shifters.

Megan nodded. "True. We really should, you know. I mean, all of us live with one foot in our world and the other foot in a completely human world. We all have a lot more in common than we don't."

Abby looked at Megan's thoughtful face for a long moment as she digested those words. Her wolf spun and whirled around in her mind, suddenly as excited and flighty as Abby's thoughts. "Huh. I never really thought of it that way."

Megan shrugged, gently tossing the flower away. She leaned back on her hands as she lazily surveyed the woods around them. "Well, it's surprising that we really don't hang out with other shifter types that much. Then again, we're the only ones who spend a lot of time in Durango. Since technically this is our territory, and the bears and big cats and whatnot don't seem to come down here that often. It's too bad, really. I meet a couple now and then. Sean actually knows quite a few of the bear shifters. But," she shrugged, "I guess there's more mingling in California. So many more shifters there."

Abby smiled at that. After he'd met Megan, Sean had left behind his northern California pack for a new life in Colorado. He always said that over there, shifters inter-mated all the time. Small town Colorado living, though, was different. Abby didn't know a single inter-species couple.

None at all.

Yet even that didn't stop her from thinking about Quentin Walker, the sexiest, strongest, most amazing bear shifter on the planet, pretty much every second of the day. Even though she knew it was hopeless. Around here, bears and wolves just didn't mate.

"So." Megan suddenly switched gears. "What about the hunter's moon run? Are you ready for that?"

The abrupt change of subject, and the echo of Quentin's mention that morning about the run, brought Abby up short. Feeling her heart flutter in her chest, she twirled the aspen leaf in her hands, her gaze roving over the tall, thick pine trees and the bright scatter of aspen trees whose leaves were turning at significant rates. "What do you mean?"

"I mean," Megan said in a gentle tone, "are you ready to possibly get mated during it? There'll be a lot of guys from other packs here for the run. You're pretty, fun, and a good catch, Abby. Some wolf is bound to have his eye on you."

The strangest sensation gripped Abby at those words. She felt vaguely like she was suffocating, perhaps on the verge of having a mild panic attack. Her breath shortened, her chest squeezed, and her mind constricted into a cacophony of angry barks and sharp whines as she thought about the formal hunter's moon pack run.

The full moon of every October was commonly known as the Hunter's Moon. Wolf packs, which naturally hunted, over the centuries had adopted the long light of this full moon night as an ideal time to bring together members from different packs for joyous runs in the mountains or deserts or canyons wherever they lived.

It was also a well-established run during which many lifelong mate pairings were made, as wolves from different packs met new potential partners. A chase that was a mixture of playful yet serious allowed wolves to prove that they could be a worthy mate. Naturally, a mating wasn't going to occur unless the pair was actually meant to be. A lot of run hookups simply ended up as casual liaisons, or simple fun as friends ran together or caught up with members from other visiting packs.

But plenty of them resulted in true, lifelong mate pairings. Enough so that each hunter's moon run was met with a certain amount of expectation. Of anticipation.

Abby was of an age when plenty of wolves mated. She had yet to meet her mate. He certainly wasn't in the Black Mesa pack, she would have known by now. She hadn't found him yet in any of the packs she'd ever visited in the vicinity, or even during her college stint on the East Coast.

So the chances of meeting her mate during a hunter's moon run like the one coming up was better than not. While wolf packs all over the country and the world set up private hunter's moon runs at this time of year, the Black Mesa Wolf Pack hosted what was by far the largest public run in the entire southwestern United States, drawing members from easily twenty or thirty other packs who traveled to spend a long weekend here. Plenty of them were already in town, staying either at hotels, or, if they were family members or close friends of Black Mesa wolves, invited to den here on the property itself.

So far, not a single one of the solo male wolves newly in town had caught Abby's attention.

Only because she hadn't run with them yet, she murmured to herself. That had to be it. Feeling Megan's eyes on her, Abby managed to say, "I should definitely meet a wolf I'll like during the run." She tried to make her voice sound convinced, even as her wolf still bafflingly pummeled her mind with what seemed to be sheer vexation. "You're right. I'm ready to be mated." Gaining steam, she sat up straight, nodding her head. "For darned sure. I mean, what wolf wouldn't want to join the Black Mesa pack? And I'm a catch. Heck, I'm a great catch."

Even as she finished talking, Abby couldn't help her voice as it dissolved into giggles at her semi-pompous tone. Megan snorted, then joined her, their laughter being answered by the scold of a bird in a nearby tree, which set them off even more. Eventually, silence settled over them again. The breeze flipped through the trees with that increasing sharpness that every day portended the deepening of fall. Abby closed her eyes, tipping her face up to the beams of sunlight coming through the branches above.

After another long moment, Megan spoke again. "Abby," she began, then paused. She took a breath before continuing. "Abby, I just want to ask you something."

Unconcerned, feeling lulled by the fading warmth of the light on her skin, Abby mumbled back, "Mm-hmm?"

But Megan's next words had her snapping her eyes open and straightening up.

"Are you sure, absolutely, one hundred percent positive, that you haven't already met him? Your mate?"

Abby shot Megan a look as her heart seemed to spasm again. Her wolf swept her tail through her mind, sending agitation skittering along Abby's nerves.

21

"Because if I asked you right now whose face you're picturing when I said that, whose would it be?"

Abby stared at her best friend, who was definitely not pulling her punches in this conversation.

She saw nothing but Quentin's face. His broad, laughing grin, the hearty laughter that rumbled out of him when they were in bed together, when he was hanging out with his brothers and the other bear shifters over in Deep Hollow, when he was just enjoying his life up in the beautiful place he'd created on the mountain at Silvertip Ridge. His huge, burly strength, different from that of a wolf yet so intensely, oddly familiar and comforting that Abby felt more settled around him than any wolf she'd ever met. His strong hands as he held her close. His fingers, so big and thick yet so incredibly tender and dexterous as they explored every centimeter of her body, drawing out sensations and sounds from her that she'd never realized she was capable of producing before she met him.

Quentin Walker, bear shifter. Gorgeous, caring, sexy, safe.

Yet he was also a *bear* shifter. Not from her pack. Not from any wolf pack. He was just a guy she was dating. Yes, a guy she really, really, really liked. One whose face she could picture waking up to every morning, going to bed with every night, spending every second with for every day of the rest of her life.

But he wasn't a wolf shifter. Abby didn't know a

single mated wolf who was not mated to another wolf shifter. Sure, they existed.

Just not in her pack.

Taking a deep breath, shaking her head to clear her visions of him, she answered in a voice she meant to be steady. But it came out shaky and uncertain no matter how hard she tried. "No one's face. I—I don't see anyone else's face when I think of a mate."

Megan studied her again for a long moment, eyes crinkled at the corners. She seemed on the verge of arguing. Abby never could keep a good poker face, and Megan knew that. In the end, though, all she said was, "Okay. Shall we head back to the den?"

Abby nodded, knowing that Megan had seen straight through her. During their entire, silent run back to the den, all she could do was see Quentin's face in front of her. And think of the hunter's moon run coming up in just a few days. The run during which she might meet her mate. Her wolf shifter mate.

Yes. Because any other shifter was just out of the question.

3

Quentin glared at his brother as he lifted his end of the huge beam, muscles and sweat popping out all over him. "Put your back into it, man! What are you, a half-grown cub? How the hell you can actually rescue people when you go out on your calls is beyond me, as scrawny as you are. It's a damn wonder more of them don't die out there with you on the beat."

Cortez roared in fury, the sound of his bear bellowing out of his mouth. He put more than his back into it, he put every last remaining ounce of his strength into hefting the cut beam that might as well be an entire tree.

Hey, they were bear shifters. They could wrangle entire trees when they really wanted to. Like right now. Quentin grinned to himself, though he didn't let it show on his face. Yeah, kicking his youngest brother around a bit had always been the way to get more out of him. It had been that way since they all had been cubs, and probably would be that way the rest of their lives.

"Orgh—ugh—aaaaargh!" Quentin's grunts and groans joined Cortez's as they wrestled the enormous beam up the stairs and managed to lug it through the double front doors of the main building on the property. A wild party last week had resulted in cracking one of the ponderosa beams in the huge dining room. Quentin had been less than thrilled. Okay, he'd been pissed as hell. He'd grumped about it to every single bear and half the humans in town. He, of course, hadn't been around for the party, having gone to Denver for a quick supply run. No, his youngest brother had gotten some stupid wild hair up his butt and invited the entire search and rescue crew he worked on, plus about ten extra people per crew member, up for the party. Apparently, it had been a raging success.

Quentin wondered if his brother still thought as highly of his antics now that he had to help Quentin repair the damage.

The beam thunked on the floor with a resounding boom after the brothers had maneuvered it to the middle of the room and set it down as carefully as they could. Which meant to say they dropped it. Wiping sweat from his brow and muttering darkly about the idiocy of letting heavy bear shifters swing from a wooden beam while they were drinking, Quentin sat down on the beam to catch his breath. Cortez flopped down beside him, gasping in his own breath with exaggerated drama.

Quentin narrowed his eyes at his brother. "We've still got a lot to do today, replacing the broken one up there." He jabbed an accusing finger at the cracked beam overhead. Their parents, who had run the Silvertip Lodge resort since shortly after they had first been mated many years ago, were in the middle of a year-long, worldwide tour. Quentin, responsible elder of the brothers not to mention already manager of the lodge, had been left in charge during their absence.

Well, damn him for being responsible. Even though he was the oldest of all the hellion Walker siblings, he never quite appreciated how hard it was to wrangle his brothers until their parents had blithely taken off on a long-delayed sightseeing tour of the countries they'd always wanted to visit but never had been able to due to the endless responsibilities of running a small guest resort that was open year-round. Quentin had been the property manager ever since he'd come into his maturity. Yet all that experience hadn't quite prepared him for the dubious honor of riding roughshod over his siblings. They were all grown ass men, for crying out loud. But they acted like damn spoiled babies every time he asked for a little bit of help.

Scrubbing a hand over his eyes, he enjoyed the sharp breeze coming in through the open door. Moving the beam from the yard had been a lot of work, and he and Cortez were both dripping with the sweat equity to prove it. The change of season finally seemed to be spanning over the mountain, a little later this year than usual. Fall was Quentin's favorite season. Something about the crisp air, the changing color guard that swept through all the trees on the mountain, the new life that tickled through the town down in the valley as everyone seemed to emerge from the lazy days of summer into the renewed pace of fall life always made him feel alive.

He was a bear in the mountains, and his life was perfect.

Well. Almost perfect.

After another few moments of catching their breaths, Cortez finally grunted, "How much longer till they get back from that crazy vacation of theirs?"

"Seven months, three weeks, two days, and a handful of hours." Despite himself, Quentin's voice was grim.

Another beat. Then Cortez started laughing. Shaking his head, between increasingly mirthful sputters, he said, "You know they did this to you on purpose, big brother. They wanted to teach you what it's like to have cubs of your own."

"Full grown cubs, and you sure as hell aren't mine," Quentin retorted, but he couldn't help the grin sliding over his own face. "Though you darn well better listen to every word I say, you scalawag." That had been a favorite word of their mother's for all of them as they grew up. It was still apt.

Cortez was probably right. Their mother and father had often bemoaned the fact that almost none of their sons was yet mated, let alone anywhere near to producing cubs of their own for their doting grandparents to dandle on their knees and teach how to search for berries and honey in the woods. In fact, during a family dinner the night before they left, their mother had severely mandated an order to the five Walker sons. "Every single one of you had better be mated and about ready to have a cub show up from that union by the time your father and I get back. Or else," she ended threateningly at the shocked silence and dropped mouths that greeted her statement.

She'd been joking, of course. Well, probably only half joking. Maybe only a quarter joking? Riley, of course, got a pass. He did have cubs, and he wasn't in the market for a mate ever again. That subject was closed. Everyone else, though, got a very stern look from the most ferocious mama bear any of them had ever met.

Now, Quentin shrugged. To be honest, he agreed with her. He wanted nothing more than to be mated. Maybe not cubs, not quite yet. First, he just needed his mate to acknowledge that she actually was his mate. If he couldn't get Abby to understand how serious he was about that, he wasn't sure what to do next.

As if he could hear Quentin's thoughts, Cortez

stopped laughing. He gave his brother a fairly compassionate look. "What's your plan for her, anyway?"

Quentin narrowed his eyes at his brother and snapped, "Plan for who?"

"Abby, of course. You need to get her here somehow. I figured you had some sort of plan to make her understand." Cortez shrugged. The fact that Abby was Quentin's mate was plain as day to all the bear shifters around here. His brothers really liked her anyway. They'd each privately told him that she was cool, and could hold her own in a rough and tumble bear clan.

Glaring at his brother, Quentin felt his bear grumping around inside him again. "What, I'm supposed to become some sort of cave bear and just drag her off to my den without more than an *if you please?*"

Cortez shook his head, answering in a fairly serious tone. "No, she'd probably just rip out your innards with her super sharp lady wolf claws. Wolves are fast, you know. You wouldn't be able to stop her in time."

"Hmph," Quentin muttered.

"Oh, come on, man." Cortez reached out for a brotherly punch on the shoulder that nearly drove Quentin off the beam. "You're driving the rest of us crazy. You've been a total asshole. Seriously, you need to chill out. And there's only one solution for that."

Caught up short, Quentin stared his brother for a long moment as his brain scrambled around trying to figure out how to answer that. Finally, he said in a low, dangerously soft rumble, "Asshole? Really? First of all, Cortez, you're the reason we're in here replacing this damn beam." He slapped the offending beam with his hand. "Better not ever bring that dumbass party boy crew of yours up here again. Swinging from the rafters," he muttered, shaking his head. Like frat boys or something. As Cortez drew breath to speak, Quentin shook his head and held up a hand. "No, hang on a second. Next, I want to know what the hell you mean. Some sort of asshole? What the hell does Abby have to do with me being an asshole?"

This time, it was Cortez's turn to stare at Quentin, brows furrowed in surprise. "Because she's your mate, and you won't get her to come over here," he said. "You're pissed off about it. Thus, you act like an asshole. Asshole," he added in a companionable tone.

Quentin ground his teeth. "There's a plan," he said tightly, lying through his teeth. He had no idea what to do. "I'm not an idiot."

"Fine," Cortez said, quirking one eyebrow as he shook his head at his brother. "So you do have a grand scheme to get Abby over here for good so you can be happy, your bear stops being a grumpy old fart, and we can maybe survive the rest of the next seven months and three weeks and whatever days and hours that you're in charge till mom and dad get back?"

Clenching his jaw, Quentin got up and went over to the large east-facing window, where he shoved his fists onto his hips and glared out at the best view on the entire property. Well, he liked to think his own cabin had the very best view. But of course they never said that to guests. His bear rumbled about his mind, alternately irritated at Cortez, at inter-species shifter politics, but mostly frustrated at not being able to just charge across the mountain to grab his mate and bring her back here to his den, safe and sound where she belonged.

Quentin liked to think of himself as a gentleman, even if he was a big bear. If Abby had plans for her own life, in her own pack, he couldn't just stomp over there and demand she change everything for him. Even if that was the only thing he wanted to do.

Quentin took a measured inhale, held it, exhaled. He did it five or six times. Finally, he replied to his brother's question when he figured he could talk without his bear growling through his words. "Fine. There is no real plan. I'm just pissed because there's this thing going on this weekend. Tonight, actually," he admitted, looking back at his brother.

Cortez raised his eyebrows, gesturing for him to go on.

Reluctantly, feeling his ire heat up even more, Quentin went on. "So her pack has this thing. They do these pack runs all the time, right? They go out, run around under the moon. You know. It's a wolf thing."

Cortez grunted from where he had stayed seated on the beam. Now he was peering up at the cracked beam overhead, critically and maybe just a bit sheepishly. He saw Quentin looking at him and waved a hand in his direction. "Go on, go on. Running. Full moon. I'm listening."

Quentin looked back out at the fiery race of color zigging and zagging all over the mountains. Despite his inner agitation, he felt slightly soothed by the sight, as always. "This weekend is a big one. It's the hunter's moon tonight. Happens every October. Each wolf pack in the country goes out for a full moon run. Some packs do it just by themselves, but others invite wolf shifters from all over the place to come join in. Kind of like a pack gathering sort of thing." Quentin shrugged. "Abby's pack is a big deal. They have a huge run for this full moon every year. Wolves come from all over the place to run with them."

"Mm-hmm," Cortez said. His boots thumped as he walked the floor across what sounded like the length of the overhead beam.

"So they run," Quentin went on, "and they hunt deer and stuff, just hang out and have fun. Wolves running in the moonlight. And," he hesitated. "And sometimes they meet their mate during the hunter's moon. They go hunting for a mate. Hunter's moon."

"Okay, cool, yeah," Cortez's voice came from the far end of the hall. "Sounds like you have a plan after all. You can go over there, run with them, and officially mate with Abby. Boom and done, right?"

Quentin managed to talk around the sudden tic in his cheek. "Not quite. It's a wolf mating thing. Meaning they might find their destined wolf mate at these things a lot of the time. Abby is at just the right age when a lot of them apparently meet. Magical mating hunter's moon, blah blah blah."

This time, dead silence greeted his words. Quentin turned around to see his brother standing stock still at the other end of the room, staring back at him. By his posture, Cortez was completely focused on what Quentin had just said.

"A wolf mating thing," Cortez slowly echoed. He cocked his head to the side. "A wolf mating thing." This time, his voice somewhat mocked the words.

A glare began to bracket Quentin's face again. "Yeah. So?"

"Are you serious?" Now, Cortez's voice was incredulous. It was also a bit challenging. "It's a wolf mating run, and you're gonna let Abby run in the middle of it with a bunch of male wolves who are looking for their mates? Abby, the woman you keep telling us is your mate? The woman we all *know* is your mate?"

"She doesn't want me there. It's a wolf pack thing."

Cortez shook his head, a small curl on his lip saying what he really thought about that. "Where the hell are your balls, man? You're letting her get away."

Quentin roared as his fury rampaged through him. His bear side suddenly threatened to burst out of his every pore. "Hell, no, I'm not!"

"Yeah!" Cortez egged on.

"You're right." Quentin slammed one fist into the

palm of his other hand as sudden clarity bloomed. "I can't let her be there without me. So I'm gonna show up, too. Show up for that hunter's moon mating thing, because Abby damn well is my mate."

Cortez strode across the room until he was close enough that Quentin could see the shining of his eyes that meant his own bear was close to the surface as well. "Let me get this straight, insane big brother of mine. You plan to go over there tonight, to a huge wolf shifter gathering thing, that's one of their big deal things that they do, and just walk in there, a lone bear shifter, and what? Grab your wolf shifter mate out from under their noses? There's no way they'll let you get away with that." The challenge still rose in his voice, though. He was totally encouraging his brother to do just that.

Quentin glared. "I don't really think they're that bloodthirsty. Besides, look at me. I'm a fuckin' grizzly bear. A grizzly bear! Wolves might mess with me, but they can't take me down."

Sharply, Cortez said, "Yeah, they can. If there's like a couple hundred of them."

His bear marching through his mind in renewed rage, Quentin roared even more loudly as his thoughts filled with images of a hundred young, mate-hungry male wolf shifters eyeballing Abby like she was some sort of prize. "A hundred male wolves? All there for this mating run thing, the same thing Abby is going to be at?"

"Oh, yeah!" Cortez said, pumping his fist in the air like some enraged Spartan warrior of old or something. "And they're all gonna take a look at that Abby of yours, decide she'd be the perfect mate for them, then snatch her out from under *your* nose instead! You can't let that happen."

"Hell, no, I can't!" Quentin roared back, feeling the bear hairs bristle out of his human skin as his equally enraged bear thundered and walked around just beneath the surface. "That's my mate we're talking about!"

"Your mate!" Cortez agreed, glaring with nearly as much fury as Quentin.

Then, "Shit," Quentin muttered. "How could I let her go back there by herself? Probably a ton of wolves already in town, ready to start sniffing out their new mates."

Cortez nodded. "Damn right there are," he agreed. "If I were you, I'd get my ass over there right now. For all you know, she's already been sizing one up, and that's why she's been reluctant to come live over here with you."

At that, Quentin saw nothing but dark, angry red. This time, though, it was at his own brother's words. "She'd never do that to me." His voice was so dangerously still, so dangerously quiet, that Cortez froze right where he was.

Then, to Quentin's surprise, instead of looking nervous as Quentin advanced on his brother, Cortez smiled instead. "Course she wouldn't," he said, so easily that Quentin paused mid stride. "She's your mate, man. She's been brought up to believe that she can only mate with another wolf. But look here. I don't know a lot about women—"

Quentin snorted at that. Cortez was a renowned ladies man. He might not know much about mates, but he sure knew a lot about women.

"—but I can tell you this much. She may not think she's waiting for you to come get her." Cortez's voice was suddenly serious. "But she is. Trust me. You show up there, do whatever the hell it is you need to do during that run thing, and let her know that you can handle not only it, but also what she needs."

A sharp wind swirled into the room through the still open front doors as Quentin stared at his brother. "And what exactly is it that she needs?"

Cortez leaned a little bit closer, as if he was about to share the deepest secrets of the universe. "What she needs," he said in a low tone, "is for you to show up, be there, and let her know you're never gonna walk away from her again."

Quentin growled. "I'm not the one walking away from her. She doesn't want me to follow her."

Cortez rolled his eyes and flung up his hands in seeming despair. Then he advanced on his brother and shoved a strong finger into Quentin's chest. "Listen to me. Yeah, you have been the one walking away from her. You haven't shown her that you mean business about being her mate. That you take it more seriously than anything else in the world. I'm not talking about showing her who's boss, hell no. Now, that would be some stupid cave bear shit. No," Cortez went on, settling back on his heels as he placed his own fists on his hips, pinning his brother with a glare, "I'm talking about you not being afraid to show up in front of her entire pack, and however many other packs are there, and not letting her run by herself. I'm talking about you showing that wolf shifter mate of yours that you sure as hell are her mate."

Quentin stared at Cortez for a long moment as his mind tripped over itself at the simplicity of what his brother said as well as the stupidity of Quentin's own thought process for the past several months. Damn. Well, he sure as hell was acting like some big, stupid, lumbering bear, wasn't he?

Not anymore, he wasn't. Turning for the door, Quentin abruptly sprinted for it, his steps shaking the floor.

"Hey!" Cortez called after him. "Where are you going? What about the beam?"

Quentin shook his head, still running. "You're right," he flung back over his shoulder. "Get some of those lazy ass search and rescue crew mates of yours up here to help you fix this. I," he thumped himself hard on the chest as he burst out the open doorway and took the stairs four at a time down to the parking area, "need to go get my mate before it's too late."

Drifting behind him as he ran like a crazy guy for his truck, Quentin thought he heard his brother mutter, "Finally. But you'd better come back in one piece after tangling with a wolf shifter pack. And you need to bring your mate back here with you!" Cortez called out more loudly.

But Quentin had already jumped into his huge diesel truck, gunning the engine as he tore out the long dirt drive from the property to go down the mountain, then all the way across it.

To go to the all-wolf shifter hunter's moon run happening tonight, and prove to his wolf shifter mate as well as her entire pack that he was the only one for her.

4

*A*fter the first ring, it went to voicemail. As the sound of Quentin's deep voice rumbled into her ear, Abby couldn't help the small shiver that rippled through her. His voice always did that to her, even when it was just a recording. She listened to his brief message, then hung up before the tone sounded. She'd already left him a voicemail earlier that day. And texted him. Twice. There was no need to throw herself at him like a lovesick puppy more than she already had.

Her wolf lightly protested, *Not a puppy,* though it was a whisper in the back of Abby's mind. Abby let a smile ghost over her face as she moved down the bustling sidewalk of downtown Durango. No, she'd left puphood behind quite some years ago. She was a grown woman, capable of making her own decisions and sticking with them, consequences be damned. So some of those decisions involved thoughts of a sexy, strong, rough, tough, utterly fascinating bear shifter. So what? She could think about him. She liked to think about him, no matter what she might have said to Megan. Quentin tingled her toes, sent zips of electricity through her body, made her sizzle and sparkle every time she was around him.

Yes, she could think about him. She'd finally broken down and admitted to herself she was wondering what his mysterious plans were this weekend. What? She could be curious about his activities when they weren't around one another. She could casually wonder what he was up to, how he was spending his time away from her.

Even though tonight she planned to join the pack's hunter's moon run and possibly find her own wolf shifter mate.

Her wolf snarled in her mind, this time with firm intention. She swiped a claw over Abby's thoughts, causing Abby to gasp a bit, which in turn made a few passing humans look at her curiously. Pasting a vague smile on her face, she turned into the shop she'd been heading toward. The Steaming Bean was a Durango institution, a small but busy coffeeshop on Main Street that boasted crowds day and night. The autumn chill in the air had made Abby crave a cinnamon latte.

Fingers clenching around the silent phone in her pocket, she joined the line of chattering customers also seeking a cup of delicious warmth. Almost immediately, she noticed the two other shifters there, getting their drinks at the front of the line as they laughed and flirted with the cute barista. Two male wolves, young and unknown. Usually, unknown shifters were cause for potential alarm in Black Mesa Pack territory. But during a pack run, especially this most significant one, strange wolves in town weren't cause to alert the pack Guardians to the presence of outsiders.

Instead, it was an opportunity to study them as potential mates.

Mates, her wolf whispered in disgust, giving the wolfish equivalent of rolling her eyes at Abby. *Cubs. Not worthy.*

They're hardly cubs, Abby thought back in mild exasperation. *They're grown wolves. Ready to take on responsibility. They're just looking for the same thing I am. A mate.*

With another disgusted bark in Abby's mind, and a flashing image of Quentin throwing his head back, mouth open and teeth gleaming as he laughed that deep laugh of his, her wolf smartly marched to the back of her mind and sat down, back turned to Abby. *Quentin,* was all she thought at Abby, the name laden with significance. *Quentin is mate.*

Abby dug her nails into her hand. Quentin was wonderful. He was fun. He was sexy. She thought about him all the time. She enjoyed spending time with him. But he wasn't a wolf shifter. He couldn't ever be her mate. She had no idea how to have a mate who wasn't a wolf.

Resolute, ignoring her wolf's tail lashing inside her

head, Abby smiled when one of the strange male wolves half turned and caught her eye. He smiled back, eyes alight with sudden interest. He was a little young, sure—*Pup,* her wolf murmured again with slight derision—but he was cute, strong, looked sane, and was solvent enough to at least buy a cup of coffee. Those were all good things, right?

Unfortunately, there was no zing as he looked back at her with appreciation. No flare of returned interest inside her, no real desire to go over and say hello to him or his friend. No wish to strike up a conversation, asking where he was from, if he was looking forward to the full moon run.

He just wasn't Quentin. Dang it. Sighing, she shrugged and looked away.

By the time Abby managed to order and pick up her coffee, a few tables had emptied out inside the popular little place. She snagged a small one by the large front window, settling down to sip her latte and look outside at the bright day and the passersby. The door rattled and squeaked as it was shoved open again, spilling more customers into the small but brisk business.

"You're from the Black Mesa Pack, aren't you?" The deep, slightly eager voice sounded above her ear, its words masked by the patter of laughter and conversation nearby.

Abby started, twisting a bit in her seat to look up. It was the young male wolf who'd smiled at her in line. He hovered beside her table, his friend right on his heels, clearly waiting for an invitation to sit down. Manners prompted her to automatically smile again. Drawing breath to speak, she didn't even get a single word out before being interrupted by another deep voice.

This voice, though, was familiar. So familiar it sent that aching, delicious zing right down into her bones, rattling her teeth and making her wolf sit up to keen attention.

"What's it to you if she is, pup?" the voice huffed out in a light snarl, as its owner pinned the young wolves with a dark look.

Quentin. Right here, beside her.

QUENTIN GLARED at the wolf who hovered too close to his mate. A look more of shock than fear sprinted over the wolf's face as he took an automatic step back. Abby's beautiful eyes, wide and guileless, darted between Quentin and the young pups who dared to put their bold moves on her.

Moves it seemed hadn't worked too well. Or that she'd even really noticed.

Good.

"Just making conversation with a pretty lady is all." The young wolf said the words in a smooth, conciliatory tone. This might be wolf territory, but Quentin was a bear shifter. He was bigger than either wolf, somewhat older, and much more savvy to a good old-fashioned throw down. He looked like he could fight anyone at any time, and he knew it. The others did, too. He relaxed—until the pup's next words. "It's the hunter's moon run tonight. It's something just for our kind, you know?"

No real menace underlaid the wolf's words, who clearly was appreciative enough of Quentin's greater size and strength to not really push it. Yet a flicker of challenge stirred there. Enough of a flicker to bring Quentin's bear roaring back to the surface, ready to take out any fool who thought to get in his way. He knew his eyes were likely beginning to glow, as did all shifters whose animals came so close to the surface they threatened to dominate their human side.

It would be so nice to show this young upstart who was really in charge here. Who was the boss of the situation. Who was really Abby's mate.

Yet years of being the oldest brother in a clan of rowdy bear shifters, not to mention the fact that he was indeed right in the middle of wolf territory, tempered his response as he forcefully shoved his bear back down. He opted for a charged verbal response, while keeping his body language non-attacking. "And what kind would that be? The young and disrespectful?"

With that, Quentin dismissed the pups by turning his back on them. It was a clear sign of mild contempt in the shifter world, the willingness to turn one's back on any perceived threat or enemies. He'd basically just called their bluff and demonstrated they weren't even worthy of a defensive stance.

Abby's lips trembled. Quentin let his own mouth curve up into a smile. He knew her well enough to know that she was covering up a grin. Buying herself some time, she lifted her coffee to her lips and took another sip. Smile abruptly wiped off his face, he stared at those full, pretty pink lips as they melded themselves against the rim of the mug. Just like the way they sometimes wrapped around his—

"Quentin. What are you doing here?" Her voice lilted out against the background clamor of the busy place as she looked up at him with those mesmerizing eyes.

He took a deep, slow breath in through his nose before he answered. All the long drive over the mountain into Durango, he'd had the opportunity to think about his impending actions. Since he'd charged off half-cocked, egged on by Cortez's ribbing—and darn that troublemaking little brother of his, trying to stir up drama and reaction as usual—he realized he'd get to town many hours before the run actually began. He'd passed the Black Mesa Pack den, headquartered north of town, rolling down his windows and trying to scent Abby as he cruised by. Knowing he'd look idiotic, if not somewhat threatening, if he tried to go onto the property this early, he'd opted instead to head to town and take a walk to cool himself off.

When she'd called him, he'd almost driven off the

road at the sight of her name on the screen. But he made himself let it go to voicemail. He wasn't sure yet how to approach letting her know he'd be there tonight. Telling her on the phone definitely wasn't the way to do it.

Besides, he really liked the fact that she'd called him. Then texted. Because it meant Abby wasn't with another guy. She wasn't going to find a mate at this full moon run, or even just a casual liaison. Abby was his, and he knew it. She did too, deep down inside. He'd realized he just needed to be cool about the situation. Not as cool as he had been. No, he'd been too laid back about his feelings for Abby. The woman had to know he was her mate, and he'd let her know loud and clear. But he didn't need to tear up a coffeeshop in downtown Durango because some juvenile wolves thought they had a shot with a magnificent she-wolf like Abby. Abby, whom he'd unexpectedly and very thrillingly had scented as he rambled down Main Street. Her flash of bright gold hair as she sat in the window had caught his eye when he snapped his head around trying to find her.

She was a gem, Abby Kenyon was. And she was his.

His bear grumbled at him, but Quentin held firm. He didn't need to give any wolves any more ammunition to think that bear shifters were oafish, always ready to fight, and just too brutish for a wolf shifter. He'd simply prove to them all tonight the exact opposite. Calmly, he replied to Abby. "I have things to do here. Errands. I didn't expect to run into you. I thought you were busy this weekend," he couldn't resist adding. He wasn't going to pick a fight with any wolves, but he also wasn't above teasing his sexy little Abby some more.

That cute little red flush tiptoed across her cheeks. "I was, ah, I mean—" she tripped over herself.

Damn, she was beautiful. Those curves, that voice, the strength he knew rested within her, despite her current flustered state. Quentin enjoyed the sight of her for another long moment, drinking her in, before he rescued her from her own floundering. "I saw you sitting here and decided to stop in to say hi."

His voice was low, but expectation thrummed along it. Abby was caught by that note, her eyes snapping over to his and her mouth abruptly shutting. She swallowed at the expression on his face, which he knew was suddenly taut and filled with a longing.

And an implacable certainty.

"I thought," he said more slowly, dragging out the words and deepening his voice, "I'd come in for just a minute so you could see me. So you could get my scent."

Abby swallowed again. Her nostrils flared a little as she took his scent in. Quentin was aware of the two young wolves, still at his back, watching everything with what was likely great interest. But they stayed silent.

"So you could know I mean for my scent to be with

you as you go to the hunter's moon run tonight, Abby." Quentin's voice dropped to such a low register he knew no human ears could hear him. "So you could know the truth."

A short pause held them together. The sounds of the little coffeeshop bustled and rolled over them, but the space surrounding Quentin and Abby was like a tiny, insulated island of quiet.

Of anticipation.

"What—what truth is that?" Her voice wavered as she spoke, but it was from curiosity. No fear touched her words. Only what he hoped was a tightly-leashed hope.

"The truth," he breathed, leaning down closer to her, "that I'll be giving all those wolves a run for their money tonight, beautiful. Because you won't be running alone. No way in hell am I allowing that."

This time, he was so close to her he could hear the little click in her throat as she swallowed again, could feel the heat of her skin pulsing out toward him. Could see the fathomless depths of those brilliant aqua blue eyes of hers, locked on his like he was the only man in the room. The only man in the world.

She looked as stunned as he'd felt earlier, when the truth of what the run meant had hit him. When the realization that he had to be there to run with her had settled onto him.

Satisfied, Quentin straightened up. Tossing her a sudden grin, he forced himself to step away from her and turn toward the door. The two young wolves, mouths now slightly open and eyebrows raised, just stared at him. Quentin simply said in a cheerful voice, "See you tonight, Abby. Boys," he added, nodding at the other wolves.

It half killed him to leave her sitting there with those young pups, but he knew they had zero chance with her, no matter what they might try to say. Not when he'd seen the same hunger in her face he'd felt while talking to her.

The hunger of a mate, ready to run under the full moon with the only one strong enough and fast enough to catch her.

5

*A*bby held her breath for a long moment as she glanced again at the eastern horizon, waiting for the giant hunter's moon to rise above the shadowed ridges of the mountains. A definite chill braced the air around her, heightening the scents of the quaking aspen trees and the stately ponderosa pines that ringed the huge meadow. Letting her breath out in a long exhale, she took in an equally deep inhale, closing her eyes as she allowed her wolf to pull in the multitude of layered smells through her sensitive shifter nose.

No question about it, autumn was her favorite season. It seemed like it had just fallen with a decisive snap in the last twenty-four hours. The air had turned super brisk, the sky so bright and clean it practically shone, and suddenly it seemed that every single deciduous tree in town had burst into flaming color overnight. Reds and golds sprinkled through the streets and dashed up the hillsides, causing Abby's heart to pound with an extra ounce of joy and a nearly constant smile to stretch over her face with unfettered delight.

The only thing she had missed all day was Quentin. Then she had seen him, and her day had exploded into an even more complicated depth of emotion, whirling around inside her as his huge presence had filled the entire room in the coffeeshop earlier. Their interaction had been so brief, yet the enormity of the bond between them had been undeniable even within those few moments. Her wolf had danced and hummed in her mind, gleeful at the knowledge that her mate had come for her.

He'd been so—so manly. So bear shifter manly huge and amazing. The two wolves also there had faded completely out of Abby's consciousness, so much so that she was literally surprised to see them still standing there after Quentin had left. She was sure they were perfectly nice, but she hadn't given them another thought the rest of the day.

Quentin had been the only shifter on her mind since she'd seen him, his scent lingering with her all day. *I'll be giving all those wolves a run for their money tonight, beautiful. Because you won't be running alone. No way in hell am I allowing that.* His words drifted through her head, echoing over and over.

He wouldn't really show up. Would he? With all these wolves? A lone bear shifter, ready to run among hundreds of wolves? That was crazy. He hadn't meant it. He was just saying it because—because he was Quentin. Because he liked her. Not because he was— because they were—

She could hardly finish the thought, even to herself.

Because they were mates.

Her wolf danced and howled in her mind, slamming image after image at her of Quentin roaming the mountains in his enormous grizzly bear form. *Mate. Mate,* she insisted, gainsaying Abby's own thoughts. Abby glanced around the meadow. No. Dang it. Now wasn't the time to be thinking about other shifters. Not even Quentin. She couldn't think about him. He wouldn't be here. This was the annual hunter's moon pack run, the largest one in the country.

Tonight was all about wolf shifters. It had to be. She didn't know any other way.

Narrowing her eyes as her own wolf's high-pitched howl, then almost vicious snarl, rang through her head so sharply the sound of it hurt, Abby let her glance slowly pan over the many wolves in attendance from different packs. From as close as the neighboring affiliate pack to as far as those who had come down from the northern reaches of Montana and even the far western coastal forests of Washington state, wolves mingled, prowled, and laughed with one another, every single one of them waiting for the rising full moon and the call of the Black Mesa pack alpha to begin the hunt.

The hunt which for some of the wolves here would be for a mate.

"A lot of likely-looking candidates for you here, Abby." She startled slightly at the deep, friendly voice at her shoulder. Turning her head, she smiled at Sean as he walked toward her with his arm casually flung over Megan's shoulders. His tone was easy, his stance relaxed as he held his mate close to him. There was no question that the two of them would run together tonight. As a mated pair, they would enjoy the evening together before slipping off to some secluded glade to have their own fun. Abby smiled a bit wistfully, even as she nodded in agreement.

"Definitely a lot of new guys here," she said, glancing out at all the strange wolves again before she looked back at Sean and Megan. Her best friend gave her a far more dubious glance than Sean had. But she said nothing. "I'm sure there will be a lot of new mate pairings tonight," Abby casually added, trying to sound excited about that.

To her utter shock, fierce growls laced her words, deepening her voice and rippling through her entire body with a tensing effect. Sean reared backward, his hackles raising more from startlement than any actual defensiveness. Megan rubbed a soothing hand along his arm, murmuring, "She's just on edge. Sometimes there's a bit of expectation at this run. Your home pack's hunter's moon runs were probably a lot more casual than this one, weren't they?"

Abby rapidly blinked her eyes, breathing steadily to settle herself and her suddenly outraged wolf, who smacked her mind with angry lashes of her tail. "Wow, I'm sorry, Sean. That wasn't directed at you." She shook her head, trying to clear it. "I don't know where that came from. Megan's right. I'm a little on edge, I guess."

Sean shrugged and waved it off, the automatic wolf glow of his eyes settling back into their normal human color.

"True." He grinned down at Megan, his equanimity restored. "Our hunter's moon runs were a lot smaller, pretty much just for fun. It's a good thing you never met some other guy during one of these, love," he added, a possessive tone creeping into his voice as he leaned down to soundly kiss Megan on the lips.

Abby watched with more wistful longing. The image of a huge, dark silvertip of a bear rumbled through her mind even as she tried to shove him out.

After she could come up for air, Megan answered in a teasing tone, "Definitely not. No, I was holding out for a certain sexy guy from the big city." She smiled at her mate, allowing her own wolf to roughen her voice with a similar amount of possessiveness at the simple pleasure of her mate's existence.

Abby bit her lip and sighed to herself. She wanted that. More than anything. She wanted to be mated, settled, part of the well-working team that was her pack. Settled with a wolf shifter mate of her own.

Her wolf howled so angrily inside her that Abby

gasped. An answering gasp rippled through the crowd around her as her wolf continued to howl inside her. Mortified, she fought back against her wolf with every ounce of strength she had, fighting for control, closing her eyes for a second as she struggled. But the gasps around the clearing rippled out to every edge, leaving in their wake only a stark, shocked silence. Her eyes flew open, expecting to see everyone staring at her. Instead, the eyes of every single shifter in the glade, several hundred of them, were fixed on a point behind her. Even Megan and Sean had turned, also staring. Abby felt the sudden danger twisting and rippling throughout the glade. The instant nervousness and protectiveness of every single wolf there.

Someone was here who didn't belong.

Whirling, Abby looked in the direction everyone else faced.

Quentin Walker, bear shifter, strode through the glen full of wary, agitated wolf shifters.

Heading straight for her. Just as he'd promised.

Abby's heart slammed into her throat, stifling another gasp as what seemed like a bucket of cold water, followed by a hot, sizzling sensation ripped through her. It took her a long, disorienting moment to find the exact emotion she felt. To name it. Her wolf still howled inside her, this time with an exultant thrill that surged through her with every beat of her heart. She recognized the feeling for what it was.

Joy.

Quentin lumbered with easy grace yet deliberate strength right into the midst of all the wolves, his huge form moving with unerring purpose as he headed right for her. A bear shifter, alone among the wolves.

"Wow," Megan breathed beside her. "That's pretty hot, Abby. And it's all for you. You sure he's not the one we were talking about the other day?" Her tone was pointed, but kind.

Abby swallowed hard, staring as the guy she couldn't get out of her head bore down on her like a freight train. As he came toward her, his long, shaggy dark brown hair topping his sexier-than-hell eyes, the mouth she wanted to feel whisper over her skin, brand her every inch with its kisses, the beard she delighted to feel each time he nuzzled it in-between her legs, Abby felt the very air seem to settle into a charged, expectant hush.

Into the wild, tight silence, Quentin drew up to within a mere foot of her, practically causing her nerve endings to burst into flame just from his electrifying presence. Without waiting another second, he crushed her to his chest and claimed her mouth with his. Startled at first for a split second, angry at his audacity in showing up here when he knew it was a wolf thing, she still couldn't help herself from almost immediately melting into him. It was Quentin, after all. Tall, strong, shaggy-haired, rough and tumble and just—himself. Unashamedly, unreservedly his bear shifter self.

She fell into his kiss as naturally as she breathed air.

Feasting on her like she was the last drink he would ever take, like she was the most delicious thing he would ever taste, Quentin kissed Abby in front of the whole pack till she felt boneless and senseless from it.

When he finally released her, she just stood there, staring at him, legs shaking and fire banking deep inside her. Hot, bright, and focused on him.

Only him. Angry, yes. But also filled with an unmistakable lust.

Dammit.

"I'm here for the hunter's moon run," Quentin said, the deep, dark rumble of his words carrying to each corner of the meadow, although he didn't take his eyes off of Abby. "I'm here to join in the hunt. Right next to this woman." He lifted his hands toward her, palms up, the move somehow screaming pure alpha male possessiveness. "Right next to Abby Kenyon. Because," his voice snarled out in a booming growl, turning around so she was tucked behind him as he swept his glance over all the other shifters there, "She's mine."

6

*Q*uentin stood in front of Abby, arms crossed in front of his massive chest as he surveyed the wolf shifters around him. He probably looked like some kind of caveman, shown up to grab his woman by the hair and drag her away to his lair, but at the moment he didn't really care.

Abby was his mate, dammit. He knew it, her wolf knew it, she knew it deep inside even if she wasn't ready to admit it. Just like he'd told her earlier today, no way in hell was he going to let her participate in this crazy wolf run without him. He was going to show her, and everyone here, that he was the one for her. The only one.

He was a silvertip grizzly bear shifter, surrounded by hundreds of wolves. If they wanted to, despite his size and strength, they could easily rip him to shreds simply due to their sheer numbers, just as Cortez had pointed out. It didn't matter. He would fight to the death for Abby if he had to. He didn't know much about wolf pack law. But they sure were about to get a taste of bear shifter law if it had to come to that.

As the dual shocks of his appearance and his kiss must've worn off, Abby stepped around from behind him, tugging at him with one arm and thwapping him with her other. He looked down at her sexy, adorably furious face with the snapping blue-green eyes. They were ringed with a bright glow, a sure sign that her wolf was rising hard and fast in her. Though he kept his features settled into an expression that told the wolves around him *don't mess with me,* Quentin smiled inside. His sexy little mate was a hell of a little she-devil.

One of the many things he loved about her.

"Quentin!" She finally found her voice. A little ragged, a lot confused, bound with anger as well as what he was pretty sure was excitement, it raced over him like heated little kisses. "What on earth are you doing? You can't just come here like this. Acting like a —doing what you—I mean, kissing me, and then—" Her voice sputtered to a halt, though she still ineffec-tually tried to drag him away. To where, he had no idea.

His heart suddenly thumped out of whack again as he realized just what she was trying to do. His sweet, sexy little she-devil of a mate was trying to protect him. She was trying to protect *him,* an enormous grizzly bear shifter, king of the woods, from her pack of wolves.

His heart swelled, about bursting in his chest from pride.

She was going to make a hell of a mate. That is, as long as he could convince her of the truth of that fact.

Quentin sensed the tension in the glen sharpening with every moment. Then a male voice spoke. Quiet, measured, collected.

"You are welcomed here, silvertip shifter."

The soft voice carried across the meadow with a potency Quentin suspected had to do with some crazy old wolf shifter stuff that he didn't understand, and didn't need to. Clearly, it came from an alpha. Despite the matter-of-fact tone, not to mention that nobody here could claim to be *his* alpha, Quentin sensed tremendous power emanating from the voice. Well, that was damned impressive. He sharply turned his head to look for the source he instinctively knew was the alpha wolf of all alpha wolves.

Silently, with not a watchful eye leaving Quentin, the small, tight clusters of shifters parted like smooth water to allow the male wolf who had spoken to easily stroll across the meadow toward Quentin. The man was tall, rangy, and definitely a savvy, cagey old wolf. As he came closer, Quentin could see silver strands in the dark hair. Wolf shifters could live a hell of a long time. Looking at this one, he guessed the man's age had to be at least a few hundred years. Maybe more. But no threat emanated from the shifter, even though every single wolf he passed seem deferent to him. Abby closed her mouth and stopped tugging at Quentin, giving the approaching shifter a single quick glance before dropping her eyes. Even so, she stepped around so that she was slightly in front of Quentin.

Still protecting him.

This alpha wolf wasn't challenging him, though. Quentin was in the man's house, so to speak. He would play by the same rules.

Keeping his voice as respectful as possible, though his bear rumbled and huffed just beneath his words, Quentin replied, "Thank you. My name is Quentin Walker. I come from Deep Hollow, over the mountain. And I want to join your hunter's moon run tonight."

The approaching wolf studied him as he drew closer, coming to a casual stop several feet away. Spreading his feet about shoulder width apart, casually tucking his thumbs in the front pockets of his pants to indicate he wasn't offering any particular challenge, the alpha nodded. "My name is Channing Bardou, and I am alpha of the Black Mesa pack. I know who you are. I know everyone in the Walker clan. Your parents and I go quite a ways back."

Despite himself, Quentin couldn't help the soft huff of surprise that left his lips. Even his bear stopped restlessly pacing as Quentin focused his entire attention on the wolf in front of him. Well, almost his entire attention. Part of him remained utterly aware of the fact that Abby stood next to him. Standing her ground with him, even in the face of her own alpha.

"I see," he said after a long moment. "Then I guess you'll understand that my stated intentions for being here are honest. I'm here for Abby. She's mine, and she will run with me tonight. Only me."

Quentin's voice fell into the silent clearing with the ring of authenticity he knew everyone here would recognize. Shifters weren't mind readers, but they were damned good at knowing when someone spoke the truth. Quentin meant his words with every molecule of his being. He was here for Abby, and that was all.

The older wolf, Channing, regarded him for another long moment, quietly assessing him in what was still a nonthreatening manner. Quentin had to admit that if he wasn't here for Abby, he might feel a little uncomfortable under that gaze. Okay, fine. He'd probably feel damned edgy with those eyes pinned on him. But he wasn't here to pick a fight. He was here for his mate, no matter how that would be received. He knew what he wanted. He'd never been more sure of anything in his life. Quietly, he waited for the wolf pack's alpha to come to whatever conclusion needed to be reached.

After another long silence, the alpha shifted his mild gaze to Abby. "Abby Kenyon," he said softly, just the sound of his voice jerking her head up to look at him. Even so, she only managed one quick, direct glance at him before she moved her gaze to settle in the general vicinity of her alpha's shoulders. Quentin understood what that meant. In wolf hierarchy, the most dominant wolf controlled the others to the extent that looking directly into a more dominant wolf's eyes was viewed as a challenge.

Abby knew her place in the pack, and she recognized the power her alpha wielded. Though he bristled a bit inside, Quentin stayed silent. If he wanted Abby to be with him, he knew she had to play by the rules of her wolf pack, the only way she knew how. While he'd done his part in showing up for her—and dammit, but his little brother had been right about that—this part wasn't his own battle.

Even so, the alpha's next words startled Quentin as well as apparently every other wolf there.

"Do you fully understand why this man is here, Abby? That this bear shifter has come to claim you as his mate?"

A low hiss whispered through some of the surrounding wolves, but not a single one of them said more. Unperturbed, the alpha continued.

"That he wishes to prove to not only you, but to the pack, and even himself that he is strong enough to take you on as his?"

Quentin's jaw opened a little bit as he stared at the alpha. The next words shocked him even more.

"And do you understand, Quentin Walker," now the alpha's inscrutable gaze shifted over to Quentin, the power behind his eyes so quietly intense that Quentin actually rocked a bit on his feet, even though he still stood right where he belonged next to Abby, "that not only must you prove this to her, but that she must prove that she is also worthy of being your mate?"

Well, damn. He hadn't thought about it that way.

Apparently, neither had Abby. She drew in a shaky breath and looked at Quentin. Before she could say anything, though, the alpha turned his head to the eastern horizon where light began to gently spill into the clearing.

"Ah." Satisfaction rippled through alpha Channing's voice. "The hunter's moon rises. Come. It is time for all of us to run under its light."

With that, he looked one more time at Quentin and Abby. Nodding at them, he then threw back his head. The deep, rich timbre of his wolf's voice loosed through his throat in a full-bodied howl that was echoed by the other wolves there.

Quentin set his jaw in determination. Ready or not, the hunter's moon run was about to start.

7

*A*bby couldn't tear her eyes away from Quentin. Her big, sexy, burly bear shifter, standing in front of her, surrounded by wolves. Their excited, high-spirited howls and yips in answer to the alpha's opening cries swirled up through the crisp October night air as the heavy orange glow of the very full moon slowly rose on the horizon.

Despite the eerie sound of hundreds of throats, both human and wolf, unleashing their wild animal sounds, Quentin didn't waver for a second. He stayed planted in front of her, ready for whatever came next.

Ready for her.

Taking a deep breath, Abby took a step back from Quentin and quickly began stripping off her clothes. Quentin stared at her, a startled yet pleased expression coming onto his face.

"Really," he said, one corner of his mouth lifting up in a grin.

But Abby shook her head at him. "You heard my alpha," she said in a soft, low tone. The husky sound of her wolf rippled through her voice as she went on. "On this hunter's moon run, you have to catch me. And wolves are fast. Really fast. You're going to have to work hard for me, Quentin Walker," she added, her voice deadly serious.

As she let the last of her clothes drop to the cold ground, stepping away from them and standing before him utterly naked, Abby smiled, letting her wolf's teeth gleam in the dark as she shifted into her wild, four-legged shape.

"I know you can understand me in this form," she said in her pure wolf's voice. All around the glen, human forms were shifting into wolf, baying and howling and setting off in all directions to run. No one paid the two of them any more mind, having been clearly warned by the Black Mesa pack alpha that the decision of what to do with Quentin was up to Abby, and Abby alone. "Are you ready for this?"

Quentin's response was to open his mouth and roar. In a flash, he let his grizzly bear burst over him, ripping and shredding through his clothes. He shook them off his furry shape, his massive jaws working as he bellowed again. Several of the wolves paused and looked at him, instinctively answering in snarls and growls and howls. The low, commanding voice of the alpha rose above them all, urging them to their own runs. To their own hunts.

Leaving Abby and Quentin alone.

"You'd better be fast, my gorgeous little wolf," Quentin said, stepping toward her on his massive paws. "I intend on catching you."

With a delighted yip at the challenge in his voice, Abby turned tail and raced away, dashing after the streaming forms of wolves as they spread up and over the mountain into the chilly forest as the moon slowly rose in the sky above them all.

As she raced through the flashes of stark white bark of the aspen trees and the dark, tall shapes of the pines that made up the bulk of the forest, she felt Quentin at her heels. The ground shook behind her where he ran. He was fast. Really fast. She hadn't expected him to be that fast. They'd run together before in their animal shapes, playing and racing through the beautiful lands by his family's property, but they'd never been so focused. They'd never been at such a dead run before, with one goal in mind: for Quentin to catch Abby.

She sensed it was a goal he was taking more seriously than anything ever before. The knowledge spurred her on, even as she flung her head up for a short, sharp howl that stabbed through the trees along with the howls of many wolves both near and far. Behind her, Quentin bellowed the roar of a grizzly bear, the noise of it reverberating through the same air to lend a deep bass note beneath the howls of the wolves. A brief silence greeted his unexpected sound before the multiple choruses of many wolves began again. Abby smiled as she raced along. Quentin was staking his claim on her. He was warning off all the others.

He was warning them off of his mate.

As she ran, Abby felt her human side blending into her wolf side, relaxing and accepting and enjoying the deep knowledge she finally began to embrace. The knowledge that Quentin was indeed her mate. The knowledge that he could be a permanent part of her life.

If, her human said with an impertinent sniff, *he can catch me.*

Letting her tongue loll out in a wolfish grin, Abby added a staccato *yip yip yip* as she leapt and raced through the trees, leading Quentin ever onward and up the mountain. Through the far reaches of the forest, far beyond where humans would dare to go at night. Far beyond where any of the other wolves on this cold October run would go.

Leading him to her.

MILES HAD PASSED before Abby began to slow in front of Quentin. He admired her lithe shape racing around tree trunks, under bushes, over downed logs and scatters of boulders. In his bear shape, his sense of smell was superior even to her acute wolf senses. The scent of his mate running in front of him, leading him to her, was so crisp and clear he felt as if he had the strength of twenty bears.

He would never stop until he could catch her. His mate. His Abby.

Abby flashed around an enormous boulder that gleamed faintly in the moonlight, disappearing behind it. With a roar, Quentin put on another burst of speed, barreling around the enormous granite boulder, thundering over the ground as he tried to catch up with her. But he raced into a tiny, empty meadow filled with nothing but the sharp, clear bathe of moonlight. Slamming himself to a halt in the middle of it, his claws leaving deep gouges in the earth, Quentin lifted his head as he opened his mouth in a roar, simultaneously bellowing out his cry and searching the chilly night for his mate.

There. Her sweetness called to him from the left. Snapping his head around, he looked into the shadows between the trees. Sitting there, panting, was the light, beautiful shape of his she-wolf. He paused for a long moment, tipping his head in the other direction as if he wasn't sure where she was. Lifting his nose a bit more as if he'd caught another scent, he moved off to the right instead, pointedly sniffing in the direction of the trees directly opposite from her. Moving as quietly as he could, he listened as hard as he was able. Yes. She was following him into the middle of the glen, probably planning a surprise leap onto his back to startle him with her agile wolf ways.

He'd see about that.

Pausing almost at the other side of the tiny meadow, still ostentatiously sniffing in that direction, Quentin waited until it sounded like Abby was about halfway across the glen. Far more swiftly than he knew she expected, he whirled on his powerful hind legs, standing up on them and roaring his might into the moonlit glade.

Shocked, she shied back from where she had indeed been right in the middle of the glen, her teeth baring and snapping her surprise. Quentin let himself stay up on his hind legs for a long moment, giving his saucy little love a good glimpse of how strong and powerful and brave he was. Then he dropped back down to all fours, the ground thundering beneath him as he landed. With a shake of his massive head that rippled over the huge hump of his shoulders and across the dark cinnamon and gold of his coat, Quentin shifted back into his human shape.

Striding fearlessly across the glen toward Abby where she stood still in her wolf form, the look of surprise comical on her face, he reached out his hand to her. "Fair and square, Abby? You caught me, then I caught you. Right?"

Quietly, he waited for her reply.

8

*A*bby stared at Quentin as he shifted into his human form and waited for her. Damn, he was fast. And smart. And hers. At that thought, she let herself shift back into human form, stepping across the pretty little glen in the cool moonlight to him. Her shifter genes didn't let her feel the cold nearly so much as a human would, though she still reveled in the delightful snap of the air against her bare human skin. Quentin was the same way, but he ran even hotter than she did. As she stepped close to him, she could practically feel the furnace of his body both heating her and beckoning her even closer.

"Yes," she said, feeling utterly at ease as both her human and her wolf side accepted the truth of what was happening right now. "Yes, Quentin. Right now."

With a groan, her big, burly man took the final step over to her and gathered her into his arms, pressing her close to him. His lips found hers, seeking and ravaging with all the pent-up energy of the run they had just experienced together. She was just as amped up as he was, and answered him stroke for stroke. Her tongue tangled with his, her teeth clashed against his as her lips tried to devour every inch of his mouth. He tasted strong, feral, and utterly divine.

"Abby," he groaned, the rumble of his bear still muttering beneath his voice. "Mine," he growled, swallowing her answering cry.

His broad, strong hands smoothed their way over her skin from her shoulders down her back, to the swell of her hips. His fingers tightened over her rear, pushing her hips against his, where she felt the heavy thickness of his dick pressing against her. The sensation made her lightheaded. Her entire body was already completely aroused from the run in the deep, wild magic of the moonlight around them. The fingers of his hand eased around the front of her hip, pressing between their stomachs and down between her legs. She let herself ease back a bit so he could find what he sought. As his exploring fingers encountered the dampness already heating her from between her legs, he groaned again with an almost desperate sound.

"Abby," he said, pulling his head back slightly so he could look at her eyes in the moonlight. His own eyes were dark, almost completely swallowed up by his pupils so soon after shifting. "I need to be inside you right now, gorgeous. Right now."

The dark, sexy need of his voice shuddered its way through Abby even as his thick fingers pushed deeper inside her, another one sliding in, then a third squeezing around the other two. She felt deliciously stretched, moaning as he began circling one of his fingers inside her.

"Okay," she said in what she knew sounded like little more than a breath. "Sounds like a great idea." She sounded inane, but she didn't care. She wanted the same thing. She wanted him inside her.

If this was what a hunter's moon run was supposed to be like, then she was in. All the way. Never in her life had she had a run like this.

Then again, never before in her life had she run with Quentin like this. On a mating run. A full hunter's moon mating run.

Gently and urgently, Quentin suddenly scooped her up, causing her to squeal a little bit. He very gently laid her down on the floor of the meadow, following with his own body. He snugged her into his side, warming her even more. She opened her mouth to speak, but he shook his head. "Let me touch you for just a minute, Abby," he whispered. The sheer need that made his voice shake trapped her own voice in her throat as she stared at him. "Let me touch you first."

Trembling, she nodded. It took everything she had to not just grab his head and pull it down for another kiss, but she resisted. He knew what he was doing.

73

Whatever it was, she wanted to be there for every second of it.

Quentin smoothed his hand down over Abby's body, gently running his fingers from her collarbone over her breast, her stomach, her hip, the top of her thigh. Then he ran his hand up the other side, as if he were feeling her for the first time ever. His hand trembled with effort. Effort, she knew, that was him keeping himself from just taking her.

That was what she wanted more than just about anything right now. Fine, he wanted to touch her first and she would let him, but—

"Oh!" Abby gasped as Quentin suddenly leaned his head down to lick and stroke one breast while his other hand moved back between her legs, his fingers diving back in to her wet, needy depths. "Oh, okay. That's good. Oh, wow. Quentin." She knew she sounded totally nonsensical, but she was beyond caring. His touch sent fire blazing through her, as if her nerves were made of molten liquid that shivered and trembled and grew ever hotter beneath his touch. Between her legs, she felt the ache deep in her core that told her she needed his touch desperately. Now.

"Abby. So damn beautiful." Sheer worship colored Quentin's voice. She half giggled, half gasped as his voice and his beard tickled over her breast, then moved to the other one.

Her hips began moving almost of their own volition, gently swirling and circling and lifting off the ground. The moonlight poured over both of them, seeming almost as bright as day, although it cast inky black shadows, giving a mysterious, momentous cast to the little meadow. Abby dug her hands into Quentin's hair, clutching his head, pressing him closer to her breast. He lightly bit the nipple, making her gasp, then did the same to the other one. Back and forth he went, even as his hands whirled and stroked inside her. She was getting so wet there she could hardly stand it. She was ready for him. More than ready for him.

She'd never been more ready for this man in her life.

"Quentin," she said, her voice nothing more than a trembling gasp.

"Yes," he finally said, lifting his head from her breast and shifting his body so that he was completely on top of her. "You're so wet for me, Abby. I'm not going to be able to hold back," he warned. "It's half killing me to hold back this much."

"Don't hold back anymore," she commanded as best she could in her still shaky voice. "Don't you dare hold back on me, Quentin."

Groaning, Quentin said, "Never. I'll never hold back on you again."

With that, he reached down to guide himself to her entrance. Abby spread her knees, lifting her hips toward him as she looked into the wild darkness of his eyes.

"Now, babe," he said. His voice roughened into a

growl of anticipation. "Now!" With a roar, Quentin plunged himself into Abby, his steel-hard dick sliding into her. It filled her so full that she screamed from the stunning delight of it as her hands moved down to grip his shoulders with a strength she vaguely thought might bruise him. But she didn't care. Her Quentin, her lover, her mate, was plunging in and out of her, diving into her with deep strokes.

Claiming her fully as his.

QUENTIN THRUST himself into Abby's welcoming heat again and again, his head about ready to explode from the sound of her eager cries as she moved with him. Like a dance partner he'd known forever, who knew his every move and joyfully met them with her own. He didn't think it was possible, but his dick seemed to get bigger and harder, encased in her slick wet heat as he thrust in, then out, then back in. Her hair, an outflung wild golden mane around the face he could tell even in the moonlight was flushed, begged for him to gently grab on and hold. So he did, even as she held onto his shoulders and back so hard he felt as if she were burning her very fingerprints into his skin.

As she clenched slightly around him, her voice took on the sexy, guttural quality it always did as she approached orgasm.

"Yeah, babe," he said, barely holding himself back

from spilling his seed inside her. He wanted her to come first. He wanted to feel her spasming around him in her wild release so he could enjoy every second of it as he plunged over the edge himself with her.

"Come for me, Abby. Come for me, beautiful." He thrust into her faster, cupping one hand around her head as he bucked against her in the crystal clear moonlight. Far off in the distance, he heard a few wild echoes of wolf howls spiraling up over the mountainside. Abby arched her back, her sweet inner walls abruptly clutching him tightly as she suddenly shrieked out, the sound of her climax spilling out of her mouth in a sweet, joyous call that he couldn't help but echo himself seconds later as he fell right over that same damned beautiful edge with his mate.

White fire seemed to lick through Quentin's body, jumping over to Abby and binding the two of them together tightly under the moonlight as their bodies moved and exploded and melted together as one. Her hoarse cries shouted along with his into the night air, her wolf howling beneath her voice even as his bear roared beneath his as the two of them claimed one another. As the two of them mated beneath the beauty of the magical full moon.

As the lingering, delicious shudders ebbed and flowed and finally rolled away from both of them, Quentin gently lowered his body slightly to the side of Abby's, keeping his arm and leg flung over her while the bulk of his body rested on the ground so as not to crush her. He listened to her breathing as it steadied along with his. A deep sense of peace and satisfaction spread through his limbs like never before.

After more long moments, during which Abby's hands gently rubbed his back and arms and basically every inch of skin she could touch, her face nuzzled into his neck, the heat of her body mingled with his combating the slight chill that both their shifter genes already protected them against, she softly laughed.

"What's so funny?" he asked, his own mouth slipping into a smile at the sound of her sweet laughter.

"Me," she said, shrugging beneath him. "You. Both of us. This," he could tell she was waving a free arm around, indicating the glen in the moonlight and the distant echoes of wolf howls in the mountains. "Us. I'm laughing," and she nuzzled her face into his neck even more, lightly kissing him, "because this is perfect. Because it's what I needed. What we both needed."

Quentin leaned back a little bit, tipping his fingers under her chin gently so that she looked up at him. He could see the luminous blue-green of her eyes even in the moonlight, enhanced by the glow of her wolf. "Because you're finally ready to admit that I was right?" He let his grin tumble into his words. "You're finally ready to admit that I'm your mate, even if I am just a big, gruff, bumbling bear?"

So quickly that it took his breath away and wiped away his grin into a serious, heartfelt expression, Abby said, "You're not bumbling. What you are is the fastest, strongest, most incredible man I've ever met. Bear, wolf, it doesn't matter. Wait," she interrupted herself, looking at him with a tiny frown on her forehead. "It *does* matter. It does matter that you're a bear. It's part of what makes you *you*, Quentin," she added so firmly that the sound shivered its way into his soul.

"My wolf shifter mate," he said, wonder touching his voice even though he'd already known the truth of it for a long time. "I don't know what it is about tonight, if it's full moon magic and pack run magic and who knows what else, but I know more strongly than I've ever known before that you're exactly that for me, too. My mate. That I'm yours," he added just as firmly as she had.

Abby smiled up at him, her sweet, full lips curving up with the luscious intention that slayed him every time he looked at her. "Some kind of magic for sure," she agreed.

"Of course," he said lightly, though every part of him felt buoyant and free, "it was because I was fast enough to catch you. Faster than you thought I could be, huh?"

"Oh, yeah?" The sweet, teasing challenge in her voice whispered over him as she threaded her hand back into his hair. "You only caught me because I let you."

"Is that so," he murmured, leaning down to her lips again. "Well, since you did, my sexy wolf shifter mate," he added, smiling again at the immense joy that word sent through him, a joy he saw reflected on her own face, "then I suppose we have the whole night ahead of us to keep seeing who's caught who."

"I think you're right. My sexy bear shifter mate," she said, smiling up at him.

He proved the truth of that to her over and over again, all the amazing night long.

The End

Thank you for reading *Hunter's Moon!* I loved writing a crossover story between the Black Mesa Wolves and Silvertip Shifters worlds, and Quentin and Abby were the perfect characters for it.

What's next for the **Silvertip Shifters**? Shane & Jessie's story in ***MOUNTAIN BEAR'S BABY: SHANE.*** Turn the page to read it.

MOUNTAIN BEAR'S BABY: SHANE

*L*ips pursed, eyes slightly narrowed in critical assessment, Jessica McMillan reached forward to touch a gentle finger to the shining star on the tree. Almost holding her breath, she pushed it just the tiniest bit to the left. It snuggled perfectly into place at the very top.

There. Letting out a huge breath of relief, she turned to her friend Livy. "I think it's just right now. What do you think?"

Livy's shiny dark hair bounced on her shoulders as she nodded. "Definitely perfect. In fact, I think that's the best Christmas tree I've ever seen in my entire life. Without a doubt." She gave another decisive nod. "Absolutely."

Jessie awarded her friend a sharp look. Livy had never been one for a good poker face. Dissolving into more giggles, she neatly sidestepped Jessie's playful swipe at her shoulder. "Don't mess with me," Jessie protested, although she let herself smile as well. "It's my first Christmas tree in my own place. Like, ever. It's a solemn moment."

With appreciable solemnity, both women regarded the two-foot-tall tree nestled into a cushion of red velvet atop the kitchen table that doubled as a writing desk and bill holder in a corner of Jessie's tiny apartment. Carefully, Jessie stepped forward to plug the small string of lights on the tree into the wall socket. With a festive little burst, they twinkled to life amidst the deliciously piney scent of the small, needled branches. She sighed with delight as Livy made admiring noises.

"See? It is perfect. I have everything I need here."

As if on cue, a slightly outraged wail punctuated her words. With the blissful rush of love that infused her every time her little angel made a noise, whether it was indecipherable baby babble, a loud burp, a rumbly fart, or even the incredibly loud screams when her sweet darling was really hungry, Jessie turned and took the three short strides to the other end of the room. Grant's chubby little legs, extending from his diapered butt, stood firmly by the low table he clung to. He futilely reached his little hands up in an apparent attempt to scale it. As Jessie reached down to pick him up, he looked at her, a small frown slicing across his brow as he once again let out an irritable string of sound, smacking one uncoordinated hand on the table leg.

Behind her, Livy said, "Wow. It's such a good thing we got you here when we did. That cute little booger is gonna be such a handful. I am so glad we were already friends, Jess. If you hadn't told me what was going on..."

Jessie, her arms now full of squirming, sweet smelling, very strong and solid little baby, turned toward her friend as she nestled her face into the top of Grant's head and breathed in his sweet baby smell. Her son. Her world.

Her own little baby *bear shifter.* Which was the Craziest. Thing. Ever.

But which also happened to be true.

Looking at Livy and her suddenly serious expression, Jessie nodded. "I can't imagine what I would've done if I hadn't known you. If you weren't from here." She waved her hand around, indicating the small, cozy little town of Deep Hollow, blanketed under snow outside her apartment. "What about the women like me out there in the world who don't have friends like you? Friends who know about, uh, shifters? What do they do, if this ever happens to them?"

Brown eyes slightly troubled, Livy stepped forward so she could cootchie-coo Grant's little belly. He loved Livy. Seeming to forget about his battle to climb the table, he giggled and smiled and shrieked up at her with joy. "That sort of situation is really rare. You and Grant were kind of the exception to the rule."

Jessie sighed. Quickly, Livy caught herself. "I'm sorry. That was insensitive." She didn't stop tickling Grant, who still giggled and squirmed, but she scrunched up her face in an apologetic expression at Jessie.

With a reassuring smile, Jessie shrugged. "It's been my reality for over a year now. Well, more like two years if you count from when I found out that I was pregnant. It's okay, Livy," she said gently to her friend, who looked genuinely contrite at having put her foot in it. "You got me *here.* I have a new family now. Seriously, who could want anything more?"

Despite the fact that she had at least a ninety percent conviction in her words, what she didn't say hung in stark relief between them.

The father of her child. That was the only thing more she could ask for. Well, that was an impossibility that was never, ever going to happen. In her experience, families didn't work. She'd accepted it, and moved on.

Mostly.

"Come on," Livy said. She brightened. "Let's get your little bundle of joy here dressed up in that cute outfit his auntie Livy got for him. Didn't she get that for him, oh, yes she did, who's the cutest little thing ever, huh?" Her voice took on the ridiculous baby voice babble adults tended to adopt around adorable little, uh, babies. "Because we have a cookie exchange to go to, don't we, little Mr. Grant baby bear cutie pie. Huh, don't we? We sure do. Even though you can't have any cookies, my sweet little boy. But your auntie Livy sure can, oh, yes, she can."

Jessie couldn't help but shake her head and smile at Livy as the two of them bundled Grant into the adorable little purple and gray snowsuit Livy had gotten him. Livy said eventually he wouldn't feel the cold nearly as much as humans did. But until he began to shift into his bear form on his own, which should be happening pretty soon since it usually started right around the time shifter kids were a year to a year and a half old, for now he still needed the warmth of as many outer layers as a human would wear. There'd been an enormous snowstorm last night, and although the roads were plowed, it was still easier to walk to Livy's sister's house, where the holiday cookie exchange was happening.

Glancing at herself in the little oval mirror she'd hung by the front door, Jessie sighed again. Well, it didn't matter that she basically looked like a disheveled new mom. It wasn't like there would be any guys at the cookie exchange, for pete's sake. Livy had said it was a girls' thing. Even if there were any men there, they sure wouldn't look twice at a woman toting around a kid. Single moms weren't exactly in vogue in the dating world.

Fifteen minutes later, they had Grant swaddled in

his snowsuit, diaper bag packed, and the batch of cookies each had baked that morning tucked away into containers they took with them. The second they stepped out into the winter wonderland, Jessie couldn't help but take a deep inhale of the air, pulling the crisp cold and the deep forest scents of the Colorado winter into her. The smell was heavenly.

With Grant tucked securely against her back in the baby carrier that had been one of the many items the local bear clan—wow, did it still feel kind of funny to be thinking about things like that now—had bestowed upon her when she first came here to live in Deep Hollow with her half-shifter son, Jessie stepped through the thick drifts of snow in front of her door to the groomed sidewalk before it. "You are so lucky you grew up with this," she said to Livy, letting soft envy buff her words. "I grew up with the smell of diesel and oil and dirty big city." Just thinking about it made her wrinkle her nose slightly.

Livy laughed as they walked down the salted sidewalk. "There are plenty of reasons to leave Deep Hollow." She ticked them off on her gloved fingers. "Jobs. Men I didn't grow up with since kindergarten. Adventure. You know. The sort of opportunities you can only get in a big city."

Jessie rolled her eyes at Livy. They had diametrically opposed dreams. She knew Livy yearned for more excitement, but as far as Jessie was concerned, cities were ugly and gross and way too noisy. "I can hardly imagine moving away from this adorable little town." She shrugged. "It already feels so comfortable to me."

"Even after barely a week?" Livy teased.

Jessie nodded. "I can't really explain it," she said softly. "Deep Hollow just clicked for me. Besides, it's definitely where Grant needs to grow up." Grant cooed behind Jessie's head in the backpack carrier, one of his hands tightly catching strands of her hair that popped out from beneath her warm hat.

Livy nodded without answering. That, she understood.

A friendly silence held them the remaining block to their destination, although it was filled with Grant's endless nonsensical chatter of delight and what, Jessie decided, had to be some sort of running commentary on their surroundings. His voice warbled along in the cooing word-like noises of babies who weren't quite old enough to speak yet, but who grasped enough of language to understand they would be able to communicate that way.

As they walked, Jessie took in the holiday-filled scene of the little town, sighing with contentment. For the whole ten days she had been calling Deep Hollow her new home, she'd been utterly charmed by its mountain feel, the genuine friendliness of the residents, and something else she couldn't quite put her finger on.

Something that indeed felt like *home.* Even without Grant needing to grow up here, surrounded by his own bear shifter kind and taught by them, she would have loved this place. She felt more soothed here than anywhere she'd ever lived in her life. Like it had called to her.

Right now, covered in piles of billowy white snow that sparkled in the sunlight of the clear day, it was even more enticing. The old-fashioned lampposts on either side of the lone main drag as they turned down it were festooned with lights and holiday decorations. Pine trees and several of the homes on Main Street were equally decorated, along with the fronts of every single shop on the way.

Jessie hadn't known she was a mountain girl before she came here, but now she was in love with everything about it. Some of the funny town stories Livy had regaled her with let her in on some of the small, harmless secrets about the locals, making her feel even more like she belonged here. The people she was already beginning to know made her feel welcome. People like the gracious Clara who owned the post office, Lindsay the bartender/server at the local watering hole called The Tank, and Peregrine, the high school kid who was bagging groceries at the town's sole tiny grocery store full-time during his winter break to fund what he had told her with earnest excitement was a new pair of skis for his younger sister's Christmas present. Jessie knew he was a shifter. She'd yet to work up her nerve to ask how a bear shifter could be named after a bird, but she figured there was an interesting story there.

Then of course there was Maddy, Livy's sister and the owner of the bakery café where Livy had set Jessie up with a job. It didn't pay much, but it came with the apartment. Maddy was also perfectly happy for her to bring Grant to work since he was such a well-behaved baby, and everyone instantly fell in love with him.

As they strolled along Main Street, occasionally waving at people on the other side whom they knew, Jessie felt the familiar sense of amazement that just about everyone in town knew that bear shifters lived among them. Livy had told her, with a deadly earnestness that almost scared her, that in general, telling humankind about the existence of shifters just wasn't done. That was pretty obvious, since Jessie had never heard of them in her entire life. Shifters weren't nearly as common as humans in the world, Livy had confided in her. It was a given that if shifters were ever discovered, they'd be dissected to within an inch of their lives. Studied, examined, spirited away to god-awful labs where who knew what would be done to them.

Humans were pretty good at being scared of what they didn't know.

Jessie felt fierce protectiveness wash through her again at the thought of anyone ever daring to want to do such a thing to her son. Jessie had not yet witnessed him turning into a bear. But he definitely was going to. She had seen his tiny claws extending and retracting from her fingertips, dreams in which he growled in a low register that no human would naturally do. Once or twice he'd sleepily blinked his little eyes at her and she could see the shadow of his bear within them, romping around somewhere inside her son.

Seeing his little claws come out two weeks ago had been what finally sent her lunging for her phone to call Livy, almost desperately accepting her offer of a new place to live. A place where Grant could grow up among his own kind, mentored by them in how to be the bear shifter he was. True to her word, Livy and two strapping male friends of hers had hopped a plane from some local private airstrip and flown to Jessie's latest home in Minneapolis, part of her years-long hop, skip, and jump around the country trying to find a good place to settle herself. They gathered up the rather pitifully small amount of her worldly belongings, threw them all into a rental truck, which they had paid for over her strident protest, and driven everything back to Deep Hollow.

She felt a tiny shiver slip down her back as she recalled the small demonstration they'd given her right as they arrived in Deep Hollow. Just after they entered the town limits, they'd pulled over in the snowy woods off the winding little mountain road. One of the guys from the local bear clan, whom Livy had introduced as Beckett, cheerfully showed Jessie his ability to shift from his human form into an enormous grizzly bear. She'd been ready for it, since Livy had been prepping her since before Grant was even born. Even so, to see the guy be human one moment, then a giant creature the next, standing there with them as nonchalantly as any person would, had been a stunning experience.

He'd opened his giant maw and yawned with an impressive show of gleaming sharp teeth—for which he got his shoulder smacked by Livy, who scolded him that he was going to scare Jessie.

"Wow," was all Jessie's stumbling brain had been able to come up with.

After a moment, Livy had gone to the moving truck, took Grant out of his car seat, and walked him over to the giant, humpbacked bruin. Despite herself, Jessie had stiffened and automatically reached for him, a protest rising in her throat. But before she could do or say anything, Grant stared at the giant bear, then chortled with glee and excitement as he reached out his chubby little hands. Beckett the grizzly bear had extended his nose forward very delicately, allowing Grant to feel and slap and tickle him without even moving, though he blinked his furry eyelids several times when Grant landed a fairly good one on his snout.

"Grant knows what he is, Jessie," Livy had said, throwing an understanding smile her way. "Even though he's half human, trust me. He's going to shift, and it's gonna happen really soon. It's a very good thing that he'll be around his own kind full-time," she'd quietly added.

They were safe here. Jessie again inhaled the scent of the wild, snow-covered woods as they turned down another street and up the walkway of a large Victorian style house nestled back in the trees. "Livy, this is absolutely the best gift I ever got in my life." She smiled happily as they went up the cleared walkway to the large, ornate door of Maddy's house. "I finally feel like I can relax."

Livy smiled. "I'm so glad, Jessie." She gently chucked Grant under his chin, the dopey smile that everyone in town seemed to get every time they looked at him coming across her face as he uttered his usual cute little baby coos and gurgles at her. "You deserve some stability and quiet after everything you've been through."

"I sure do." Jessie sighed with contentment as Livy knocked on the door.

Almost instantly, it opened, sending out a whoosh of warmth, the happy chatter and laughter of many voices inside, the delicious scents of baking cookies.

And a deeper, darker, far more intense something else beneath it all.

A *something* that swept through Jessie like a delicious, icy wind of alertness and clarity. A touch musky, yet crisp like snow, wild and rough, the scent slammed through her with an intensity she'd never before experienced.

"Hey, Shane," Livy said in oblivious cheer as she pulled off her scarf and hat, stepping toward the door. "I thought you were still out of town. Did the big ole manly grizzly bear come back just for our girly cookie exchange?" she teased. Then she gestured at Jessie. "This is Jessie, she's new here. Jessie, meet Shane, another one of our resident hulking shifters."

Jessie stood rooted in front of the door, staring at the enormous guy filling the entire frame. Her jaw dropped as her eyes slowly traveled upward to find his. The guy was massive. Just like all the other male bear shifters she'd met so far, but he seemed even bigger. He must be 6'5", she thought to herself in a daze. A half-wild tousle of golden brown hair on top of his head was at odds with the darker, neatly trimmed beard and mustache that bristled out from his granite hard, drop-dead gorgeous face. Light whiskey eyes that seemed familiar looked back at Jessie with as much startlement, his strong lips somewhat parted and sending the bizarre image of absolutely ravaging her with kisses as Jessie stared back at him, completely frozen.

Whoa, she thought, still dazed, *he's a freaking sexy as hell bear shifter lumberjack god of the woods.*

Except lumberjacks had never looked this sexy, she was pretty sure. Especially—

Especially ones she recognized.

Wait a minute.

Holy.

Freaking.

Nuh-uh.

He looked like—

"Maverick?" Jessie's voice was strangled as the name she had often thought about for the past two years managed to shove its way out of her mouth. She sensed more than saw Livy's smile falter as her head suddenly swiveled back and forth between Jessie and Mr. sexy lumberjack bear shifter dude. "You have a beard now," she whispered stupidly.

His own voice rumbling out so deeply it vibrated through her body, he replied in an equally shocked tone, "Jessie? What—what the hell are you doing here?"

Grant chose that moment to emit one of the screeching little kid cries of those not quite into toddlerhood, demanding the attention come back to him. Obligingly, three sets of eyes clamped on him, though all Jessie could see was the corner of his face since he was still ensconced in the backpack carrier. He waved his snow-suited arms around, almost seeming to reach forward to Mav.

"Who—what—no, no, no. That's *Shane*," Livy stuttered, eyes about popping out of her head. "He's the handyman up at the lodge. You said the guy's name was Maverick. And that he was some sort of fighter dude on the underground rings." Her wide eyes darted between them. "No way."

Seeing Jessie's expression, then that of the sexy guy Jessie knew as Maverick, Livy's face slackened. "Oh, my god," she breathed. She looked from Grant to Jessie, then back to Grant. Then she gestured at the huge, gorgeous man taking up all the space in the doorway. "No freaking way. This is him? For real? *He's* your baby daddy? Shane Walker from Deep Hollow is Grant's father?" Her voice dropped to a stunned whisper.

Jessie shook her head, completely lost as she stared into the achingly familiar face of the man she'd been looking for ever since she found out she was pregnant.

The man with whom she'd spent the most erotic, blissful, exciting three days of her entire life.

The man who was the father of her bear shifter son.

2

---

*S*hane stared at the woman who'd uttered his former name in such a completely dumbfounded tone it would've been almost comical. Except, of course, that he was just as dumbfounded.

Memories of a sex-filled, sensual, wild weekend of amazing physical union and the most bizarre joy he'd ever felt in his life crashed over him with a clarity that made him catch his breath. He'd never expected to see sweet, sexy, curvy Jessie again. He never saw any of the women again. That was the point.

But something about her had left him unable to shake her from his thoughts for the past two years. Her sweet lips, smiling up at him with languorous satisfaction after yet another delicious romp in the hotel bed they had shared for three nights. The luscious decadence of her body, which had called to him to sink into her and claim her during every second he spent with her. The beautiful gray-blue eyes, which he'd caught glancing at him several times that weekend when she hadn't expected him to turn so quickly to look back at her. She'd been watching him, with a funny, almost awestruck little smile on her face, when he woke up from sleep in the mornings.

It was that look in her eyes that had told him he was doing the right thing by jetting as usual without any contact information. Sweet, sexy Jessie had known the score. She wasn't looking for anything more than some casual fun herself. When they parted ways, they hadn't even known each other's last names. She hadn't even known his full name.

Then again, almost no one had.

Back then, he lived a wandering life that was disconnected from others except to fight them, and he liked it that way. Besides, he'd been passing through Denver with his old brawling crew at the time. Something pretty ugly had gone down at the underground shifter fight rings that had meant he and the other guys needed to jam out of town early. But if he were really honest with himself, he had to admit that the abrupt need to leave so quickly had irritated him for reasons more than the fact that the crew of guys he'd been hanging out with had been proving to be assholes and idiots.

It also had to do with the fact that his bear had just not wanted to leave Jessie. Something about her had drawn him, with the sweetness that masked a deeply sensual woman who had utterly blossomed beneath his touch during the three days they got to know one another's bodies so well. They'd actually gotten to know one another fairly well too. They talked an awful lot during those seventy-two hours.

He never talked to women like that. Ever.

The little baby strapped to her back now chortled again, reaching toward him. Livy said in a low gasp, "No way." Shane's gaze snapped over to the kid. Amber eyes looked back at him, filled with an innocence and gentleness he sensed the kid had gotten from his mother. Something else was going on back in there too. Something that he knew was—

What the hell.

"He's a shifter," Shane muttered, so shocked now he almost felt numb.

The baby also looked just like Jessie. Shane dragged his gaze back up to her. She still stared at him with opened mouth.

Livy's voice sliced through again in a shaking whisper. "Grant is obviously Jessie's son. He looks just like her. But his eyes—his eyes are *yours,* Shane. They're exactly yours. I would never have noticed unless I saw you both together. Holy smoked mackerel on a cracker," she breathed.

Shane felt his entire world shake, rattle, and roll.

Before he could say anything else, Jessie blurted out in a voice as stunned as he felt, "I've been looking for you. You said you lived on the road. That you didn't live anywhere in particular." Her voice wavered. "You told me your name was Maverick. You didn't—you weren't telling me the truth?" She sounded utterly crushed.

Livy rounded a suddenly ferocious glare at Shane. He narrowed his eyes back at her. Though she was human, she had grown up knowing about bear shifters, as did most of the humans who called Deep Hollow their home. Naturally, she didn't back down an inch.

"Well, apparently he didn't. Holy shit, Shane. Did you *lie* to her? You knocked her up, then lied to her?" Livy was in full-on outraged mode, poking her finger into Shane's chest. "What the fuck is this *Maverick* bullshit?"

That was too much.

"What the hell, Livy!" He took a deep breath to calm the angry bear he felt slamming around inside him. "I may have done some shady things in my past, but I'm not a fucking liar." He ground out his words. "You don't know my life story, anyway." He pinned her with a darker glare before taking another deep breath so he could continue more calmly.

"I never once lied to you," he said, looking back at Jessie. Damn, her eyes were beautiful. Even more stunning than he'd remembered. "My full name is Shane Maverick Walker. Everyone just called me Maverick or Mav when I was growing up. It stuck. That was my name, back when I met you. But when I moved here to Deep Hollow earlier this year, I'd decided to cut all ties with my old life. So I introduced myself as Shane, and that's the name everyone knows me by now. It is my actual legal name," he added, tossing a dark frown at Livy before looking back at beautiful Jessie. "I don't use Maverick anymore. That guy is dead as far as I'm concerned."

Under Jessie's astonished gaze, his heart beat so hard it felt like it might pound its way right out of his chest. Livy started to say something, but he plowed on.

"And yeah, when you and I met, Jessie"—whoa, just saying her name did crazy things to his insides—"I didn't have a place I called home. The road *was* my home. But things changed. They had to. So I ended up here. Deep Hollow is my home now."

She just stared, still open-mouthed, with the sweet, gorgeous face that had haunted his dreams ever since he'd left her in that hotel room they'd filled with sex and secrets and a closeness he'd never before experienced. Just looking at her made his heart jump. What the *hell* was that about? He felt his bear rising hard. Agitated. Unruly. Like his out-of-control bear of old.

He channeled the surging feelings into his words, hoping to calm his bear. "If that little kid is actually mine"—ah, damn, just saying that sent the craziest jolt through his entire body, making his head rattle and his thoughts jumble even more—"then this is a private matter between me and Jessie. So you can march your ass into that house and leave us alone, Livy."

Jessie finally spoke again, the husky sweetness of

her voice scraping over Shane's nerves in a sexy, rough little rasp that managed to inflame them even more. "Hey, she's my friend. Don't talk to her like that. *Shane,*" she said with emphasis, now looking somewhat more rankled than crushed. Those gorgeous eyes of hers squinched up into a fierce scowl at him as she took a step back, her shoulders straightening.

As if she was trying to protect the cub from him.

At that show of motherly bravado, he snorted and threw his hands up in the air, still struggling against his bear. "Trust me, if he's part shifter, he'll be more than able to hold his own. Especially," and abruptly, the shock of the entire situation thundered down onto him again, making his voice even more dark than usual, "a cub that's my son."

Complete silence held all of them, even the little boy, as Shane's growled words hung in the chill early afternoon air, punctuating the enormity of the situation. Yeah, he had to admit it. He was shocked as shit. But there was no question about it. The kid's eyes looked exactly like his. And he clearly was a shifter.

He, Shane Walker, had a son.

And he knew somehow, he'd manage to fuck it up.

As if she could read his thoughts, Livy said in a firm voice, "Jessie is one of my best friends in the world. So even if you are a big, bad grizzly bear shifter, I'll shoot you, mount your head on my wall, and use your fuzzy skin for a rug if you even think about hurting her or Grant."

Shane barely noticed her threats. "Grant," he said, briefly distracted from his agitated thoughts. "Grant Walker. That's a good name."

Quietly, Jessie corrected, "Grant McMillan. I didn't even know your last name, so he got mine instead."

Shane felt an inexplicable sensation coat him, lacing his voice with more darkness. It felt close to rage, though that wasn't quite it. "If he's mine," he growled, "his last name is Walker."

Shit. His bear was freaking out and he still had no clue why.

Jessie stared at him, her blue-gray eyes now more uncertain despite her brave face. Shane's vision abruptly blurred, then blackened a bit at the edges. His bear rampaged through him. Bewilderment and that odd, stunning emotion Shane couldn't quite place blasted through every sense he had. One thing was certain: his bear wanted out. Wanted to explode into being, roar and rage in some sort of maddened fury. Desperately trying to hold himself steady, wondering what the fuck was going on, Shane focused on his breath as he tried to regain some sense of stability.

"Jessie," he managed to say, wanting to sound normal. In control. But it came out so low, so heavy and contorted by his bear's clawing dominance, that her eyes widened with the one thing he didn't want to see.

Fear.

Even Livy was caught short, staring at Shane with

her mouth open. Damn it all. This was useless. His bear was about to literally burst out of him, roaring and growling and demanding to rip something apart. Out of control and aching for battle, the way he'd been his entire life before finally moving to Deep Hollow and settling into a calmer, more quiet life. He couldn't scare the shit out of Jessie like that, letting her see him as a terrified, enraged bear. The barely restrained bear he used to be. He also couldn't let his *son* witness that.

Instead, he muttered in a savage growl that was no longer completely human, "I'm sorry."

Desperate to escape before his grizzly took over, he lunged around her and the wide-eyed baby boy, thundered down the steps, and bolted away toward the snow-covered pine trees of the deep mountain forest with the prickly feeling of his shocked, raging bear scraping beneath his skin.

And with the bizarre, unexpected sense of being ripped away from the two most important things in the world.

3

*J*essie smiled with automatic friendliness as the bell over the door jingled at the arrival of the next customer, even though her stomach was still in tight little knots. "Welcome to The Mountain Muffin! I'll be right with you."

She cringed at her own sickeningly cheerful voice, but no one else seemed to notice how fake it was.

The family that had walked in stood in a little cluster by the door, taking off hats and stamping their snowy shoes on the heavy rubber mat that covered the floor at the front of the bakery. The father smiled at Jessie as she turned back to the espresso maker, whipping up some lattes and mochas for the small gaggle of college-age kids who'd come in a few moments earlier. The little shop buzzed with morning activity, though it was not yet 8 a.m. on a Saturday. Holiday cheer sprinkled throughout the place, which Jessie had helped decorate a few days after she and Grant arrived in Deep Hollow.

Holiday cheer that had taken a decidedly sooty feel for her on the turn of a dime. Her adoration of all things wintry and festive, from pretty lights to pine trees to carols to gifts to spiced cider, felt jostled with the shock of realization that Maverick—no, Shane—was *here*. He invaded her every waking thought, and had padded through her dreams the past few nights on the big, clawed paws of a grizzly bear.

To say her mind wandered today was the understatement of the year.

Maddy, her pile of auburn red hair pulled back into a messy bun that just accentuated her natural beauty, leaned over from where she was rinsing a spoon in the sink to whisper, "Those are the Calhouns. They have a place about three blocks from here. Super nice family, been here forever. Shifters, of course."

Jessie nodded, still focused on the drink she was making. During her work days, Maddy had been slowly introducing her to all the locals as they filtered into the bakery. By this point, she'd met quite a few of them, seeing as how Deep Hollow boasted only a few thousand residents, and they all seemed to like coffee and baked goods. She glanced over to her right, where Grant lay snuggled up in his little travel seat, which made a handy nap spot for him when she came to work. Jessie simply carried him in the travel seat to the shop each morning, which was easy since she lived about twenty feet away from it. She had a blanket pulled over the top of his seat so the lights and bustle of the bakery wouldn't disturb him quite as much, though she didn't really need to. Every mother she'd met had exclaimed how lucky she was that he slept so soundly through the activity and noise of the bakery. They were downright jealous when she said he also slept a solid eight, nine, or even ten hours a night, every night, without waking up once. And yes, he was perfectly healthy and developmentally where he should be.

Every visiting tourist human mother was jealous, that is. All the locals simply smiled and whispered that it was normal. Bear shifter babies slept long and hard, particularly in the winter. Something to do with the natural hibernation rhythms in shifter systems.

Maddy, now beside Jessie at the other espresso maker filling a paper go cup, noticed her glance. "So. How you hanging in there? I swear, Livy is about ready to kill Shane."

Jessie startled badly, her hand knocking the steamer and sending steam whizzing off to the side. Maddy quickly flipped the switch off and smiled apologetically. "Sorry. I take it you're still pretty rattled."

Blowing air out of her mouth in a long breath, Jessie gave a brief nod. "It's just so weird, you know? Here I've been, resigned to the fact that I'd never know where Grant's daddy is, that he'd never know he had a son, and boom. He's been living here, right under my nose."

Pushing some silver tinsel out of the way where it hung a little too close to the coffee mug rack beside the sink, Maddy shot Jessie an understanding look but didn't interrupt. She seemed to sense that Jessie was talking it out to herself.

"I want Grant to know him, of course. I never had a dad, and that was pretty hard on me. I never wanted to raise a child alone either, but I didn't have much control over it." Jessie sighed as she set down the second latte and started to fix a holiday-themed peppermint mocha, complete with a miniature candy cane sticking out of it. "And he seemed almost *angry* when he took off like he did. Do you—" Jessie hesitated, though her hands kept working on the drinks. "Do you think he'll come around? I just need to know he'll show up for Grant. That he'll want to be in his life."

Maddy sighed. "He was just as shocked as you, from what Livy said. Reverting to the animal side was just a self-protective measure. Give him some time. Besides." She smiled impishly at Jessie as she went back to what she'd been working on. "Maybe the magic of the season will soften him up to the idea a bit."

Jessie smiled at the encouraging words but didn't reply. She loved Christmas herself, but she doubted it would have any sort of magical effect on a tough, burly bear shifter like Mav—Shane. He seemed like the sort to mutter *Bah, humbug* at all the holiday trappings she loved.

Surrounded by happy, chattering people, a plethora of sparkly and jingly holiday decorations, and the overwhelming sense that everyone in here was celebrating the holidays with their family all conspired to darken Jessie's mood even further. *You're being melodramatic,* she firmly told herself as the strains of the Nutcracker Suite with its dancing sugar plum fairies came on over the speakers. *Just be grateful. You still have everything you need here.*

Well, if that were true, why did it feel like the one thing she wanted most at the moment was probably off somewhere in the snowy woods, having a bear-sized freak out about the unexpected holiday gift she'd abruptly dumped on his doorstep yesterday?

Biting the inside of her cheek, she rolled her eyes at herself for her continued melodrama—it hadn't been *his* doorstep, for crying out loud—and turned back to the espresso maker. After she finished the drinks for the college kids and rang them up, the shifter family, the Calhouns, stepped up to the counter. She greeted them pleasantly, trying to observe them without staring as she waited for their orders. The man was tall, brawny, stupidly attractive, and had that funny little thing about him that she had come to recognize as meaning he was a bear shifter. It wasn't anything she could put her finger on. It simply was as if he wore a wild edge that set him off as being different. As being somewhat more than human.

Just like—Shane. It was funny to think of him with

that name, when for three days she'd known him as Maverick. But she could tell he'd told her the truth the other day. That was his name then, and Shane was the name he went by now. He hadn't lied to her. It was weird, but she *knew* that deep down, with an unshakeable surety.

She had recognized his innate wildness during the three days she had spent with him in bliss-soaked pleasure in his hotel room all those many months ago. She had no clue what that had meant at the time, of course. All she really knew then was that he was the most exciting, fascinating, sexy, and wild yet gentle guy she'd ever met. She'd been temporarily living in Denver, he'd been rolling through town, they met at a bar. It had seemed like a simple pick-up, until it turned into so much more.

She'd also sensed something in him that seemed to be hurting. Not so much a secret pain, nothing so dramatic as that. It was more an overall defensiveness. A wariness he draped about himself like an impenetrable cloak. Even though during the days they had spent in one another's company, literally never taking any time away from the other, they both had lowered their defenses, she'd known he wasn't sharing all of himself with her.

"Okay, I think we've decided what we want." The deep voice of the father of the little shifter family pulled Jessie back into the present moment. She wasn't really surprised when he added, "You're our newest resident, aren't you? And your son?"

Feeling a little shy, she nodded. The woman next to him, presumably his wife and also clearly a bear shifter, gave her husband a thump on his upper arm before smiling back at Jessie. "Ungracious oaf. Don't let him scare you off. But yes, everyone here knows who you are. We're all really excited to have a new little baby in town."

The father of the small clan gave a self-deprecating smile. "Forgetting my manners. I'm Bain Calhoun." He gestured with pride at his family. "My wife, Helena, and our daughters, Willow and Laurel."

Next to him, one of the daughters, who was probably around 14, gave Jessie an eager smile. "Is it okay if we go say hi to your baby? What's his name?"

"We won't wake him up," the other one added solemnly, who looked exactly like her sister. Jessie realized they must be twins. "We just want to see him. We love babies."

The mother, Helena, admonished her girls to be more polite, but Jessie shrugged it off with an easy smile. She had to admit that anyone who wanted to look at Grant with such enthusiasm made her more than pleased to show him off. Behind her, Maddy added, "These two young ladies will also make excellent babysitters if you ever need any, Jessie. They sit for every family in town that has little ones. They come as a package deal."

Jessie smiled at the girls, who both sported the piercing green eyes of their mother and the unruly brown hair of their father. "Of course you can see him," she said. "So far, he seems to love meeting everyone here. His name is Grant."

Bubbling out *thank yous,* the girls darted around the corner of the counter and bent down, very gently pulling back the blanket that covered Grant's little cocooned seat. Jessie looked over and saw him blink his eyes and smile up at the girls. The two of them immediately started making faces at him, *oohing* and *awwing* over his soft skin. They definitely seemed comfortable around a baby his age. She glanced at Maddy, then back to the Calhouns. "Why exactly does this town seem so enamored of babies? I mean, *I* happen to think he's kind of special, but has there been a baby shortage or something?"

There other three laughed, shaking their heads. "Nothing of the sort," Maddy assured her, grabbing some napkins to stick them in the to-go bag she was preparing for another customer. "We're a tight-knit town, and besides." Her voice lowered a bit. "Shifters are not exactly the most common inhabitants of this planet. Every new one, especially ones we didn't know about, is a reason for celebration." She gently squeezed Jessie's arm while the Calhouns smiled at her. "Another cause for celebration is that you're here now. With him, where you belong. No matter what happens."

She gave Jessie a gentle smile, which the Calhouns

clearly caught. It led to a slightly uncomfortable lull in the conversation, oddly punctuated by the cheerful holiday tunes lilting out of the speakers set in the walls and the bursts of happy laughter that dotted the little bakery.

Jessie bit her lip. The elephant in the room, the man who'd had a major bombshell dropped on him and not surprisingly had sped off by himself to deal with the reality of a certain little adorable bouncing baby, was also the subject Jessie was pretty sure everyone in the café as well as the town also knew about by now. Even though it had been just a few days, she knew word got around fast. Livy, who'd still been ticked off at Shane and presumably herself for not realizing before that he was the daddy bear in question, had told Maddy and everyone else at the cookie exchange about the thunderbolt moment of realization at the front door. And they'd all probably told their spouses and siblings and cousins and nieces and nephews and kids and who knew who else.

Jessie didn't begrudge them any of that. They were all Grant's extended family now, too. They just wanted the best for him. This was a different world. Besides, she noted dryly to herself, shifters seemed to like gossip just as much as humans did.

To cover the slight awkwardness, Jessie said to the family, "Let me finish taking your order so you can get on with your day. What can I get for you?" Maddy gave her a relieved little grin as the Calhouns began ordering. Inside, though, Jessie still felt the prickle of oddness. Almost an ache of longing. As she watched the shifter parents finally round up their girls after a last session of cooing and smiling at Grant so they could all grab one of the few remaining free tables, she felt a sudden bite of longing slide through her entire being. They sat there as a family, laughing and talking with the easy familiarity of those who loved and cared for one another.

Wow. Seeing Shane hadn't prepared her for how much it would trigger her desire for exactly that thing. Family. Sure, she and Grant were family, and Livy was practically her family, and the whole town had embraced her anyway. But to have a core family of her own, one that stayed true through thick and thin, was what she really wanted.

And a guy. But not just any guy. Seeing Shane once again had brought a roar of longing through her that she realized had been banked ever since their last encounter with one another. She'd never stopped thinking about him anyway, Grant's existence notwithstanding. Shane had walked into her heart during those three days of passion they spent together, and now that she'd unexpectedly found him again, that same heart was dancing with an utterly ridiculous hope and joy. The heart that had wondered about him for months after their magical weekend together.

Magical, and pretty dirty, too, she remembered with a blast of heat in her cheeks. He'd fit her just perfectly and revved her motor like crazy. No wonder she hadn't been able to stop thinking about him. If only...

"No. That's just getting mixed up with sugarplums," she muttered to herself, trying to talk some sense into her girlish fantasies that were getting tripped up by all the holiday jingles and seasonal delight with which she'd been filling her days.

Maddy shot her a startled look, busy back over at the griddle preparing one of the simple breakfasts they offered. Jessie shook her head. "Nothing. Just thinking out loud to myself."

With a smile, Maddy said, "As long as you don't go off your rocker, girl, you can think out loud all you want."

Jessie sighed as she began fixing more holiday drinks. "I'm not going to go off my rocker. I'm just trying to make sense of everything without it all turning into gigantic mush in my brain."

Maddy's expression softened even more. "Jessie," she said in a kind tone, "honestly, from my perspective there are only two things that have to happen right now. One, just give him more time, as well as yourself. You've both had a shock. I'm sure he's out there with the same kinds of things running through his head right now, too."

"Agreed," Jessie murmured.

"And two," Maddy continued, "you need to decide this: what is it that you really want? In your heart of hearts. Be really clear about that, and I think it will help you find some peace."

"Sure hope so." Jessie's eyes yet again snagged on the Calhoun family. The immense pride on Bain Calhoun's face as he sat with his little family unit once again struck in her a sharp longing to experience that sort of sweet closeness for herself.

With Shane. Who, she had to admit if she was going to be utterly blunt with herself, was a lot more than just the guy who was the father of her child, no matter how important that was in itself. He was more than the mystery that had dogged her for nearly two years now. He was more than the memory of three days so unforgettable that she would always have thought of him with a smile anyway. No, she had to admit that Shane's importance to her had to do with something she'd never before in her life experienced, not even with her long-ago boyfriend of several years, or any of the guys she'd ever gone out on a date with in hopes of finding that spark she didn't actually believe existed.

She'd fallen in love with Shane Maverick Walker during those three magical days.

So deeply, in fact, that it had about shattered her when they parted ways without exchanging any sort of contact information. Even though now she tried telling herself she'd only fallen in love with a fantasy, because of three days of totally amazeballs sex, because of the lifelong loneliness that she simply wanted to be filled, she understood the truth after the wild flare of emotion burst out of her chest after seeing him the other day.

She was *still* totally in love with him. Which was very likely the stupidest, most heartbreakingly pathetic schoolgirl daydream she could think of.

Pasting cheer back onto her face, she shoved her thoughts of Shane Walker to the back of her mind for the moment. She had work to do, and a little boy to take care of. For right now, it had to be enough.

At the end of her shift in the late afternoon, Jessie collected Grant and walked back next door to her little apartment. Though the place had felt like the perfect little home yesterday, now it felt strangely lacking. As if something very important were missing. Fluttering out a little sigh, she glanced down at Grant's face in his carrier and smiled at him with deliberate cheer. "It's still our place, little man. Just you and me, and that's just fine."

Grant yawned up at her, his face scrunching up in the most adorable manner. Her smile melted into a more real one as she headed around the corner of the bakery and up the walkway to her front door.

And right smack into one hella sexy mountain of a bear shifter man who stood there waiting for her and his son.

4

Shane paused at the edge of the clearing, lifting his massive snout and sniffing. Was that—? Did he smell—? Oh, yeah, he did. Beef stew. Delicious hints of spices, veggies, potatoes. Crisp, fried, buttered russet potatoes if he wasn't mistaken.

Lunch was being served. Just in time. He'd raged around the forest long enough, having his bear-sized crisis. It was time to man up. But starting with a full stomach could only help.

Dropping back to all fours, he loped to the back of the main lodge building at the edge of the clearing, shifting from his enormous grizzly form back into human form in the space of a few strides. As he let himself in the back door, he paused to shake his head and entire body to dislodge the last of the snowflakes that covered him from having run too close under a tree branch covered with the stuff. Kicking the door shut behind him, he went to a row of little cubby boxes set into the wall of the mud room. The one marked *Shane* held an abundance of folded, clean-smelling clothes. Appreciative, he tugged out a pair of jeans and a long-sleeved blue and black checked flannel shirt, pulled them on, and padded barefoot down the hall-way, up the few stairs to the main floor, and into the kitchen of the lodge. Elodie Walker stood there, quiet and calm as always. Matriarch of the local Walker clan, she was also his aunt and the reason he was in Deep Hollow in the first place. She and his uncle knew about his wild past, his old way of life. They were the only ones here who did. They'd been willing to give him a chance to start over, with the slate of his past wiped clean.

Two places were set at the large kitchen island. Decorated to the holiday nines with wreaths and tinsel all over the place just like the entire Silvertip Lodge, the kitchen smelled like a giant vat of spiced cider along with the stew. Not turning around from the stove where she ladled the aromatic beef stew into two enormous bowls, his aunt said, "You're right on time. The bread is almost finished baking, I just put the pota-toes out, and there are little cherry tartlets that will be ready in about fifteen minutes. Have a seat."

Shane shook his head, grinning as he pulled out one of the stools around the kitchen island. He'd been here for a year and still could hardly get used to having such an abundance of food, love, and consideration at his disposal any time he wanted to walk into this house. "You're amazing, Aunt Elodie. Uncle Oberon hit the jackpot with you. I hope he appreciates that."

Elodie turned around from the stove, carrying a large blue ceramic soup bowl over and setting it onto the place setting in front of him. The smell of her amazing beef stew hit him even harder. He swallowed hard to keep himself from drooling. He might not have grown up with manners, he might've chosen a hard-scrabble life until recently, but he wasn't about to be a total cave bear in her house. But she must've somehow been able to sense it. She laughed gently, urging him, "Go on, just tuck in. I'd rather you enjoy it while every-thing's still hot and fresh."

"Thanks. I'm pretty hungry." He lifted a spoonful of soup to his lips, taking a generous sip and groaning with delight. "No wonder guests come back to stay here again and again," he said after he politely swal-lowed. "They're treated like kings and queens with every meal."

Returning with her own bowl of soup, Elodie settled onto her own stool with a pleased smile. "I just like taking care of everyone. Guests, of course. Yes. But especially," and she reached out a gentle hand to pat the back of his hand, "family. When my family needs to be taken care of, I like to give them good, nourishing food."

They ate in companionable silence for a while, although Shane's thoughts turned and rumbled and twisted. Yeah, his Aunt Elodie knew he was going through some shit right now. After seeing Jessie and Grant the other day, Shane had run straight to the woods, changing into his huge brute of a bear in a painful forced shift almost in the middle of Main Street. Then he'd blindly run up the mountain and stayed out all night.

And all the next day.

And all the next night.

Plain and simple, he'd run away from Jessie and the kid, but he'd had to. He'd been so shaken, his bear so ready to blindly slash and burn, he didn't know what else to do in the moment. His old way of being, the way of the cunning street fighter and angry brawler and pure survivalist, emerged so quickly in reflexive self-protection he hadn't even been able to control his own shift. Just the memory of that made him wince.

At least this morning he'd finally woken up realizing he'd attacked all the trees, tramped all the trails, and picked all the raging mock air fights with fiercely scolding birds that he possibly could. His bear was physically spent and emotionally way more settled. He was also hungry as hell, since he'd not found much to snack on in the wintry woods while he wrestled his demons. Whatever the hell those demons were. But at least he'd finally been able to shift back to human just now.

How Elodie had known to expect him was beyond his understanding, but she seemed to have an uncanny sense about every member of her family, even someone like Shane. He wasn't her direct blood relation, since her husband, Oberon Walker, was Shane's father's brother. But that didn't matter. Somehow, Elodie was attuned to the feelings and needs of the whole Walker family, from her sons to nephews to those even more removed.

Shane shrugged to himself. The was little sense in trying to understand it. For the moment, he was just grateful that he had a delicious meal to help settle him after the mass chaos his life abruptly had become.

"So tell me," Elodie began. She gently folded her hands under her chin.

Despite himself, Shane tensed slightly in anticipation of her question. Instead, she asked, "Is there anything we need to tack onto the supply order for spring? I was going over the budget last night and just want to see where we are with the latest numbers to make sure we're not going over."

Shane relaxed. The Silvertip Lodge, the one his aunt and uncle ran and at which he helped out as a handyman when needed, was gearing up to build several more cabins this spring to be ready for people to stay in by late next summer or early fall. One of Shane's duties had been to help out with the custom orders, which was why he'd been gone for the past few weeks. He'd traveled to Denver to meet with some of the suppliers they worked with, going over the specifics of what was needed. The lodge was a cozy place, but a top-notch one. They didn't skimp on anything. Exacting attention to detail was something the craftsmen in the city were held to when fulfilling orders that couldn't be taken care of locally. Shane had traveled there to make sure the specifications were clear and the details understood.

He'd stayed at the same hotel where he and Jessie had holed up for three days. Hoping against completely insane hope that somehow, he'd miraculously see her again. Not in his dumbest dreams would he ever have imagined finding her right here in Deep Hollow. Where apparently she'd been while he was back in Denver, thinking about her.

The craziness of it all made his brain hurt.

"We just need a few more things," he answered Elodie, then went on to list them. They casually stayed on that topic for the next little while, all the way through finishing their lunch and diving into the tart little cherry pies straight from the oven served with warm cream.

Frigging delicious.

Finally, empty pie plate pushed away and sipping on his third huge glass of water to help him rehydrate after his snowy rampage through what felt like half of the San Juan Mountains, Shane took a breath. It was time to face reality.

Looking at Elodie, who regarded him back with a serious yet encouraging expression as she waited for him to speak, Shane said in low voice, "What happened is exactly why this won't work."

"Why what won't work?" The words were very gentle. Neither censure or sharpness underlay them.

"Me. Jessie. I mean, there's a—a kid. I'm a father, Aunt Elodie." He shook his head at his aunt, feeling that truth slap into him again. *A father.* "Just the thought of it freaked me out so badly my bear wanted to react by ripping something apart. I was furious." Shame rose in him at the memory. "I was about to shift into my bear right there in the middle of town and—and I don't even know what. Go berserk."

"Shane, it was an enormous shock." She smiled in gentle understanding. "Nobody thinks less of you for having left. Everyone knew you would be back to man up about it."

"Everyone except Jessie." Shame leaked through his words. He shoved his hand through his hair, pressing his head into his palm for a second and closing his eyes. "Any other shifter in this town would be psyched beyond belief to find out he had a kid he didn't know about. But I don't feel excited about it." He opened his eyes again, feeling the bleakness behind them. Even though he had grown up without his aunt's gentle presence in his life, he'd come to trust her so much during the past year, knowing she would never blab his secrets and was always there to provide very wise counsel, that he let his guard down around her more than anyone else in Deep Hollow or Silvertip Ridge. "I'm absolutely terrified."

Her face still soft and understanding, Elodie quietly asked, "Of what?"

During the silence as Shane hesitated before answering, the large grandfather clock in the Walkers' living room boomed out twice, signaling the mid-afternoon time. Jessie and Grant had appeared in Shane's life forty-eight hours earlier. Two days in which his life had been tossed into a blender, turned on high, and shredded completely.

He gave his head a savage shake before answering. "Terrified that I'll be like him."

There was another short pause. They both know what "him" he was talking about. Elodie drew breath to speak, but Shane beat her to it. "Besides, even without that role model of fantastic gentleness in my life," he couldn't help the bitter note at the old hurts that crept into his voice, surprised though he was to hear it since the ugliness of his cubhood was many years back, "I've only been responsible for myself my whole life. Shit, I've never even had a dog. Or a plant. What the hell do I know about taking care of a kid?"

At that, Elodie straightened up. With a precise edge to her tone, she said, "I don't want to ever hear you say that sort of bullshit again."

Whoa. Shane eyeballed his aunt. She wasn't the type to let loose with bad language. Ever.

She narrowed her eyes, which were getting the

colorful intensity that meant her bear was scratching at the surface. "You are nothing like him. Don't you dare hide behind that as an excuse to cut yourself down and not live up to your potential. I won't hear of it."

With that, she folded her arms across her ample bosom and gave him a challenging look. Mouth slightly open, for a long moment Shane could only stare back at her. Finally, he muttered, "It's not an excuse. I'm not hiding behind anything."

"You had better not be. Because the Shane I know, the one I've watched create a solid life for himself here over the past year, is much too smart and much too honest to do that."

Shane snorted out an irritated laugh. "I'm honest now, yeah. But for a lot of my life I didn't care about anyone or anything. If I had to lie to save my ass, I did. So I'm capable of it."

Elodie shook her gently silvering ash-blond head. "Everyone is capable of doing the worst possible things depending on what situation they're in. People who say they would never lie, never steal, never do anything bad, are people who've never been tested beyond what they should be. At heart, Shane," and now she softened a bit again, the smile creeping back onto her face, "you're a gentle, kind soul."

"Oh yeah? How do you figure that?" Shane glared down at his hapless pie plate, curling and uncurling his fingers on the table. But his aunt's next words had him snapping his gaze back up to her again.

"Because of who you are now," she said simply, settling back into her chair. Her smile grew broader with every moment. "If deep down you actually were the way you behaved for all those years when you lived as an outcast without clan, without family, just scrabbling for survival the best way you could, you would still be like that now. You would have fleeced us all. Lied, stolen, possibly even killed."

She got up and went back to the stove, glancing out the window as a small sheet of snow dropped down the pane in the day's bright sunshine. "Instead, you proved yourself to be a hard worker, a productive member of this community, an extremely valued member of this family, and you never say a bad word about anyone. Except," she turned to look back at him, "about yourself. Stop doing that. You're a father now."

Her voice sharpened. "One of the most important things you can role model to that adorable little boy is that you value yourself. By doing that, he'll be well on his way to growing up as someone who values himself also."

Shane sat in thunderstruck silence as Elodie got two cheerful mugs out of the cupboard and ladled some of the spiced cider into each of them. Along with her uncanny ability to sense when anyone she cared about needed some nurturing, she also had a highly developed ability to see right into people and note their true character. She was an excellent judge of others, even without knowing them very well. She also said things like they were. Elodie Walker would never blow smoke up his ass.

Well, hell. That exploded his ideas about himself as a big, badass bear shifter. Thoroughly disgusted with himself, Shane snarled. His aunt just laughed. "You knew when you came to me that I would listen to you, but I'd also give you brutal honesty."

"True that." Shane unclenched his curled fingers and drummed them instead. "I guess I've just been so busy working here." He spoke slowly, articulating his thoughts even as he spoke them. "I wasn't paying much attention to anything outside the day to day. That's what you're saying, right? That it's possible for us to change."

Elodie turned back around with two steaming mugs. She placed one in front of Shane and settled back onto her stool with her own mug cradled between her hands. To his surprise, she shook her head.

"I believe that it's not so much that people change, as that they actually become more of who they really are," she said. "They get closer to their true self as they learn that trust exists in this world. As they realize they don't need to look at life like it's a constant battle."

She shrugged as she blew on her drink to cool it. "People's true selves will show when given a chance to. And they always come back to that true self eventually. No matter what."

Shane frowned. "What if that just means that my time here hasn't been long enough for my true self to show up again? Now that Jessie and Grant are here, maybe it means I'm just gonna go back to being an asshole. Just like my dad."

"I don't believe that." Elodie took a thoughtful sip of her drink. "I think you know the right thing to do. Because," she eyed him carefully, "you really do want to go see them, don't you?"

"Yeah." His voice was gruff. His bear thumped around inside him, somewhat agitated. It still made Shane nervous. "I don't know what the hell to say to her, don't know what the hell do with him, but I do want to see them both."

Now his aunt gave him a knowing smile, her eyes soft. "Because you never stopped thinking about her, have you? She was the one that got away."

Shane let the silence stretch again for a long moment between them before he could admit the thing that had been gnawing at him for the past two years. The thing he thought he'd kept hidden from everyone, had never once mentioned, and had tried to forget by enjoying the same mindless hookups that had been a constant part of his life up till meeting Jessie. But they'd all left him cold, and he'd dwindled in the past several months to no contact with women at all.

The only woman he could think of was Jessie. He'd been stupidly desperate to find her again. Only her. Apparently, it sure as hell was some sort of fucking Christmas miracle that she and his son had shown up right here in Deep Hollow.

Looking back at his aunt, he held her eyes as he said what might've been the truest statement of his entire life. "You're right. I've never forgotten Jessie. I've never been able to stop thinking about her. So why is it that now she's here, I'm," he paused before shoving the word out, "afraid to see her again?"

Elodie smiled with such compassion and understanding Shane felt it smack his heart. Leaning forward again to touch him, this time covering part of his big hand with her own, she gently said, "Oh, my sweet little boy."

He snorted at that, especially since he towered over his not-small aunt by nearly a foot and easily outweighed her by about a hundred pounds. Yet her next words slammed him sideways.

"Shane, it's because you love that girl. She's your mate."

Her words dropped between them with all the force of an atomic bomb. Shane reared back on the stool, mouth agape. A crash of wild heat spread throughout his body as the word *mate* seemed to shimmer in the very air before him.

Elodie's smile engulfed her entire face. "You couldn't acknowledge that when you met her, because you probably didn't even understand what the bond would feel like. Trust me, it's why she somehow found her way here. The two of you are meant to be, just like that adorable little Grant was meant to be born. It will all work out. Don't you prove me wrong now," she added in a teasing chide, playfully shaking her finger at him.

All Shane could do was sit there blinking at her. The truth of it spread over him as certainly as the planet spun on its axis.

He had a mate. A real mate.

And a son.

With his mate.

That was why his bear had almost gone crazy. Had burst out of him, uncontrolled, totally freaking out. Not because he was reverting back to his brawling days, his days of fighting on the shifter circuit, of fighting in back alleys, of raging and crashing through a life that had never treated him fairly.

No, it was because his bear had recognized Jessie as his mate and Grant as his son. He knew that, and wanted to protect them with every ounce of possessive pride he could. His bear wasn't out of control again. His bear now had a purpose. Shane just hadn't been able to understand it.

His job now, his purpose, was to be with Jessie, to raise Grant, and to keep them safe. Always.

He sat there unmoving for another long moment as everything ticked over in his brain. Then he exploded into action. Urgency gripped him so badly he thought his heart would whack its way out of his chest.

"I've got to find her right now." He stood up so fast he tipped the stool over. Blindly righting it, he turned to thump down the few stairs to the mud room, skidding along the hallway in his sudden desperation to find them. Flinging open the door, he remembered to holler back over his shoulder, "Thanks for lunch!" as he shucked off his clothes and galloped off into the snow, his bear form bursting back over him as he ran. This time, though, it was more controlled. Focused. Driven by purpose.

Somewhere behind him he thought he heard a delighted laugh, but he barely paid attention.

He was on his way to find his family. Hopefully, it wasn't too late.

5

"Hi, Jessie." Shane's deep rumble set things aflame inside Jessie and zipped shocked little shivers down her back. Standing there in her little yard, he looked like some wild creature of the woods, all burly and big and just outrageously—manly. He smelled like the snowy forest mixed with spicy, sexy man. Jessie felt suddenly almost dizzy from his scent.

He also seemed slightly out of breath, like he'd been running. Her mind was so boggled she couldn't get out any words. She just gaped at him like a dumb fish or something. His next words about knocked her flat as well.

"I'm sorry. I was a total ass the other day." The words suddenly fell over themselves, like he'd been thinking them over and over and just needed to get them out. "Can I come in? I want a do-over on meeting my son. And on saying hi to you again. In a much better way than I did before." His voice dropped on that last sentence, seeming to wrap around Jessie with a sensuality she remembered.

From head to toe, she flushed as she abruptly recalled hours of sweat-slicked eroticism with him. The most amazing, mind blowing, exciting, adventuresome, wild, sweet, fantastic eroticism of her life. Swallowing hard, she managed to nod and finally find her voice.

"Yeah. Of course." Jessie had no idea how she kept her voice casual. She juggled Grant over to one hip and reached forward with her free hand to unlatch the little gate in the fence that encircled her approximately two square yards of snow-covered front lawn. But Shane beat her to it, taking an easy stride forward to reach out his own dark brown denim clad arm to open the gate for them. Murmuring a thank you, Jessie slipped past him toward her door.

Despite herself, she felt another flash of warmth as her body slipped past him at a distance of only about four inches. Wow. She'd forgotten how big he was. How masculine. How incredibly—dammit. Fine. Incredibly arousing. Forcing herself to remember that she held a bouncing little baby in her arms and that this was no time to be letting her thoughts go to some pretty debauched memories, she took the few steps toward the apartment and opened the door.

"So you're already embracing the Deep Hollow way of life and don't bother locking your door, huh?" Shane kicked the snow off his boots just outside her door, then entered the house behind her.

Trying not to focus too much on how much incredibly sexy space he took up in her tiny little apartment, Jessie went into the middle of the main room that basically tripled as living room, office, and dining room. She gently set Grant on the floor so she could begin getting him out of his warm layers.

"Livy told me I didn't have to worry about that here. This place literally didn't even come with the key to the door lock. Everyone's assured me that nothing ever happens here, anyway. That all the shifters in town are better than any state-of-the-art security anyone can buy, anyway."

Shane made a low sound of agreement behind her. She could hear him taking off his jacket, but other than carefully draping it over the back of the chair pushed in behind the two-square-foot table that she jokingly referred to as her impressive dining table, he didn't say anything else. She sensed him watching as she tugged the wiggling Grant out of his snowsuit.

She somehow felt extremely heated at the moment. Which could perhaps be because she was hyperaware of Shane's proximity to her. Of his amazing scent, the one that made her think of the wildest depths of mountain forests, dark mossy caves, and snowstorms whipping with gale force winds of strength.

To cover it up, she said, "Would you like a drink? I've got tea and coffee."

Jessie turned around. Shane's wild hair and dark beard made her want to rake her fingers through it. She wanted to feel it rasp against her skin as he kissed her.

Oh, for pete's sake. Dumb whacked-out hormones. She made herself smile at him. Yet even as she did, something shifted in his expression. Something hungry and possessive crept over his face as he looked back at her. The whiskey-colored depths of his eyes darkened into a bronze sheen as his tongue dipped out against his upper lip for just a second, like he tasted something good there.

As if something divine lingered on his mouth and he wanted more of it.

Jessie realized, as she stood rooted to the carpet, her son's babbling little voice muted beneath the weird roaring in her ears, that the divine something Shane wanted more of was *her.*

SHANE FELT ROCKED to his core as he stood in Jessie's little apartment. The place was tiny but decorated with such care and attention, filled with such holiday festivity, that he could feel how settled here she already felt. As he stood big and hulking in it, he felt something swelling and bursting with a combination of deep pride, exultation, still some lingering shock, yet most of all an unmistakable desire. Inside him, his bear roared and paced in the strong need to protect. The heavy footfalls of his enormous paws echoed in Shane's mind.

Something wild and hot in him just wanted to claim Jessie for his own, right then and there.

Shane took a deep breath, then released it on a long exhalation. He took another deep breath, followed by another exhalation. After doing that several times, he felt like he might have a handle on the totally crazed emotions running around inside him. He'd spent his whole life attracted to the spiky precipice of danger that beckoned for him to throw himself off the cliff into a free fall, consequences be damned. Most of his life, he willingly answered that call. It led to a lot of hard-core intensity, not to mention sheer stupidity. After the final major blow up just over year ago, the one that brought him up short and informed him in no uncertain terms that life was finite, even for shifters, he found his way back to Deep Hollow and the bear clans of his origins. He'd spent the past year slowly learning how to not go off half-cocked, but instead take his time, assess the situation, and settle into something better and deeper.

Right now, he used every single thing he had learned to keep himself in check. To not completely scare the shit out of Jessie before he could tell her that they were—mates.

It sure as hell didn't help that he easily scented her own sharp arousal, wafting through the air to him like a beckoning harbor that promised a wild mix of both safety and crazy excitement. A deep comfort for which he longed, even as he still wrestled with the reality of the situation.

It was enough to make a bear shake his head and roar, trying to figure it all out.

After another long moment, during which he tried to be as sure as possible that when he spoke he wouldn't have the growl of his bear beneath it, he responded, "No, thanks. I'm fine. I really just want to spend this time talking to you and," he tore his gaze from Jessie's clear blue-gray eyes and looked down with an almost equal fascination at the blond little boy playing with his own toes at her feet, "Grant."

Jessie's voice went soft with the gooey sort of adoration he'd heard all the women in town and most of the shifters, whether male or female, adopt every time they talked about a shifter baby. "Sure. He is pretty amazing." She gracefully sank to the floor, sitting crosslegged beside Grant. Shane followed suit, allowing himself to be entranced with the chubby little bundle cooing between them.

Then the kid let out the loudest fart, giggling uncontrollably as he did it.

Jessie rolled her eyes, and even Shane couldn't help his own snort of laughter. At the sound, Grant's little head turned up toward him, his tiny mouth circling into an "oh" of interest as the bright amber-brown eyes stared at him.

"That's your daddy, Grant." Jessie's voice was soft. Tentative. "He's your daddy."

Shane felt something bizarre clutching his chest, spreading a different kind of warmth over his body than he felt each time he looked at Jessie. This warmth was like nothing he'd ever experienced before. He instinctively knew that it was the protective pride of being a—father. The same sort of pride a guy had to feel when he reached the top of Mount Everest or something. The tiny prickle of happiness was something he recognized as well. It had taken him a few years to identify that particular emotion. It wasn't something he'd ever known in his life until he got to Deep Hollow. But he could recognize it for what it was.

Happiness and pride in *his* family. And his sexy as hell mate.

Glancing up at Jessie again, he was able to furtively study her because she now was engrossed in tickling Grant's tiny feet and listening to more of the kid's wild giggles. The curve of her breasts under her shirt as she bent toward their son, the creamy smoothness of her neck, the dark blonde hair that tumbled down her back, the soft, inviting swell of her hips all tugged at him.

Jessie glanced up too quickly for Shane to pull his eyes away and caught him staring at her. Her giggles died in her throat as she saw what had to be an intense expression on his face.

"Sorry." He kept looking at her, though. "I'm just still amazed that I'm seeing you again."

"Me, too," she said, her tone soft. "It's like a dream. I often wondered what you were doing, what it would be like to see you again. I even imagined—"

She cut herself off so suddenly, eyes widening, that Grant stopped giggling to stare at his mother with a concerned little frown on his face. Shane glanced at the kid. "He really watches you. He's attuned to every single thing you do."

Tucking her hair behind her ear, Jessie nodded. "It's a survival mechanism. Babies depend on their mothers for safety. He definitely watches me all the time," she added with a small laugh. "I never had any idea how all-consuming taking care of another human being could be until I had him."

"Fuck, I wish I'd been there to help you do it. Dammit!" Shane winced. "Gonna teach him bad words before he's even old enough to talk." He looked down at Grant. "Some role model I'll be."

This time, Jessie snorted out an actual laugh. Shane glanced back up at her, surprised and happy to hear the sound. He remembered her laughter so well. It'd rippled through his mind time and again for months.

"Believe me," Jessie said, still laughing, "this child has heard it all. His delicate little ears are well-accustomed to bad language by now. Don't worry, you won't make it worse."

Gently, Shane reached out his huge hand to touch

Grant's cheek. He was ridiculously soft. Grant looked back at him, occasionally blinking his big eyes. Softly, Jessie said, "Smile at him. He'll smile back at you."

"Seriously?" Even as he said that, Shane smiled at the chubby little bundle of roly-polyness.

After second, Grant smiled back, dimples appearing on his face and his chin doubling as he grinned in delight at Shane.

"Wow," Shane breathed, staring at the child he'd somehow managed to make with the woman he'd only known for three days. "That's pretty cool."

Jessie laughed. The gentle tones of it rippled through the room, mingling with the Christmasy scent that suffused the whole place. The piney smells came from the tiny decorated tree she had sitting on the table shoved under the window. She seemed to really like the holiday.

"So." Shane gently stroked Grant's cheek again before taking his hand away, leaning back on his arm so he could just observe the little boy as he reached down and began playing with the cuff of Shane's jeans. "His bear's been starting to come through, hasn't it?"

Jessie nodded. "Yeah. I knew it would start to happen, Livy told me all about it, but it still totally freaked me out. He had claws a couple of weeks ago. That's why I'm here now. I finally understood what she was trying to tell me." She gave a resigned shrug with one shoulder. "I can't raise him on my own. Away from—his kind."

Silence held them before he decided to just out with it. "The thing is," he said, struggling to express the words without sounding like a complete jerk, "that's exactly what I'm afraid of. That I'll make things worse for Grant, and for you. Oh, don't worry," he added quickly as Jessie flicked a serious gaze at him. "I'm going to be in this kid's life. He needs a dad. I get that. He needs a hell of a good one, too."

"Because," Jessie said, watching him very carefully, "of what kind of a father yours was to you? Or rather, wasn't?"

Another very long silence, interrupted only by the sound of Grant blowing little spit bubbles with his mouth, already having distracted himself, held the two of them. Well, shit. He'd forgotten that he told Jessie about that. He'd opened up to her so much during those three days.

Because he trusted her. Which was what one did with a mate.

Feeling his brows lower, he answered, "Yeah. That bastard was no kind of father. Beating the hell out of me on a regular basis till I was big enough to fight back. Then leave home." His voice came out shorter than he intended. Jessie caught it and looked away. Ah, hell. This was harder than he'd thought it would be. But his bear nudged and snarled at and prodded him to take action. He needed to man up.

"Anyway," he said, forcing himself to soften his

voice. "So you've been learning a lot about bear shifter life since you got here."

She nodded uncertainly, clearly not getting where he was going with this.

"How much do you know about—bear shifter mates?"

He let the word just drop into her tiny little apartment. Let it hang in between them and the oblivious, cheerful little boy sitting between them still practicing blowing spit bubbles.

A rapid succession of emotions raced across Jessie's face. Confusion, then a flicker of understanding. For a long, breathless moment, he saw something else that whipped over to his own heart like a shimmering cord between them.

Pure, unadulterated hope and excitement, mingled with a rush of joy. Quickly covered by a carefully blank face.

Like she needed to hide her hope.

"You mean, like Elodie and Oberon Walker? The Calhouns, or," and she rattled off a couple other names of mated shifters who lived here.

He nodded. "Yes. Like that. You understand what it means?"

"I think so?" She spoke slowly. "It's two shifters who are meant to be together. Like a soulmate thing, like humans have. Uh, human people. I mean, just people." She flushed deep red, which oddly made her even cuter. "Something like that?"

Shane nodded, feeling abruptly weary as a long-ago image of his own mother and father fighting bitterly and angrily flashed through his head. "Yes. Like that."

Her gaze softened. "Not everyone gets to have that, I take it."

Shane took a deep breath. Now or never. "No," he said, keeping his gaze firmly on hers. "But some do. Some are lucky. Like us."

Jessie looked at him, her expression still cautious. Shane huffed out a breath, frustrated with his inability to properly explain. He tried again.

"Jessie, what I mean is that you and I are *mates.* You're my mate. We're bound together." Something flickered in her eyes. "I never thought it could happen to me. I thought I was broken. Thought I was too much of an asshole—aw, shit. Dammit," he muttered savagely, looking down at Grant.

Jessie shook her head, ignoring his language. "Bound to each other? Like, you mean, forever?"

"Yes. That's exactly what I mean."

A long silence spun between them, broken only by Grant's occasional noise as he rediscovered the interest of playing with his toes. Jessie's face was once again that proverbial open book, but emotions zipped across it so fast Shane wasn't sure what exactly she thought.

Finally, though, she simply said very softly, "Forever? Are you sure? Because that doesn't happen."

Her voice was so small, so filled with pain, that Shane saw red. He wanted to kill whoever had made her feel this way. Even as the rage fell over him, though, he knew where her sadness came from. Their hours of soulful conversation back in that hotel room had stayed etched on his brain. Every single secret they'd shared with one another.

"Your family, right?" He just barely kept the growl out of his words. "I remember, Jessie. They left you to raise yourself."

Her voice was low when she answered. "Yeah. When I was barely into my teens. Do you think we can do better by this little boy?" She stroked the back of Grant's head with such fierce tenderness that it wrenched at Shane's heart again. Before he could respond, she added, "And you don't have to include me in it. We're mates, or whatever. But I just want you to be there for him. Me—that's not important."

The red haze dropped over his mind again. She really, truly didn't believe that he could want her. That she was his mate.

Shane's bear roared through him. Possessiveness and confusion whirled around. Battling himself and his bear, he closed his eyes for a long moment, knowing they'd likely be a simmering gold with the proximity of his incensed animal. He wasn't handling this well. He didn't want to scare her again.

Not really sure what would come out, he opened his mouth and heard himself say, "I want you to come up to the lodge. My cabin's up there. Bring Grant. It's his home, Jessie. The place that will feel most comfortable to him in the world, even more so than down here in town. I want to try to do this right. I promise," he added in a soft voice that nevertheless held tremendous conviction, "I won't freak out again. I won't leave again. I mean it, Jessie."

Jessie looked down at their son. A few dark golden strands of hair fell into her face as she slowly nodded. "Okay," she said softly. One of her hands stroked mindless circles on Grant's back. "I'm on the work schedule for the next two days, then I have a few days off. I can bring him up there then? We can—you can—we'll see how things go."

Despite her agreement, he didn't feel as elated as he should have. He'd done it again, going off half cocked and blurting out to his beautiful, sweet, very human Jessie that she was his mate. Expecting her to just trust in it based on the concept of shifter mates that she didn't really understand.

Way to go, dumbass, he snarled to himself. His bear snarled in response. Shane shoved the brute down as best as he could. What he wanted to do more than anything right now was grab Jessie and kiss her sweet lips until he couldn't think anymore. But somehow he managed to hang onto the last tiny pieces of sanity and dignity he possessed. So instead of making things worse, he just nodded.

"Okay. It's a date."

Jessie smiled at him. "A date," she said softly, nodding back at him.

But the nervous silence between them made his bear roar in frustration and worry. Silently, he vowed to himself to make it work when she came up there. He had to prove to her that they were true mates. That he wanted her, and only her. And that he would be there for both of them, always. "Okay," he echoed, hearing the seriousness in his voice. "It's a date. A real one, Jessie."

Looking at her face as he said that, he put every ounce of conviction he had into his voice. A date with his mate. The most important date of his entire life. He would make sure it was perfect.

6

*J*essie caught her breath as she rounded the final snowy curve and the property of the Silvertip Lodge opened up in front of her. Despite the threatening storm that had turned the sky dark gray, the place was absolutely gorgeous. She'd thought Deep Hollow was a winter wonderland. A snow-covered fairytale of charming mountain life. It was, but the Silvertip Lodge was like the most fantastical dream come true. The huge stone and wood building nestled against the rising flank of the mountain, looking like something straight out of those glossy magazines about fancy homes. Despite its immense grandeur and beauty, however, it still seemed incredibly inviting. Welcoming and warm rather than off-putting and haughty.

As she drove in, she passed several small cabins set well back from the road with a cleared driveway leading up to each one. Smoke gently spiraled out from the chimneys of a few of them. Shane had said several shifters lived here, but there were also quite a few guest cabins, all of which were actually full for the holidays.

The road from town up to the lodge should've been hairy and scary, and she supposed it was during a bad storm, but it had been immaculately groomed and easy for her to drive up in the truck she had borrowed from Livy. She'd had it in four low the whole way up, of course, but Livy assured her she would make it with no problems. And if for any reason she did get stuck, they would come down and get her shortly. She even had cell service, she noted as she glanced down at her phone. Amazing. They really planned for every contingency.

In the back seat, Grant made funny little half snuffling, half giggling noises. He'd been doing it the entire twenty minute drive up. Jessie glanced at him in the rearview mirror. Although he couldn't see out the window from within the depths of his car seat, his head was turned toward it. He looked up at the trees and stormy sky as they drove, seeming fascinated.

"We'll be spending a lot of time up here, little man," she said to him. He glanced toward the front seat, his chubby little face breaking into a grin at the sound of her voice. Then he immediately looked back toward the window. It was as if he knew he was getting closer to his daddy's home, the heart of which Shane had told her was one hundred percent shifter land.

Silvertip Lodge, as it turned out, was open only to shifters. The website was hidden from human eyes, being password protected and only findable on shifter forums and other shifter-only sites. Although people talked about it in town, and the casual human visitor to Deep Hollow might hear of it, or see a lodge brochure at one of the many town businesses, they would only be told that it was a private community.

Despite her own nerves at seeing Shane, at the craziness of what he'd said to her the other day about being mates, Jessie couldn't help a smile of excitement as she drove into what was practically a secret kingdom. This was the life her son was going to know about. Surrounded by his own kind, all different kinds of shifters in fact, and always feeling free to be himself. The thought made her incredibly happy.

Taking a quick look at the directions Shane had scrawled on a piece of paper for her, she started counting driveways after she passed a huge, stately barn, which she was told held snowmobiles and snow-shoes and cross-country skis rather than animals. Apparently, horses and other livestock were perfectly manageable by many shifters. But not all of them, and since the ones who came to the Lodge weren't exactly screened for their horse whispering abilities, it was deemed safer for everyone involved if there no animals on the property.

Except, of course, the shifters themselves.

At the third road past the barn, she turned left. The

road twisted and turned through the trees, bending around a few times before it ended in a little turnaround in front of the most freaking adorable cabin she'd ever seen. The sharply angled roof was billowed over with snow. A large stone chimney hugged its side, curls of grayish white smoke puffing out of it. Large wooden beams held up the roof over the porch. A large window ran the length of the porch. It was the picture of a perfect little mountain cabin.

"Oh, wow." But Jessie's exclamation didn't come because of how darling the cabin was. No, she gasped as she slowed the truck to stop and killed the engine because Shane was waiting for her on the porch.

Half naked Shane, that is.

He stood there wearing nothing but a pair of tan-colored work jeans. They clung to his muscled thighs, practically molded there. His feet were bare, as was the rest of him from the waist up. And holy freaking moly, his naked chest was a thing of beauty. Muscles rippled across it in a mesmerizing display of what was his pretty much perfect masculine physique.

Jessie's brain showed the first signs of actually melting.

It wasn't like she'd forgotten how freaking hot he was. Of course not. She'd dreamed about him every single night since Grant was conceived. But to see him standing there in front of her, for real, took her breath away even as it sent hot sizzles zipping throughout her entire body. Mr. sexy lumberjack mountain bear shifter god of the forest indeed. It was almost as if she could feel his desire leaping across the space of the little yard from where he stood on the porch, his expression serious, to where she sat frozen in the seat of the truck.

The spell broke when Grant emitted one of his screechy little demands. He wanted out. Right now. Taking a deep breath to get control of herself, because wow, were her hormones hammering at her right now, Jessie exited the truck and practically fell to the ground because the thing was lifted so darn high.

"Glad you got here before the storm." Shane's voice rumbled deep into the heavy, storm-threatening air. He came down the wooden steps and walked across the snowy yard, barefoot.

"Your feet—" Jessie began. Shane flashed a smile at her, making all her girl parts sit up to attention. Despite knowing that forever wasn't real, couldn't be real, her ovaries suddenly clamored that making more babies with him was a great idea.

"Bear shifter," he reminded her, his grin getting a little bigger. His eyes slipped past her to Grant in the backseat. "He'll be doing the same thing once his first shift comes."

Flustered by her female reaction to him, Jessie opened the door to the backseat of the truck and got Grant out. Impulsively, she suddenly thrust him out to Shane. "Here. Will you carry him in? I'll grab our stuff."

Shane's arms automatically came out for Grant, his smile dissolving into first surprise, then pleasure.

As soon as Grant was safe in Shane's hands, Jessie took a step away so he couldn't hand the boy back. But he didn't seem to want to. He held Grant away from him at arm's length, little boy and big man both locking eyes with one another for a long moment. The smile came back onto Shane's face just as it did onto Grant's. Jessie caught her breath again. Not only were their eyes the same, so were their smiles. He pulled his son in close, holding him awkwardly but safely in his arms.

She went around to the other side of the truck to grab her little overnight bag and the three other bags that held Grant's mountain of stuff.

"Can I help you carry something else?" Shane asked, though he was engrossed in Grant's fascinated pulling of his beard. Damn, he was the most gorgeous man she'd ever seen. Despite her own doubts, she couldn't help but notice the tingly pulses her lady parts gave each time she looked at him.

Jessie shook her head even though he couldn't see her. "No. You have the most important thing. I've got the rest of it."

"Yeah." Absolute awe tinged Shane's voice.

She couldn't control her own smile as they all walked towards the little cabin and inside. Carefully, making sure Shane couldn't see her, although he was so caught up in Grant he probably wouldn't notice anyway, she lightly pinched the inside of her skin on one wrist. Just in case she was dreaming, she wanted to make sure would wake up now and not be disappointed.

The pinch hurt. This was all real. Daring to let her smile get bigger, she walked up the stairs and into Shane's cabin.

The inside was manly yet adorable at the same time. Rough-hewn logs made up the walls and ceiling. A smooth wooden floor was clean, covered only by a few pieces of simple yet very well-made furniture. To the right of the front door, a huge window offered up a view of the snowy field outside and the darkening forest beyond. Jessie sighed with delight. "This is so cozy. Better than life on the road?" she added shyly, nibbling on her upper lip as she glanced at him.

To her surprise, he seemed a little nervous as well. Running a hand through his spiky brown hair, he nodded. "Yeah. I like it here a lot. Come on, let me give you the grand tour. It has five whole rooms." He huffed out a chuckle at that.

She relaxed at the sound. Still holding Grant, Shane swiveled his free hand around and said in a grand voice, "Behold the living room."

Jessie couldn't help her giggle. Shane then gestured through a door that framed a coal-black cast iron stove. "The kitchen. Where, I admit, not much cooking goes on. I tend to eat leftovers from my aunt because she often takes pity on my lack of culinary skills."

Feeling the grin stretch over her face at how silly he

was being, and at how Grant's giggles indicated he was
enjoying being held in Shane's powerful arms, Jessie
nodded for him to go on. Shane pointed at another
door down a short hallway and said the bathroom was
behind it. Indicating the open door next to it, he said,
"Guest room. There's a crib in there." He sounded
abruptly diffident. "My aunt gave it to me. I figure that
can be Grant's room? When he's here, I mean."

Those whiskey eyes fixed on Jessie's, now more
direct. He ignored Grant tugging at his beard. "And
there's also the bedroom." Without waiting to see if
she'd follow, he went down the hallway. As if mesmerized, Jessie followed. When she entered through the
last door behind him, she caught her breath. A huge,
dark oak sleigh bed was centered neatly against the
main wall, which was made up of large, smooth gray
and tan river stones. Covered in a rich chocolate
brown comforter, a deep royal red blanket folded over
its foot, the bed looked extremely masculine—and
extremely inviting. Nearly floor-to-ceiling windows
and a door that was all window panes itself made up
the east wall, revealing a stunning view of the storm-
tossed mountain slopes beyond.

She'd had no idea his place opened up to such an
incredible vista. Or that she would feel so at home in it.
The cabin was gorgeous, classy in an understated way
that didn't make her feel like a poor city mouse. Just as
she thought that, Shane turned to her with a small
shrug. "It's a nicer place than I've ever lived in my

whole life, and it's nothing compared to the main lodge. But I felt at home here right away. Like it was meant for me." Tipping his head down to tickle Grant's face with his beard, he added, "I want it to feel the same way for this little guy. And for you." He looked up at Jessie, his eyes thoughtful under his thick brows.

Before she could respond, he said, "Snow's coming. I have to batten down a few hatches outside before it gets dark. I'll let you two settle in. You and I," and his heated gaze went right to Jessie's insides, lurching them sideways with a delicious tingle, "have all night to really catch up with one another."

"Um, okay." She blinked at him, feeling the tingles race up and down her body. While she was pretty sure *forever* wasn't in the cards, no matter what he'd said about mates, the sensual promise in his eyes was something she wasn't about to ignore. Despite her nerves, she wanted to kiss him more than anything.

Okay, fine. She could admit it. Despite everything, the nighttime couldn't come fast enough for her.

Shane was making her insides flip and melt and explode with desire. She wanted to enjoy every single second in his presence. Even if it ended up being only physical, *mate* thing or no.

SHANE WATCHED with slightly hooded eyes as Jessie turned away from the soundly sleeping Grant. Outside, the night sky howled with the force of the winter storm that tore up the mountain, but the cabin was snug and secure. They were perfectly safe in here. Dinner was done—thank god for Elodie still taking pity on him, though she'd mentioned with slanted eyebrows that he really should learn to cook one of these days—and the dishes were clean.

All that lay before them now was the promise of the night. A night in which Shane meant to do everything in his power to prove to this spectacular woman that he wanted nothing more than to have her in his life. And, of course, that he'd also really desperately like to taste her sweetness again. He'd been wildly craving it ever since she'd appeared back in his life.

The stunning woman in question walked back to where Shane stood in front of the fire he'd laid in the hearth, her every movement graceful and sort of liquid. He could sense the desire buzzing through her, almost as if it glowed out from beneath her skin. The firelight lit up her face and throat as she approached him, adding to the sensuality of the moment. Shane knew he was staring at her, but she didn't look like she minded in the least. During the late afternoon and evening that they'd spent playing with Grant, talking about their respective last few years, and eating dinner, she'd relaxed more and more.

Her arousal had also spiked ever higher, which Shane had scented so clearly it had him struggling to not just ravish her already. Only the presence of his amazing little son, as well as his awareness of the delicate balance of the situation with Jessie, had kept him reined in.

But now Grant was sound asleep, Jessie was giving clear signals that she more than welcomed Shane's advances, and he was more than ready to claim his woman.

Finally.

Her sweet scent reached out to envelop his senses as a little smile tugged at her mouth. "He's out cold," she murmured. "Kind of funny, isn't it? This isn't exactly like the way things were the last time you and I spent in each other's company."

Despite himself, Shane snorted. "I'll say." Yeah, having a baby sleeping in the other room was definitely different. Every single protective instinct Shane possessed was on the alert, tipped toward going to overdrive at a moment's notice.

Yet he was also achingly aware of the gorgeous, sensual woman standing beside him. Her lips were slightly parted, plump and glistening in the firelight. She gently worried her lower lip between her teeth. Glancing up at him with those blue-gray eyes, she looked like a sexy angel.

To hell with being careful. He needed to ravish his gorgeous mate until she couldn't even remember her own name. "Everything I want is right here, right now," Shane said, a possessive growl shattering his words.

Before she could say anything, he added, "And it

starts with a kiss." With that, he reached out and pulled her succulent, very willing body towards his, holding it against every hard inch of himself and reaching down to claim her mouth with his.

Jessie moaned as he finally tasted her lips, the sound swallowed between them as her arms went up behind his neck, pulling his head down closer to hers. Her eagerness only excited him more, and he slid one hand down her back, rubbing small circles until he got to the bottom of her shirt. He slipped his hand under it to feel her silken bare skin just above the top of her jeans. Gently running his fingertips over the skin at her waist, Shane groaned.

He pulled back just long enough to murmur, "Fucking hell, Jessie, you're just like I remembered. Only better. You're the sexiest woman I have ever laid eyes on in my entire life. I'm doing my damned best to be quiet, babe, but I can hardly think straight right now."

Her half-lidded eyes gazed up at him as she shamelessly thrust her pelvis against his. "It's okay," she whispered, her voice slightly ragged. "Grant is a really sound sleeper. He won't wake up. Whatever it is you want to do to me, you have my full permission."

Shane's dick jumped at that, swelling even more with a blast of excitement that was almost painful. "Sounds perfect." Without another word, he easily scooped Jessie up into his arms, grinning as she gasped. He carefully deposited her into the soft, synthetic rug in front of the roaring fireplace, gently nestling her into it before straddling her with one leg on either side, sinking down onto his knees and resting his weight on her thighs where he trapped them between his legs. Jessie's eyes widened even more in her mouth opened as if to speak, but he shook his head, gently placing a fingertip against her soft lips.

"No talking, beautiful. I just want to show you how you make me feel." His own voice was ragged as he said those words. He knew he was going to have a bit of a time reining himself completely in. Her masses of golden hair waved around her face, a few strands caught on her cheek and mouth. He gently pushed her hair away from her face. Curving his hand along her cheek, he slid it down the side of her neck, over her collarbones, to the front of her shirt.

Pausing, he quirked an eyebrow at her and let his grin turned dangerous. "Well, just a little more talking. How attached do you feel to this shirt of yours?"

It was a pretty peach-colored number, with a silky row of pearly buttons down the front. Jessie shook her head, clearly confused. "Not very. Why?"

Shane gently traced his hand over the sweet swell of her breasts beneath the blouse, this time eliciting a sharp gasp from Jessie. "Because of this," he growled, and in one smooth quick move ripped the blouse open, scattering buttons like shimmering little seeds.

"Oh!" Surprise but, more importantly, breathless anticipation punctuated Jessie's voice. Her beautiful breasts, encased in a black lace bra festooned with a tiny rose at the center, lay heaving and exposed in their creamy beauty before Shane's fascinated gaze.

His dick throbbed even harder as every sense he had seemed to roar to life, sweeping through him with a tingling electricity he hadn't felt since—well, since the last time he'd had this glorious woman all to himself for three incredible days. He managed just enough control to shake his head at her, murmuring, "I want to hear the sounds you make as I touch your body."

Without waiting for an answer, he reached his head down to her breasts, sliding his hips back down her legs a little bit to give him enough space to dip his face down and trace the swell of her skin where her tempting breasts curved out of the top of the bra. She didn't disappoint him in her response, groaning and gasping and breathing happily all at once in a delicious staccato of sound that rippled out along with the crackle of the flames and the occasional beat of snow on the windows outside as the wind raged around his cozy cabin. He glanced up at Jessie. Her stunning eyes were wide open, fixed on him, her mouth also open with her keening gasp as she lifted herself partway off the soft little rug so that her breasts met his tongue.

Shane smiled, spanning his broad hands over her waist, his thumbs tracing a delicate circle over her bellybutton as he slowly dropped kisses on the tops of her breasts and her collarbone. Jessie arched her chest toward him, putting her hands on the back of his head and pressing it down. Closer to her.

Good. She was loving every second of it. Pretty sure she would be a little less happy if he ripped her bra off the same way he'd done with her blouse, he moved his hands underneath her and up her back, finding the bra's clasp and easily undoing it. He slid it off her arms, tossing it to the side so the bounty of her breasts could fill his hands.

Shane just stared at her breasts, gently running his thumbs over her nipples, which gratifyingly hardened even more than they had already been. The beautiful pink rosebud tips crowned the silken creaminess of her breasts. Jessie was breathing fast, her eyes still fastened on him. Smiling at her, he dropped his head down again. This time, he lapped at one nipple with his tongue, then lightly nipped it with his teeth.

Jessie whimpered and moaned. Hearing her voice soften and stretch, yet also tense and tauten as she gave herself over to her wilder, rougher side, made Shane's dick throb so hard it almost painfully strained against his jeans.

He moved his head to her other breast, lavishing the same ministrations upon it. Tasting, teasing, nibbling. Losing himself to the incredible wonder of having Jessie with him again.

This time, he wasn't losing her. Never again.

Sitting up, he rocked back on his heels, then stood. Jessie's eyes opened as a protesting sound left her throat. She stared up at him from the softness of the rug, pushing herself up on the backs of her forearms to watch him as he stepped to one side of her. Hastily, not caring if he shredded his own clothing, he ripped off his shirt. Throwing it somewhere behind him, he unbuttoned the fly of his jeans so fast he heard the denim rip at the bottom. Careless, he shrugged them down his legs and kicked them off, leaving himself standing in front of her utterly buck naked since he never wore anything under his pants if he could help it.

"Oh, my god." Jessie's voice was a jagged, tumbling waterfall of womanly appreciation. "I thought my dreams remembered how amazing you are. But I forgot. You're much more amazing."

He was so incredibly turned on just looking at the stunning woman in front of him he was almost afraid he was gonna blow like an untried teenager. Flexing and unflexing his quads and toes in an effort to distract himself, he growled to the fucking hottest, most amazing woman he'd ever met, "I'm going to tear your jeans off now, Jessie. Then I'm gonna go to town feasting on you, because I want to taste you when you come in my mouth. How does that sound to you?"

7

*H*ow did that sound to her? How did that *sound* to her?

Holy freaking yowza yum was what it sounded like.

Jessie stared up at Shane and his gorgeous, rock-hard cock, a single pearly drop of liquid shimmering on the end of it. Before she could help herself, before she could even think, she sat up all the way.

Then she leaned forward and took that beautiful length into her mouth.

Shane's breath whooshed out of him on a gasp as she turned the tables on him. Jessie pulled his smooth, velvet-encased hardness into her mouth, licking and twirling her tongue along it all the way. He tasted divine. She could hardly get enough, licking him up one side and down the other. Catching the fluid at the very tip, she swirled it over her lips, opening her eyes to look up at him as she did so.

"Fuck me, that feels good," he growled. His hands reached down to her head, catching her hair and burying themselves into it. His fingers clutched her skull, very gently pushing down as he groaned. "Careful, Jessie." His warning was half laugh, half serious. "It's been a while for me. I'm gonna have a hard time holding back if you keep doing that."

She smiled around his thick length, pursing her lips over the head and sucking out the salty-sweet drop. Shane gasped, his fingers almost painfully convulsing on her head. Pulling back, she whispered, "It's been a long time for me, too. Since you, actually," she admitted. She was too excited to care how pitiful that sounded.

Shane's grip on her head tightened again. "Good." The word was a pure growl. "I'm caveman enough to like that no one has touched you since me. Though I'm damned sorry it's been that long. You deserve to have your body worshipped every single day."

He looked right at her as he spoke. Even though she was the one on her knees, she felt like she was the one on top. The one in charge.

The one truly being worshipped by this stunning woodland god of a man.

"Shane." His name was a whisper on her tongue as she stared back up at him, mesmerized by the sincerity of his voice and his eyes. Their gazes locked for a long, heady moment, the world narrowing down to the two of them in this snowbound cabin, their baby sleeping soundly in the other room, everything right.

Then he sank to the soft rug beside her, leveling the playing field. "Jessie," he groaned. "It's so damned good to have you to myself again."

Without another word, he flipped her onto her back in the plush softness of the white rug. She gasped as his fingers traced her skin. They skimmed over her hip bones, along her thighs, back over to caress her stomach and hold her breasts. Her nipples tautened as she pushed herself into him.

"Yes," she gasped. "I've missed you so much."

Shane's amber eyes seemed to glow, his entire face rippling with his desire as he slowly bent his head down once again to the soft bounty of her breasts that he held in his hands.

MOVING his fingers out of the way, Shane first lapped one, then the other sweet nipple, circling his tongue around the hard little peaks. Jessie's fluttering breaths and gasps sounded musical to his ears. The fire crackled in the hearth, the wind roared and whistled outside as he gently scraped his teeth over her nipple. Soft cries of encouragement fell from her lips.

Bit by bit, Shane felt his control slip as he slowly quested his way down her generous body with his lips and tongue. Her fingers curled again into his hair, urging him on. Her hips lifted upward beneath his shoulders as he worked his way down toward them.

When he hovered his face over her closely trimmed golden curls, inhaling her scent like the ambrosia it was and feeling dizzy from it, he paused.

"No!" she protested, pushing his head down.

Shane chuckled, then leaned down to lightly huff a heated breath over the sweet damp folds that awaited his touch. Jessie's answering cry was inarticulate.

Without waiting another second, Shane plunged his tongue into the delicate, glistening folds that awaited him. Honey and nectar, cinnamon and spice, everything that made this stunning woman so very nice, flipped inanely through his brain as her sweet taste exploded into his mouth. He feverishly licked her sweet crevices and folds, dragging his tongue up and down and around in rhythm to her keening cries and gasps. Pulling his head up once, he growled, "I've missed your taste so much, Jessie," before diving back down again into her succulence.

Jessie trembled and shook beneath him as he worked his tongue thoroughly over her slickness, then into her hot depths. Licking and stroking, he swirled and twirled his tongue, hummed his lips over her clit, and lazily circled her inner walls with one thumb.

"Shane, Shane, Shane," she began chanting, her voice rasping over his name, hardening his dick even more. Her taste subtly changed, becoming more intense, with a savoriness to it that he lapped up with the greed of a starving man.

With a groaning cry, she fell over the edge, her inner walls clenching and flexing around his thumb, her voice keening through the walls of the cabin on the billowing waves of her ecstasy. Her voice pulsed and echoed slowly back down until she finally relaxed back against the rug, her ragged breath and the crackling flames the only sounds in the room.

Reluctantly, Shane left her sweet center and pulled his way back up her body until he rested over her. Her eyes, their shade now close to a navy blue, blinked at him, sated. He let a corner of his mouth wing up in a grin. Both satisfaction and promise tumbled through his voice as he said, "That's just the beginning. Because I have to be inside you so badly right now that it hurts."

Her own lips tipping up into a smile, she whispered, "Then come in. Please." With that, she reached down to guide him inside her.

AT HER BOLD INVITATION, Shane's eyes turned to molten gold. The sight of it, the evidence of the animal he harbored deep inside him, should've scared her. But it didn't. Instead, she simply felt more excited at her power in arousing him. At the clear knowledge of how much he wanted her.

She about felt her own eyes roll back in her head as

he pushed that huge, hard length into her, centimeter by centimeter. She could tell he was struggling to hold himself back, not just slam into her. It felt so good, and she was simultaneously both so relaxed and yet further roused by the orgasm he'd just wrung out of her with his lips and tongue, that she reached her hands down to the delicious hardness of his ass to press him into her.

"Don't hold back," she whispered, looking right into his eyes. "I've missed you. I want to feel how much we want this."

With a ragged groan, her name sliding out of him like a prayer, Shane nodded once. Then with a quick thrust of his hips, he pushed himself into her all the way to the base of his thick cock.

Despite herself, Jessie gasped. He was so damned big. But the delightful sensations of him finally being inside her again simply intensified into a spiraling deliciousness that she wanted to climb. He paused briefly, halted by her gasp, but she frantically shook her head.

"No. It feels good. It feels amazing. Don't you dare stop," she ordered.

A chuckle rumbled out of him as he complied. He stroked in and out, going faster and harder as she encouraged him by lifting her hips with his each stroke. She wrapped her hands around his broad back, hanging on to him for dear life as their synchronized movements slid her along the rug like the incredible power of an ocean wave slipping and bobbing them both along.

His eyes shifted and pulsed with the golden lights in them, capturing Jessie and holding her in them. She could see his bear dancing in there, along with Shane's own powerful presence. Everything scary, everything hard, everything that could possibly be wrong between them melted away into the openness and vulnerability she remembered from their time together when they first met.

"Love," she whispered, saying the word like it was a name for him. Saying it like it was the most natural, obvious thing in the world.

Shane's mouth loosened and his eyes softened even more. He gently gripped her shoulders in his massive hands. "Oh, yes," he whispered in a ragged groan. "Jessie, my mate. My love."

In a powerful, blinding white heat, another orgasm soared through Jessie, shaking and shattering her. Making her shriek out with the beautiful force of it. At the same time, she could feel Shane tighten inside her and then pulse, releasing shots of his beautiful liquid heat deep into her as his guttural voice boomed out her name in his own pleasure. Their eyes never left one another, locked together as the sensations gripped them both at the same time, shooting up and around and binding them together in what Jessie could sense with every molecule of her being was exactly the right thing. Exactly the right way to be.

She was his mate. And he was hers. This was exactly where she was meant to be, and it was right.

As the tremors slowly ebbed and waned, gradually draining away to leave Jessie feeling boneless, Shane gently tipped his face down to kiss her. Long, deep, luxurious, he savored her lips with the taste of her still on them. His beard tickled her face, making her smile in languorous delight as the endorphins still flooded through her body.

Long moments later, when he gently rested of the weight of his body on the floor beside her, keeping one arm and leg flung over her, his face nestled into her neck, the soft rumble of his voice vibrated against her skin. "Exactly where you belong, Jessie. With me. You and me and our son under the same roof. Together. Safe."

The sensation of being lovingly cocooned into the warmth and safety of Shane's snowbound little cabin in the middle of a winter storm filled her every sense. It all felt perfect.

"Now then," he said, sitting up. Without warning, he scooped her up into his arms as if she weighed no more than a feather. She squeaked in surprise. Cradling her close against his sexy rock-hard chest, Shane strode to the bedroom and gently put her down onto his gorgeous sleigh bed. Staring up at him with a startled anticipation, Jessie's breath sucked in with delight as he said, "We've still got a lot more night ahead of us, beautiful. And I fully intend to hear every last one of the gorgeous sounds you've got to make."

"Mmm," was Jessie's only reply as Shane made good on his promise.

8

How did that sound to her? How did that *sound* to her?

Holy freaking yowza yum was what it sounded like.

Jessie stared up at Shane and his gorgeous, rock-hard cock, a single pearly drop of liquid shimmering on the end of it. Before she could help herself, before she could even think, she sat up all the way.

Then she leaned forward and took that beautiful length into her mouth.

Shane's breath whooshed out of him on a gasp as she turned the tables on him. Jessie pulled his smooth, velvet-encased hardness into her mouth, licking and twirling her tongue along it all the way. He tasted divine. She could hardly get enough, licking him up one side and down the other. Catching the fluid at the very tip, she swirled it over her lips, opening her eyes to look up at him as she did so.

"Fuck me, that feels good," he growled. His hands reached down to her head, catching her hair and burying themselves into it. His fingers clutched her skull, very gently pushing down as he groaned. "Careful, Jessie." His warning was half laugh, half serious. "It's been a while for me. I'm gonna have a hard time holding back if you keep doing that."

She smiled around his thick length, pursing her lips over the head and sucking out the salty-sweet drop. Shane gasped, his fingers almost painfully convulsing on her head. Pulling back, she whispered, "It's been a long time for me, too. Since you, actually," she admitted. She was too excited to care how pitiful that sounded.

Shane's grip on her head tightened again. "Good." The word was a pure growl. "I'm caveman enough to like that no one has touched you since me. Though I'm damned sorry it's been that long. You deserve to have your body worshipped every single day."

He looked right at her as he spoke. Even though she was the one on her knees, she felt like she was the one on top. The one in charge.

The one truly being worshipped by this stunning woodland god of a man.

"Shane." His name was a whisper on her tongue as she stared back up at him, mesmerized by the sincerity of his voice and his eyes. Their gazes locked for a long, heady moment, the world narrowing down to the two of them in this snowbound cabin, their baby sleeping soundly in the other room, everything right.

Then he sank to the soft rug beside her, leveling the playing field. "Jessie," he groaned. "It's so damned good to have you to myself again."

Without another word, he flipped her onto her back in the plush softness of the white rug. She gasped as his fingers traced her skin. They skimmed over her hip bones, along her thighs, back over to caress her stomach and hold her breasts. Her nipples tautened as she pushed herself into him.

"Yes," she gasped. "I've missed you so much."

Shane's amber eyes seemed to glow, his entire face rippling with his desire as he slowly bent his head down once again to the soft bounty of her breasts that he held in his hands.

Moving his fingers out of the way, Shane first lapped one, then the other sweet nipple, circling his tongue around the hard little peaks. Jessie's fluttering breaths and gasps sounded musical to his ears. The fire crackled in the hearth, the wind roared and whistled outside as he gently scraped his teeth over her nipple. Soft cries of encouragement fell from her lips.

Bit by bit, Shane felt his control slip as he slowly quested his way down her generous body with his lips and tongue. Her fingers curled again into his hair, urging him on. Her hips lifted upward beneath his shoulders as he worked his way down toward them.

When he hovered his face over her closely trimmed golden curls, inhaling her scent like the ambrosia it was and feeling dizzy from it, he paused.

"No!" she protested, pushing his head down.

Shane chuckled, then leaned down to lightly huff a heated breath over the sweet damp folds that awaited his touch. Jessie's answering cry was inarticulate.

Without waiting another second, Shane plunged his tongue into the delicate, glistening folds that awaited him. Honey and nectar, cinnamon and spice, everything that made this stunning woman so very nice, flipped inanely through his brain as her sweet taste exploded into his mouth. He feverishly licked her sweet crevices and folds, dragging his tongue up and down and around in rhythm to her keening cries and gasps. Pulling his head up once, he growled, "I've missed your taste so much, Jessie," before diving back down again into her succulence.

Jessie trembled and shook beneath him as he worked his tongue thoroughly over her slickness, then into her hot depths. Licking and stroking, he swirled and twirled his tongue, hummed his lips over her clit, and lazily circled her inner walls with one thumb.

"Shane, Shane, Shane," she began chanting, her voice rasping over his name, hardening his dick even more.

Her taste subtly changed, becoming more intense, with a savoriness to it that he lapped up with the greed of a starving man.

With a groaning cry, she fell over the edge, her inner walls clenching and flexing around his thumb, her voice keening through the walls of the cabin on the billowing waves of her ecstasy. Her voice pulsed and echoed slowly back down until she finally relaxed back against the rug, her ragged breath and the crackling flames the only sounds in the room.

Reluctantly, Shane left her sweet center and pulled his way back up her body until he rested over her. Her eyes, their shade now close to a navy blue, blinked at him, sated. He let a corner of his mouth wing up in a grin. Both satisfaction and promise tumbled through his voice as he said, "That's just the beginning. Because I have to be inside you so badly right now that it hurts."

Her own lips tipping up into a smile, she whispered, "Then come in. Please." With that, she reached down to guide him inside her.

At her bold invitation, Shane's eyes turned to molten gold. The sight of it, the evidence of the animal he harbored deep inside him, should've scared her. But it didn't. Instead, she simply felt more excited at her power in arousing him. At the clear knowledge of how much he wanted her.

She about felt her own eyes roll back in her head as he pushed that huge, hard length into her, centimeter by centimeter. She could tell he was struggling to hold himself back, not just slam into her. It felt so good, and she was simultaneously both so relaxed and yet further roused by the orgasm he'd just wrung out of her with his lips and tongue, that she reached her hands down to the delicious hardness of his ass to press him into her.

"Don't hold back," she whispered, looking right into his eyes. "I've missed you. I want to feel how much we want this."

With a ragged groan, her name sliding out of him like a prayer, Shane nodded once. Then with a quick thrust of his hips, he pushed himself into her all the way to the base of his thick cock.

Despite herself, Jessie gasped. He was so damned big. But the delightful sensations of him finally being inside her again simply intensified into a spiraling deliciousness that she wanted to climb. He paused briefly, halted by her gasp, but she frantically shook her head.

"No. It feels good. It feels amazing. Don't you dare stop," she ordered.

A chuckle rumbled out of him as he complied. He stroked in and out, going faster and harder as she encouraged him by lifting her hips with his each stroke. She wrapped her hands around his broad back, hanging on to him for dear life as their synchronized movements slid her along the rug like the incredible power of an ocean wave slipping and bobbing them both along.

His eyes shifted and pulsed with the golden lights in them, capturing Jessie and holding her in them. She could see his bear dancing in there, along with Shane's own powerful presence. Everything scary, everything hard, everything that could possibly be wrong between them melted away into the openness and vulnerability she remembered from their time together when they first met.

"Love," she whispered, saying the word like it was a name for him. Saying it like it was the most natural, obvious thing in the world.

Shane's mouth loosened and his eyes softened even more. He gently gripped her shoulders in his massive hands. "Oh, yes," he whispered in a ragged groan. "Jessie, my mate. My love."

In a powerful, blinding white heat, another orgasm soared through Jessie, shaking and shattering her. Making her shriek out with the beautiful force of it. At the same time, she could feel Shane tighten inside her and then pulse, releasing shots of his beautiful liquid heat deep into her as his guttural voice boomed out her name in his own pleasure. Their eyes never left one another, locked together as the sensations gripped them both at the same time, shooting up and around and binding them together in what Jessie could sense with every molecule of her being was exactly the right thing. Exactly the right way to be.

She was his mate. And he was hers. This was exactly where she was meant to be, and it was right.

As the tremors slowly ebbed and waned, gradually draining away to leave Jessie feeling boneless, Shane gently tipped his face down to kiss her. Long, deep, luxurious, he savored her lips with the taste of her still on them. His beard tickled her face, making her smile in languorous delight as the endorphins still flooded through her body.

Long moments later, when he gently rested of the weight of his body on the floor beside her, keeping one arm and leg flung over her, his face nestled into her neck, the soft rumble of his voice vibrated against her skin. "Exactly where you belong, Jessie. With me. You and me and our son under the same roof. Together. Safe."

The sensation of being lovingly cocooned into the warmth and safety of Shane's snowbound little cabin in the middle of a winter storm filled her every sense. It all felt perfect.

"Now then," he said, sitting up. Without warning, he scooped her up into his arms as if she weighed no more than a feather. She squeaked in surprise. Cradling her close against his sexy rock-hard chest, Shane strode to the bedroom and gently put her down onto his gorgeous sleigh bed. Staring up at him with a startled anticipation, Jessie's breath sucked in with delight as he said, "We've still got a lot more night ahead of us, beautiful. And I fully intend to hear every last one of the gorgeous sounds you've got to make."

"Mmm," was Jessie's only reply as Shane made good on his promise.

9

*J*essie floated up out of sleep. She was somewhere softer than she'd ever been before. Soft, deliciously warm, completely comfortable. In Shane's bed. In his cozy little mountain cabin, tucked deep into the sheltering forest. Memories of the night she had spent with him flooded through her, coloring her cheeks, making her face split into a smile even though her eyes were still closed.

Shane's home. It all felt so incredibly right that she simply stayed nestled into the bed for another several breaths, just enjoying the sensation. Finally, she lazily turned over and reached out her arm, patting the bed to find him.

He wasn't there. Eyes opening, she sat up. She had the huge sleigh bed to herself. He must've gotten up early. She knew he wasn't going to be the type to make her breakfast, or probably even coffee. Though the cabin was not nearly as tiny as her apartment, it was still kind of small. She tipped her head so she could hear.

Nothing. In fact, no sounds of the storm, either. Reaching to the window, she fumbled with the heavy blind and whipped it up. Gasping, she stared outside. Bright sunshine streamed into the room. Everything out there was utterly smothered in snow. It settled in heavy drifts on the bowed pine branches and blanketed the ground. The sky was robin's egg blue.

It was absolutely beautiful.

Somewhat reluctantly pushing the warm covers off of her, she swung her feet around and slid off the tall bed. Luckily, the cabin was warm. Stepping into the small living room, she grabbed up Shane's long button-up shirt that had been tossed onto the floor, smiling as she shrugged it on. It smelled like him. Then she glanced around. No sign of him. She looked into the kitchen. Nope, definitely not there either.

Turning toward the little room Grant slept in, she walked over, her face ready to smile at the sight of her baby boy snuggled up in there.

Instead, she sucked in her breath at the sight of the empty bed. "Grant? Baby?"

Nothing. He wasn't here.

"Shane?" Her voice pitched more loudly than she intended. Quickly, she checked each of the five rooms in the place again, just in case it was possible to miss a gigantic man or her little boy.

They weren't here. They were gone.

Sudden panic clutched at Jessie's stomach. Whirling, she ran toward the front door of the cabin, flung it open, and darted onto the porch. Swallowing desperately against the dryness in her throat, she screamed out Grant's name—then almost strangled on her own voice as she looked across the field of snow toward the nearby treeline.

A baby grizzly bear cub clumsily tottered out from the trees on the other end, loping and tumbling straight toward her in an uneven line. The fuzzy little mouth was open, his entire little body bouncing with excitement as he shoved his still uncoordinated limbs through the deep, fresh snow toward her. He made funny noises that sounded like a bizarre mix between grunts, bellows, and shrieks of pure joy.

"Grant?" This time, Jessie's voice was disbelieving. Yet almost instantly, she also felt a pure knowing that it was him.

Her son.

Grant was a baby grizzly bear, bouncing right toward her. The cutest, fluffiest, darlingest one ever.

He reached the bottom of the stairs, smacked right into them because of his uncoordinated forward momentum, and tumbled back into his fuzzy little rear. Emitting a squeak of surprise, he looked up at his mother.

Jessie laughed even as she darted down the steps and knelt beside him. He immediately burrowed into her side with his little nose, nuzzling and snuffling and making funny little whimpers that were similar to the little sounds he made as a human baby. He gazed up at her with pure adoration as well as excitement.

"Grant, oh, you're amazing, little one! Look at you! You are such a handsome, wonderful little bear." Jessie laughed through her words, crazily proud of him for doing this.

Another movement at the edge of the woods caught her attention. Grant swiveled his little head around, too, falling over completely backward as he did so. The trees seem to be moving. Or rather, a single tree was moving? One giant tree rustled wildly at the edge of the woods. It stood out because it was more green than white, unlike the others.

The fact that it was also being dragged by the most gigantic bear Jessie had ever seen in her life kind of made it stand out too.

She froze for a second, instinct slamming into her that there was an enormous, dangerous wild animal right there. But then Grant, her own little baby bear cub, righted himself back onto all fours. Unevenly, he started plunging through the snow straight towards the huge grizzly bear. Who, Jessie's more logical mind realized with a flash, of course was Shane.

For some reason, he was dragging a pine tree toward his cabin.

Standing in the snow, she abruptly realized her bare feet were going numb. Going back up onto the lowest step to the porch, she stared at the giant grizzly and the little baby one tumbling around his huge paws, grabbing onto pine needles with his tiny teeth and trying to help drag the tree. The enormous grizzly, with its distinctive hump and wash of burnished golden-brown coat, made a muffled roar as he tripped over bumbling little Grant.

Jessie couldn't help but burst out laughing. Her smile just wouldn't quit as she watched. Finally, the two bears and one big pine tree were at the edge of the porch. In the slip of a heartbeat, the enormous one shimmered and cracked and broke back into the shape of a man.

"Holy shit," Jessie muttered, the smile falling into an open-mouthed gape.

Shane walked to her, naked as a jaybird and just as human as she was. She caught her breath again at how frigging *gorgeous* he was. Jeez.

"I got up this morning because he was making noises." Shane's voice was wrapped in a smile. "He'd made his first shift into his bear, right there in his crib, and was doing his best to eat the damn thing trying to get out of it. So we went outside. I didn't want to wake you up just yet," he added, "you were sleeping so soundly. I know I wore you out last night." Sheer masculine pride edged his tone.

Jessie blushed.

"So, I had a thought." He paused at the bottom of the shallow set of stairs. His eyes were that same molten gold they'd been the night before, his hair wildly sticking up on end and his face guardedly hopeful.

Grant bumbled toward her as well, shifting back into a little human baby halfway up and tangling himself in his own feet. Jessie reached down to pick him up. He felt warm in her arms, way warmer than any baby just frolicking in the snow should have been. Cuddling him close, she looked at Shane, then at the pretty spruce tree by his feet. "Does your thought have anything to do with that tree?" Her breath puffed out cold and white in the sharp morning air.

He nodded solemnly. "Yeah. I was thinking my cabin looks a little bare. No Christmas lights and stuff like that. So I thought—maybe you'd like to help me decorate it?" His voice suddenly was almost shy, though that was a little funny coming from such an enormous, sexy lumberjack bear shifter god of the woods. He gestured at the needled branches of the spruce. "I brought a tree to put up. Because I noticed you seem to really get into the holiday spirit. I thought you might like it."

Sudden tears pricked at Jessie's eyes. This was by far the most thoughtful, sweet gift anyone had ever given her in her entire life. Well, aside from Grant, of course. "Um, okay," was all she could manage to say without totally losing it to the happy tears clogging up her throat.

Shane walked up the stairs with a purposeful tread.

He stopped on the porch, right next to her in all his glorious nakedness. Reaching out a closed hand to her, he turned it over. Uncurling his fingers, he revealed a tiny pine cone and a few bright red little berries. "It's not much till we can get some actual decorations in town, but I thought you might want to start with these. We need some holiday sparkle going on in this place. I thought you and Grant might like to help. Because you both belong here," he ended on a whisper.

Jessie sniffed, nodding. "Yes," she bubbled out through the thickness in her throat. "Yes, we belong here. With you. There's nowhere else I'd rather be," she added, feeling a huge grin split her face open.

In her arms, Grant babbled out some noises as he reached for the shiny berries in Shane's hands, though Shane kept them away from his grasp. Then the little boy clearly said, looking right at Shane with his sweet little grin, "Dada!"

Jessie gasped even as Shane's jaw dropped. She looked into his eyes, which were not only a molten gold, but suspiciously shiny. He swallowed hard, then also let a stunning smile sweep over his chiseled features. Reaching out to Jessie, he pulled her against his side and dropped a tender kiss on her forehead, their son held close in her arms.

"It means the world to me to hear you say that, Jessie. Welcome home," he added, squeezing her shoulders.

"Home." She laughed with joy as she said it, looking

out at the beautiful winterscape lit by the brilliant morning sunshine. "Yes. We're home," she whispered, her smile shining through her own watery eyes.

"Now let's get that tree inside so our family can start to decorate it," he added, and she was sure she heard a thickness in his voice as well.

"Deal, mate of mine," she sighed with utter bliss, snuggling her son and her mate close to her.

"Welcome home, mate," Shane said, and he kissed her long and deep, standing on the front porch of their home.

The End

Thank you so much for reading *Mountain Bear's Baby*! Writing about Shane, Jessie, and cute little Grant was a ton of fun.

What's next for the Silvertip Shifters? Beckett North and Pix Camden's story in ***TAMING HER BEAR: BECKETT.*** Turn the page to read it.

TAMING HER BEAR: BECKETT

1

Pix leaned in sideways to deliver the
punchline to Haley, getting close enough
to be heard over the muted roar of the crowded bar.
"You're bigger than the Titanic? Wowza, you mean like
this big?" Cackling like a loon, Pix flung her hands out
to illustrate to her bff the massive girth her blind date a
few weeks back had assured her he possessed.

Unfortunately, her drink was still in one hand. It
went sloshing out all over her arm, and apparently all
over some random stranger as well.

"Argh!" came a grumbling, masculine grunt of
surprise from behind her left shoulder.

Lurching forward, Pix sat up, her laughter instantly
disappearing. "Oh, shit! I'm sorry!" She whirled around
on the barstool.

The second she laid eyes on the guy she'd tossed her
gin and tonic all over, Pix was a goner. Total goner.

Cuz holy moly, was he beyond hot. Hot, and something amazing that curled sweetly through her body and set her inner dragon fire sizzling through her veins.

The guy was massive. Burly, strong, and built. Dark whiskey gold hair, eyes that matched, a pronounced five-o'clock shadow and muscles on his muscles. Built like a tank, but she could tell he had a stealthy grace and balance that meant he could move fast if he wanted to. He looked like he chopped and hauled his own wood to his man-cave cabin tucked up somewhere in the forest above town. In fact, he probably *did* do that, considering she sat in a bar in a quintessential little mountain town full of all sorts of rugged types.

The startled expression on his craggy, sexy face froze as his eyes snagged on hers. They stared at one another for a second that lasted forever.

So this is what they mean when they say time stops, Pix thought in a daze. *Okay. Got it. Time is stopped.*

Behind her, Haley nudged her back with a knee. It was the sort of nudge that said in bestie nudge-speak, *"You just scored! Holy shit he's hot!"*

Uh-huh, Pix thought to herself. *Uh-huh, whoa yeah crazy hot, yep.* Nothing else super intelligible materialized in her brain other than that. That, and something mysterious and intriguing that made her dragon pay very focused attention to him.

Slowly, one corner of the guy's very appealing mouth curled up into a puzzled smile. "Damn. That was pretty good aim for not looking where you were tossing a drink." His voice rumbled into her, making her insides flip and squeeze in excitement as little tingles raced with speedy shivers up and down her spine. Still looking right into her eyes, his grin slowly tucked up the other corner of his mouth. The longer she looked at him, the more the grin pulled up his entire mouth, finally lighting his face into something even more ridiculously good-looking and, well, rugged. She could tell he didn't smile like that often. He had the dangerous aura of a predator always on the lookout for trouble.

But really, he should smile more often. She liked it.

Mr. Rugged 'n Sexy gestured at his forest-green plaid button-up shirt, which sported the wet splash of her drink across one damned well-defined pec that bulged through the flannel material. "This thing's old. You can toss all the drink you want on it. But if you'd hit my boots, sweetheart, then we would've had a problem."

Despite her lingering chagrin at being a drink-tosser, Pix couldn't stop her burst of laughter. She glanced down at his feet. They were clad in work boots of some sort, scuffed up and dirty and definitely covered with way worse things than just booze.

She looked back up at him and let her bold inner flirt come out. "We wouldn't want that. They definitely look like they're in way better shape than your shirt. I mean, those are some clean, tidy boots you have right there."

Now the guy laughed, a rumble just as deep as his voice. Pix felt completely at ease, even though something deep and real still shivered inside her from the look they'd exchanged. Her dragon, usually fierce and ready to swoop into whatever action was going on, wasn't battering at Pix's brain the way she normally would, either. She stayed silently fascinated deep within, watching the man through Pix's eyes as he extended a large hand in her direction. "Beckett North at your service, beautiful."

Feeling a tingling pink paint itself across her cheeks just from the sound of his voice, Pix stuck out her own hand, watching as it was swallowed up by his. His grasp was firm, warm, and had just enough electricity that she could feel it sizzle through her. Yeah, she liked this guy touching her. Beckett. Beckett North. She liked that, too. The name fit him.

"Pix Camden." She sounded a little breathy. Shameless flirt. Happy to flirt with him. Ooh, yeah, he was sexy. Sexy man. Interesting man. Unlike any man she'd ever met before. That sounded dramatic, but it was true. This man was nothing like the men she'd grown up with. The dominating kind she'd fled.

Beckett North nodded at her. Then a super serious look dropped over his face, making it hard and craggy and ferocious in a way she felt all the way down to her lady bits. "It's nice to meet you, Pix," he said in that deep voice. It soothed over her nerves, both electrifying and calming them at once.

The dragon heat that always ran through her, some-times ready to combust, flared high, but it felt good. Not like it would be out of control. Weirdly, it felt slightly cooled by this sexy, savage man in front of her. Or not cooled, but...handled. At ease. Like her dragon's flames were calm for once, instead of wildly out of control.

Her dragon quietly murmured within her. Quiet? Her dragon? That was a first. A really big first in the history of all big firsts.

Now Pix was more than a goner. She was lost, completely and utterly lost in his fierce gaze, the strength of his voice, the certainty in his grip on her hand.

She nodded, her grin beginning to get dorkily big and goofy on her face. "Yes," she said softly. "Beckett. Hi." Inside, she cringed. She wasn't usually this stupid around guys. But whoa, his shoulders and chest were broad. He was a bear of a man. That made her perk up even more. Was he a bear shifter? Probably, consid-ering this was grizzly territory. Hmm, more and more interesting.

She was used to elitist dragon shifter prep school guys, the kind she'd gone to school with before she'd escaped those confines. They were all suave, sophisticated, and always totally uninteresting to her because all they had to fall back on was money and their family name. Yawn. Not a rugged, sexy, self-made bear shifter among them. This sexy-as-hell mountain man, who clearly was as salt-of-the-earth and no-nonsense as they came, was the most refreshing guy she'd come across in—forever. He looked realer than real. So real that the look in his eyes was making her girl parts tingle with serious interest.

Woo-eee. Her birthday week was getting better and better.

She ignored the low buzz deep inside. The nervous one. That was her old warning system, acting up out of sheer reflex. The one she'd relied upon her entire life to keep her safe. This man, she knew with a deep, unwavering instinct, was no danger to her.

Slowly, reluctantly, he let go of her hand. Looking behind her to where she could feel Haley breathing down her neck, he blinked, like he suddenly realized there were more people in the bar than just Pix. The thought warmed her. He said to Haley, "You look familiar. You live here in Deep Hollow?"

Pix turned and gestured to Haley, suddenly remembering that her best friend had been sitting there ignored. "Haley, meet Beckett North." Oh, wow. Just saying his name out loud sounded good on her tongue. "Haley's in town housesitting for the winter. I'm here on a visit."

Haley awkwardly reached around Pix to shake Beckett's hand, though she quickly let go and leaned back. *He's all yours,* she was telling Pix in silent bff speak. Besides, Haley was sort of head over heels in like with another guy. Very head over heels.

Recognition lit up Beckett's craggy face, which had become a bit ferocious when he didn't smile. "Oh! Haley. Yeah. You're the one housesitting for the Walkers."

Both Pix and Haley stared at him before Haley shook her head. "Seriously, does everyone in town know who I am? It feels like I have a neon sign on my head." She scrunched her eyebrows into a resigned frown. Poor Haley. She liked her privacy. Pix knew her friend had thought she'd be getting solitude here in a little shifter town tucked deep into the Colorado mountains.

But Beckett nodded, finally reaching to the bar top for a napkin to swipe at his gin-sloshed shirt. Pix winced slightly as he did so, shrugging at him again in apology. He waved it away, his eyes still eating her up as much as she did him even as he answered Haley. "Yeah, we all know who you are. The Walkers are the backbone of this town. That crazy old pair of lovebirds, traveling around the world like they're in their twenties." He shook his head, but a glint was back in his eye. Glancing at Haley, he added, "You know Quentin, then."

Haley nodded.

"Yeah." Beckett's eyes landed back on Pix as if he couldn't help himself. "He's the housesitter contact while they're gone because he's the responsible one. Thinks he's in charge and all that. Me, I'm way better friends with his younger brother, Cortez. That guy's a daredevil."

Haley started sharply at that name, and Pix grinned to herself. Haley sure did like Cortez. A whole crazy lot. Pix was sure it was mutual.

A teasing challenge lit Beckett's expression now as he still looked straight at Pix. "I'm more of the daredevil type myself. A wild child. How about you, Pix Camden? You a wild child, too?"

Her breath caught in her throat. Behind her, Haley bumped her again, then coughed and deliberately said, "I'll be back in a while. Gotta go to the ladies' room."

Pix barely noticed as her friend slipped away from the bar, obviously leaving them alone to chat. She looked at Beckett. Big, sexy man. Lifting her eyebrows, she countered him with a small challenge of her own. "We just came back from a day skiing at Snow Peak. That wild child enough for you?"

Beckett barked out a laugh, all gravelly and tough and definitely enough to make her fire roar inside. She could sense her dragon's wings beating against her mind now, taking the challenge from this very fascinating man. He rested his strong forearms on the bar and turned his body to face Pix. "Sure is. I pegged you for the kind of girl who could handle Snow Peak."

Snow Peak was an experts-only ski area northeast of Deep Hollow. It had backcountry runs that appealed to only the most skilled, adventurous skiers. Since Pix had been skiing almost since before she could walk, Snow Peak offered the perfect challenge for her.

"You on vacation, then?" His words were idle but his eyes probed hers. Seeing if she was just temporary. Only in town for a little while. Well, that was fine. She didn't need permanent any more than he probably did. Permanent meant a gilded cage back where she came from. Permanent was something she'd been running from her entire life. Glancing down at those brawny arms of his, she decided she sure wouldn't mind at least one night spent with them wrapped around her. That, and his voice. She could get used to the sound of his voice.

One night. Yes. She could do that much, and no more.

She nodded, curving her fingers around the still cold base of her glass to cool her heated skin. "Vacation. I grew up in Boston. I've lived there my whole life, but we always went skiing. Once I found out that Colorado had way better snow and slopes than anything back east, I was hooked. I ski out here every year, though this is the first time I've ever been to Deep Hollow. I'm also celebrating my birthday. It was yesterday."

"Really?" His sudden smile was so genuine it made her feel light. "Happy birthday, Pix. How young are you now?" His fingers curved around his glass as well. Pix's mind danced with the thought that maybe he was trying to cool his own heat.

Feeling flustered and keyed up at once, she paused before answering to be sure her voice would stay steady. "Twenty-nine. I decided it needed celebrating by doing one of my favorite things, which is skiing. Two of my favorite things, if you count visiting my best friend. Which I do count." Then she shrugged a bit self-consciously. "And maybe also to prove that I'm not all washed up just because I'm almost thirty now. So ancient!"

Beckett laughed again, the baritone sound of it tickling along Pix's body in a very pleasant way. She decided she could bathe in his golden whiskey eyes and happily drown. "Hell, woman, if you're washed up now, I'm a downright fossil. I turn thirty-three a couple weeks from now."

A fossil? Oh, heck no. Thirty-three meant Beckett was a real man. An actual grown-up, hewn from the mountains, tough and real like none of the guys she'd ever before dated. Pix smiled back, letting it turn into a laugh. It felt natural to laugh around him. "Great. We can both roll through this new year like the ancient fuddy-duddies we are now."

Beckett's expression suddenly grew serious again, making Pix catch her breath. He was really damned good looking. Crazy good-looking. The whole package of rugged mountain man made her sizzling nerve endings sit up and pay attention as if they were saluting him. She could tell he didn't bullshit around. He wasn't a political maneuverer like the guys she'd grown up with, nor was he lurching around way out on the edge of nowhere, dazed and confused, peering into the abyss and wondering who the hell he was, like most of the non-dragon shifter guys she'd met ever since she broke free of the strictly regimented ways of her family's world. No, Beckett North knew exactly who he was and exactly what he wanted.

His deep voice sent mini shock waves through her sharply attuned body. "Pix the newly minted twenty-nine-year-old, that sounds like a great idea. I'd be down to help you celebrate your birthday. I think," he said more slowly, watching her with real interest, "we should celebrate being in the prime of our lives. If you like to backcountry ski, I know a great spot up the mountain right above Deep Hollow. What do you say?"

His voice was neither overbearing nor hesitant. It was an open, direct question that allowed her to say either yes or no. She studied him for a moment longer. Well, she had a feeling he really wanted her to say yes. But he wasn't going to force it. Chalk up another reason to really like him. No pushy, overly arrogant alpha male—though she could tell he definitely had that alpha quality—he was giving her all the freedom to say yes, or to say no. Oh, she liked that. She also really liked that he knew the owners of the place Haley was housesitting. It meant they could ask around to make sure he was on the level.

Deep inside, something in her whispered that he

was more than on the level. He was the real deal, through and through.

With a big smile, Pix nodded. "I'm game. Haley has to do some work tomorrow anyway. She's a writer," Pix added with pride, because she was hella proud of her bestie for that, "so she can work from anywhere. That's why the housesitting deal was such a good thing for her. Me, though? My days are free. So," yeah, inner flirt was on a tear now, "game on for tomorrow, big guy." She watched to see how he'd react to her candor.

Beckett nodded, his eyes catching some lights in the bar and seeming to sparkle. Or maybe glow from what had to be his bear being close to the surface. "I like your enthusiasm, Pix."

Whoa, she really liked how her name sounded in his mouth. The deep tone of his voice rolled over it like he was tasting it. He cocked his eyebrows now, like he was a little worried, although a devilish little grin still played on his firm lips. "But after a whole day skiing at Snow Peak, are you sure you can still handle another day in the backcountry? Might be kind of tough for a little thing like you."

She straightened up a bit. "Them's fighting words." Something sensuous sparked in the air between them. "You tell me when and where to meet you in the morning."

He shook his head, signaling to the bartender although he didn't take his eyes off Pix. "No way. I know where you're staying. I'll come pick you up at seven. We have to skin up the mountain a good ways to get to the best spot, but trust me. It'll be worth it."

The promise in his voice told Pix he meant more than just skiing would be worth it. She swallowed hard as the spark of heat inside her turned up even higher. Nodding, she said in a suddenly thick but firm voice, "I'm in. All the way."

The way his eyes lit up even more at her words told her how very appreciative sexy Beckett North was of her agreement. The way her whole body seemed to tingle and twang, like a musical instrument about to be played, told her how freaking amazing her birthday week was still becoming.

"Sounds good." He leaned a little closer, his eyes holding hers and feeling comfortable despite the intensity. "It'll be my pleasure to show you around my mountain, pretty little badass Pix Camden."

She smiled back at him, feeling slightly breathless as the fire licked through her. She was pretty sure the pleasure of Beckett North's company would be all hers. For one day, and maybe one night. But after that, Pix Camden would be rolling on. That's what she did. Sexy, rugged guy notwithstanding, she couldn't stay here forever. Pix had a mission to stay footloose and fancy-free—and nothing and no one, not even a really interesting man like Beckett, could keep her from it.

Unless, something deep and quiet and oddly certain whispered inside her, he was the one man who could.

2

*B*eckett North kept glancing at the crazy hot woman next to him, wondering how he'd gotten so lucky to meet her. His bear softly snorted within him, a dark breath of barely controlled energy locked deep inside. Beckett frowned and firmly leashed his hot-headed animal. Not fucking now, damn it. He shook off his bear's edgy pacing inside him and made himself focus on the simple, easy pleasure of this moment.

He and Pix—such a cute name for such a cute little thing—had puffed their way up to his favorite back-country runs on the mountain, laughing and talking the whole time. He'd already laughed more times since last night than he usually did in an entire month. Pix was in killer good shape, easily able to keep up with him. Skinning up a mountain, or walking up with special "skins" covering their skis so as not to slide back down, was the price avid backcountry skiers paid to enjoy a winter paradise few others would ever experience. He knew sexy little Pix could ski like a pro, since she said she'd skied at Snow Peak, but huffing it up an alpine mountain on foot, at elevation, was another thing entirely. Frankly, he was impressed.

He wasn't usually into small women—being a bear shifter, he was six and a half feet tall and built stouter than the mountain itself, and he liked women who could handle that—but she just felt *right* beside him. His bear grunted in approval, also just as taken with the sweet little thing even if he was being a surly bastard at the same time. Beckett grunted back at himself. Living with a see-sawing monster inside him was the norm. It fucking sucked a lot of the time, but at least he was used to it.

Once they got to the top of the first run Beckett had planned, he glanced at Pix with eyebrows raised to judge her reaction. It was a fairly burly run, with trees and boulders and a few fairly steep drops to navigate.

She pushed her goggles up on her purple helmet as she surveyed the run, which was strewn with snow-covered trees and lumps and bumps that indicated the rocks and bushes hidden beneath the blanketing white powder. Eyes widening and a grin cracking over her pretty face, she breathed out in what almost seemed like worship. "Oh, wow. Sweet spot you have up here, Beckett." Casting him a sidelong glance, her huge smile lit up the already brilliant day. Damn, he was practically halfway in love now. Or at least in lust. "A man who's willing to share freshies with me? On a run like this? Be still my heart." She winked as she said it, but her eyes lingered on him for a moment.

Skiing freshies, or laying down fresh tracks after new snowfall, was pretty much the ultimate dream for any skier. He cocked one shoulder at her, admiring her sky-blue eyes one more time before he lowered the goggles that gave the landscape a yellowish cast that allowed them to see better. "I had the impression last night you know what you're doing on a pair of sticks." He nodded at her skis. "Don't let me down now. You got this?"

She bubbled out more laughter that seemed to sparkle in the crisp late January air. Something about it seemed so free, so open, that his heart thumped again. He needed to be careful here. A date with a pretty, badass woman was one thing. Any more than that, though, was treading on dangerous territory. Everyone in town didn't call him Bang 'Em Beckett for no reason. He did one night, and no more. More was too dangerous.

His bear huffed deep inside, the sound bracketed with a growl. Beckett pushed back at the beast, hard. Fucking hell, he just wanted to ski and enjoy the day with Pix. Just one day, damn it. One rad day and hope-fully one awesome night.

Then it was time to move on, since his bear would freak her the fuck out otherwise. Little human woman like her, she'd never be able to handle how rage-y he could get when he just couldn't control his bear. Which was more days than not.

He lobbed an easy grin at her, forcing himself to keep the day light and fun. "So why is your name Pix? Did your parents hate you or something?"

She reached down, grabbed some snow, and chucked it right at his face. He ducked in time to the sound of her cute cackling. Shit, she was adorable. He could tell she had a streak of fierceness in her, though. Something about her was sort of powerful, weird as that sounded. She might be little, but he bet she packed a punch, both literally and figuratively.

"No, they didn't hate me. But I hated my real name and every possible nickname you could come up with from it. My older brother always called me a little pixie, saying I was a tiny little pain in the ass pixie." She shrugged. "I finally just made everyone call me Pix. But my mom still refers to me as Penelope."

Beckett's eyebrows shot up. "Penelope? Damn. They did hate you."

She snorted as she pulled her goggles down firmly on her face, then checked her boots to make sure the heels were well locked into her skis. "They wanted me to live up to that name. I decided not to."

Before he could respond to that, she gave him a flirtatious little ass wiggle that about caused a riot out here in the middle of nowhere. Beckett blinked rapidly several times, talking down his suddenly very interested dick. He was too busy staring at her sweet body to pay attention to her sneaky next move.

"Ready yet, slowpoke? Last one down is a cheeto-head!" She abruptly shot down the mountain, launching into graceful turns on the thick blanket of fresh powder. "And it's not going to be me!" she called back, another peal of gorgeous laughter with a streak of something wild and hot running beneath it hanging on the air as she sped downhill.

Fuck yeah. He had no idea what a cheeto-head was, but he liked her style. Fun, quirky, sexy, and as dare-devil as he was. Beckett quickly double-checked his own bindings and shoved off after her. This was more like it. A hot, interesting woman who knew what she was doing. A woman, he quickly realized as he watched her expert moves, who not only could keep up with him going up the mountain but might actually pose a real challenge in beating her down to the bottom. She moved like she'd been born on skis. He might have to put in some serious effort to stay close on her tail.

And what a sexy tail it was, he thought as he admired her ass while they caromed downhill. His bear rumbled with approval. At least they agreed on that.

The run went by in a thrilling blur of bright blue sky, dazzling white snow, and laughter. She was amazing. When they reached the bottom, Pix in the lead, Beckett could honestly say he could have beaten her down—but just barely. She shushed to a stop just as gracefully as she skied. Beckett smoked a fancy circling stop around her, sending up a little rooster tail of snow as he did.

"Show off." Giggles still trembled in her voice as she said it. Her smile was big and bright, and definitely appreciative of his move.

Beckett doffed an imaginary hat and sketched her a half-bow. "For you? Absolutely. Going all out on my best today. I'm working hard to impress you, Pix." His tone was easy, but he felt some tension inside him as he said it. He meant his words.

Her expression got equally serious. "I don't impress easily," she admitted. Her cheeks were full of color from the exertion and the bright chill of the day. "You're doing a great job so far."

As she still studied him with that intense gaze, Beckett thought she might have more to say. Instead, after another silent moment filled only with the stinging sharp air and her pretty lips slightly parted, she suddenly shrugged. "Race you down the next one?"

Beckett huffed a grin, his breath showing white. "Let's do it."

Eyes sparkling, Pix turned her head to search the trees ringing their little snowfield. "Okay, badass Beckett. Which way to our next run?"

Beckett let his laugh echo over the trees. Damn, this girl was flat-out amazing. He tried to remember the last time he'd had this much fun with a woman, genuine fun that didn't mean only a tumble in the sheets. He couldn't think of one single time. As she swung her head back to look at him, thick braids swishing over her jacketed shoulder, he tipped his chin to the right. "There. This run's got some more challenging terrain, and there are a couple sections where we can do a little jump. You game for those?"

In response, Pix immediately glided off in that direction. "You better bet I'm game!" drifted behind her.

With a laugh that happily busted up out from his gut, feeling as genuine as anything ever had, Beckett slid behind her and into the lead to show her the start of the run. When they got to the section where the trees opened up slightly, exposing the swishing flash of dazzling white snow blankets below interspersed with dark pockets of trees and a couple of drop-offs that were the jumps, he glanced at her. He suddenly felt crazy daring. "Last one down has to give something to the other one."

Pix's grin was still wide as she looked at him. "Like what?"

Beckett shrugged, pushing down a flash of nerves at what he was about to say. *Be bold, dick,* he muttered to himself. *This chick's cool.* Even if it would be just for a day and a night. His bear grunted inside him, the sound indecipherable as to whether it was in agreement or irritation. "An answer to a question. A real question about the other person. Something you wouldn't necessarily tell someone you just met." Fuuuck, he couldn't believe he'd just said that. But he had.

Everything fell silent as the world seemed to hold

its breath while he waited for her answer. He didn't know why it was so important that she agree to it. It just was. The skin crinkled up above her goggles in the tiny strip visible beneath her helmet. She must be raising her eyebrows at him. Finally, she nodded. "Sure. And what about the first one down? There should be an incentive for that too, shouldn't there?"

Beckett opened his mouth to answer, but Pix suddenly plunged on. "I know. First one down gets to ask about *two* things from the other person. Two real things." Her voice was soft as she said that.

Without waiting for his answer, she whipped her head back, slightly bent down, and shot off into the unknown. He grinned and raced right after her. One way or another, he planned to catch her and her sexy ass.

3

*B*eckett shoved off after Pix in the space of half a heartbeat, racing ahead to guide her down. Damn, if he got to ask for two things from this crazily intriguing woman, he'd work his tail off to get there first. His bear flipped him an image of the barely-there tail of a bear, accompanied by a gruff rumble of bearish laughter. Huh. His bear seemed to be in good humor. That was weird, but nice. He'd take it.

The cold air whipped by as he skied like a fiend to keep up with Pix. He could tell she wasn't pulling her punches at all. He made a mental note to ask her if she'd ever been on a ski race team, because the girl knew what she was doing out here. Her small, lithe form whipped in between the trees so easily it was almost as if she flew.

There was a slight leveling out before one of the areas where they could jump, or turn more to the right to stay connected to the earth while they kept hurtling downhill. He looked at her, all beautiful, fearless woman that he didn't even know but wanted to get to know more than anything he'd ever wanted in his life. "That's the jump," he called out, slowing slightly as he waited for her decision.

Without missing a beat, she called back, "Let's do it! Your lead."

For some completely stupid reason, the fact that she wanted him to show her the way made him ridiculously proud and puffed up. Focusing on the jump, he aimed for the best takeoff point. When he reached it he easily leapt into the air, crouched over his skis, letting the short, light blast of wind whistle over him. Aside from making things with his hands, skiing was Beckett's favorite way to feel completely alive. He let out a whoop as he landed, looking back to see how Pix did. Before he could even turn his head all the way, her own happy holler burst out, joyous and laughing. She thumped down seconds after him, her laughter still dressing the air.

The rest of the way down was just as awesome. Beckett felt buoyant and excited as he skied with a woman who could keep up with him, one who seemed just as thrilled with this wild country as he was. As they zipped downhill, he furrowed his brow together for a moment. He really liked her, and he barely knew her, but he was already wondering how she would react if she found out he was a bear shifter.

But that was crazy talk right there. She wasn't from Deep Hollow. The humans in town knew about shifters. Outsiders didn't. That was a secret that had to be kept. He couldn't tell her he was a shifter. And this was a one-day, plus hopefully one-night, thing only. Shaking his head, he pushed away his dumb thoughts of sharing everything with this amazing woman and just leaned into the wild moment on the mountain.

At the bottom of the hill, they went into an all out race for the copse of trees Beckett pointed out. He hollered, "Finish line, baby!"

"Then you'd better give it all you have!" Pix hollered back. She skied hard and surged ahead. Hell, yeah. Now it was a flat out battle to win, even with Beckett's bear shifter strength. She was just that good of a skier.

Right at the end, Beckett paused for a split second, weighing the options of the outcome. Let her win and get the two questions, like something called a "gentleman" would do? "Hell, no," he muttered to himself, watching Pix's sexy ass just ahead of him. She wasn't giving any quarter. Neither would he.

They raced across the flat, the momentum of their downhill trajectory zooming them along. Beckett whipped past the first tree in the little grove a hair's breadth ahead of Pix. But she was right on his heels. He hit the brakes, turning his feet and sliding to a crisp stop. With a whoop, Pix slid to a halt beside him and thrust her fists into the air. She yodeled out, "I declare there's no such thing as second place! There are no losers! We are both winners!"

Beckett laughed for what must have been about the fiftieth time so far today. His face felt funny. Oh, right. His muscles weren't used to smiling so damn much in one day. "That's crazy talk, woman. If we're both the winners, how do we know who gets one question and who gets two questions?"

Pix's smile seemed brighter than the sun. Beckett figured he might end up getting burned by it, standing so close. To his surprise, he didn't care. He was still having too good of a time with her.

"Well, I just made it the rule that there are no losers, so I can also make up the rule that we both get two questions each." She settled her fists on her hips and turned her head, taking in the rolling view of the mountains. "Whoa. Pretty stellar, Beckett. You definitely know how to take a girl on a good date."

He lifted his eyebrows. "Huh. This a date? Most girls would complain about there being no fancy food, no bouquet of flowers, shit like that." Beckett took a step closer towards the slope in front of them that had a killer view of Deep Hollow and the San Juan Mountains flinging out in every direction. "But yeah, there's some pretty stuff to see from here. I thought you might like it," he added. He felt bashful for a half second.

Bashful, for fuck's sake. What the hell.

Pix laughed again. It sounded like it was made up of crystals, of snowflakes, of beautiful shimmering things.

She smiled at him, still carefree. "I'm a girl, you're a guy, we met at the bar, you asked me out to do something." She lifted one shoulder and spread her hand out, palm up. "So yes, this is a date. Although it's kind of a funny date so far because we don't know the most important things about each other yet. But now," she drawled, "it's time for two questions."

Quirking his brows back down, Beckett went for a sort of goofy response. "So we play this like twenty questions, but not, right?"

Boom. She laughed again. He thought he might want to make it his full-time mission to hear this woman laugh every day for the rest of his life. He'd never get tired of it. Her laugh defined the word *beautiful*. Open, free, and purely unaffected. "You're really real, you know that?" Aw, shit. He'd just said it without even thinking. It was as if he *wanted* to get all open book with her.

His bear growled. Yeah. Right. No open book here. Not his style. Even so...he really wanted to know more about her. To know everything about her. Which was batshit insane.

Pix cocked her head at him. "It took me a long time to get here." Her voice was suddenly serious. "Sure, I'm just barely twenty-nine, so I'm not ancient yet. But even so, it's felt like a long lifetime to figure out who I am."

Whoa. Deep time now. "And who are you exactly, Pix Camden?" Beckett's voice was low. Suddenly wanting to see her eyes, he shoved his goggles up on his head. Despite the bright sunlight, it was worth it. Slowly, Pix pushed her own goggles up. She was squinting too hard for much of her irises to show, but he caught a glint of their pretty blue-green.

"That's your question number one, Beckett North," she said softly. "You sure picked a big one."

She went quiet for a moment, waiting for him to respond to that, but he hardly dared breathe. He didn't want to miss a single word she said in reply. After another moment with them just looking at each other, both all squinty-eyed from the sun, she raised her eyebrows and made a small noise like she was thinking about how to say everything.

"I'm... I'm a wanderer." Her voice slowly got firmer with each word she said. "An explorer. Explorer of life." She waved a hand. "Yeah, that's kind of woo-woo, but I am. I never felt like I fit into the family I was born into, ever since I was a little kid." He thought maybe a tiny splinter of pain stung her words, but she went on too quickly for him to be sure. "I was always trying to figure out who Penelope Adelinda Tanith Camden really is."

Beckett cringed back in horror. "Fucking hell. It should be criminal to saddle someone with a string of names like that. Even if they're kind of pretty." He himself had two names. Beckett, and North. Simple. He liked simple.

She nodded. "Damn right it should be criminal. But

that's how it is where I came from. Anyway, when I finally figured out I was a Pix, and always had been, a lot of other things fell into place for me." She gave a little shrug but didn't break eye contact. "I was a rebel as a kid." She flashed him a quick grin. "A wild child, for sure.

"A rebel, huh? What did you rebel against?"

Grinning, she shook her head at him. "That's question number two, Beckett."

"Hey, dirty pool—" he began, though he couldn't help grinning back at her.

Cute little Pix, strong little Pix, shook her head. "Nope. You accepted my made-up rules by agreeing to them. You have to abide by this. But I'll admit I was an angry teenager."

"Are you still angry?" Beckett kept his eyes locked on her.

Carefully, as if she was really considering the question, Pix shook her head again. "No. Not really, not anymore. Honestly, if anything, these days I'm more restless than angry. Restless Pix," she said softly. "Anyway. The anger got taken care of by running away from everything my family wanted. Instead, I created my own life. With my own rules. It worked." Something dark flashed over her expression, gone almost before he caught it. "I know who and what I am, and I accept it. My question now," and suddenly her eyes were tight on his, her head now tipping to the side in a way that was half playful, half challenging, "is do you know who and what *you* are?"

That was easy. He was a wild mountain man who liked small town living. He knew enough about how hard it was to control his bear that he stayed away from anything serious with a woman. Inside, his bear rumbled and muttered at him.

Before he could open his mouth though, Pix gave him a smile that matched her stance. Playful, provocative, challenging. "Wait, Beckett. I actually have a really good guess about what you are."

"Oh, yeah?" By this point, she'd probably easily pegged him as the broody mountain man who would be fun for a weekend fling. "Sure, go ahead. Tell me what I am."

Pix suddenly leaned a little closer, the smile dropping from her face. As serious an expression as Beckett had yet seen made her features still, her eyes now more adjusted to the sun and wide enough that he could see bright green flecks sparkling in their blue.

Then she said the last thing in the world he'd ever have thought.

"You," she pointed a steady finger at him, "are a bear shifter, Beckett North. I know you are."

4

*F*ucking fried shit on a shingle. It was a favorite expression of Beckett's best friend, for who knew what reason. He'd used it so often over the years that it stuck with Beckett. Right now, it fit the situation.

How in the fuck did Pix know about shifters?

His mind churned for a long second, his bear for once quiet. He stared at her so hard he knew it probably was making her squirm. But she stood quietly, seeming unconcerned with the big-ass guy she'd just called out as a bear shifter standing a mere foot or so away from her.

"What did you call me?"

She raised her chin up a bit. "A bear shifter. Because you are one." Her voice was calm but firm.

"How the hell do you know about bear shifters? We don't talk to humans about it." His voice came out a little more of a growl than he planned. He winced, but Pix didn't seem that worried. She didn't look remotely scared of him.

She shrugged, still staring at him with a steady expression. "I just know about them. Were you gonna tell me?" She unsnapped her chin strap and tugged her helmet off her head, which was covered with a thin purple fleece hat. Woman sure had a thing for purple.

Beckett gave her a look, then uttered a disbelieving snort. "Tell you? If you know about shifters, then you know that it's kind of burned into our brains that we don't publicly talk about being shifters."

Most of the world didn't know shifters existed. Some shifters, like the wolf pack on the other side of the mountain, even had such crazy old rules about never telling humans that shifters existed that if they did, they'd have to kill the human they told. Bear shifters weren't that rigid about it. Even so, they didn't run around sharing the truth of their lives with most humans. That was a dangerous thing in this world that didn't know about shifters. Bad things could, and sometimes did, happen if the information got out. The humans living in Deep Hollow knew about shifters, of course. Half of them were mated to shifters anyway. But Pix wasn't from Deep Hollow.

She gave him another long look. Tendrils of hair blew out from beneath her fleece hat to swirl around her face, her braids bouncing on her shoulders.

"Wait a minute." He narrowed his eyes at her.

"You're not some kind of reporter or something, are you?"

But she was already shaking her head at him, a line slicing between her eyebrows. "No. Do I really look like a reporter to you?"

Beckett stared at her for another long minute. His bear wasn't insanely riled. He didn't feel the surge of growling and roaring that he would if she was lying. His bear was really good at telling when people were lying, since shifters could sense untruths pretty easily. "Sorry." His voice was gruff. "We get suspicious here. We've had some bad shit happen with the outside world before. I didn't mean to accuse you of being some sort of spy here to out us."

Pix offered a sudden sigh. "It doesn't matter that much to me if you're a bear shifter. I just wanted to know if I was right." She half smiled. "I've always lived in big cities. We don't have many of the apex predators living in big cities, so I wasn't sure about you. But you sure look like a big bear to me."

Beckett stared at her. "Apex predators? You sure as hell know your shifter lingo." Then he felt something silly coming on. Despite the startling moment, she seemed to bring out the smile in him. "No big shifters in the big city. Huh. So do you guys just have chipmunk shifters or something like that back in Boston?"

Now she finally cracked up. That laughter rolled out of her again, open and free. The sexy vibe was still there between them too. The sort of vibe that was making the front of Beckett's pants kind of tight. He liked all of it.

"No, you big goof, we do not have chipmunk shifters in Boston. At least I don't think we do." She suddenly looked bemused.

Beckett started to laugh, for about the seventy-third time so far that day. Oddly, it felt fantastic. "You might. Most shifter groups stick to themselves. I'm pretty sure there's a shifter for just about every animal out there. But yeah, you're right." He relaxed even more as he said out loud to her the truth she already knew. "I am a bear shifter. Grizzly bear. This is our home, here in Deep Hollow." He jerked his hand out over the vast snowy landscape that spread out below them. "Got a couple other shifter types around here, but we're the main type. This is bear territory. So." He eyeballed her. "How'd you learn so much about shifters if you don't have that many in Boston?"

She sighed, biting the inside of one lip. His gaze caught her little white teeth gnawing at that pretty pink lip. Man, what he wouldn't give for it to be his own lips touching hers. He lifted his eyes back up to her face. Very slowly, Pix pulled off one of her gloves and extended her bare hand out toward him. Beckett wanted to ask what she was doing, tell her to put her glove back on because it was too damn cold out here for temperature-sensitive little human hands, but he couldn't. His heart suddenly was thumping hard, tingles racing over his skin, and his dick was interested. Definitely interested. He was a horny bastard, that was for sure. For a second all he could think about was her pretty hand touching his dick, just like the caveman he was. Well, he lived alone in a cabin in the woods for a reason.

"Beckett." Her hand gently landed on his chest, her fingers splaying out as she pressed her palm into him. "I still haven't asked you my second question. Here it is."

As he watched her, the green lights flickering in her eyes seem to get a little brighter. "The second question to you is, how far do you want to take this?"

5

*B*eckett stared at her like she'd just asked if he'd marry her. The heat she could feel rising from him, even through the layers of clothing between her hand and his chest, seemed to intensify.

"What," he said in that low rumble of a voice that set her on fire, "do you mean by that?"

Uncharacteristically flustered all of a sudden, Pix shook herself. She needed to focus. "I mean, how far do you want this to go right now? Through the evening and into the night?" Based on the smoldering attraction they'd had going on since the night before in the bar, she felt comfortable asking this. His eyes looked back and forth between hers, as if wondering if he would find a different answer in each one.

He startled her when he asked, "Why didn't we start last night? The energy was there. We could both feel it."

That was an easy question. "Because I stopped

doing that a long time ago," she said simply. "Picking up a random guy I just met and taking him home, then casting him out in the morning. I did tell you I actually managed to grow up a little bit in all my worldly years. Besides," she turned her head to glance back out at the mountains, "I needed to check up on you first. Just to be sure."

She could sense him bristle slightly. "Check up on me?"

"Of course. I had to know you're not some psycho." The deep knowing inside her that he was the safest guy she'd ever met flashed through her again. Her dragon hummed with satisfaction. Hmm. Interesting. "This is a small town, and you said you knew the Walkers. So Haley called someone she's gotten to know here in town and asked him about you. Cortez Walker."

At that, Beckett groaned. "What did that smartass have to say about me?"

"He said something about you being a grumpy ass old dick, but that you sure as hell aren't dangerous." Then Pix grinned. "I think at first he thought Haley was asking for herself. He was kind of pissed about that. I think he's got a serious crush on my bestie. Or maybe more."

"Hmm," was all Beckett would say about that, but she thought he looked pleased. Ah, good. Haley was her best friend and deserved true happiness after all the shit she'd been through. Cortez seemed like he might be the right guy for Haley, and if Beckett thought the same, that was a positive sign.

Silence settled around them again. Pix kept her gaze trained out over the sprawl of snowy mountains that seemed to extend as far as the eye could see. It was so amazing out here. She found herself idly wondering how many of the local residents might buy her paintings. Sharply, she reined herself in. Nope. Not going there. She was a free spirit these days. Nothing was holding her back from moving on anywhere she wanted, anytime she wanted. Nothing kept her rooted anywhere. Not here, not anywhere. Not even stunning mountains, great ski runs, and a sexy guy she hadn't even kissed yet. Though she knew when they did, it would tingle her down to her toes and back. Deliberately, she faced Beckett again.

Oh, wow. His eyes glowed bright amber in the sunlight. It was his bear, stirring inside him. He was letting her see the real him. All of him. Her dragon stirred back, seeming very intrigued.

His words slow but deliberate and clear, Beckett said, "Yeah, Pix. I'd like this date to go on. As far as we both want it to go. I have to work this afternoon, but I want to take you out this evening. There's a fun event going on in town tonight, a midwinter tree-lighting thing. You probably already know about it."

Feeling slightly dazed by the magnetism of his eyes, Pix nodded. "Uh-huh. Haley's going to it with Cortez already and I got invited along. Though I'm pretty sure I'll be a third wheel."

Beckett shifted his weight from one muscled leg to the other. Geez, this guy was stouter than an oak tree. "You're coming with me. As my date."

The certainty in his voice caught at her breath. He definitely knew what he wanted. Mm-hmm. Oddly enough, it didn't at all bother her like it would have from any male dragon shifter.

"Then afterward, I'd like to take you back to my place, which you know is safe since you checked up on me and all." Sudden mirth flashed into his eyes, although his expression remained deadly serious. "You'll stay with me all night long, beautiful. Because I can feel something sizzling between you and me, and it feels pretty fucking good. I want us to be able to spend time to explore that. Then in the morning…" Finally, he hesitated.

Quietly, Pix finished for him. "In the morning, we'll have a lingering goodbye, especially if it was a good night—"

"Oh, it'll be a good night." The deep, dark certainty in his voice shivered and danced through her entire body.

Well, then. Oh, my. Okay, then. Yes, please.

"Okay," she stumbled a bit, her thoughts stuck on short words. "Yes, okay. Ahem. Uh…" She paused to focus before she could go on like someone who could actually speak in complete sentences. "So in the morning, we'll say our goodbyes and move on. Because," she paused again for a long moment. Letting her face soften, not taking her eyes from his, she finally plunged on, determined to be open with this man. This big, sexy bear who was turning her inside out and setting all her nerves on fire in the most delicious way. "Apparently you're also known as Bang 'Em Beckett, or so I hear."

Oh, god. It sounded so stark, so mean, when she said it out loud. It was an awful, cruel nickname. But Pix hadn't gotten to this point in her life by shying away from things that should be discussed. She needed to know how he felt about it. If he wanted something as no-strings-attached as she did.

This time, the silence wasn't as comforting. When it lengthened into something that might border on uncomfortable, she carefully went on, "You said you wanted the questions to be real. I don't really do more than one night either, Beckett. And that's okay by you. Right?" She kept her eyes trained on his as she spoke.

Beckett's face was like granite. She couldn't read it at all. But his eyes flashed in anger. His bear was looming just beneath his skin. She could feel it. It was as if he had his animal barely under control. Dangerous.

Several more heartbeats passed before Beckett ground out, "Cortez didn't tell you about that. About what people call me."

She shook her head, caught by the way his pulse ticked beside his left eye. "No. He's your friend, and it's

231

clear he thinks highly of you. It was some asshole at the bar last night who said it after you left. Pretty sure it was another bear shifter."

Beckett stared at her again for another long moment. Anger simmered and coiled in him, seeming ready to boil out. Pix stood steady in the face of it. That crass nickname bothered him. Maybe even hurt him. But she wasn't afraid of his anger. It wasn't directed toward her and she knew it.

Finally, he snarled out, "He was right. I don't do more than one night, and I shouldn't even go that far with you. It's too dangerous. For you."

"Why?" she countered. She didn't take her eyes off his face. The brightness of the day harshly emphasized the stark conversation they were having.

"My bear," his voice hardened, "doesn't do well after spending too much time with anyone that way. So I made the rule that I just do one night. Also because I don't want to get serious and hurt someone by mistake." He nailed her with those eyes. "I have a feeling you don't want to either, restless Pix."

Bam. Zinged right back. Restless Pix. Pix who didn't do more than one night, either.

She felt her ears heat. A rueful smile crept onto her face. "Well, then. Now that I'm on the receiving end of the real questions, I have a little more sympathy for you being in the hot seat earlier."

He unexpectedly shot out, "I like you, Pix. You're genuine, and fun, and interesting."

Wow. That was a surprise. A nice one. "I like you too, Beckett."

They stared at each again for a long moment, just like when they'd met last night. The air between them swirled with promise, with excitement, with something deep and real Pix couldn't look at more closely.

Feeling flustered again, she shoved her goggles back down on her face and pointed her skis downhill. "Okay then. If you have to go to work this afternoon, we'd better keep racing each other down. Because I want you to work as fast as you can, so we can get to our evening as quickly as possible. Our one, single evening together."

One evening with this sexy bear shifter who liked her, and that was all. That was all she could handle, and she knew he felt the same. Taking a breath, not waiting for his answer, she pushed off and swooped downhill, knowing a big, sexy grizzly bear shifter would be right behind her, chasing her all the way down.

And that felt completely, perfectly all right.

6

*T*he sign on the way into Deep Hollow had said the total population was 1,276. Pix was willing to bet that about 1,271 of them were present at the town's midwinter tree lighting ceremony. Okay, that wasn't possible because she was pretty sure that many bodies couldn't fit, but there definitely were more people crowded around the cute town square than she'd seen so far during her several days here. "Wow," she said, impressed. Apparently small towns liked to turn out for things like this.

Next to her, Haley nodded. "Everyone loves the midwinter celebration, or so they all keep telling me. There also are a bunch of tourists here. Silvertip Lodge up on the mountain advertises it. It's one of their big draws this time of year."

Haley had told Pix about the lodge. It catered to an exclusively shifter clientele. Looking around the square, Pix had a hunch that well over half of the people here were shifters. It was true that back in Boston there weren't many of the big predator shifters like bears, so she didn't run into them that often. But she could recognize them, the same way she'd recognized Beckett as one. Their scent, their aura of something slightly dangerous and definitely big, whether male or female, gave them away. She was lucky her dragon didn't do the same. Flying under the radar was Pix's way of living ever since she'd left the dragon world behind, and she liked it that way.

Inside, her dragon rumbled and flamed in irritated little bursts. She'd been doing it off and on all day. The feeling was unsettling. Her dragon hadn't been this active for some time now, ever since Pix had hit the road and started her rambling life. It was as if she now responded to something like what Pix had left behind, with all her irritation and desire to shift and fly and flame.

Pix frowned. Tonight was about having fun, not thinking about her past. Hushing her own thoughts, she made a mental note to shift into her dragon soon and fly over the huge expanse of wild mountains. Aside from Haley, no one here knew she was a dragon shifter. Even so, she didn't neglect that side of herself. She loved being her dragon, even if she had no interest in being part of the restrictive dragon world. This place, she thought with delighted satisfaction as she looked around at everyone else here enjoying themselves in the cold night air, was much more her style. Relaxed, fun, and no one watching her to make sure she did the "right" thing.

Haley stood on one side of her, watching the activities with interest and a lot of happy laughter she shared with Cortez. Watching them together, it was very clear he was just as interested in Haley. On Pix's other side stood the warm mountain of wildly hot man flesh that was Beckett. Oh, did she like feeling him there. He leaned into her more as the crowd pressed around them. Her entire left side was on fire from where their bodies touched. The town plaza was filled with enough people that everyone had to shove together, elbow to elbow.

"That's the town mayor coming up that ladder to the top of the tree." Beckett jerked his chin in the direction of the enormous tree in the middle of square. Pix turned her attention to it. A woman was climbing up the ladder as nimbly as a monkey, with what looked like a bulky messenger bag slung over her body. "She'll put the town star up on the very top, then signal the lighting crew down on the ground when the switch is ready to be flipped. The whole thing will light up. It's pretty." He grunted as if half embarrassed he'd just said that. "Then there's gonna be total madness as all the kids in town race forward to get the presents under the tree.

Pix frowned. She had noticed a ton of little munchkins in the crowd, all hopped up on hot cocoa and presumably general excitement about the activity. "Presents? Nobody told me about presents. Were we supposed to bring some for them?"

On Haley's other side, Cortez answered her. "Nah, townies take care of that. We supply all the cute little gifts under there. It's sort of like a second Christmas. But this is better, because nobody expects this kind of fun stuff at the end of January. That's why we started it about five years ago. Everyone loves it."

"Yeah, till they open up the dumbass little gifts you probably brought, Cortez." Beckett leaned forward to sling his insult around the two women standing between him and his best friend.

Cortez good-naturedly said to Haley, "Hey, tell your friend Pix to slug Beckett for me, would you?"

Haley laughed. Pix smiled at the sound of it. Haley hadn't really laughed in a long time. "I don't think she's trying to establish a fighting relationship with him."

"Huh, weird. Works for me. I've been slugging that big lug since we were kids." Cortez shrugged while Haley laughed again.

"Here." Pix look down to where Beckett pressed something warm against her hand. It was a thermos. "Hot chocolate, spiced up with something a little fiery. You can share it with Haley and that bozo down on the end if you feel like it."

Pix smiled so big her cheeks almost hurt. This was so much silly, easy fun. This adorable little town, smelling like pine trees, fresh snow, excited people milling everywhere, with her happy best friend and her friend's new potential love interest on one side and Beckett, mountain bear of a man Beckett, on her other side. It was just comfortable and—homey. She could get used to this.

She shoved the thought away as she brought the thermos to her lips in a cautious sip. Whoa, that was good. "What did you put in there?" She took a few more gulps before handing it off to Haley.

"Marshmallow vodka." Beckett sounded nonchalant about it.

Pix almost choked on her next sip. Not that it wasn't good, it was delicious. But she gave Beckett the hairy eyeball. "A big strapping guy like you puts something weenie like marshmallow vodka in his hot cocoa?"

"Hey, now." He nudged her with his arm. "It's for you girls. You in particular. It's about twenty-two degrees out here and only supposed to get colder." Dropping his voice, he moved his mouth close to her ear. "I wanted it tasty enough you'd drink it up, and zinged up enough it would warm you up. Figured I should start warming you up now."

Pix's entire body definitely flushed with heat. Inside, outside, all around, heat enveloped her. Her dragon made little noises inside her. Noises of approval. Oh, it was going to be good, this night with Beckett. She knew it, Beckett knew it. She had a feeling Haley and Cortez knew it, too. Then again, she thought as she cast her happy, totally-absorbed-in-Cortez friend a sidelong look, she also suspected they didn't much care. She'd bet they had similar plans for the evening.

"It's working," she murmured to Beckett. His leg pressed against hers.

Suddenly there was a commotion up front by the tree. A ripple of new excitement rumbled through the crowd. A high-pitched whine came from the speakers, immediately followed by answering cries of pain from the audience as people clapped their hands over their ears. An amplified voice boomed out, "Sorry about that. Okay, everyone, we're about ready for that star to get up on that tree. You ready up there, Clara?"

In response, the woman on the ladder leaned toward the tree, pulled the object she'd drawn out of her messenger bag, and securely nestled it onto the very top of the huge spruce. Exclamations from the crowd, including a, "Yeah, that's my girl!" accompanied her actions.

Beckett murmured to Pix, "That's Clara. She's the postmistress as well as the mayor. Some kind of bird shifter. So heights don't bother her."

Pix sighed happily as Haley passed back the spiked hot cocoa and Beckett leaned into her from the other side. This all was small town charm at its best. Things like this never happened back in Boston. Glancing at the huge mountain man to her left, a guy she'd just met yet already felt like she knew better than some people she'd known for years, she let the feeling of familiarity and belonging suffuse her in a relaxed glow. It felt pretty darned awesome.

The voice on the loudspeaker crackled out again. "And a one. And a two. And a three… Light 'er up!"

Abruptly, thousands of sparkling white lights lit up the huge spruce, showcasing its beautiful glory. An admiring gasp swept over the crowd, erupting into cheers as Clara the bird shifter pumped her fist in the air at the lit tree, then agilely climbed back down the ladder.

"This year's tree is a beaut, folks," whoever had the mic told the crowd. Pix couldn't quite find the source. "We have Beckett North and Cortez Walker to thank for bringing it down from the mountain for us all to enjoy. Beckett, Cortez, where are you two lumbering oafs?"

Another giggle rippled through the crowd. An older woman with a pretty smile standing on the other side of Beckett, her arm tightly threaded through the arm of the handsome gentleman beside her, helpfully called out, "Here! They're right here." She pointed to Beckett and Cortez.

Hundreds of eyes turned their way as people craned their necks looking. The announcer cheerfully said, "There you boys are. And you each have a girl on your arm who's prettier than any of the decorations we have on this tree. How about you, the young lady right next to Beckett? Would you care to come up and do the honors of starting the present scramble this year?"

Pix realized everyone was suddenly looking at her, smiling huge and urging her on. "Uh, what?"

Haley laughed next to her, gently shoving her forward. Beckett smiled down at her and said, "All you have to do is get up there and say ready, set, go, and all the kids are gonna come racing up for those presents. They pull a random person from the crowd every year to do it."

"Oh, cool. Sure, I can do that." Pix grinned. She loved little kids. The evening was getting better and better. She pushed her way up to the front of the crowd, everyone there smiling and laughing and enjoying the event just as much as she was. When Pix made it up to the front, a guy standing at the bottom of the ladder gestured for her to step up the little wooden stairs onto a small platform to the side of the tree. Atop a little box up there was a folded piece of silvery-white cloth with a shimmer of blue stars on it.

"That's the present-running flag," the guy explained. "Just go on up there and hold it in your hand above your head. Then just shout out *ready set go* and drop your hand down with the flag in it. Like starting a car race. But instead of cars, there'll be a zillion kids running like mad to grab the presents under the tree."

Pix laughed, completely thrilled with the whole thing. Eagerly, she ran up the stairs, grabbed the flag, and turned around to face the crowd. Tons of breathless little kids' faces looked up at her from where they'd gathered close to the tree. Half of them looked shaggy and wild, like the bear shifters they probably were. Uncontained and unrestrained, just allowed to be little kids having goofy fun in a way she'd never been allowed to as a child growing up in her dragon culture.

Darn it, she was loving this little town more and more.

Briefly glancing out over the crowd, her gaze unerringly shot straight to Beckett. The look on his face was so relaxed, so happy, and so bizarrely proud as he looked right back at her that her chest squeezed for a minute. This all felt like she was caught up in some sort of awesome winter fairytale. A sexy, really interesting guy looking at her like she hung the moon, a cute little town that had just cheerfully invited her, a complete stranger, to participate in one of their beloved traditions, and just the whole sense of community and belonging as the lights on the giant midwinter tree brightly sparkled beside her, made her eyes almost prickle for second. Well, that was crazy.

Before she could do anything ridiculous like shed a tear, she grabbed the flag and waved it in her hand above her head. Before the kids could even gasp with excitement, she hollered as loudly as she could, "Ready, set, go!"

On the word *go* she dropped her flag hand back down to her side, letting the long cloth flutter and whip through the crisp night air. Screaming with joy, the wave of children launched toward the tree, grabbing at the hundreds of little presents that were scattered around down there. Several adults were interspersed among the kids, watching to make sure that each kid only grabbed one present as they'd been instructed to do.

A little boy with the fattest, reddest cheeks Pix had ever seen, a shock of black hair pushing out from beneath his bright blue fleece hat, plunked himself down practically right under the little platform she stood on, starting to unwrap his present before his butt even hit the ground. Pix watched him, entranced by the fun of seeing an eager child open a gift. As he hastily unwrapped the packaging and ripped open the box, scrabbling through the tissue paper in it, Pix took a deep inhale of the pine scent in the cold night air, the snow coming off the mountain, the hundreds of happy, chattering people gathered together. Everything all mixed together smelled so good it squeezed at her chest again. She closed her eyes for a second, just breathing it all in and feeling something that felt like...home.

Then the little boy shouted, "A Beckett Bear! Wow!" making Pix snap her eyes open again to look down at him.

She watched as the little boy's eyes lit up and turned big as saucers. Almost reverently, he pulled a fairly large wooden figurine out of the box. Pix echoed after the boy, "Oh, that's really cool." It was a beautifully carved black bear, sitting on its big butt with its paws wrapped around a bucket of overflowing honey, a dopey smile on its face. The detail was incredible from what she could see in the light of the midwinter tree. The boy then pulled out two other carved bears, one climbing a tree and the other plopped in the midst of berry-covered bush, happily stuffing its face with little carved red berries. He gasped. "Three Beckett Bears! Whoa!" Clutching the carved wooden animals to him like they were the world's greatest treasures, he swiveled his head around. "Mom! Where are you? Come see what I got!"

From directly behind Pix, a deep voice rumbled almost into her ear, making her jump. "You got a nice view from up there? Pretty nice view from behind, too. Your ass is sexy in those tight little jeans."

Feeling heat flush through her from head to toe, Pix spun around to see Beckett standing right there. "Why, thank you," she said, batting her lashes at him. She reached for the hand he extended to help her down, not like she needed it. But she definitely enjoyed feeling little tingles thrum through her at his touch. Feeling another surge of wildly overheated hormones at his gaze and the lazy grin playing on his lips, she curved her lips up. "Ah, thank you. And yes, the view from up there was great. So much fun. This whole little town, it's so—it's so homey. So cute. And fun."

"It's not too bad here." One of those smiles crinkled up his face again.

Another voice from behind them suddenly said, "Beckett! Orson, hon, Mr. Beckett is right there. Go say thank you."

Pix and Beckett turned around. A woman, her black hair and a flash of something wild in her eyes telling Pix she was a bear shifter, gently nudged the boy with the wooden carvings in Beckett's direction. As the boy saw who stood there, his eyes lit up even more.

"I got your Beckett Bears, Mr. Beckett!" he said in a whisper-shout of joy. "I've wanted them for forever! Thank you for bringing them as midwinter gifts," he added a little more shyly, suddenly realizing Pix stood there as well. His little face looked down to the prizes he tightly clutched in his arms as bashfulness apparently seized him.

To Pix's surprise, Beckett stepped forward, then knelt down beside the boy. The boy's black hair escaped the cute winter beanie he wore as he looked up at the huge bear shifter. Beckett had to outweigh the kid by a couple hundred pounds, but his entire body expressed such careful gentleness that Pix caught her breath. He was a big guy with what seemed to be a dangerous inner bear, but clearly he was a really nice guy, too. And—what on earth was a Beckett Bear, anyway?

Reaching out to gently touch the carved wooden toys the little boy held, Beckett said very softly, "You enjoy these, Orson. I'm glad they went to you." Leaning closer and whispering, though the general crowd around them was so active and noisy no non-local human could have heard him, he added, "Every little black bear boy should have some black bear toys to remind him of how cool his inner animal is."

Winking at the kid, who now gazed up at Beckett with a worshipful expression, Beckett stood, nodded at the exuberantly pleased mother, and turned back to Pix. He took her hand to lead her away through the crowd. As they walked, she asked, "Beckett Bears, huh? You carved those? They're amazing."

Pix knew her expression had to be mimicking the worship the little boy'd had on his face when Beckett abruptly looked—bashful. Bashful Beckett? Huh. She wouldn't have guessed that.

After another moment as they pushed through the milling crowd of happily shrieking kids and laughing, chattering adults, Beckett gave a half shrug. "Yeah. I've been carving things since I was a kid. It's how I make my main living now. They sell in stores here in town, and other places too."

"Other places?"

He nodded. "Yeah, stores in other towns. Telluride, Durango, Park City, Aspen, Denver, Santa Fe—"

"Whoa, hold on there a minute." Pix tugged him to a stop and turned to face him. She held up her hand, pressing it against his chest. Mm, big, strong chest. "Those are some fancy towns you just named." She suddenly narrowed her eyes at him. "How much do those sell for?"

"Uh." He looked at the ground, then at the sky above. Hmm. Bashful Beckett again. Fascinating.

Pix folded her arms and gave him what she internally called her dragon stare, which basically meant a stern look. "You'd better tell me right now, backwoods mountain ski man."

Beckett looked back at her, his bear faintly glowing in his eyes. "Oh, I'd better, huh?" But his tone had become light. Bantering with her again. She liked bantering with him.

She nodded, letting one corner of her mouth curve up.

He shrugged again, not taking his gaze from her. "Every single piece is unique. I hand-carve them all, and they each take time. A lot of time. Each one is different. They got really popular, and people started to collect them. Then some high-end stores started to hit me up to carry them after someone began posting them on whatever social media site a couple years back. The demand was crazy, there was no way I could make enough. I'm back-ordered for about three years right now."

Pix felt her jaw drop. "Three years!"

He nodded slowly, then gently reached out his hand to tuck some of her hair off her cheek. She felt a deep, thrilling tingle skitter up and down her body, though she made herself stay still. "I sell each one for about three grand."

Now she thought her jaw might break as it fell open even more. "Three thousand dollars each!"

He grunted softly, shaking his head. "Yeah, and then the stores sell them for even more."

She stared hard at this bear, this huge man with a darkness inside that tore him up, and thought about how gentle he'd been with the little boy who'd gotten his Beckett Bears. "And you just gave them away here, three of them, so some little kid could have them, and love them like crazy, and probably keep them for the rest of his life. You're a good man, Beckett North," she whispered.

Without even thinking, she leaned up on her tiptoes to drift a kiss on his check, just barely grazing the side of his mouth. When she pulled back, Beckett's eyes devoured her with an intense softness that had her dragon fluttering with a whirl of excitement inside her.

His voice low and tempting and only for her to hear, he said, "Come on, Pix Camden. Let's get out of here."

7

*B*eckett wrapped a big arm around Pix's waist, pulling her close to him as he navigated their way back through the people everywhere towards the outer edge of the crowd, kids still giggling and exclaiming with joy as they opened their presents. She caught another smile on his face as he watched the scene. "Even though you keep to yourself, you do like it here, don't you?"

He squeezed her waist. "Shh, don't go telling everyone my secret. But yeah, it's a cool little town. I like it."

"Then why do you live in your man-cave cabin in the woods instead of down here in town?"

She felt Beckett's assenting "Hmm" rumble through her as he guided them out of the crowd and towards the quaint Main Street. Even though they were free of the crush of people now, he kept her pulled in close to his side. She really liked that. "Just because I prefer to live like a hermit doesn't mean I don't like this town. There are a lot of good folk living here." He shrugged, the movement of his shoulder scraping along her body and sending a tingle through it. "But I like my space. Bears like the room to roam. Mine in particular."

Although they were out on the street now, only a few people trickling past them as they made their way back out to where Beckett had parked his truck, Pix reflexively glanced around her. "You said that out loud so casually," she murmured. "Everyone who lives here knows about the shifters, but what about all the tourists?"

They strolled past the cluster of little stores here on the main drag, the streetlamps casting a cozy light. "It's not like we shout about it around them. We're usually careful. But if people don't believe in something, they won't hear it, even if it's being spoken about right front of them."

That was a good point. Big cities all across the country had dragon shifters living in them, but no human not deeply involved in their world would ever believe they were real. Not even if they could see them fly, which thankfully they couldn't. Pix listened to the snow crunching beneath her feet, feeling warm despite the cold snap of the still air on her face. "So," she abruptly switched the conversation. "Is this the part where we're about to do what we've been flirting about all day?"

Beckett turned his head to look down at her. Moonlight glinted off his teeth as he flashed her that grin. The one that changed his features from craggy and cold to breathtakingly hot and inviting. The one she could feel shiver its way through her entire body. "Huh. What exactly is it that we've been flirting about all day?" A knowing caress smoothed itself through his words even as his arm tightened around her.

Pix was usually really confident around guys, but Beckett already had a way of making her thoughts tangle and her tongue stutter. Almost breathlessly, she answered, "You know. The part where we act like adults and do very adult-like things with one another?"

They had reached Beckett's truck, a huge but unassuming work vehicle with dings and scratches visible even in the dim light. Beckett led her to the passenger side of it that was illuminated by the nearby street lamp, and leaned her up against the cab. Pix's breath momentarily halted in her throat as he placed his arms on either side of her, bracing himself against the truck with his hands. He splayed his feet out so that she was comfortably enclosed in his massive embrace, although he wasn't touching her. Yet. Lightning bolts seemed to spark through her entire body, rising to a combustible pitch. She felt her dragon rumble inside her.

In a low voice, the serious look back on his face, he said, "Oh, hell yeah, you sexy badass woman. Maybe I'll start right here," he gently curved his hand to the back of her neck, his fingers threading up through her hair under her fleece hat, exploding the tingles in her body into about hundred more tingles, "with a kiss."

Pix felt boneless with the fire sizzling through her. Beckett brought his lips down onto hers, feather gentle at first. Questing, exploring, tasting. She murmured a pleased sound into his mouth as his tongue traced her lips, then pushed inside her mouth.

As he kissed her, he curved up his other hand on her neck, then brought both hands around to cup her face. His hands were so huge against her, so all-enveloping. He was harder, earthier, stronger than any guy who'd ever held her or kissed her before. So much so that the memory of every single one of them was instantly lost from her mind as she kissed this one back. Oh, could Beckett kiss. He groaned against her, leaning forward until his entire body leaned into her, his chest pushing against her breasts, against her abruptly super sensitive nipples. His hips pressed hard and firm against hers, making her gasp against him. His thighs, which basically felt like thick tree trunks, pushed into hers. It was like being held by a mountain. Each stroke of his tongue inside her mouth sent more fire dancing along her veins.

"I like kissing you, Pix," he said against her lips, the words vibrating into her head.

She blinked her eyes open, feeling heavy lidded and half drunk with desire. "I like kissing you too, Beckett," she whispered back. Looking right into his eyes, feeling the mingled lust and like and need swirl through her, she added, "I like everything about you." It was too much to say, too soon. But she said it anyway.

As he looked back into her eyes, Beckett suddenly frowned. The planes of his face hardened, going granite cold in a nanosecond. Muttering, "What the hell?" he reared back from her. Taking the warmth and strength away. As he stepped back, staring hard, his entire body suddenly stilled into that of a predator that had just scented danger.

What the... Understanding suddenly washed over her. Shit. Her eyes. She was aroused, not thinking. Pure, wild instinct had taken over, and her eyes had changed because Beckett was kissing her. Her dragon had roared into her eyes, and he could see it.

He grabbed her chin and turned her face up, staring into her face as shock cascaded through his expression. She knew exactly what he was seeing: her eyes, a suddenly bright silver, the irises thin vertical black slits. Like a cat's eyes. Except that she definitely wasn't a cat.

Deliberately, he sniffed the air, knowing she could tell what he was doing. Contrary to popular myth, canine shifters like wolves didn't have the best noses. Bears actually had superior olfactory systems, and Beckett was using his right now. "You don't smell like a shifter." His voice was pure gravel. Dark gravel filled with anger.

No, no, this wasn't going like it should be. Feeling cold splashing in and out of the heat in her veins, Pix reached for him, but he shook his head. Hard. Blinking back against the freeze that seemed to be filling her from the inside, she said, "And what if I am one? Would that change things?" Her voice sounded scratchy.

"I can't scent you. You can't be a shifter." His voice came out flat. She could sense his bear rumbling beneath his skin, close to the surface. "But clearly you are one. What the hell are you?"

She forced herself to look right at him, although inside she suddenly felt like she was wilting. She was so stupid. She should have told him earlier today. But she was so used to not talking about that side of herself anymore, so accustomed to *not* being judged solely for being a dragon shifter any longer, she'd just pretended she didn't need to say anything. In a low voice, she pushed out, "I don't have a scent to other shifters the way your kind does."

A shiver rocketed through him. "My kind?" His bear roughened his voice, making a growl roll through it.

"Bear kind. Furred kind."

"Furred kind? What the fuck does that mean? You don't have fur? What the hell are you?" His voice was so low it came out almost more rumble than words.

"I mean," she pushed out despite the tight band that seemed to be constricting around her chest, "the kind that are mammals usually found on this planet. The kind with fur. Or hair. Not my kind." She should have done this sooner. Inside, her dragon bellowed. Pix felt her abruptly tenuous control over that part of herself loosening even more.

Face dark, his jaw tight, Beckett just stared at her, chest heaving as he breathed hard. His eyes glowed bright with his agitated bear's presence.

"Beckett." She stopped, caught by the hardness of his stare and the angry heat in his eyes. This was even harder than she'd thought. Inside her mind, wings flapped hard and angry. Just as enraged as Beckett's bear seemed. "Beckett, haven't you met one of my kind before?"

Before she could finish her sentence, he guessed.

"Dragon. You're a dragon shifter." His flat voice bumped between them, sending a sudden chill through Pix. "What the fuck, Pix. Why the hell didn't you tell me that?"

She held his gaze even as it felt like ice replaced all the fire inside her. Her dragon screamed inside her again, wanting to do—something. Pix wasn't sure what.

Beckett ground his teeth. "You knew from the beginning I was a bear shifter, and you were hiding something as big as this the whole time? You just let me think you were human? Was this some sort of fucking joke to you? I thought you were real. Honest, and real. Not a liar." Though he still kept his voice low, the darkness in it rolled over her like a relentless shadow. Darkness, and something else. Something that went deeper.

Pain.

She had hurt him.

"No! Shit. I'm sorry." She felt colder by the second, not to mention she also felt like a total fool. "This isn't how I meant to tell you. Let me explain—"

But he was already shaking his head, his expression almost wondering in its anger. "Fuck, Pix. No. No way. I like you, and I like kissing you, but I can't hang with someone who can't be honest with me from the get-go. Not even for just one damn night." His tone deepened with every word, getting rougher, as craggy and wild as the mountains around them. "If you can't be honest with me about something as big as this—" His words disappeared, swallowed into the growl of his bear.

Shit, he sort of looked bigger. Growlier. Was he losing control?

Pix felt a tremor in her jaw. His words hurt more than they should have. She barely knew the guy. He had no pull on her. Right? This was just for fun. No one had control over her. Not even a sexy, funny, kind, fascinating bear shifter who set her completely on fire every time he looked at her.

But it did hurt. The same way she'd apparently hurt him. What did that even mean?

Her thoughts dropped, hollow, into a mind staggering under the weight of her dragon's insistent unraveling of her composure. Shit shit shit. Her dragon was pissed as hell. She clutched her hands to her head.

"Beckett," she began, forcing her words out, "wait, just give me a minute. I can explain. I just need some time." She gasped as her dragon screamed again, wings beating hard against her thoughts, making then scatter. She wildly swung her head, then looked at Beckett. She could feel her dragon trying to lunge out of her eyes, trying to rip through her skin. Holy shit, *she* was about to lose control. What was going on here?

But he stepped back even farther from her, his own eyes wide and glowing. A snarl ripped out of him, then another. He kept backing away from her, staring at her eyes and shaking his head. "No," he growled, his voice almost not human anymore. Pix didn't even notice if anyone else was around. She didn't care anymore. "I have to get away from you."

With that, he abruptly turned and stalked off down the street, away from her, away from his own vehicle, away from the town, away from everyone. His feet picked up the pace until he was loping, his steps heavy and hard on the ground as he raced away from her and the part of herself she'd been stupid enough to try and hide from him.

Oh, that hurt. Watching him race away from her and the out-of-control beast she had inside. *I have to get away from you.* Her breath shuddered with how much those words hurt.

She barely knew him, and already he could hurt her. How was that even possible?

Her dragon screamed again, the sound ringing with violent fury throughout Pix's mind.

Damn it. She had to let her dragon out. Now.

Whirling around, she lunged for the shadows cast

by the buildings over the sidewalk, then ducked down a side street dimmer than the rest. Her dragon bellowed and scratched inside her, desperate to be free. She would force the change in seconds if Pix didn't allow it. Damn it, this was too much.

Fighting hard against the change, struggling to hold it in, to rein back her enraged dragon for just a few more moments, Pix bolted hard to reach the end of a little driveway outside a dark house. Trying with all her might to keep the dragon sounds inside, gasping in spite of herself, she finally allowed her dragon to burst out of her.

The change ripped over her, fast. Painful. It was so fast it actually physically hurt, making her cry out as tears welled up in her eyes. She gritted her teeth and tried to let it flow over her, giving way to her dragon. Silver flashed in the night as her wings snapped out, unfurling almost to the houses on either side of the darkened little street. Pix launched herself skyward, letting the downdraft shove her up out of little Deep Hollow, above the shifter town, away from Beckett.

Beckett, the big man who carved beautifully detailed toys for kids, who spiked hot cocoa with marshmallow vodka, who'd just moments ago been kissing Pix like they were meant to be doing that for the rest of their lives. Like they knew one another in a way she'd never thought possible.

In a way she now might have screwed up from ever being possible at all.

As she soared through the dark, flying toward the emptiness of the wild mountains, she glanced down, looking for the shape of a large bear galloping through the town below. But she didn't see him. Keeping her angry-sad cry choked inside her, she waited until she was far from the town, soaring over the empty, snow-covered forests. Then she screamed into the night, the massive sound booming through the air. Long, sad, angry, and a little frightened. Just the way her heart felt, beating hard inside her massive chest as she flew ever farther away. Away from Beckett. The fascinating man who had irrevocably changed her entire life in less than twenty-four hours.

The man she now knew without a doubt, despite the pain of having screwed things up, she for sure would see again. There was zero chance she could ignore the powerful connection sparking between them. The thing that told her he was much more than a one night stand.

As her dragon, she could recognize the truth that kept echoing inside her: *Mate. Mate. He is my mate.*

---

8

*B*eckett shoved his way out of Deep Hollow's small, solo grocery store, hauling his several shopping bags to his truck. His bear rumbled and grumbled and itched beneath his skin. He knew his eyes would be glowing with the strong emotions racing through him. He'd been wearing sunglasses all day, even inside every store he'd entered. Those who knew him, which was to say the whole town, knew it meant he was probably having problems controlling his bear. As usual. Despite the fun of the tree-lighting ceremony last night, how he'd been there and been calm and easy and kept smiling like some happy lunatic, today everyone kept out of his way. Aside from the cue of his sunglasses, he knew his irritation just poured off of him, and every townie could sense it. Anger, aggression, and a bizarre restlessness were his vibe today, and that made him dangerous.

Restless. That was what Pix had called herself, at least one of the things she'd mentioned. One thing she hadn't said, he thought as his strides began to speed up, was that she was a dragon shifter. A fucking dragon shifter. What the damned fuck. Her eyes, all bright silver with the slitted irises, had chased him all last night, through his dreams, and all this morning. He'd found his way back to his cabin on all fours, shifting into his furious, roaring bear as soon as he was out of the town proper and in the woods. He'd been so afraid he might actually go after Pix in his bear shape he'd had to run from her.

Like a giant fucking coward. A furious, hurt one.

How the hell could she have not told him she was a shifter? Worse yet, how could he not have realized it? Sure, dragons didn't have a scent to pick up. He'd known that, but he'd never really thought about it before because he didn't know that many dragon shifters. They stayed as guests up at the Silvertip Lodge sometimes, just like every other shifter type that existed, but Beckett didn't work at the Lodge, and he didn't spend a ton of time there. There was a lone dragon shifter who lived in town, but he kept to himself even more than Beckett did.

His steps pounded even faster on the parking lot that still had patches of snow here and there despite the best clearing efforts of the grocery store staff. He'd been so enthralled with Pix, with how funny she was. How badass, how interesting, how totally—herself. He

261

grunted under his breath. Herself. She was herself, but she had a part of herself that she hadn't wanted to share with him. His bear roared, twitching under Beckett's skin.

And why the fuck he gave a fuck was beyond him. *Bang 'Em Beckett, that's the name,* he thought savagely to himself as he tossed his groceries into the back of his truck. Except this time, he hadn't even had a chance to bang her yet.

But fuuuck him, how he still wanted to do just that. Bang her. Except that calling it that just felt weirdly crude when it came to Pix. He more wanted to kiss her all over. Lick her, stroke her, pull her down on top of him, hold those small, sweet curves close. Okay, fine, he wanted to have crazy hot wild sex with her. He wanted to fuck her till she screamed her release, mindless with pleasure because of him. But he also wanted to hold her close, to be tender with her, to cradle her in his arms and never let her go.

Fucking hell. Clearly, he was losing his damned mind.

He started to yank open the driver's side door when someone called out his name.

"Beckett. Hey man, hold up there."

Ah, shit. Cortez. He'd been ducking Cortez's phone calls all morning. No avoiding him now, though. Growling, he turned around and glared at his best friend. "What?" he barked.

Cortez shook his head as he ambled up. "I'm gonna be straight with you, dickwad."

Beckett snorted. Typical Cortez style. He didn't beat around the bush.

"So I just barely met Haley, right?" Cortez drummed the fingers of one hand on his thigh. "She's awesome. I like her a lot. Then her best friend comes out to visit her, somehow meets your dumb ass, and for some even crazier reason, seems to like you."

Beckett felt a growl rattle through his throat. His bear clawed at his chest.

"Then for some other who-knows-what reason," and now Cortez was narrowing his eyes at Beckett, "something went down with you guys last night that wasn't good. So now Haley's really upset, too. She's upset that her best friend is sad, she complains to me, and worse yet, she got so distracted when Pix came back last night, all alone and also upset, that I didn't get any sweet loving from that sexy woman like I'd wanted. That means now it's personal, man." Cortez's jaw was set as he leveled a glare at Beckett. "I don't like to interfere in your shit, but seriously. I have to respectfully ask you to get your head out of your ass and fix whatever it is you have going on with Pix, because you're ruining a good thing for me with Haley."

Beckett growled. "I didn't ruin anything. She did. Pix, I mean." Saying her name was hard. He grunted. This was ridiculous.

Cortez gave him a squinty-eyed stare. "Nope. I

know you. It was all you. You ruined it for sure. And you did it before you even spent one night with her. You trying for a new track record?"

Beckett clenched his fists at his sides as his bear roiled thunder inside him. Cortez was pushing the envelope, hard. But he wasn't Beckett's best friend for no reason. He knew Beckett well enough that he could stare his friend in the face, say something like that, and know that Beckett wouldn't rip him to shreds.

After another long, tense moment, Beckett shook out his hands to try and release some of the tension. In a low voice still pocked by snarls he said, "No. She ruined it. She's a fucking dragon shifter, Cortez. A dragon shifter." He glared at his friend to emphasize the seriousness of it. "I couldn't tell. You know dragon shifters don't have a freaking scent like normal shifters do. She knew I was a bear, and she didn't bother to tell me she's a shifter, too."

Cortez's mouth opened and his eyebrows raised in gratifying response. "A dragon shifter? That itty-bitty thing? That's nuts. You sure you heard her right?"

Beckett jerked a single nod. "I tried to scent her again after she told me. Finally thought I could smell something like brimstone." He frowned.

Rolling his eyes, Cortez snorted. "Overactive imagination, dumbass. You sound like a power-mad preacher saying words like that. Dragons don't have to use brimstone, they have their fire naturally inside them."

"Whatever." Beckett growled. "I saw her eyes shift last night. Dragon eyes. Glowing silver and slit like a cat's. But cats don't have silver eyes. She's a dragon."

Cortez stayed silent for a long moment, mulling it over. Finally he said, "Haley didn't mention that to me. The dragon shifter part."

Beckett scowled even more. "See? Pix can't even tell the truth to her best friend, and she wouldn't share with me even though she knew I was a bear shifter. Someone like her can't be trusted." His bear snarled as he thought that. Beckett shrugged it off with an angry jerk of his shoulders. He was pissed off, damn it, and he wanted to stay that way.

"No, dumbass. I didn't say she hasn't told Haley, I said Haley didn't tell me. There might be a reason she doesn't want people to know she's a dragon." Now Cortez gave him another look. "Oh, hell. Wait a minute. You planned to spend a single night with her, but now you're saying you really care if she didn't tell you? Nope." He grinned big. "No way. There's more to it. "You like her. You really like her. Holy shit, Beckett. You *like* her." Cortez tucked his thumbs in his belt loops and rocked back on his heels, starting to laugh as he slowly shook his head.

Beckett took a shuddering breath, which rattled up as a growl in his throat. "I do not like her."

"Do so," Cortez retorted, laughing past his words.

"Do not."

"Do so."

"Do not." Beckett clenched his fists as he snarled the words out like they were kids on the playground having a tantrum fight. The thing was, he was lying to himself and he knew it. Damn it all.

"Do so, and I'm right. Come on, man, don't you get it?" Cortez stopped laughing, looking at Beckett more seriously now.

"What?" Beckett snapped.

Patiently, as if outlining something to a child, Cortez said with slow enunciation, "She's a dragon shifter, Beckett. A dragon."

Beckett just glared at him, shaking his head in a "get to the damned point" way. Cortez threw his hands up in the air in disgust. "Look. Your big issue is that your bear is a grumpy old sourpuss who likes to rage and snarl around half the time. You have real trouble controlling it."

"Yeah?" Beckett snapped. "What's your fucking point, Freud?"

"Beckett." Cortez huffed out a sigh. "Are you that blind? Who better to help you control your bear than a goddamned dragon shifter?"

Beckett blinked. His bear abruptly stopped rumbling, seeming as stupefied as Beckett felt. "A dragon shifter," he repeated dumbly, as if he'd just thought about it.

"Yeah, top of the predator heap?" Cortez lifted his hand way up in the air as if to show how high up there they were. "Biggest, baddest creatures out there?

Even if they do worship gold and useless shit like that."

"A dragon shifter," Beckett repeated again. Cortez shook his head in despair, waiting for Beckett to come to his senses.

It didn't take long.

"She's a dragon shifter. Holy shit." Beckett blinked as the simple truth of that hit him. Well, hell. He was the one being an asshole. Not Pix. Definitely not cute, sassy, strong, badass dragon shifter Pix.

"Holy shit, man," Cortez agreed, sounding somewhat cheerful again. He leaned forward, socked Beckett in the arm, and started to walk away. "Don't waste your chance," he called her over his shoulder. "Unless you just want to live with your grumpy-ass bear for the rest your life."

But Beckett had already turned on his heel to stride back toward the grocery store. Cortez must've turned his head to look back at him. He called out, "What, is your brain so addled you forgot some groceries?"

Beckett shook his head, yelling over his shoulder, "I figure I better buy some flowers since I have to go see her and tell her I'm sorry for being an asshole."

Cortez's laughter rang behind him as Beckett charged back into the store, feeling oddly different. Lighter.

It took him until he had paid for his purchase and gotten back to his truck, sunglasses now shoved on top of his head, to realize what it was: he felt a lot less like his bear was about to burst out from him in an uncontrolled frenzy, and a lot more like his bear was quiet and content beneath his skin.

His bear kept rumbling a word at him that seemed crazy but certain. *Mate.* Ah, holy shit. Just the thought of the word had his entire body leaping with a crazy lightness he'd never before felt.

He wanted to be with Pix more than anything he'd ever wanted in his life. He was going to find her, tell her he was sorry, and hold onto her. Maybe even forever, the thought lingered in his head as he roared his truck out of the parking lot to go get his sexy, badass Pix.

His sexy, badass *mate.*

9

*P*ix stared at her website, feeling flat even as she should be really excited. "I sold another painting," she called out to Haley, who was in the kitchen. "That really big one you told me to put a higher price tag on. You were right. Raise the prices and suddenly people want to buy."

Haley squealed with delight. A few seconds later she appeared in the doorway to the living room, two steaming mugs held in her hands. "Awesome! You needed to find a way to really support yourself on your own, and in style. I bet your dragon is happy. Come join me in the sunroom and we'll talk about the rest of your life over coffee."

Pix gave her friend a half smile as she stood up to join her. The sunny little nook, situated on the south side of the house, was one of the many perks of this beautiful housesitting gig Haley had managed to snag.

She accepted a hot mug with a murmured thanks and settled into one of the cushioned wicker chairs. Haley eyeballed her thoughtfully. "You're not as happy about this as you should be. It's good news, after what that jerk did to you last night."

Reflexively, Pix murmured, "It wasn't his fault, I told you. It's my fault. I wasn't honest enough with him, and he didn't like that."

Haley shook her head, a strand of her messy blonde hair slipping out of the makeshift bun she'd shoved it into this morning. "You don't like that part of your life. It reminds you of the past, and that past is over. It wasn't any of his business what you chose to tell him or not tell him about yourself. Besides, it's not like he needed to know every last detail about you just for a casual hook up. Right?" She gave Pix a shrewd gaze while innocently sipping her coffee.

Pix felt the heat coiling and burning inside her. That was her own out-of-control beast, just like Beckett had referred to his bear. There was a reason she didn't share that part of herself with most shifters. Once she'd renounced her formal dragon shifter ties, knowing she'd simply never fit into that world, she tried to live her life in a way that meant others had to take her at face value. Not because of her family name or that she was at the top of the shifter heap, being a dragon. "Yeah, but even so, when I asked him point-blank if he was a bear shifter, he told me. And I never mentioned my dragon to him. That wasn't right," she said softly.

Pix sipped her coffee in silence, looking out at the lovely view of the Walkers' backyard. The more time she spent in Deep Hollow, the more she liked it. But in a town full of shifters, she'd really made a huge misstep by not telling Beckett what she was. He'd been right to stalk off in a rage.

It wasn't like her to feel as undecided and unhappy as she felt right now. Ever since she had cut ties with the expected route for a dragon shifter, even though she stayed close with her own family, particularly her mother, she'd felt a sense of freedom as she forged her own path in life. There had been hard times as she tried to make a living for herself, no longer able to exist in the lap of her family's monied luxury. It had been eye-opening to say the least. But she liked her life much better this way. It felt real. True to herself.

A snap of hot lightning forked along her veins. She grimaced. She wasn't always true to her dragon soul. Her dragon had gotten more and more unpredictable, until Pix finally realized she needed to leave Boston and get away from all the dragons in that big city. It also meant she couldn't land in another big city, since dragon shifters preferred the high life generally afforded to them by the large companies they tended to own, which usually had to be run from large urban areas. It was a good thing dragon flight was invisible to human eyes. Because Pix always loved flying as her dragon.

Her dragon screamed, sending fire flipping along Pix's veins.

Deliberately, she switched the subject. "What are you doing today?"

Haley brightened. "I'll be out most of the day with Cortez." Her smile got dreamy as she said the name of the guy making her smile and laugh so much lately.

Pix gave a genuine smile back to her friend. "I'm glad to hear that. Say, do you know—"

The chime of the doorbell, followed by loud, gruff knocking, cut her off short. Haley bounced up, eyes sparkling. "He's early!" she said as she hurried to the front door.

But when she came back to the sunroom two minutes later, face wary and protective, it wasn't Cortez who was following her. Beckett filled the space of the doorway.

"Hey, Pix," he said in a low voice. He shifted from one foot to the other. "Look." He cut a quick glance at Haley before turning back to Pix. "I suck at this kind of thing, so I'm just gonna say it straight out. I didn't give you a chance to explain last night why you waited to tell me about your dragon. But it wasn't my call. It wasn't for me to tell you what to do, or when to tell me. Your story is your story. I had no right to expect you to tell me everything at once. Or even ever, if you don't want to. But I hope you do." His eyes were bright with his bear when he added that. "So I was an ass. I'm sorry. I still really like you. Here," he added, thrusting out a bouquet of flowers wrapped in brown paper tied with a pretty ribbon. "I brought you flowers. Girls like flowers."

Something happy sparkled through Pix at every single word he said. "Not all girls like flowers, you know," she couldn't help teasing him. Then she looked closely at the bouquet and drew in a sharp breath. Silvery purple roses, festooned with pretty little white daisies. "Oh, Beckett, they're really beautiful. Thank you," she added with soft sincerity. "I'm sorry, too," she began to say, but he cut her off.

"You don't have to explain right now. I'd rather hear it when we're alone anyway." He looked again at Haley, who was surveying the scene with the air of a mother hen ready to peck his eyes out if she needed to.

Pix said to Haley, "It's all right. We're good now." She looked at Beckett again, letting a smile sweep over her face. It was more than good. Being in his presence lit her up like that tree last night.

A smile nudged the corners of his mouth. "Okay. You can tell me anything or nothing you want over dinner. Tonight. My place. If you still want to come over." He looked at her steadily as he said all that. Once again giving her the choice, even though he pretty damn clearly wanted her to say yes.

She jumped on the chance to lighten the moment. "You're telling me you know how to cook? A backwoods bachelor bear?" She infused as much skepticism into her voice as she could.

It worked. His mouth relaxed even more. "Hell, yeah, I can cook. Six o'clock okay for you?"

Before Pix could speak, Haley jumped in. "She'll be there. Since it seems like she doesn't want me to kill you, I guess that means she'll give you another chance. And," Haley cast a quick smile at Pix, "sounds like you'll give her another chance, too. Pix is awesome, and you probably don't deserve her, but I guess you're lucking out."

Beckett nodded, still looking at Pix. "Yeah, I'm pretty sure you are damned awesome, Pix. So dinner, and the entire night is still on the table. If we both want that."

Pix finally let a bigger smile flood over her face as her dragon fluttered around inside her, stretching her wings out, blasting heat throughout Pix's body. "Yes. It's probably still on the table," she managed to answer in a steady voice.

The look in Beckett's eyes made her go weak in the knees. "Then I'll see you tonight, badass Pix. I'll text you the directions."

"Okay. It's a date, badass bear," she said in a suddenly breathless voice, her entire body feeling deliriously light with happiness. "I'll see you tonight."

*A*s soon as Beckett's "little cabin" in the woods came into view, Pix's mouth fell open. Wow. She'd literally expected a little cabin, maybe even somewhat ramshackle, all rough-hewn and man-caved out. This was anything but ramshackle. It was so beautifully made it looked like it easily would stand for another two hundred years. And it was a lot bigger than she'd thought it would be. It was the size of a regular house, nicer than a cabin. She could tell every inch of it had been lovingly crafted. By hand, apparently. She knew from the carved toys that Beckett was good with his hands.

That thought made her blush, then giggle at herself. She felt nervous but excited and calm at the same time. Stepping out of her car, she grabbed the bottle that rolled around in the little brown bag on the passenger seat. She'd been raised to believe that it was polite to bring something to someone's house when invited to dinner, and it was a part of her background that she couldn't shake. The bottle held golden whiskey.

She walked up a driveway that was clear of snow, despite the piles of it lining both sides. Spying a snow shovel leaning up on the side of the stairs going up to the front door, she suddenly imagined Beckett's strong arms working hard as he scooped the snow off his driveway. He probably did it while stripped to the waist, muscles flexing beneath his skin. Picturing Beckett naked from the waist up did something really delightful inside her. Whoa there, she thought to herself. Dinner first.

As she headed up the wide sweep of wooden stairs she brushed her hand over smooth, solid rails on the side. When she saw his huge front door, she laughed. The door knocker was a massive grizzly head, mouth open wide in a snarl. It was like he enjoyed having his angry bear greet the world. *Well,* she thought as she firmly rapped it several times, *let's see what he does when he faces a dragon that's gonna be a lot bigger than he probably thinks it is.*

About three seconds after she knocked, Beckett opened the door. He must have heard her pull up. Bear shifters had excellent hearing. She was taken for a breathless moment by the way his eyes drank her in, then burst out with more laughter when she saw the apron he wore over his jeans and long-sleeved shirt. *I'm the Chef. If You Don't Like the Food, I'll Bite Your Face Off.*

She instantly felt even more at ease. His sense of humor matched hers. "Do you wear that every time you open the door when you invite someone over for dinner?"

"The only people I ever have over for dinner are already my friends. They know I'm an asshole, but they also know I'm good at slaving over a hot stove." He grinned at her. Seeing that sexy grin, knowing how few got to see it and letting it remind her of all the fun they'd had yesterday, relaxed her even more. "Come in, Pix." His voice deepened as he ran his eyes down to her toes and back up to her face again. "Damn. You look really good."

"Why, thank you, kind sir." Giving him a flirtatious wink, she pushed past his huge, yummy-smelling bulk standing in the doorway. She'd decided to dress up. She wore a little black dress, slinging a form-fitting dark gray jacket over it that cinched nicely at the waist and emphasized her figure. She'd even styled her hair a little bit, brushed a hint of mascara onto her lashes and dabbed some color on her lips. It felt really good that he noticed the effort she'd put in.

As soon as she stepped all the way inside his house, though, his reaction to her appearance was completely forgotten. She stood riveted in the tiny entryway that

277

opened up to a spacious, incredible living room. "Whoa, Beckett. This place is amazing." She blinked as she looked around his home, shrugging off her coat so he could take it and hang it up on a carved wooden coat rack by the front door. A coat rack he'd probably made himself too.

He closed the door behind them. "Yeah. It's still my man cave, though."

Pix spluttered, still looking around in appreciation of the place. "Man cave? Then it's the most beautiful, upscale man cave I've ever seen."

"You been in a lot of man caves?" His voice suddenly sounded possessive. He moved past her back into the open kitchen to stir the incredible-smelling something bubbling in a huge silver pot on the stove, letting a hand slide over her waist as he passed. Warmth flushed up through her.

"Nothing ever in my life like this," she assured him. Sure, she'd grown up in enormous privilege, but this place was built by hand. To her, that meant it surpassed any house she'd ever see before.The floor plan was open, the smooth, shining cherry wood of the floors seeming to extend for miles. The kitchen, which flowed into the living room without walls to separate it, featured an enormous stainless steel island, behind which stood an industrial-sized stainless steel stove and a stainless steel refrigerator so big it probably could hold enough food to feed Beckett and about a hundred of his closest friends. His popular, pricey carved toys obviously had meant he could splurge on this place, and he clearly had. The ceiling angled upward in an airy slice, making the place feel even bigger. She saw a faint glow coming from around a corner.

"Fireplace," Beckett said, seeing the direction of her gaze. "It's in the sitting room."

"The *sitting* room?" She looked at him, the gruff, tough bear shifter, then swung her head back toward his so-called sitting room. "What, do you receive your royal guests in there and offer them crumpets with their tea?"

He barked out a laugh, followed by another. The ease of it made her laugh, too, as she glanced back at him again. "Yep, the queen sits in my big leather easy chair and we exchange palace decorating tips." Without missing a beat he added, "That's another thing I like about you, Pix. You're funny. I've laughed more times around you in the past few days than I usually do all year." He headed over to the kitchen island, where a salad sat in a large bowl made up of large criss-crossing stripes of different-colored wood.

She shook her head, watching as he casually chopped, added, stirred things. "People just don't know you, do they? You're the funny one. And you seem to laugh a lot."

"Only because you've been bringing it out in me," he said simply. The look he gave her was charged with something that made her shiver in anticipation, though the half smile lingered on his face. Then he turned back around to the stovetop and clanged a spoon against the pot.

Pix sniffed appreciatively. "What did you make for dinner? I'm pretty hungry." On cue, her stomach rumbled loudly. She snickered at herself.

The sound was echoed by Beckett's deep laughter. "It's just spaghetti. But the sauce is a secret recipe I came up with myself. That'll soothe the hungry beast in your stomach."

She snorted another laugh, then licked her lips. "I haven't even tasted it yet and I already think you should open a restaurant. Oh, I also brought a bottle of whiskey. You look like a whiskey drinker." She crooked an eyebrow at him.

Beckett eyes lit up. "I think I like you more and more every minute." Something quietly deep and true sounded under his words. A brief silence lasted for a long moment, during which Pix felt her heart bang hard inside her chest and her nerves twitch with liquid fire. The word *Mate* once again whispered through her veins, her self, her soul. She was too nervous to bring it up out loud yet, but something in his gaze told her he'd been having the same thought.

He broke the silence by saying, "You're actually perfectly on time. It's ready to serve right now. Hand me the bottle. I'll pour us drinks to have with dinner. You," he pointed at her, "just go sit. There," and now he pointed at a chair pulled out slightly from a set place at the casual but highly polished farmhouse table in the middle of the open space between the kitchen island and the living room.

She nodded, floating herself over to the chair. The buoyant feeling inside her, she suddenly realized, was partially from just being here, around Beckett, but also partially from her dragon. Her dragon, who was strangely calm and quiet. Watchful, but peaceful inside Pix. "She's quiet right now," she said out loud, pitching her voice so Beckett could hear her.

He'd been heading toward her, carrying two glasses filled with dark gold liquid. "Who's quiet?" He lightly clunked the glasses onto the table, one in front of her. Mm, whiskey.

"My dragon." Pix felt the slight flap of dragon wings inside her as she said that, and the usual fire, but not the agitation that had been more her companion for years now since she'd decided to become restless Pix. She liked this new calm.

"Hmm," he said, returning to the stove to bring back two plates heaped with spaghetti, the tantalizing sauce, enormous meatballs, and a tiny side of salad each. But instead of asking more about her dragon, he just put the plate down for Pix. "Eat, beautiful. I want to see you appreciating my food."

Her first bite of the amazing pasta dish he'd prepared for her made her happily moan in a way that did interesting things to Beckett's expression. "You definitely should open a restaurant. But you definitely have to be in the back of the house. You'd need someone much more cheerful for the front of the house. Although," she paused to take another big bite, closing her eyes as she savored every last taste sensation of the amazing sauce and cheese combination he'd put on it, "this food is so good, customers might forgive you for being surly."

When she opened her eyes, Beckett was staring at her, the light in his eyes more pronounced. She swallowed a sip of the whiskey, then demanded, "What? Do I have spaghetti sauce streaks on my face?"

He huffed a laugh. "I like that you can eat food in front of me and not care what you look like. Most girls aren't like that."

She quickly shot back, "As you may have noticed, I'm not most girls. In fact, I really am different in that I have a dragon in me. I bet you don't have any of those living here in Deep Hollow."

To her surprise, he said, "Actually, we do have one. If you think I'm surly, you should meet him. I've got nothing on his cranky old ass. He keeps to himself more than I do. But yeah, otherwise, no. Dragons seem to favor cities. Like Boston."

Like Boston. The city she had been born into, and the city she'd finally left. Cocking her head, she carefully watched him over the rim of her glass as he dug into his own meal. "I know I told you I was on vacation. I am. Sort of." She took another bite of food and swallowed. "But I'm also actually on a journey of sorts."

He contemplated that for a moment, then nodded. Ooh, she really wanted to reach out and touch the sexy stubble on his face. "You know who you are, but you're still trying to figure out where you need to be. That right?"

She took a deep breath. "Yes. Part of why I didn't tell you about my dragon is because she's really wild. Hard to control sometimes." Her dragon smacked her wings against Pix's mind and screamed. She winced slightly. "Like that. She's pitching a fit inside me right now."

"Why does she do that?" He sounded genuinely curious.

Pix swirled some spaghetti strands around her fork. "I don't really know. Growing up, I never felt like I fit in my own skin. I mean, I mostly do. I am happy with who I am. I wasn't lying when I told you you that. Since dragons are almost impossible to scent, I just stopped telling anyone that I'm a dragon shifter. But my dragon pushes back at me sometimes. She's strong. Really strong."

"That sounds familiar." Beckett took a slug of the whiskey, uttered a satisfied sound, then gestured at her fork. "Keep eating. I don't want you to do all the talking and not enjoy my best easy dish."

Pix started to shake her head, meaning to protest, but he nodded more firmly at her food. "Let's enjoy our dinner, Pix." He sipped the whiskey, the color of his eyes matching the liquid in the glass. "I want you to have your energy."

She coughed, carefully swallowed her next bite, and gave him a look from under her lashes. "Mr. North, are you planning to seduce me?" Despite her light tone, she felt the sweet heaviness move through her limbs, pool into a flash of desire between her legs.

He slowly smiled back in a Cheshire grin sort of way. "Anything's possible, beautiful."

The temperature in the room raced up. She forced herself to focus on the food—which was easy to do, really—and the moment. As they relaxed into more casual conversation, Pix felt her body humming with awareness. But it was an easy, light awareness, not the tenseness she often experienced with her dragon. Letting laughter bubble up out of her as easily as breathing, she let herself enjoy this dinner with Beckett just as she'd enjoyed skiing with him.

Eventually, the dishes were carried back to the sink and Pix got a little tour of Beckett's house. The sitting room in particular was her favorite. Huge windows ran from the ceiling to the floor, showcasing a dark sky filled with stars and the rounded tops of the pine trees outside still covered in fluffy snow. The ceiling by the window domed up, creating its own nook complete with a wide, long buttery leather couch, a few plush easy chairs, standing lamps that cast a soft golden glow, and a fireplace that was ridiculous. "Tiny fireplace you've got there," she observed in a droll tone, craning her head to see the top of the stonework that made it up, which towered over her head by an easy ten feet.

Beckett laughed again, but this time there was a small edge to it that she caught immediately. She glanced at him, feeling a skitter of tension roll up her spine as well. He looked at her for a long moment, his expression once again hard to read. Finally, "Come outside with me, Pix," he said in a low voice, extending a hand toward her. "I need to show you something."

She raised her eyebrows but didn't hesitate. Putting her hand in his, she let him lead her outside. As they left the house, the sharp cold slapped against her face. He stepped out onto his wraparound deck, then turned around so he faced her, letting her hand slide away from his. His expression had gotten more intense. More wild.

Suddenly, she knew exactly what he planned to do. "Beckett, you don't have to show me." Her voice was quiet but steady as she looked at the sexy mountain man, the surly man people in town sometimes skirted with a wide berth, the man who'd already slid into her heart. "I can handle your bear."

He shook his head as he went down the stairs. "I need you to see all of me, Pix. You need to know my bear, too. If he can't handle you, I'll know right away. He won't hurt you," Beckett added with a ferocity that glowed in his eyes.

"I know he won't. Trust me, he can't." Her soft voice sounded loud in the quiet of the night.

Beckett nodded, then closed his eyes. With an enormous sigh, he abruptly let the shift drop over him, letting his bear burst out of him while Pix watched, unmoving. Oh, he was enormous. And stunning. He had a glorious golden brown hide, the huge hump of his shoulders indicating his power and strength. Quietly, calmly, he stood in the driveway, dark eyes trained on Pix. Opening his mouth, he bellowed out a call that echoed through the woods, shaking snow down from trees and probably freezing the blood of tiny animals burrowed into their little winter dens. His huge claws clicked on the driveway when he slowly backed up, his head swinging down, snorting at Pix.

She smiled and walked down the steps. Straight for him. "You don't scare me, Beckett North. Your bear is stunning. Strong, and beautiful"—his outraged snort at that made her chuckle—"and fierce and protective." That part she said with sheer admiration. "But trust me," she added softly, still slowly walking toward him before she pulled up with a good amount of space still between them. "I can handle you. I just hope you can handle me."

Pix opened her mind and let her eager dragon flood through it, take over. She burst out of Pix's skin with a bellowing roar of excitement, crying out to the quiet forest that she was here. Pix spread her enormous silver wings, luxuriating in the feel of them. The freedom. Eagerly, she turned her head. There was space here. So much space. She could fly, and dive, and hunt, and play out here over these mountains. She could swoop freely above them, claiming them as her own. Her own place.

Opening her mouth, she shrieked out a wild burst of elation, calling out again and again, flapping her wings and creating mighty downdrafts of air.

A bellowing cry answered her, cutting her short. She swung around her head, and looked at him. At Beckett. The huge bear, standing on his hind legs, roaring out his own call. His own claim to these woods. His own strength and vitality.

Calling out his invitation to share the mountain, the forest, his home—with her. Pix flung her head back, letting the chilly air ripple over her silver hide with a delightful sensation of aliveness. She cried out in answer, her bugle ringing through the forest, answered by his own roaring bellow. Their voices mingled, together.

Beckett was inviting her to be here. To stay here with him. Accepting her into his home.

Yes. Oh, yes.

After one last bellow, Pix curled in on herself, flowing back down into her human form. She stood on her two human feet, utterly naked and vulnerable in front of him. In half a heartbeat, Beckett shifted from his bear back to human, striding toward her on his long, strong legs. Also wonderfully, gorgeously naked. He scooped her up into those arms she'd imagined holding her and cradled her close to his broad chest as he leapt up the stairs two at a time, back into the house.

"Yes," he growled with soft, insistent intensity against her hair as he carried her toward the sitting room and that giant, soft leather couch. "Yes, my beautiful Pix. You can handle me. Now, let's get to know each other even better."

*B*etween her legs, the delicious pressure ached, feeling full to bursting as Beckett gently set her down, his hands lingering on her body. He was completely silent, his eyes drinking her in. She was so keenly attuned to his presence she could sense his undeniable need as loudly as if he were yelling it.

He pulled in his breath, then breathed out her name in a reverent whisper. "Pix." The intensity in his eyes touched Pix on an equally deep level. Her dragon stared back at Beckett through Pix's eyes with an avid, bright hunger. With acceptance, excitement, joy. Pausing only for a second, Pix let go. She let her dragon lead this most instinctual of dances.

"Oh, yes," she breathed back, nodding her head once. "Beckett. Please."

As a groan spilled out of her huge, sexy bear's

mouth, he crushed her to him in an embrace that tangled their lips and tongues into an erotic dance. Pix felt electric tingles shiver up and down her limbs as Beckett's mouth descended on hers, demanding an entrance she eagerly granted. His wild, purely masculine scent catapulted her senses into overdrive. She moaned in helpless bliss as his tongue explored her, her legs shaking as her dragon flooded her in a delighted response to the sexy bear shifter ravishing the hell out of her.

Beckett slid one large hand down her back, cupping her ass and squeezing. She gasped, letting her wild dragon side take over, guiding her movements with a sensuous thrill. He tilted his head forward and lightly bit at her neck, his teeth skimming over her skin and sending more jolts of desire skittering through her.

"Oh, fuck yeah, Pix. I like it when you make noises like that. I had a feeling you might make some interesting, sexy sounds." His voice rumbled against her throat, the sound of it seeming to vibrate through her.

"Did you now?" Her voice came out as a jagged whisper. Thinking wasn't happening now. Sensation and being purely in the moment were her top priorities.

"Hell, yeah. Ever since the moment you threw your drink all over me at the bar."

Her eruption of giggles at his words stopped quickly when his lips traveled up her neck, slowly exploring. Each tiny kiss, each small nibble, caused more of the sweet, almost unbearably pleasurable sensation to ripple along her skin. She'd never before realized her neck was so sensitive. When Beckett's mouth found her ear and gently played with it, the exquisite sensation made her tremble in his arms. Quivering desire pulsed between her legs with such strength she thought she might come right there. That would be fine. So fine. So damned good.

"Pix," he murmured, sounding almost awed. "I fuckin' love the way you respond to me." He growled those words, pulling her tightly against him. "Sweet woman," he groaned, his entire body taut against her. "Sweet, sexy, powerful dragon," he whispered, tracing the words on her skin with his lips.

She let her head loll back as Beckett kissed her all over, the feeling of it like being set aflame in the best way possible. The huge, hard length of his dick pressed into her thigh. She let expectant shivers rattle up and down her spine, whimpering a bit from her sheer need for this man. A wave of lust rolled through her, seeming to melt her bones, her mind, her entire self into a heated coil of pure sensation.

Still trembling, she felt emotion that was more than just lust rocking her entire body. Oh, this man. This sexy-ass bear shifter. This man she'd just barely met but who had already seen right into her soul. Who'd greeted her dragon with an equal strength.

"Beckett," she whispered, watching his eyes light to the bright amber shade of his bear. This impressive, stunning man she was about to get very naked with. With her breath catching in her throat, she rubbed her hands up his huge arms. He shivered in response, making her smile with pure female satisfaction. He could hold her so easily, keep her safe in those huge arms. She lightly ran her fingers up to his shoulders, experimentally squeezing. An equally satisfied male groan told her how much he enjoyed it when she did that.

"Sexy man." She whispered the words, watching him closely as she let her hand travel up to his neck, curving around one side of it. His pulse jumped under her touch. "I need to feel you right against me. Just like this." She pushed herself up against him, nestling into him as hard as she could. They both gasped from the feel of it.

Beckett gently pushed on her until she let herself lightly tumble into a lying down position onto the couch. He leaned on his arms above her, looking into her eyes with a savage urgency she knew her own eyes matched. Silence wrapped around them the entire time, although Pix's heart beat so loudly she was positive he had to hear it.

"Pix," he finally murmured.

"Mm-hmm?" She said it breathlessly, wondering if her heart might not bang its way out of her chest.

He groaned, the rich sound of it stealing her breath. "I can't hold back anymore."

She arched herself into him, her desperate need for

his touch driving her every word. "Then don't. Don't hold back with me, Beckett. I can take everything you've got. I'm strong enough for you. And you're strong enough for me."

As he let another small groan ripple out, Beckett kissed her shoulder, then gently bit it with his teeth. Pix gasped, instantly flooded with a wet heat between her legs, her core pulsing with her desire. Beckett gazed down at her breasts. Muttering a low, "Fuck, you're beautiful," he reached down to cup one of them in his hand.

Pix uttered a wordless cry as her nipple stiffened just from the touch of his fingers. Swirls of hot sensation made the nipple tighten even more as he began to play with it.

"Pix, my beautiful, powerful woman," he muttered. She closed her eyes, spinning in the sensations his light touch caused. "Look at me," he suddenly demanded.

She opened her eyes, feeling her dragon cascade fire throughout her body.

"Too much, too soon?" He swirled a finger around her other nipple, drawing more gasps from her.

"No. It's perfect," she gasped. "I want more. Much more." She reached up her arms to him, pulling him down to her for another long, deep kiss.

Beckett tasted just like his scent: wild bear, deep forest, luscious and powerful and hers. All hers. His hands explored her body, one lingering on her breasts, exploring first one, then the other. His other hand traveled down her hip, tracing her leg. He slowly swirled his fingers, heating small infernos under her skin and pulling more small cries from her throat.

Mine, she thought in a firm rush of possessiveness. Her dragon roared in agreement. *He is mine. My mate.*

*B*eckett pulled back to look at Pix with an intensity she felt dive deep into her soul. "Beckett," she said, her voice low and needy. Reaching her hand toward him, she dragged her fingers down his sculpted chest, which made him gasp. In a low, urgent voice, she said, "I want you. Right now. Don't you dare hold back with me."

With a sharp inhale, he slowly grinned. It was purely devilish, with a hint of worship in it that made her heart explode with desire and joy. Abruptly, he stood up on the couch, putting his legs on either side of Pix's body. "Anything you say, my sexy, stunning woman."

Oh, holy wow, she thought as she stared up at Beckett standing naked above her in all of his glorious maleness. Her brain completely stuttered to a halt at the sight of his huge, strong legs, his chest covered with rippling muscles, and that gorgeously huge part of him she was suddenly desperate to touch. Reaching out to him, struggling to sit up, a tiny gasp tore out of her throat when Beckett suddenly jumped back down to stretch his body along hers. His hard dick pressed up against her inner thighs, which she parted with a needy moan. But Beckett shook his head at her, letting just a touch of that teasing grin still play at his lips.

"No. Let me lead you now." His voice tipped at the edge of control.

Oh, yes. With a quick nod, she eagerly waited for his next move.

Beckett caught both her hands and pulled them over her head, where he lightly held them together. Pix gave a token struggle to test his strength, then another. He tightened his grasp in small increments, still watching her carefully despite the roiling need she saw in his eyes. But she let a pleased smile linger on her face so he knew how she felt about being held down by him.

She loved it. She wanted nothing more than to let him claim her in a way she'd never before allowed. Never before had known she wanted. She'd never wanted a man to control her—but Beckett North, her mate, was the sole exception. She absolutely wanted him to hold her, to possess and cherish her, in a way she'd never thought she would.

She trusted him entirely, and wanted to open to him completely. "Yes," she murmured, the word almost lost in the ragged breathing that filled the room. "Yes, Beckett. Anything for you."

He groaned again. His teeth nipped at her ear once more, then traveled down her neck. Letting his other hand slip over her body, he first fondled her breasts, then gently tugged at her nipples with his fingers, setting off more quivering shudders of bliss deep inside her. His hand danced over her ribs, slowly curved over her side. The sensation of his teeth gently scraping over her skin made her want him to do exactly that farther down. Right between her legs, where she was afire with the aching need to be filled by him.

"Beckett, please," she said, her voice a mix of pleading and demand. "Now!"

He pulled back, shaking his head and looking at her with a shuddering desire she could hardly believe he was managing to contain right now. "I'm in charge now, beautiful Pix. I'm leading this."

Thrashing against him, bringing her longing hips up against his, she practically wailed, "No!" She spread her legs so she could wrap them around him, trying to pull him to her. Trying to *make* him take her. But Beckett was too quick for her again. He firmly pushed her legs back onto the couch, one at a time, and covered them with his knees to keep her still. She fought again, breath heaving with her completely uncontrolled need, until his hand suddenly went right to that one spot she wanted him to touch more than anything. She instantly stopped struggling. As soon as his fingers touched her wet folds, Pix moaned. "Ah, yes, right there. Right there." Her voice was ragged.

Beckett groaned as his fingers explored her, one slipping inside and stroking her there while another gently twirled around her clit, driving her beyond wild. "You're so damned wet for me." The deep baritone of his voice was bracketed by a rough edge that teetered on the loss of control. His gaze held hers, strong and soft at once. "I can't hold back, beautiful. Need you now."

"Don't hold back," she demanded. "Get inside me, now. I need to feel you inside me." She was shamelessly begging and she didn't care. All she wanted was to have his gorgeous cock deep inside her, filling her with his hugeness, making her his. All his. "Beckett. I need to come." She barely whispered the words, already so close to the precipice but unable to fall over it until he was inside her.

"That's what you need from me, beautiful? Me deep inside you, filling you all the way?" His heavy-lidded eyes looked into hers as he stroked her, his long finger making a beckoning motion inside her.

She thought her head was about to shoot off her body from the sensation. Her hips rolled in time to the rhythm of his touch. All she knew right now was him, this gorgeous man holding her close, teasing her to the point of explosion with his deliciously talented finger. She needed to shatter apart right now, with Beckett inside her. Claiming her as his.

"Yes! Please," she whispered, her eyes locked on his.

"Pix," he groaned. "Anything for you. Everything for you."

He reached down to push her thighs apart, his fingers sliding along the slickness that had dripped there from inside her. Bracing his hands on either side of her, he looked at her with an expression that was purely feral. Hungry. Longing, and certain.

"Now," he growled, driving himself deep into her hot center, slamming into her with such stunning force they both cried out. Just as quickly he pulled back, then thrust in again. Pix was so slick that he entered her without any resistance. Beckett filled her completely, fitting inside her as if he'd been made to do so. As if they were made for one another.

He slammed in and out, holding her gaze the entire time. The relentless need on his face captured her, spiraling everything inside her higher, higher. She grasped his back with her hands, urging him into her again and again. Sheer lust shuddered through her entire body as Beckett's eyes, still brightly lit by the glow of his bear, kept her grounded in the moment that was about to explode her into a million spasms of pure joy.

"Pix!" he snarled, cupping her face with one hand so gently, even as he thrust into her so hard they both slid across the couch. Then he swelled inside her even more as his hard length suddenly spasmed again and again. Roaring out a deep, guttural noise, Beckett kept his eyes open and on hers despite the shudders wracking his body and the cries he didn't bother to rein in.

Then, fast and sure and fearlessly, he swung down his head and bit her hard on the neck, his suddenly sharp teeth breaking her skin, claiming her as his. Claiming her as his mate.

Pix tumbled right over the edge as her own orgasm slammed through her, making her scream. Her entire body lifted up, slamming back against Beckett even as his teeth still gripped her. Her fingers held onto his back, her body heaving and shaking with the glorious force of it. She cried out his name, followed by a sense-less babble of noise as the entire world seemed to explode into brilliant shards of light and a joy she'd never felt before.

Her mate. Her mate.

Slowly, so slowly, the rush of ecstasy gently ebbed away. In its place, a powerful wave of calm and connection spread throughout her. A sense of true belonging like she'd never felt before. Nuzzling at his neck, kissing him, she clung to him with a contentment that filled her very soul.

Only their heavy breathing surrounded them for long moments. Pix still felt aware of nothing else in the world but the sensations gently leaving her body, and the gorgeous man now gently settled on top of her. Slowly, she let the world come back in piece by piece, returning to her consciousness in small bursts of revelations as she remembered everything else that existed. She'd been so focused on Beckett and what they were doing that she'd literally tuned out all else.

He stirred, gently rubbing his stubbled face on her shoulder. "I'm halfway surprised we're still on this planet." His voice rumbled into her body. "I almost forgot it existed."

In answer, she just squeezed him closer. Beckett. Huge, sexy, strong, gentle and soft for her. Her mate. The beast that matched her beast. Her dragon softly rustled with agreement inside her. The man who felt comfortable and exciting at once, wild and docile at the same time. She traced mindless designs on his back with her fingers, feeling her breathing match his. Nuzzling her face into his neck, she murmured, "I know. I forgot, too. You're safe, Beckett North." She pushed her head back into the pillow so she could look into his face. "Safe, and mine. My dragon says you are mine. My mate."

His eyes, still bright, looked back at her with a smile in them. "My bear says the same about you. Mate," he whispered, the word filled with awe.

She sighed, feeling her face crack open into an enormous smile. "Well, then." Her voice stayed soft, but the strength in it echoed through the room with its crackling fire, the array of stars she could see through the floor-to-ceiling windows, the moving shadows of the pine trees outside. The cocoon-like feel of the whole place seemed—perfect. "I guess that means I need to stay here then, huh?"

Beckett stifled a yawn, his body heavy on hers. "You're definitely staying the night." He tightened his arms around her, nuzzling her back now. "I want to see your beautiful face looking up at mine in the morning."

Pix smoothed his back with her hand, marveling at the feel of his corded muscles rippling as he hugged her. "I mean," she said, feeling a sudden giddy joy spreading over her, "I need to stay here. With you, forever. In Deep Hollow, Beckett. If you're my mate, after all, I guess I need to stop wandering."

His arms froze around her, as if she were a fragile piece of porcelain he needed to handle with the most delicate care. "Stay? Restless Pix?" He pushed himself back, leaning up on both his arms so he could study her face, his own abruptly serious. "Tell me this is real. Because I don't do half measures. You're my mate, Pix, that's for sure. But I won't hold you somewhere you don't want to be, even if it kills me." His expression was a mixture of uncertainty, longing, and wild hope.

She nodded as her giddiness bubbled up into a smile. Pulling her hands out from under his arms, she reached up her palms to cradle his face. "Neither do I. Neither does my dragon." Her dragon bellowed and called inside her, firmly echoing Pix's joy with a steadiness she'd never before felt. "She says you're mine. She's meeting your strength head on with her own." She paused, then gently added, "And your bear? What does your bear think about this?"

Beckett paused, seeming to search inside himself. "My bear," he said in a wondering tone, "doesn't want to rip down walls and get so crazy I can't control him. My bear says you're mine. And that's making him quiet, because he's happy now. You're soothing the savage beast, Pix. You tamed my bear." Laughter rolled out of him, joyful and excited. She let it pour through her as well, until they both shook from it, laughing like happy lunatics at one another.

With one another. Forever.

"Well, okay then. Welcome to Deep Hollow, Pix," Beckett said after the burst of laughter finally faded away. "Welcome home, my gorgeous dragon shifter mate."

"Yes. I'm home." She let the contentment of that deep truth, its absolute rightness, fill her every cell and molecule. "Home with my sexy bear of a man. With my mate. Now, kiss me again, Beckett North. Make me forget my own name for a while."

Smiling, he leaned down to do just that.

I hope you enjoyed *Taming Her Bear*! Pix & Beckett
made me laugh, smile, and cry as I wrote them.

What's next for the Silvertip Shifters? Cortez & Haley's
story in **RESCUE BEAR: CORTEZ.** Turn the page to
read it.

RESCUE BEAR: CORTEZ

*O*ne pivotal scene could alter the course of Haley Adams' entire life. It needed to be the best damn one she'd ever written.

Fingers poised over the keyboard, immersed in the climax of the book in which the heroine was about to rescue the hero after he'd been cold-cocked by the bad guys when he'd come to rescue *her,* her pulse thrummed wildly. This was it, the magic was about to happen, she could just feel i—

BAM BAM BAM.

"Shit!" Haley whacked her knee on the underside of the table and almost fell out of her chair.

Someone pounded on the front door so loud it sounded like they were planning to bring the thunder right into the house. Her heart joined her pulse, galloping hard enough she was half afraid it might jump out of her chest. She looked at the big grandfather clock in the corner of the living room. Six-thirty in the morning. Who was out there scaring the crap out of her at freaking six-thirty in the morning? Making her lose focus on the book she had to finish, or else she'd lose the tiny toehold she'd fought so hard to gain during this past year of shitasticness?

A-ha. She remembered now. The property manager had told her he would come over today to fix a slow leaking pipe in the upstairs bathroom. Great. She hadn't thought he'd meant this early. Or that he wouldn't call her first to let her know he was on his way. Sighing as real life took over the made-up-but-oh-so-real-feeling one she'd been working on, she took a quick glance down at her clothes.

Oh, fabulous. She was wearing her favorite ratty orange robe over her fleece jammy bottoms, the red ones that had little purple and black penguins sprinkled all over. Better yet, she also had her big old fuzzy moose slippers, complete with antlers and huge eyes, shoved onto her feet. They were her good luck ones that she liked to wear when she was writing.

Basically, she looked like a disheveled madwoman.

Oh, well. She'd met the guy the day she came to town, when he'd shown her the house she would be sitting for a year while the owners, his parents, traveled around the world. He had struck her as polite, professional, and totally uninterested in her. Which was completely fine by her. After she'd had her entire life blown up last year, men were the last thing on her mind. All she cared about right now was working hard to write the best damned book of her career. It was clear all *he* cared about was making sure any handiwork that needed to be done to his parents' house while they were gone got taken care of. So neither one of them should care about her hair or her unfortunate choice in sleepwear. Plus, it was six-thirty in the morning. What else should she be wearing?

Automatically smoothing her hands over her hair anyway, she frowned harder as she realized it was in a ridiculously messy bun caught at the nape of her neck. Great. But she shrugged as she went to the door. Writers at work looked scruffy and neglected sometimes. Dude would have to deal.

BAM BAM BAM! She jumped again mid-stride as the pounding sounded once more, even louder. It sounded like it could crack the door in two.

So rude. Now she was just plain irritated. "Hold your horses!" As she yanked open the door, she started to say in a pointed voice, "You know, there's a perfectly good doorbell—oh!" She chopped off her words. "You're not the property manager." She stared at the mountain of a man standing outside the door.

Big, huge mountain man with golden-brown eyes and muscles that bulged out even from beneath his tawny shearling jacket. Hoooly shit. He was really, really big. Light brown hair cropped close, a bristly beard that spread over his lower cheekbones and chin that she really wanted to scrape her fingers through to feel the scratch of it, eyes that gazed steadily at her from beneath a tussle of eyebrows. Jeans that fit him well, scuffed up but nice cowboy boots on his feet, a collared blue checked shirt that opened up just enough at his neck to show skin. Did she mention that he was huge? He took up the entire doorway, which was already supersized. Wow. Bear shifters sure did make for big humans.

He stared back at her, seeming just as surprised to see her. A beat up black toolbox he held in one hand bumped gently against his thigh. There was a moment while they both just looked at one another, Haley's mouth open. Finally he shook his head, still looking at her like she was spotted with purple dots. "Not the property manager, no. I'm his brother. Cortez. He had something come up, couldn't make it. Said there's a leaky pipe that needs fixing?" His voice rumbled through her like dark gravel, shuddering through her body and sending sweet chills dancing up and down her skin that had nothing to do with the cold air outside.

Haley finally remembered both her manners and to shut her foolish mouth. She stepped back so he could come in. *Focus,* she ordered herself. Right. Men were not to be trusted. Not at all. But this one, though, oh, he was kind of interesting. He was big and sexy and smelled really good, all woodsy and manly, but not like fake cheap cologne. No, he smelled like an actual forest, like pine trees and deep, rich earth, with a streak of something wild running beneath it all.

Something wild like a bear shifter.

And here she was, wearing her ratty orange bathrobe with big fuzzy moose slippers on her feet. Great. Damn. She sternly told her inner girl not to care. Her world was all about her for right now, orange bathrobe and all. It had to be.

"Upstairs." She finally found her voice as he headed down the hallway with a quick stride, clearly familiar with the place and maybe in a hurry. "I'm Haley. I'm housesitting for your parents the rest of the year." Okay, stating the obvious. She clamped her lips down tightly so nothing else dumb could slip out.

Cortez stopped and turned back around to her. A slow, curious smile pulled at his lips, his eyes looking at hers with a careful friendliness that also seemed wary. *Well, that makes two of us, buddy.* Like he'd just thought of it, he reached out a big hand to shake hers. Although Haley had never considered herself to be a tiny woman, like her best friend Pix, she suddenly felt absolutely minuscule next to Cortez.

His hand wrapped around hers, warm and strong and just so darned big. "Sorry. That was rude of me to just barge in without properly meeting you." Ooh, his voice. Okay. She really liked it. "Hi, Haley. That's a pretty name," he added, almost as if it were an afterthought. But his eyes lingered on hers, like the faint smile on his face.

"Thank you." His searching gaze made her want to babble. "Actually, I always hated it because there was a girl in school more popular than me whose name was also Haley, and she told me no one was allowed to call me Haley. She was the only one allowed to be called Haley."

He tipped his head to the side, still studying her. "What did you do?"

Haley shrugged, somewhat self-consciously pulling her robe tight around her as if to shield the memory of nasty Haley, with whom she unfortunately had gone to school all the way through junior high. "There was nothing I could do about it. She was top of the heap, I was bottom of the heap. I tried once to speak up about it, but her little girl gang jumped me after school and slapped me around."

Now Cortez's eyebrows rose up, practically brushing his sandy golden brown hair. "Slapped you around? So they beat you up? But girl style?"

Haley couldn't help the snort that slipped out. "Girl style? What's that supposed to mean?"

Cortez leaned back against the wall, grinning. He lightly kicked the heel of one booted foot up behind him. "You know. Like a regular fight, but girl style. Slapping and pulling hair and stupid shit like that."

Haley's mouth dropped open again. Just before she snapped out an outraged protest, she noticed that while his words were challenging, there was a devilish little glint in his eyes. She narrowed her eyes back at him, but then her mouth smiled as she found a come-back. "Oh, I could show you girl style, but you'd end up knocked off your feet and all embarrassed because you'd lose all your street cred with the guys since a girl took you down." Teasing him back felt right. It felt comfortable.

Now Cortez laughed. Really laughed. Head thrown back, a deep, booming laugh rolling out of him and echoing around the room. Whoa, that kind of gave her the shivers. *Trouble,* Haley thought as she drank up every last detail about him. He was sexy. She could notice that, couldn't she? Didn't mean she would do anything about it. She'd just look at him and enjoy doing it. That was all.

"Haley," he finally said, laughter still teasing the corners of his mouth, "I don't have to worry about street cred with the guys. They all know I can wipe the floor with their sorry little asses."

Haley could definitely picture that. Then again, this was a shifter town, so… "I bet most of the guys around here are your size, though. And just as strong. And sort of—brawly. Right?"

Now Cortez folded his arms in front of him and studied her more critically, the teasing grin slipping off his face. "Uh-huh. So you know we're shifters."

Haley nodded, her fingers picking at the frayed end of her robe. "Yes, but I take it I'm not the only human in Deep Hollow who knows about you all."

In the very hallway they stood in, a large framed

photo that seemed to be a family group of grizzly bears hung on the wall. Six adults and two adorable little cubs. No normal human family would have photos like that on the wall. Then again, Haley's housesitting gig hadn't landed in her lap from a normal human family.

The Walkers were bona fide grizzly bear shifters, every last one of them. Elodie and Oberon Walker, the parents and owners of this house, had decided it was time for them to go have some worldwide adventure. They'd taken off to travel around the planet for an entire year, and in fact had left months ago. Their grown sons had apparently gotten their hands—their paws?—too full to keep watching over the place themselves, so Elodie placed an ad seeking a full-time sitter while they continued their worldwide adventure. It was a third honeymoon, she had confided in Haley with a girlish giggle during their Skype chat. Haley had swallowed at that. Bear shifters lived longer than humans. Quite a bit longer.

And Cortez here was one of them.

His gaze seemed to drink her up as well. She could almost feel the warm caress of it on her skin. Dang it. "Yeah," he said, "but they all grew up here. They've known about shifters their whole lives, just like their parents and grandparents and great-grandparents before them. But you're not from Deep Hollow. So how'd you find out about shifters, Haley the mysterious house-sitter?"

Haley giggled, then tried to swallow it. She hated it

when girls giggled, but she couldn't seem to help it around big, burly Cortez. Big sexy bear shifter, big sexy guy. "I'd tell you, but I can't just give away all my secrets at once, can I?"

She prayed that the Walkers, Cortez's parents, had not yet made true on their excited promise that they would tell everyone in town she was an author who wrote romance books. They were thrilled to have a real live writer staying in their house. But while she was proud of her work, she might die on the spot if Mr. Hottie Forest-Smelling McSexypants here wanted to read one with all the kissing and sex in it. Well, her one and only book at the moment, which wasn't even finished yet, let alone published. But Cortez just grinned back at her, shaking his head.

"I guess you can't," he agreed in a soft voice that rubbed over Haley's nerves like sweet, dark velvet. "Even so, I'm gonna find out some of your secrets, Haley. I have a feeling they might be worth it."

Silence spilled over them, but it wasn't awkward. It was close, warm, nice. *Safe.* That was new.

But safe didn't exist. That was one hard truth she understood. Carefully directing the conversation to more neutral ground, she said, "Do you know which bathroom it is? With the leaky pipe."

"Sure do. The guest one on the second floor." A cocky little grin now as he slowly pushed himself off the wall, bringing his alluring woodsy scent much too close to her. "So, pretty Haley. You need someone to show you around town? I know all the fun stuff to do. Adventures on the mountain, or parties in town. Whatever tickles your funnybone. What do you like to do?"

Taking a small step back from him, because that insanely sexy smell was going to her head and she couldn't be dumb, Haley nodded toward the desk she'd set up in the corner of the living room to be her workspace. "I like to write. I have to write, actually." She was babbling again, but she couldn't stop. "It's my work. My only work, the only work I know how to do. I write all the time, and it takes up a lot of time. About sixty hours a week, including all the marketing and management details. Well, there's no marketing yet. It's not published yet. But it will be. And then I'll have to work even harder." Whoa, stop, enough info. She snapped her lips shut and pasted on a smile.

Those sexy, thick eyebrows raised again. "Sixty hours a week? Shit, that's crazy. So all you do is sit at the computer all day? Come on, pretty Haley, there's not much fun in that. Where's your entertainment?" He slid a slow, easy grin at her. Careless, clueless grin.

The smile fell off her face like it had been slapped away. Utterly stung with something that hurt from way deep down, something that had nothing to do with this man because he wasn't *that* man, the one who had hurt her, but this hurt like crazy anyway for who knew what reason, Haley snapped back without thinking. "I have a perfectly active imagination and can entertain myself just fine with my stories, thank you very much."

A sudden smile burst over Cortez's features, lighting him up. "Uh-huh. Right. Mom said you write romance novels. Guess those are pretty entertaining. I hear they can be kind of hot." He winked at her. It was charming, cute, inviting. *He* was kind of hot.

Haley froze, little zips and zings of mixed embarrassment and some sort of wild attraction thing flickering through her body as he flashed another grin at her, then turned to go upstairs. She watched his sexy butt in those jeans as he climbed the stairs, her mind stuttering. Oh, my god, he really knew she wrote romance novels? And she just said they kept her entertained? Like, as in, physically entertained?

Haley never turned red from embarrassment. Instead, when she was on the spot or shocked about something, her mind usually froze up so she couldn't think of anything to say. No snappy comebacks from her. Great. Outed as someone who enjoyed the sexy times in her own books *and* unable to zing him back.

Mind still blank, she returned to her desk and plopped back down in the comfy office chair she'd hauled all the way out here from Boston, dismantled in the back of her car for the journey. She couldn't work without it. Then she stared at her manuscript open on the computer, paying way more attention to the sounds of banging upstairs. She imagined that big bear shifter up there with a hammer, pounding the errant pipe into submission. All she could think about were how big his hands were. Big hands. Really big hands. Which meant he also had a big—?

Nope. Stop. Stop right now. Her thoughts were confusing. He was confusing. Oh my god, she was losing her mind over a guy she didn't even know. What was wrong with her?

Scrubbing her hands over her face, she shoved away the direction of her thoughts and focused on her irritation. She was still pissed at how he'd brushed off her work ethic like it was nothing. She'd always been a hard worker. Always. And for the past several months she'd been working even harder than ever before, stretching her limits almost to the breaking point, learning something new, doing everything herself because she had to. Frowning at the screen, she stabbed out a few words with the keyboard, but they made no sense. Glaring, she highlighted and deleted them. Great. Now she couldn't even work because she was so mad at that big, galumphing, irreverent jokester of a bear up there, banging around her peaceful sanctuary and breaking her concentration.

Darned big, loud, nice, good-smelling bear shifter of a man.

By the time he jogged back down the stairs fifteen minutes later, Haley hadn't written a single word. She was ready to wring his big, distracting neck. Springing up from her chair as he strode to the front door, she marched after him. "You know," she blurted out to his bristly face, his warm eyes, the overall bigness of him as he turned in surprise toward her, "I don't have time to play while I'm here. That's not why I came here and took this amazing house-sitting opportunity." Passion exploded through her chest, making the words come faster. Why did she even care what he thought? But she did. "I work really hard! I have to. I have to support myself, I'm my sole support, and I'm building something from the ground up again because I have no choice."

He stared at her. Words tumbled and spilled from some place she hadn't realized still ached so much. "This is what I choose to do. It's my choice to work as hard as I do, and I like it. Life isn't all about parties and having fun, Cortez Walker." She said his whole name for effect as she pointed at him, then popped her fists on her hips, breathing hard, still frowning at him.

Feeling almost naked like she'd just shared something so deep with this guy, and she didn't even know him.

He stood still, just looking back at her. Face now expressionless. She waited for a cocky response. Or defensive anger at her sudden crazy girl act. Instead, something so shadowed and troubled dropped over his face that her breathing hitched. "Yeah," he finally said in a low voice. "Yeah, I do know that. Really well, in fact. Which is why I think having as much fun as we can before we die is so important. Because one day, without any notice, it's all over."

Wait, what? Haley's lower lip fell away from her

upper one. Oh, shit. She'd said something without knowing, and it had zinged him. But zinged the wrong way. The air between them was heavy and dark, like his voice. Behind her, the grandfather clock quietly ticked.

"No second chances to have fun, pretty Haley." His voice got softer, but still just as serious. "This life is your one and only shot, and there are no guarantees how long it will be. So." He cleared his throat and seemed to shake off the odd flash of darkness. "See you around town, maybe. Hope you get all the work done today that you need to. If that's what you want to do." A small twist to his lips that passed for a casual good-bye, then he was out the door, gently closing it, his steps quick on the stairs and then gone.

Gone, just like that. Leaving her with cryptic words. Words that made her suspect Cortez Walker might have just as much of a dark past as she did, one that was just as painful.

2

*C*ortez watched the clients as they stalked away from him, all graceful and panther-y like panthers supposedly were. Fucking *panthers,* his ass. He quietly snorted so they couldn't hear him. They'd said they were panthers from back east somewhere, nothing at all like the mountain lion shifters who lived here in Colorado. Yeah, whatever. Same damn things, but these two were insistent on being called *panthers,* like they were some kind of big cat royalty. And he'd pissed the hell out of them this morning by being an hour late. An entire hour. Fuck.

Quentin would kill him when he found out. Hell, Cortez was angry enough at himself about it. He'd been so late, when here he'd thought he'd be early, even be able to get in a little paperwork before the clients showed. But they'd been waiting for him at the lodge, tapping their feet as they sat by the roaring fire inside the main building, angrily drinking fancy coffees that Abby, Quentin's mate, had made for them. Gratis, of course, since their day had been upended by his being late.

Cortez the perpetually late, the irresponsible youngest of the family. Your basic screw up, if anyone asked his brothers. Awesome. He'd pasted on his best game face, apologizing and explaining that he'd forgotten he told them 7:30 am, he thought he'd kept it at the usual 8:30 am. But no problem, he'd add an extra hour to their Winter Wonderland Sleigh Adventure (cheesy name, but he was trying to collect customers with every hook he could use since he desperately needed the business) and all would be well. Right?

Oh, fuck, no. Nope. Too damned bad for him, they had to leave early today to catch their flight out of Durango, which was why they'd set the meet time an hour earlier. So he'd had to cart around pissy, snooty *panther* shifters all morning, showing them the "secret" spots up on the mountain with the most spectacular views of the snow-covered San Juan mountains sprawling out in every direction, perfect for pictures and snuggling under the blankets in the back of the sleigh while he sat up front, holding the long reins on the horses as they trotted and jingled through the snow.

Better yet, the horses who pulled the sleigh, Paxton the sweet gray mare and King Lear the grumpy sorrel gelding, who Cortez was sure was perpetually grumpy because he'd only been gelded a few years ago and probably remembered his stallion days with frustrated longing, had today of all days decided they didn't like the smell of big cat shifters. Even more fucking great. They'd been snorting, prancing, eye-rolling snots the entire time, sometimes lunging forward in their harnesses when one of the *panthers* had screeched with laughter at something the other said. He'd had a hell of a time controlling them while trying to pass off their behavior as high spirits due to the especially cold day.

Fucking panther shifters. Cortez decided he hated them. They needed to get their stuck-up asses back to Florida or wherever and never come back here again. Not that he could actually say something like that, ever. No, he had to grit his teeth and pull out his Cortez-the-bumbling-good-natured-bear-shifter schtick for these clients. The Silvertip Lodge belonged to his parents. It was one of the premiere shifter-only destinations in the whole country, beloved for its down-homey mountain feel and the fact that it was utterly secure. Shifters could roam around the hundreds of acres in their animal forms all day if they wanted to, and that was a huge draw. So not only would he never do anything to endanger the impressive business his parents had built up over the years from a start of absolute nothing, but his cash flow was close to nonexistent right now.

And the pissed off panthers hadn't even tipped him. Miserly jerks.

Fuck his life, sometimes. Fucking fried shit on a

shingle. He didn't even know what the hell that meant, but it usually summed up bad moments pretty well. He sighed and rolled his shoulders, trying to shake off the tense irritation. He'd been prone to irritation and snapping for months now. Even though he knew why, it was getting old. Really old.

The only thing keeping him going at this particular second was the pretty smile and careful, solemn eyes of that Haley girl the other morning, the house-sitter. He'd been so damn taken with her soft skin, her big green eyes, that wild mop of hair gathered into some kind of messy ponytail thing on her head, and her *laugh.* Her laugh was just so—pretty. So open. He'd spent longer minutes talking to her, teasing her, just to hear her voice. She was super cute. Even with that ridiculous orange bathrobe—orange, for crissakes, but she actually looked good in it—and the enormous fuzzy moose slippers on her feet. He wanted to—kiss her or something. Take her out. Show her around, like he'd offered. And she'd gone and gotten all huffy on him, defending her crazy work hours like they were all she had.

Cortez could tell her about work hours. About how work wasn't the only thing in life. About how life was about having fun, about enjoying it before it was over. Fuming, wishing he was having fun right now, he savagely locked the runners on the sleigh before turning to unhook the horses, who were still skittish. Which was ridiculous because they'd been raised up here at the lodge, like all the horses they had, so they'd be used to shifters from birth. Something had crawled up their butts today, and they'd just decided to react to the panthers.

Damn, he needed to get a handle on his temper today. He could feel his bear rumbling and snorting beneath the surface, driving his anger while also feeding off it. That was no good. Not at all.

"Hey!" a cheerful voice called out behind him.

Turning, he saw Abby walking over to him, a steaming mug of something in her hand. "I brought you some hot cocoa. And I tossed a slug of whiskey in it." Her voice was sympathetic as she handed him the hot drink. "Figured you might need a little pick-me-up after those two."

"You mean to give me strength for when Quentin finds out what an asshole I was today." Cortez took the drink with a grunt as a thank you, forcing out a lopsided grin. Abby was really cool. He had no gripe with her. She was a wolf shifter, from the insular wolf-only Black Mesa pack on the other side of the mountain, but she fit into the Silvertip bear clan like she'd been born to it. She also managed to keep Quentin from getting too riled up when his youngest brother pissed him off. Again.

Abby gave him another compassionate smile, then reached out to stroke King Lear's neck. The gelding had settled down now, looking like an innocent pussycat who'd never shy at anything.

Jerk.

"I'll try to head Quentin off at the pass for you," Abby said, leaning forward to kiss the gelding's soft red nose before turning to Paxton and gently rubbing behind the mare's ears, which were sweaty and probably itchy from where her headstall had been. "They already left a review on Yowl." She said it casually, not looking at Cortez, but he heard the careful note in her voice.

"In the past five minutes? Ah, fucking fried shit on a shingle." He yanked the straps off of Paxton more forcefully than he needed to. The mare cast him a wounded look. "Sorry," he muttered at her, which was dumb because she was just a horse, not a shifter. Even so, Cortez liked the horses. He wasn't a horseman, but ever since he'd officially taken over the lodge's sleigh rides in a bid to build up his own brand-new business, he'd spent enough time with them to start really enjoying their mostly quiet, calm equine company.

Horses couldn't give him shit like everyone else did.

"And?" He kept untacking, not looking at Abby. Yowl was the shifter app for business reviews, where everyone could review their favorite—or most hated—shifter establishment and let the entire rest of the shifter world know what they thought. Complete with growly faces of their animal avatars for a thumbs down.

Abby fidgeted, murmuring in Paxton's fuzzy ears as she rubbed them. Cortez chanced a sidelong glance at her. Sensing his gaze, she sighed and shook her head. "Well, they five-starred the lodge. They loved their stay here, and they plan to come back again."

"That's good," Cortez muttered, looking back at what he was doing. If he didn't pay attention, he'd tangle up the long reins and harness as he removed it from the mare's back. Untangling that stuff wasn't something he had time for today.

"But they weren't as thrilled with the lodge-recommended Tooth 'n Claw Tours. They gave it a snarling panther face."

Cortez clenched his jaw. He'd just begun his outdoor tour company last year. He couldn't afford a single bad review.

"They then proceeded to dismember your good name, with some choice comments about your attitude and tardiness." Abby gently chucked the mare under her chin, then looked at Cortez with a troubled expression. Her mate Quentin was the lodge manager, in charge while the elder Walkers were gone for the year. She liked Cortez, but her mate was her mate. Plus she worked here at the lodge now, so it was her reputation as well.

Cortez exploded. "My attitude? My attitude was just fine for those highfalutin *panther* shifters." He shoved as much disdain into the word as he could. "I bent over backwards being nice to their snobby asses. No way was my attitude off." He stomped over to the small tack room inside the barn to put away the harness.

Abby huffed in agreement. "I believe you, Cortez. I had to cater to their every need for the whole week. They were definitely a pain in the ass, and they're clearly more used to high-end places than a lodge like this." Her tone was arch.

Cortez began to protest, but she waved it off. "You know what I mean. The lodge is incredible, but they wanted major upscale pampering and ass-kissing." She gave a short, wicked little chuckle. "No one here is very good at that."

He settled the harness onto its wall hook. "That's for damn sure. We advertise as a great place to come and let your inner animal loose. We don't advertise that we're going to groom it and serve it caviar and bubbly on a silver platter every night at dinner."

Abby's own laugh rang out, lightening the mood more. "Definitely not. Anyway. I've got to get back inside, we've got some new guests checking in soon. Hang in there," she added, smiling at him as he emerged from the tack room with brushes in hand to use on the horses. "You went through something awful, and you're still working your way back." Her eyes on his were suddenly serious, though her voice was soft. "Quentin knows that. He might yell at you, but then he'll cut you some slack."

Cortez heaved a sharp laugh. Abby had taken him under her wing like the big sister he'd never had. She liked to mother him. But he knew better. Quentin would just kick his ass five ways to Sunday.

"Yeah, right. He won't think I deserve some slack." Starting with Paxton, he groomed her in small circles on her side with the curry, feeling her relax with a contented sigh under his hand. A small thunk sounded outside the barn as a pile of snow must have slid off one of the pine tree branches in the warming midday sun.

He could feel Abby's sharp gaze on him as he brushed the mare. "He's not the one who has to cut you the most slack, Cortez. That's on you." Her voice was firm.

Ouch. That stung. Surrogate big sister-type truth usually did. He listened to the sound of her footsteps as they crunched away back to the lodge, the drip of melting snow outside the barn, the snuffling sounds as King Lear nosed around for some hay.

In his head, he suddenly pictured Haley's pretty green eyes, her wild messy hair, the fiery defensiveness that covered up something small and hurting inside. Just like him, though he tended to cover his by going balls-to-the-wall with fun and adventure.

Cortez felt his bear rumble around inside him, like a dark shadow filled with brooding energy. Fuuuck. This was the darkest secret he carried right now. Sure, on the surface he was lighthearted, fun, living for the moment. And prone to fucking up left, right, and center. But that was because he was at polar opposites with his bear right now.

His bear was anger. Shame. Rage. Sadness. There was so much darkness inside him, he had to balance it somehow or else he'd go crazy. He couldn't let anyone see the angry bear inside. Not until he got his shit straightened out. If he ever did. Quentin would have his head, and every antsy shifter in town that wanted a good throw down would challenge him to a brawl that would end much worse than they usually did. Cortez had seen it happen with his best friend, Beckett, who was a cranky asshole on the best day. Beckett didn't have much control over his very dominant bear. It was why he pretty much hid out on the mountain, so he wouldn't destroy the town by losing control and rampaging through it as his savage animal with no restraint from his more rational human side.

Cortez couldn't, wouldn't, let his bear get to that point. Because if someone like pretty little Haley knew about the darkness buried inside him? He'd hurt her somehow. He wouldn't mean to, but he would none-theless. His bear was on a thin leash right now. She was cute enough, somehow fascinating enough, that he wanted to see her again. But he had to be careful. He could tell she already hurt from something. He wasn't about to add to that.

Swallowing more swears, shoving it all into his bear's dark threats rumbling deep inside him, Cortez pushed it all away. Stupid panther shifters, angry brothers, a business that might fail before he even got it off the ground. He needed to focus on right now, right here. Just brushing the horses, relaxed and quiet, until his bear subsided and all he was left with was a calm surface. The part of him that just wanted to go out and have a good time and forget about everything else. Especially the worst day of his life, the day that ended with pain and suffering and so much anguish he might explode from it.

He brushed the horses. Listened to the quiet of the day. Definitely thought about a cute girl with very pretty eyes and a big laugh. Yeah, he wanted to see her again, real bad. But it wouldn't matter anyway. Once she saw him, the real him, fucked up and going nowhere except downward in a spiral of anger and hurt, she'd run like hell.

No one would blame her for running. Least of all him.

3

*H*aley watched the beautiful winter landscape scroll out alongside the car as it slowly wound its way up the mountain. "It's so pretty here." She sighed with contentment. "Have you gotten used to how beautiful it is yet?"

Jessie laughed. "Not for a single second. I grew up in big cities, so any snow we ever got turned all grey and slushy and yucky in about two seconds. This place still blows me away every day."

"That sounds like Boston. Grey slush and dreary winter days. But this is just incredible," Haley murmured. She couldn't drag her gaze away from looking out the window, at the sun-dazzled white snow that lay heavy on the deep green pine boughs, the occasional glimpse of jagged white peaks farther in the distance. Of course she'd seen mountains before. But they were back east mountains, the soft, sloped ones of

New Hampshire she'd gone to for weekend ski adventures with friends. The hills were short, the views were mellow, and while nice enough, overall they had absolutely nothing on the wild, stunning beauty here. When she'd arrived in Colorado the other week, she'd been so bowled over by the seemingly endless mountain ranges, the big peaks, the snow-draped forests that probably stretched on for the length of two eastern states, she'd practically forgotten her own name.

Coming to Deep Hollow had been the best decision of her life. It was a lucky break that she intended to make the most of. Forget the past, and live for her new future in these beautiful mountains.

She drank in every detail as they drove upward to the Silvertip Lodge, the main shifter tourist draw of the area that also happened to belong to the Walkers. It was an entire landscape filled with adventure and excitement, all wrapped up in a crisp newness Haley desperately craved. She'd spent the last year in a nightmare. This was a sweet, incredible dream she'd finally been able to find. She only hoped she wouldn't suddenly wake up to realize it was just as false as the life she'd been forced to leave behind.

As Jessie steered the big truck around one more corner, she glanced over at Haley and smiled. "Your expression is just like the one I had the first time I saw all this. I feel so lucky I found this place. You will too." Her voice was cheerful and upbeat, just like she was.

Haley had met Jessie at the Mountain Muffin, a cute

little bakery that was the heart of Deep Hollow. She liked to split her time between writing at the house, with its privacy and peace, then heading to the Mountain Muffin at midday to soak up the energy whirling around her as she worked on the more mundane tasks of running an online, one-woman business.

Jessie worked as a barista there. The very first day Haley had shown up, Jessie had immediately smiled at her. "You're Haley, right? You're house-sitting for the Walkers? I'm Jessie. Welcome to Deep Hollow." She'd been so instantly friendly and likable that Haley naturally liked her. Jessie was also human, but she was the mother of a shifter son, both of them living with her shifter mate, Shane, up at Silvertip Lodge where Shane worked. She told Haley she'd lived here for about a year now and that she absolutely loved this little town and its boisterous yet extremely protective clan of bear shifters. In Jessie, Haley knew right away she'd found a new friend.

Jessie had been fascinated to find out that Haley had already known about shifters, since she herself had never heard of such a thing until her son was born and she noticed something different about him. Luckily for her, her best friend was originally from Deep Hollow and immediately knew what was going on when single mother Jessie had told her that her infant son, who'd been born from a weekend fling, sometimes growled like an animal. Although Jessie curiously pried for how Haley knew about shifters, Haley was reluctant to share with anyone exactly how she'd found out about Deep Hollow.

Her best friend, Pix, was a dragon shifter who'd partially renounced her heritage. But that wasn't Haley's story to share, and Pix kept her shifter side a secret from most. So she just vaguely said that she knew a shifter back in Boston who'd hooked her up with the shifter-only online message boards through which the Walkers had been seeking a house-sitter. That was the truth. Jessie had easily accepted that, not pressing for more details.

"I think it's amazing here," Haley murmured now. "I definitely feel very lucky already."

They rounded one more corner of the road, and suddenly a scatter of cozy brown log cabins, a barn, then a building that dwarfed all the rest, which must be the main lodge, came into view. Haley sucked in a breath, swiveling her head around to take it all in as Jessie drove them toward the large building. Nestled into a small valley beneath the imposing brow of the mountain above, which she knew was called Silvertip Ridge, the mountain lodge was spectacular but not overwhelming. The place felt cocooned in the safety of its little valley, yet at the same time it also opened up to the wide open sprawl of the mountains beyond. Haley got a sudden little shiver down her spine, then another, as she realized that *bear* shifters ran around back there. All kinds of shifters, actually. This place was the ideal mashup between meeting the needs of the human side of shifters as well as the animal side. Haley had to admit she didn't really know any shifters at all except Pix. And Pix wasn't a bear.

Suddenly, Jessie's delighted laugh rolled out. "There they are! My cub, and my man." Devotion and pride filled her voice.

Haley turned to look where Jessie pointed. Involuntarily, she gasped, her eyes widening as her brain stalled out. Charging across the snowy grounds, directly for them, was a little bear cub, an actual bear cub, all cute and roly-poly and sort of disjointed as he ran in that little baby creature way. He was followed by an absolutely giant grizzly bear. A grizzly bear that had to be Jessie's mate.

She found herself wondering if Cortez, that sexy, sexy man she'd met the other morning, would be as big as this bear. Be as fierce, and strong. She couldn't stop thinking about him, which half bugged her and half keyed her up. Even though he'd left on that sad, dark note, a note that jostled into her own deepest fears and told her he had fears of his own, what she most remembered about him was his deep laugh and the sparkle in his eyes. She couldn't help but wonder if he was up here somewhere. He was a Walker, after all.

Jessie coasted the truck to a stop on the side of the road. Opening the door, she jumped out and fearlessly went straight for the huge grizzly and the little cub, clearly joyful as she knelt down and spread out her arms wide so the little bear could run right to her.

Haley just stared at the improbable but totally adorable scene, frozen to her seat with excitement and wonder. The next second, the little bear abruptly morphed into a little boy, probably around two years old, butt naked and giggling cheerfully in the freezing cold January weather. He leaped barefoot out of the snow into his mother's arms, flinging his own little arms around her neck and squeezing her tight.

Haley rubbed her eyes, blinking. Whoa. She'd met the little boy, Grant, at the Mountain Muffin several times, but there he'd always been in human form. And while she'd seen her friend Pix change into her dragon before, and it was amazing, she'd also been seeing it since they were both in elementary school. She was kind of used to it. Haley had never in her life seen bear shifters before. Her mind soaked in the details even as at the same time it could only unimaginatively come up with *Wow* as a descriptor.

The adult grizzly bear gently whuffled his nose over the boy's head, then equally gently nuzzled the top of Jessie's. Jessie reached out to rub the golden fur between the bear's fierce eyes, completely unafraid. Grinning, she gestured back at the truck, half turning to wave at Haley. Haley waved back, still nonplussed. The giant bear turned his head toward the truck, letting out a muffled roar that she really hoped was a greeting. He gently nudged Jessie one more time before turning and loping toward some sort of maintenance shed tucked around back behind the lodge.

Jessie stood up, naked little boy held tightly in her arms, and came back to the truck. She slid in, beaming at Haley. "Shane will say hi later, over lunch. We decided you didn't need to be freaked out too much just yet, so it would be better to meet him when he's human. And when he has clothes on."

"Uh—sure. Clothes are good." Haley's voice was a squeak.

Jessie laughed over her son's babbles. "I felt the same way when I first saw them in their shifted forms. Come on, let's get up to the lodge. Abby will have lunch ready for us. It'll just be sandwiches and soup probably, but it will be good. And you can meet everyone finally." She put the truck back into gear and they rumbled the remaining hundred feet up to the beautiful main building.

Her head still whirling from seeing the bears, Haley murmured a delighted "Ooh!" at the sight of the stunning lodge. Huge windows spread from floor to ceiling while a wrap-around deck the size of the Titanic ran the full length of the building. Stately pines, the ones Haley had learned were ponderosas, rose to dramatic heights on either side, their limbs covered with sparkling snow. Jessie pulled up and parked in the lot beside the lodge, shifting Grant in her arms as she got out of the truck and headed toward the front doors. Haley followed up the cleared walkway, which lined by fluffy piles of snow all the way. It was fairytale beautiful here.

When they reached the doors, she made a noise when she saw the carvings in the wood. Jessie smiled at her. "Pretty neat, huh? The lodge is open to all shifters, but it's a reminder that this is native bear country."

On the upper panels of the gorgeous oak doors, huge carved silvertips, or grizzly bears, stood on ridges surveying their domain before them. On the panels below, enormous grizzly paws decorated the wood, carefully etched in by a master hand. "Those are the actual paw prints of the boys," Jessie said as she pushed open the door. "Shane's is down there," she added, pointing proudly to what clearly was a newer carving. "He just moved back here a few years ago, but he's part of the Walker clan since he's a cousin. He got to have his on there too."

Driven by sudden impulse, Haley asked, "Which one belongs to Cortez?"

"Cortez?" Jessie gave her a funny look. "I didn't know you knew him already. That's his." She pointed to a block in the middle of the left door. "You can tell because he's missing a claw tip."

Haley blinked at that. "Really? I thought shifters could, uh, heal really quickly."

Jessie shrugged as she maneuvered herself and her squirming son through the doorway. "He was born that way. He's always been a little different. Abby!" she called out, waving at a blond woman behind the enormous reception counter. "I brought a new friend for us.

Abby's a wolf shifter," Jessie added. "Her mate is Quentin."

Abby had almost immediately come forward to coo at Grant, who said something that sounded like "AmmyAwwy!" Abby smiled at Haley, who couldn't help but stare for a second too long. She was pretty sure she'd never before met a wolf shifter, either. But Abby didn't seem to notice. She said in a genuinely friendly voice, "Welcome to the Silvertip Lodge, Haley. I've heard all about you. We all have."

Haley sighed. The quiet life of a writer had some-what eluded her here. But at the same time, it was sort of nice. Everyone seemed to want her to belong, even though she was just the house-sitter. They were welcoming and friendly. It was a tight-knit yet accepting community like nothing she'd ever experi-enced before.

Abby turned to the man who was taking her place behind the reception desk, saying, "It'll just be an hour, Joe, thanks." The man cheerfully flicked two fingers from his forehead at her in an *aye-aye, cap'n* sort of way, then cast a friendly yet curious look at Haley. She gave him a shy smile in return, wondering if he too was a shifter, then picked up her steps to follow Abby and Jessie as they went down the hallway. Grant walked between them on his own two legs, still stark naked.

No one seemed to notice or care that he didn't have clothes on in the middle of the winter. Then again, they were bear shifters. She knew they had a totally different metabolism and internal temperature than humans. The cold must not bother him at all. As they entered the small dining area, which by the casual, somewhat messy look of it appeared to be for staff only, she couldn't help her curiosity. "Jessie, would you let him run around like this in town too? I know everyone in Deep Hollow knows about shifters. But he's starkers."

Jessie giggled, but Abby answered, smiling as she gestured for Haley to sit down at the table. "No, not in town. It took a while for me to get used to it up here too. The pack I'm from lives closer to humans, even though on the pack estate there is a lot of privacy. But only members of that pack are usually there. So it's different up here. Here at the lodge, we welcome all kinds of shifters, from all over the world." Abby busied herself ladling out a hearty-smelling soup from the giant pot bubbling away on the stove in the corner. "I knew the lodge existed, of course, but I never actually came here until I met Quentin."

"Did I hear someone sexy and amazing just say my name?" Haley looked over as a big guy, Cortez's brother as well as her house property manager, walked in. He raised his eyebrows when he saw her sitting there, but nodded cordially. "Haley. Good to see you here." Even so, he gave Jessie and Abby a questioning glance.

Abby, who was walking the soup bowls over to the table, leaned over to brush her lips on his cheek for a lingering moment before she answered. "This girl works her tail off, even when she's hanging out at the Mountain Muffin all afternoon. Jessie's told me so. She's landed here for a whole year. Jessie and I decided it'd be good for her to come see the lodge and meet all of us."

Before Haley could say more than hello back to Quentin, a rush and tumble of enormous men sauntering into the room distracted everyone.

"Who wants to meet all of us?" The owner of this voice, a tall man with dark hair and that somewhat feral vibe Haley had come to associate with bear shifters, strode straight over to Jessie, whose face exploded into the same joy and happiness it had worn outside with the bears that were her mate and son. This must be Shane. Haley couldn't help a wistful stare as Shane kissed Jessie with all the possessive passion of a man who hadn't seen his woman in weeks, let alone about five minutes ago. Grant waved his chubby arms at Shane, obviously still recognizing Shane in his human form. And clothed, Haley noticed. Good thing he was. She was pretty sure Jessie was right and she wouldn't have had the grace to handle seeing naked adult guys running around all over.

That fascinating Cortez, though. Hmm. She might not entirely mind seeing him striding around buck naked. He'd be so big, and those legs like darned tree trunks, and that broad chest of his—

Nope. Not going there. She turned her head away. What Shane and Jessie had looked real enough, but it was also still painful to watch. Even so, she wondered where Cortez was in this gaggle of Walker bear clan guys. She also couldn't help thinking again about the sexy gold stubble on his face and what it might feel like against her cheek.

"If she wants to meet the clan of the wild and crazy, then she's come to the right place," Quentin said. His voice was mild, but Haley caught an irritable undercurrent. She remembered his mother, Elodie, had told her that Quentin was in charge of the lodge, as well as all his hooligan younger brothers while the elder Walkers were gone. Almost all of them were somehow involved with the running of the lodge. If they were all like Cortez, poor Quentin probably had a tough time reining them in.

It was probably impossible to rein in a guy like Cortez.

The noise level in the room turned way up, everyone chattering and laughing and just taking up so much space. If Jessie hadn't been right here with her, if Abby hadn't been so friendly and welcoming from the beginning, Haley might have wanted to leave the room and go hide. The energy in here boomed and ricocheted, amping up the entire space. So much suppressed wildness in all these huge men. She could sense it from Abby, too, though hers seemed more contained. Haley knew it wasn't just male testosterone filling the room. It was fierce, untamed shifter energy, brimming and curling through the room with its strength and innate power. Pix was very powerful, but her energy was more controlled. This bordered on half savage, invigorating as well as intimidating.

Abruptly, another energy tumbled in through the doorway, pulling Haley's attention like a magnet. She breathed in hard as she turned around.

Cortez.

He rolled into the room, feeling just as energetically wild as the others, but also like he had some sort of anger lashing beneath everything. Then his eyes landed on Haley. She almost choked on her breath from the sheer power of his gaze. His anger seemed to ease off and a surprised smile swept over his face. They'd left on such a strange note full of mystery and confusion, but now it felt good to see him.

Before he could say anything, another dang huge guy entered the room, followed by a pair of kids who immediately ran over to Grant and swooped him up in their arms, all three giggling at once. This guy paused when he saw Haley, his eyes narrowing. She took a nervous half step back. There was no mistaking the animosity in his gaze. It was disconcerting because he looked similar to Cortez. He must be another brother.

"Who's this?" Ooh, nope. His voice was definitely not friendly. The air seemed to chill.

Jessie, paying more attention to Grant's giggles as the two new children tickled his belly and the soles of his bare feet, said through her own giggles, "Hey, Riley. Meet Haley, the house-sitter."

Haley drew breath to say a pleasant hello to Riley, even though her entire being felt suddenly pinned by his decidedly not happy presence. Pinned like a helpless butterfly to a board, unable to escape. He didn't want her here. Why? He strode to the center of the room, staring at Haley with a look that she could only think of as being predatory. The greeting died in her mouth. Though she managed to stand her ground, she quailed back. Holy crap, he was not happy to see her. She didn't even know who he was. Cortez. Where was Cortez? She opened her mouth to ask him for help, but her mouth had dried up into something that felt like desiccated twigs.

Rocking to a halt in the center of the room, arms down at his sides, fingers slowly curling, Riley snapped, "Haley. Yeah, I know who you are. The writer. The one who likes to tell secrets."

The dark, angry thread beneath his words thunked sudden silence into the room.

"That's why you came here, isn't it? To spy on us?" His words came out flat, but with an edge beneath them. He leaned forward. She saw something not human lurch in his eyes, and she thought she might piss her pants. "You want to tell our secrets, expose our home to the whole world so more fucking humans who want to murder our kind will come here, isn't that right?"

4

*F*ucking Riley and his shit. Cortez instantly saw red at his brother's asshole move. That sweet, pretty Haley was standing stock still, clearly terrified. Cortez had instantly sensed Riley's simmering antagonism directed right at her the second his brother came in the room. His bear roiled beneath his skin, pushing hard at him. Cortez was on Riley's heels, a breath behind his brother as Riley got too close to Haley. Much too close to her with his ugly temper. Lunging the last step forward, he grabbed Riley's shoulder amidst the shocked silence in the room, yanking him back.

"Watch your mouth." A snarl underscored Cortez's words. The snarl of his bear shoving through his throat, threatening to lunge out and draw blood from his own brother if he had to. Teetering on being out of control. "She's no spy, and that's no way to greet her. Apologize to her right this second, asshole."

Jessie had clutched Grant to her, as well as Riley's own children, wide-eyed from where she crouched on the floor. Even though she'd lived here for a year, even though her own mate and her own son were shifters, overt displays of shifter aggression still frightened her. Abby was aghast, her mouth open with one hand over it. Yet her eyes were laced with sympathy. She knew why Riley was being such a prick. They all knew. But Abby had more kindness in her than Cortez felt like sparing for his brother right now. Quentin swung his head sharply toward Riley, opening his mouth, but Abby reached out to catch him by the elbow. Cortez more sensed than saw her shake her head at her mate. For some reason, she didn't want him to interfere.

Riley yanked his shoulder away from Cortez, still not taking his eyes off Haley. She'd turned bone white, but didn't move an inch. Beautiful, bold, strong woman, even in the face of danger like this. Cortez snarled again, shoved his way forward to push his bulk between her and his brother. She had no idea what was going on. She wasn't a fair target for Riley's anger. "Back off," he warned again, now staring down Riley, cutting off his brother's glare at Haley. "She's not here to cause trouble. Mom and dad would've known. They vetted her within an inch of her life."

Ragged silence still held the room. Ugly and sad, it

smothered everything and everyone there. Grant had stopped his giggling, and Laney and Finn, Riley's cubs, had also fallen silent, staring at their father. Cortez forced himself to take a breath. He needed to chill in order for this to go well. Leaning forward and lowering his voice, he grated out, "Riley, we get it, man. We all do. But she's not a bad human. Now apologize to her so we can have some fucking lunch like the civilized family we are."

Laney suddenly giggled. "Cortez, you said fu—"

"Delaney Walker, knock it off," Riley barked, though he didn't lower his baleful gaze from Cortez. "When you're older you can cuss up a blue storm, but not till then."

Finn snickered, causing Laney to elbow him in the ribs. Riley snapped again, a sharp, "Behave. Both of you." The cubs settled down.

For a long moment, Riley still stared hard at Cortez, who glared back, unmoving. Finally, Riley moved his gaze to Haley, leaning his head to the side so he could see her around Cortez. Another long, breathless moment of tension held the frozen room before he muttered, "I apologize, Haley." His voice was short. "I don't trust human strangers in our town."

He sharply bit off any more words. Finally turning away from her, which made Cortez relax, Riley strode over to the counter where makings for sandwiches had been laid out. With jerky movements, he began making himself a sandwich, stepping away from the burst of tension he'd created.

Cortez held his temper, reined in his bear's roaring as best he could. This was as good as it was going to get for Riley. For his whole screwed-up clan. Savagely, uselessly, he wished Haley hadn't seen this side of them. Maybe she *would* write about this kind of shit. Put it in her books or whatever.

Turning to look at her still-wide eyes, he somehow knew she wouldn't. Ever. She was a good person. She wasn't one to tell secrets that weren't hers to tell.

After another beat of heavy silence, Abby said in a determined tone, "Let's eat."

Haley still seemed shaken, face pinched. Cortez cursed Riley again in his head, though he managed not to say anything out loud. As everyone else began to chatter again, he looked right into her eyes, trying to read what was going on behind them. "You okay?"

Haley's teeth caught at her upper lip. Cortez couldn't help staring at those full lips before he yanked his gaze up to her eyes again. Such a pretty green and still big, they looked shadowed. She finally nodded, slowly. "Yes. Or I will be. He was scary," she added in a whisper.

"He can hear you, you know," Jessie piped up. Looking calmer now, she'd stood up again, still holding a wriggling Grant. "Their hearing is a lot better than yours and mine."

"We can fix that," said Shane, curving a possessive hand around his mate's waist. His tone was also relaxed, though he'd tensed up like everyone else. But looking at his mate and his son, he was calm. Cortez envied that sort of easy peace.

Jessie arched a brow at Shane, though she smiled at him. She curved a hand up on his cheek.

"How could that be fixed?" Haley asked, less nervous. She shot a quick look at Riley's back. "I'm not fishing. I'm genuinely curious."

Riley shrugged his shoulder, focused on making his sandwich. Another drop of tension welled, but it was quickly covered by Abby again ordering everyone to make their sandwich and have their soup before they had to get back to work. Low chatter started up again, getting louder as the cubs stampeded toward their father and pushed in to make their own lunches.

"Shane wants me to turn," Jessie answered Haley's question, jiggling Grant on her hip.

"Roast beef, babe?" Shane asked Jessie. Jessie nodded, and he went over to make a sandwich for his mate.

"Turn?" Haley looked at Jessie, clearly lost. She looked so innocent here, in the midst of his clan's craziness. Cortez felt the weirdest wave of possessive protection wash over him as he watched her.

"Be turned into a bear." The words were simple, but enormous. Cortez knew that Jessie had been considering being turned for a year now, though she'd been hesitating. It was a huge step. But he looked at Haley to see her reaction.

"Ohhh," Haley said, her eyes going even wider.

"Yeah," Jessie agreed softly, smiling down at Grant. "Ohhh."

"You'll be an amazing bear," Shane called out as he squirted mustard onto his mate's sandwich.

Cortez watched Shane for a second, then looked at Haley again. "You hungry? I'll make your sandwich." He felt kind of bashful offering it, but she nodded, the side of her mouth curving faintly into a smile. Damn, now he felt all puffed up like it was the most important job he'd ever do.

"Yes. Thank you. Is there turkey?" Her voice was quiet, so quiet in the loud of this room. But less tense now.

"Hell yeah, there's turkey. I'm making Haley's sandwich," Cortez announced to the room at large, like he'd been challenged. He marched over the counter and shoved both Riley and Shane. Riley glared at him but didn't press it. Cortez knew his brother was trying to keep calm in front of his children.

Abby, being a good-natured diplomat as usual, said, "That's nice of you, Cortez." But there was a speculative undertone in her voice.

Cortez shrugged. "It's to make up for Riley being a dick."

Shane laughed, eyeing Riley as he finished making lunch for his mate and himself. "Nothing can make up for that. Especially not making a sandwich."

Riley had relaxed more. He elbowed Shane, hard. The two of them engaged in an elbowing, shoving, foot smashing battle for a minute, to the sound of the cubs laughing and Grant's baby giggle-shrieks. Even Abby laughed. The tension in the room dissolved completely away.

Cortez made a sandwich for himself once he finished Haley's, keeping out of the line of elbows and boots. His cousin Shane was good for the clan. He'd once been a big brawler, fighting on the underground shifter rings, but finding his mate and son had changed him. Softened his rougher edges. He liked to be a peacekeeper now. He'd definitely kept the peace a lot of times. Cortez really appreciated that he was doing it now.

Maybe someday he too would be as valuable to his clan, rather than just the fuck up they usually saw.

Carefully, he carried the sandwiches back to Haley, each one set onto a paper towel. He snagged two travel mugs of hot cocoa from the counter too. Abby usually put hot drinks into travel mugs because this time of year everyone liked to take them back out to whatever they'd been working on and enjoy them through the day.

Haley smiled at him in thanks, which was pretty awesome and made the rest of the bullshit in the room disappear. Her smile was just so damn gorgeous. She took a couple bites of her sandwich, swallowed them, murmured how good it was. Her face, though, was still drawn, her laugh nowhere to be found. Cortez ate his own sandwich in silence for a few minutes, watching her carefully. She was still scared, and she shouldn't be. He frowned. Whatever was happening with her had to do with more than what had just happened here.

He glanced over the room, filled with his boisterous family, his family's mates and children. It was a bustle of energy and commotion, just like always. Everything had gotten back mostly to normal, though Abby and Jessie glanced over at Haley more than once, their expressions concerned.

Cortez made up his mind in a split second. He wrapped the rest of his sandwich in the paper towel, then stood up. Haley looked at him, puzzled. "Come on," he said. "This is great here and all, but you haven't seen the whole place yet, have you?"

She shook her head, slowly wrapping her sandwich in her paper towel even though she still looked confused.

"I'll show you around. I know a good spot where we can finish our lunch. It's not windy today, not that cold right now. Bring your jacket and gloves and all that. Okay?" Carefully, he extended a hand to her.

Haley looked at his hand for a long moment, then up at him. She still seemed somewhat wary, but he knew it wasn't aimed at him. Finally, she nodded. "Okay."

Her voice was quiet, but when she reached her hand out to his, her grasp was certain. Grinning, Cortez gently tugged her up out of the chair. "If you want to stay up here, Jess," he called out, "I'll take Haley back to town later."

Jessie nodded, a small smile playing across her face. But all she said was, "Sure. Have fun."

Cortez didn't let go of Haley's hand. This, he decided, felt damned good. Being with Haley felt good. He didn't know why, but she was someone he wanted to know.

Even more importantly, he wanted her to know *him.* Squeezing her hand gently, he led her outside. The way she let him do it, totally trusting him, made him feel like a fuckin' hero. Maybe for once, he wouldn't fuck something up.

5

*W*hen Cortez finally let go of her hand so she could shrug on her jacket just before they went outside, Haley's fingers tingled and felt kind of cold. Holding his hand felt good. *Danger,* her mind shouted at her. She shrugged her shoulders as she pulled on her jacket. So what? It was just holding hands. Just a physical thing, nothing more. It felt nice, like a good man should feel. *No danger,* she thought sternly back at herself. Then she giggled out loud because she was talking to herself in her mind.

Cortez glanced at her as he easily ranged by her side, gesturing toward a clear path that led toward the cute little cabins in the distance. A wide smile broke over his face. "What's funny?"

She liked the way his voice sounded. Every time he spoke, she enjoyed it. "Nothing really. Just having a conversation with myself in my head. It's kind of silly."

He grinned over at her and shook his head. "That's okay. We've got plenty of crazy around here. Trust me, you'll fit right in." His smile slid away a bit and his voice got more serious. "Sorry about that back there. It was a dick thing of him to do. It had nothing to do with you. Trust me, that's all Riley's—stuff."

Sunlight scattered around them as they walked through the bracing air. "He seemed really mad. I've never been that close to an angry bear shifter before."

"Have you even been that close to any angry shifter before?" He sounded genuinely curious.

Haley nodded. "Yeah, but not when they were angry at me. Was Riley—" she hesitated for a long moment, trying to frame the words right. Cortez didn't push, just waited in an easy way that made her feel relaxed. "It sounded like humans have caused some bad trouble here. For him in particular?" Cortez's knuckles just brushed the back of her hand as they walked side by side, warming her.

He sighed. "Yeah. A long time ago, when his cubs were about Grant's age."

As he spoke he gave her a long, assessing look. She looked back at him, quietly letting him examine her. She had no idea what he was about to say, so she shouldn't have anything to hide. Finally he blew out a long breath, one that mingled sadness as well as a hint of the anger that Riley carried like a brightly burning torch. "It was his mate. She was hunted down and shot by humans."

Haley gasped, stopping dead on the pathway to stare at Cortez in horror. He stopped too, looking at her steadily, his eyes darkening. "They were hunters," he said in a careful, almost bland voice. "But not hunters like you think most humans are, like going out and shooting animals for food or for sport. These were shifter hunters. They're humans who know about us, hate us, and deliberately stalk us to kill. They don't want us to exist. Some of them somehow found out about Deep Hollow and came here. They flushed out Riley's mate when she was out alone with the cubs. We figured they must have been watching her for days."

Haley's blood ran cold even though Cortez's voice remained flat as he told the terrible story.

"She stashed the cubs in their bear form up in some ledges on the other side of the ridge. Told them not to move, not to make a sound, practically not to breathe until someone they knew, from their clan, came to get them. No one else. Then she ran, in her bear form, leading the hunters away from her cubs. She could have taken them on herself, easy, except they had guns. They shot her in cold blood. They knew what she was, and they murdered her. Luckily it was far away enough that the cubs didn't have to see it, but they heard the shot. It still haunts him sometimes in nightmares." As he said that part, Cortez's voice finally cracked.

Tears burned in Haley's eyes and her throat choked. Her voice also a cracked whisper, she forced out, "No wonder he looked at me like he might hate me." She remembered the cold, haunted look in Riley's eyes as he'd glared at her.

Cortez shook his head, hard, reaching his hands out to gently grasp her arms. His grip was warm, strong and sheltering. "No way. He doesn't hate you. He doesn't even know you. It's just like he said, he has a hard time trusting anyone anymore. It's been years, but he can't shake it. He barely trusts the humans here now, even though he knows not a single one of them would ever do anything to expose us. Half the humans in town are mated to shifters anyway. But knowing that you're a writer, and that you already know about shifters—"

Haley shook her head. "I would never, ever write about shifters. I don't even know much of anything about them. My one shifter friend told me a lot of stuff, but not about bear shifters. I don't know anything about bear shifters." The shocking pain of the awful story still iced through her. "I don't know anything about you and your kind, Cortez. And I don't even like saying it that way."

He gently squeezed her arms, then let go. But his eyes still held her. "Saying it what way?"

"Your kind. Like you're different than me. Like you're *other*." She looked into his eyes, searching for the bear in them. But all she could see was the strong yet gentle man. Riley hadn't been right about her. She wasn't here to spy on shifters. But she somehow desperately wanted Cortez to know all her secrets.

Cortez crooked up the side of his mouth and one eyebrow, turning and gesturing up the path with his chin that they should keep walking. "We are different, Haley. That's why you got scared. He scared Jessie, too. It's one of the reasons why Shane wants her to turn. So she'll be stronger, so she can protect herself if she needs to. But he won't force it. It'll only happen if she wants to."

They walked in easy silence for another minute before Haley ventured, "Is that common? Like if a human gets together with a shifter, the human eventually wants to become a shifter too?"

Cortez shrugged. "A lot of them do. It can be easier that way."

Haley watched her footsteps for several strides, letting herself get lost in the way they crunched the snow and kicked up a few flakes of it now and then. "I thought about it a lot. I mean," she stumbled, "not that I would actually do it. But I have tried to imagine what it would be like." Her voice was wistful. "To be able to shift into something that wild and free and fierce. It would be so incredible. Even though it also seems really intense."

"It is, sometimes. Here." Cortez stopped suddenly at a narrow, snow beaten-down path that led off deep into the woods. "We're going this way."

Haley stared down the path somewhat suspiciously. "Where are you taking me?"

He laughed, that deep, easy rumble of sound that

seemed to roll over her very skin. Ooh, she liked it. A lot. "An overlook. You'll really like it. We can finish our lunch there." The path was just wide enough for two people abreast. He started down it, reaching down again for her hand, gently tugging her forward.

A smile rippled over her face. Cortez was a giant, yes. He was a big, ferocious bear shifter. But despite that, she instinctively felt completely safe around him. She trusted him with wherever he was taking her.

As they walked through the tall pines, some of which Haley recognized as Engelmann spruce with their blue-tipped needles and the towering ponderosas with trunks huge enough that even a group of people would barely be able to put their arms around them, she listened to the quiet sounds around them. Their feet crunching on the snow, the occasional light, warbled call of a bird in the distance, one or two muted bursts of sound from behind them that might've been vehicles starting up or doors slamming or people laughing. The sharp air held the crisp, clean scent of the outdoors that she'd come to love during the past week she'd been here. She was already in love with the little town below, and now she thought she also could fall in love with these wild, big mountains.

"It is so beautiful up here." She used a hushed voice, not wanting to break the silence, but unable keep her happiness at the simple moment to herself. "Do you live up here? Or in town?"

"I've got a place in town, but it's just a rental. I'm working on building my house."

She was impressed. "A man of many talents. Is your house down in town too?"

Cortez shook his head, the shadowed light that cut through the branches of the trees overhead glinting on his hair. "It's halfway between town and up here. It's great up here and all that, but I never worked full-time at the lodge like the others do. I wanted some distance."

"So how far along on it are you?" she asked. There was a pause. She looked at him again and caught a flash of something on his face that she couldn't quite read. She waited quietly, just like he'd done for her earlier. But instead of answering, he pointed ahead of them.

"There's our lunch spot. Go on and take a look, pretty Haley."

Haley looked and inhaled with quick delight. Ahead of them, the little trail through the trees suddenly opened up in bright sunshine, seeming as if it dropped off into nothing but blue sky. She sped up, eager to see the special place this big, different, interesting guy wanted to take her. Funny how her ex, Justin, never liked to take her anywhere. She frowned away the unwelcome memory of him and looked ahead. Cortez chuckled behind her, but his footsteps quickened as well. Grinning, she trotted the last few yards to be sure she got there first. But when she was just past the trees and could see what opened up in front of her, all thoughts about a silly little footrace left her.

"Oh, wow, Cortez," she breathed, stunned. "This is spectacular." Before her, an enormous view spread, consisting of the snow-covered San Juans spanning out as far as the eye could see, the town of Deep Hollow tucked far below them, the pine-dotted white ridges and flanks of the mountains. The bluebird sky was so deep and pure in the Colorado sunshine that it seemed almost violet, contrasting sharply with the blazing white snow everywhere. The view was so immense, so breathtaking, that Haley just stared. Cortez stepped up beside her. He looked out over the view in what she thought was an equally appreciative silence. Her skin prickled in his presence, tingly and hyper aware of him.

Very quietly, half afraid to break the enormous beauty with the small sound of her voice, she asked him the same question she'd asked Jessie earlier. "Do you ever get used to it here? To how beautiful it is, I mean."

She saw him shake his head out of the corner of her eye. "Nope. This place gives me energy. It gives my bear space to roam, and it's home. It's where I work."

She suddenly realized she had no idea what he did for a living. "Doing what?"

He gestured toward a long bench she hadn't even noticed, snugly nestled onto a block set on the ground, the base covered in snow although the entire bench itself had been carefully cleared. "We can eat here. Will you be warm enough?"

Definitely. She felt warm just at the fact that he cared. Her cheeks stretched even more into the smile she already wore. "I've got enough layers to stay very warm. Thanks." Her stomach growled and she laughed at it. Settling onto the bench, she pulled out the rest of her sandwich, still wrapped in its paper towel.

Cortez settled in beside her, a huge presence of heat and strength and, oddly enough, something that felt like *safety*. He unwrapped his own sandwich, but before he took a bite, he answered her question. "I used to do construction around town, sometimes a job or two over in Durango. But things started drying up with the housing economy taking a crap, so I had to find something else." He shrugged, and she suddenly felt him hesitate again. Like he wasn't sure how to say whatever he was going to say. "I have an outdoor guiding business. I run tours for the lodge. Just started doing it about three or four months ago."

Tours? That sounded interesting. "What kind of tours?" she asked before taking a big bite of her sandwich. Dang, it was a really good sandwich. Cortez was a master sandwich-maker.

"Just about any kind of tour. This time of year I take folks snowshoeing, or out for a ride in the sleigh."

Haley sat up straight and twisted a bit to look at him, her sandwich momentarily forgotten. "You take people on sleigh rides? Like with jingle bells and everything?" A sleigh ride in the snow sounded like the most magical thing ever.

Cortez laughed at her expression, his face crinkling into the friendliness she realized must make him a great guide. That and the fact that he probably was really good at making everyone feel safe. "Exactly like that. And yeah, people love it." His face darkened briefly. "Well, most people. Ones who aren't stuck-up panther shifters from the east coast out to have an adventure in the sticks." He took a savage bite of his sandwich and chewed like he was imagining it was a pantherwich.

Her sandwich was the last thing on her mind now. Enormous kitties with sharp claws and big teeth filled it instead. "Uh...panther shifters?"

"Yeah, it's just another name for mountain lions." *Chomp* as he savagely chewed another bite before going on. "I had some clients that were obnoxious and insisted on being called panthers. They were a massive pain in the ass."

"I wouldn't be." She imagined the sound of jingling bells, the whisper of sleigh runners over the snow. "I'd be so happy to go on a sleigh ride. I'd be the nicest client ever."

Cortez said, in a super casual voice, "Well, I could take you some time. But I don't think you're allowed to have any fun. I'm pretty sure you have to spend all your time working. Work, work, work. Nothing but work."

Haley bumped his shoulder with hers as hard as she could, uttering an indignant, "Hey!" Her shove barely moved him, though he grunted. But a big grin was on his face. Maybe a grin as big as hers.

Fine. This was fun. She was allowed to have fun for a minute, at least.

They sat in a companionable silence, finishing their sandwiches, brushing the crumbs off their laps into the snow. Cortez pulled out the little insulated bottles of hot cocoa and handed her one. As they sat and looked at the crazy gorgeous view, Haley felt more than just companionable. She felt totally comfortable. Relaxed. Like she belonged here. Here in these wild mountains, sitting beside this wild man. It just felt...right. But she did have a question. Slowly, carefully, she worked up her nerve to ask him.

"Cortez, about what you said the other morning."

He stiffened beside her but nodded. He knew what she meant. She said it anyway, just to be sure. "What you said about enjoying every day until you die. That there are no second chances at life. What did you mean by that? Was it about Riley's...mate?" She kept her voice soft and her eyes trained on the faraway dark dots that were trees on the mountains.

Her heart thumped hard as she waited for his answer. It was a big question, a personal question. She really didn't know him well enough to ask it. Then again, he'd volunteered the information himself. She did the same thing when she wanted someone to really look at her. To see her. To listen to her. Just maybe, Cortez had that same deep longing. For some reason, she wanted him to know her—and she really, really wanted to know him.

He turned his head to look at her. His face was still, the smile gone, his eyes searching hers with a piercing gaze she could feel straight to her soul. She wanted to flinch but didn't, making herself sit still and look back at him, waiting. Whatever it was, she wanted to hear it.

He took a breath, held it for a moment, exhaled it slowly. "For years, I was a volunteer for the local search and rescue team. Was actually the head of it for a long time. Whenever anyone gets into trouble in the mountains out here, just out having fun and then something just goes wrong, they get hurt or lost, search and rescue is called up and we go out to find them. All of this, everything you can see out there," he waved a hand to indicate the big expanse of mountains, "was our area. I know every inch of those mountains. My backyard, my playground, and when I was out on a call, my workplace."

His voice lowered, softened, even as his eyes went bright and hard. He was about to say something really big, she could feel it. Something dark and sad too.

"I'm supposed to help rescue people, Haley. Instead, one day last year I ended the lives of two people I cared about. Friends. Coworkers. Guys who relied on me to have their back. There was an avalanche, and I was in the lead. I was supposed to read the snow, to make a call on if it was safe to cross or not. I made the wrong fucking call. I'm well-trained in avalanche safety, but I made the wrong call." His voice was flat, almost monotone. "I was responsible for their safety, and I fucked it up. They will never have fun again. So," he shrugged, still holding her now frozen gaze, "now I have fun for them."

Silence was a huge chasm between them this time. Not companionable. Not comfortable. Haley just stared at him, words again choked in her throat.

He didn't say anything for a long moment, just studying her reaction. Then he went on. "Riley's story is bad enough, right? It's more pain and sadness than anyone needs for a lifetime. As a result, he really doesn't trust humans. That sucks and it's awful, and we all understand why he's like that. We're all trying to help him, and we hope that one day things won't be so hard for him anymore. But mine's just as shitty, in a different way. It's almost worse." The softness of his voice was a stark, almost mocking contrast to his words. "Because *I* was the one responsible. So I can't trust myself. I can't rescue anyone anymore. I'm fucking broken in that department."

He looked at her long and hard, his face still and waiting. Waiting for her to respond to that. To respond to his admission that his mistake had cost lives. That it was only a mistake, people made mistakes.

"I—you—I don't believe that." She swallowed, trying to say more, but she didn't know what. Damn it. Haley the writer, Haley the wordsmith, what a joke right now. She wanted to be able to say a thousand different things to take that look off his face, but everything jumbled up in her head and nothing would make sense. She didn't know how to say that it was okay, she didn't think less of him, that he wasn't broken.

She couldn't possibly find those words for him when she didn't have them for herself.

Finally, Cortez stopped waiting. He shrugged and looked away, back over the deep wilderness in front of them. She sensed hurt in him. And distance. "Come on, pretty Haley. You probably have to get back down to work. And I'm actually supposed to meet up with a friend and do some work on my house this afternoon."

He stood up, reaching down a hand to pull her up. She took it and tried to smile at him, but he quickly let go and started to walk back down the trail to the lodge, leaving her to follow his stiff back. She did, quiet as she tried to process everything. All the details. The only details she really cared about were the things he was telling himself inside his head. What he felt in his heart. Details she would never, ever share with anyone else. She knew everyone had to know about what he'd just told her. His family, his clan, probably everyone who lived here knew about what happened. But it still felt like he'd given her a gift: the darkest thing about himself that he believed. He'd shared something hard and painful because he trusted her with it, even if he didn't trust himself anymore.

Something inside Haley, maybe resolve, suddenly went strong as steel. She jogged slightly to keep up with his long-legged stride. Cortez might not know it, but she trusted him and, in a totally crazy way, she wanted to protect him. Not that he'd think a big bear shifter like himself needed any protection from a small human like herself. But he did, and she would.

No matter what.

6

*H*aley stretched her arms overhead and leaned back, closing her eyes as her back cracked. Oh, that felt good. The sounds of the Mountain Muffin in mid-afternoon were relatively quiet, matching her mood.

"You done with your dishes?" a friendly voice above her head asked.

Haley jerked, snapping her eyes open. Maddy, the owner of the bakery, stood beside her, smiling as she refilled Haley's bottomless coffee mug. She carried a gray plastic bin under one arm, which had a small collection of dirty dishes in it. Haley blinked, looking around. "Oh. Yes, thanks."

Maddy plucked up the small dish which had held the cinnamon roll Haley had treated herself to earlier. "Here you go. We have to fuel the creative genius brainstorming, right?" Maddy looked hopeful. She knew

Haley was a writer and loved the thought that she was writing a book in Maddy's bakery.

"The creative genius part comes in the morning, actually. I'm here in the afternoon to do things like answer emails and stuff like that." Or totally freak out about her future and sometimes lose herself into the void of social media's cute kitten videos in an attempt to distract herself from the possibility that all her hopes and dreams would be crushed as Justin had assured her they would be. "You know. The usual business end of things." She sighed.

Maddy nodded as she headed back behind the counter. "I definitely do know the business end of things. It's the tough stuff most people don't want to think about when they imagine the joys of being self-employed."

Haley laughed nervously, but she swallowed hard. She'd glanced at her bank account this morning and nearly had heart failure. If this book tanked...she'd be tanked too. The thought made her queasy.

As she fussed around with stuff on her website, adjusting the placement of photos and text so they were just so, internally thanking smart people out there who had created drop and drag websites for people like her who were totally clueless about coding, her thoughts drifted again to sexy, intriguing, heart-string-tugging Cortez. After their walk out to the beautiful spot in the mountains the other day, when they got back to the lodge Jessie was still there but ready to take Grant to town for his swim lesson at the local school's indoor pool. So Haley had gone back with Jessie, after a somewhat awkward and brief goodbye with Cortez. He'd watched as they drove away, and she turned around to wave at him. She was pretty sure she caught the flash of a smile as he casually waved back. Yeah, he was fascinating. So strong, so big. But she knew that deep down, he was also so hurting.

She nonchalantly asked Jessie about him on the way back, but all she really got was that Cortez was a great guy, always tried hard but often seem to have run of bad luck or maybe bad decisions. But he always bounced back. Jessie didn't seem super concerned about him. It sounded like no one here was.

So the other day when Jessie had been here working at the bakery, and Abby had stopped by while in town running some errands, Haley had oh-so-offhandedly asked them about Cortez. She could tell right away from the probing look Abby gave her that Abby had a feeling why Haley was asking. Even so, and even though Haley had already been able to tell that Abby sort of big sistered Cortez, Abby hadn't seemed very worried about him either. Maybe Haley was wrong? Maybe it was just her writer brain seeing too much deep internal angst and pain in Cortez, and she just wanted to do some silly girl thing like rescue him or something.

But she couldn't shake the feeling that Cortez was hiding a loss deeper than the loss of the friends he'd mentioned. Neither Abby nor Jessie had brought that up, although when Haley carefully inquired, their faces had drawn tight with sympathy. They'd simply said it was one of those sad, shocking events that had affected the town the same way as when Riley's mate had died, though this was somewhat different since Cortez's buddies from his search and rescue team were human. Then, to her surprise, Abby added that the other difference was that they hadn't died.

"Wait—I thought they did die?" Haley was nonplussed.

Abby shook her head. "No, but it was still really bad. Tim is in a coma, and the doctors aren't sure he'll ever regain consciousness. Scott lost a leg. They're both in Denver at the hospital. Scott is staying at a rehab center there to get tons of physical therapy every day. He's had a really hard time with the whole thing. Like everyone else on the team, he lived for adventure and having fun outside, being really physical. Now he has to learn how to just walk all over again. The search and rescue team, it's called a SAR team, is made up of both shifters and humans, and they're all really tight. Worked hard together, partied hard together." Her smile was sympathetic as well as concerned. "It was a devastating blow for everyone. There's still a SAR team of course, with some additional members now to make up for the loss, but they've all changed since then. And Cortez isn't on the team anymore. By his choice," she added quickly as Haley made a sound of dismay. "He's worried he'll let them down again by missing signs of another avalanche or something else that could go wrong. But that's part of the risk they take when they go out to save people." Abby shrugged, but her face was still filled with compassion. "He didn't do anything wrong, Haley. But he believes he did, which is almost worse."

After Abby had left, Haley mulled the story over in her mind, stunned and aching for him. Cortez hadn't told her all the details because it was hard for him to think about them. To relive them. That, she understood completely. It now made sense too, what he'd said about his buddies never being able to have fun again, to enjoy life again. For extremely active guys like them, they may as well have died. Her heart clenched with compassion for him. Cortez was carrying around a lot of pain over the event. While his family and friends knew that, she was still sure they didn't know how deep it went.

But she understood that completely. None of her friends or family truly knew just how deep her own emotional scars went. They thought she was dealing and would be okay. She hid the worst of it from them, because frankly, she didn't want to relive the shit she'd been through either. Sighing hard, she forced her thoughts away from the old ugly memories.

Instead, she easily called up another image of Cortez's eyes. His face crinkled up into a smile, that golden stubble on his cheeks that she insanely longed to rub her cheek against, danced through her mind. Even as she thought about him, her phone dinged with a text. Heat shot through her body when she saw the message.

Hi Haley it's Cortez. I'm sorry our lunch the other day ended like that. I know you're working hard and I bet you're at the mountain muffin cuz Jessie says you're there every afternoon so I was wondering if you have a break soon. I'm down here in town and I really want to show you something that I'm working on.

Her entire body tingled and a smile blazed across her face. Quickly she typed back, *Yes.*

When?

I could use a break pretty soon actually.

Like in five minutes?

She laughed. *Yes.*

Okay. I'll come get you.

Before she could answer, she saw the dots bouncing that indicated he was typing something else. She waited.

Thank you for not being scared of me. Thank you for being okay with it. With me telling you that stuff.

The smile on her face was so huge she thought her cheeks might break. Bouncing dots again. Then another text flashed.

Fuck, that was probably a dumb thing to say. You can ignore this if you want to. I hope you don't. You're really pretty and you smell nice and you have a big heart and I like that. I'll see you in five minutes. I'll be the big guy.

Her breath caught. Oh, my god, he was amazing. She quickly texted back, *I can't wait, I'll be ready.*

She was glad Jessie was busy with customers, because she knew she was smiling so hard she probably looked crazy and Jessie would ask what was going on. She wasn't ready to talk about this yet when she wasn't quite sure herself what it was.

As she slid her laptop into its carrying case and shoved it into the little daypack she wore to walk between the house and the bakery, her phone chimed with an incoming email. Still smiling, she grabbed her phone to check it.

Instantly, her stomach lurched and the smile fell off her face. Her ex, Justin.

Hello, Haley. Have you missed me? I've been thinking about you. You have something I want. And I'm coming to get it.

Her entire body began to tremble. Hand shaking so badly it took her two tries, she wrote back, *Leave me alone. Don't contact me again.* Then she darkened the screen and shoved the phone into her pocket. She stood up and pulled on her jacket, mind staggering. No. She wouldn't let him get to her. He was just being cruel and petty, trying to scare her. Justin was the past. He couldn't touch her anymore. He didn't know where she was anyway. He was fucking with her mind, which was what he liked to do. She knew better than to respond. If he tried again, she'd ignore it.

Swallowing hard, pushing her fleece hat hard down

her head as she headed toward the door to wait for Cortez, Haley tried to focus on the now. On the heart of this sweet, welcoming little town, the amazing community, the most intriguing guy she'd ever met.

But inside, something dark, scared, and hopeless taunted her, trying to crawl up from the ugly shadows and swallow her whole.

7

*C*ortez looked over at Haley as he pulled his truck up in front of his partially built cabin and killed the engine, watching for her reaction. She didn't disappoint. A smile ripped across her face as she looked at the half built skeleton of what would eventually be his home. It was nice to see because she'd seemed oddly distracted when he picked her up from the bakery.

"Cortez! Oh, I can see what it will look like, it's going to be gorgeous. You're doing this yourself? By hand?" She looked at him like he walked on water. His chest swelled with pride.

"Yeah. Though to be fair, a good friend of mine has helped me out a lot. I couldn't have done it without him. Oh, and Riley bangs a few nails now and then too. Sometimes Quentin and Slade help, when they're in the mood."

"Slade?"

"Another brother. He's out of town right now. There's a bunch of us."

Haley sighed with delight as she looked at his cabin. Yeah, she liked it. And he liked that. There wasn't much to it yet, but the parts that he had finished gave an idea of what it would look like eventually. It would be a sweet little pad in the woods, far away enough from both town and the Silvertip Lodge that he'd have his own space, yet close enough that he could easily head up there to do a tour. As the youngest sibling in a rowdy clan of bear shifters who were always up in each other's shit, Cortez hadn't been blessed with a lot of alone time in his life. He was pretty social, he did like being around others, but as he'd gotten older he started to realize how nice it was to have a private space he could just breathe in when necessary. Especially after the accident. The problem was, the cabin wasn't coming along as fast as it should. That was all his fault. He'd been slacking on everything, even to the point that Beckett was pissed at him for blowing off meets to work on it.

He didn't want to think about that right now. Instead, he wanted to focus on Haley. He really wanted to impress her.

Cortez reached over her to the glove compartment, feeling the heat from her body and that sweet smell of hers that turned him on so much as he leaned across her. At the slight hitch in her breath, he thought she

379

might like this closeness as much as he did. Allowing a cocky grin to slip over his face, he opened the glove compartment, pulled out a sheaf of papers, and sat back in his seat. He crinkled the sheets open, Haley watching curiously. The open papers revealed the cabin plans. She let out a delighted breath.

"Oh, wow. It's going to be so cute."

Cortez turned his head and gave her a dubious glance. "Cute? Woman, you take that back. This is a man cabin. There's nothing cute about it."

She laughed, the sound of it spilling through the cab of the truck. It made him want to thread his fingers through her golden hair, touch the back of her neck, stroke her cheek and see if it was as soft as it really looked. He forced his eyes back down to the paper, then held it up in front of them so they could see the actual building over the top of it. "Okay. It's got stairs going up to the front door since it's built kind of into the hillside, which I did on purpose because I wanted to try to catch some of the view through those trees behind us."

Haley turned to look through the back window of the cab. "Whoa, that is pretty." It wasn't nearly as good as the views from the lodge, but it definitely wasn't half bad for this little parcel tucked back up in the woods like he wanted.

"You can see how the deck will wrap around the cabin." Haley turned her attention back to the page. "It'll have a loft upstairs, which is where I'll sleep.

There'll also be a basement area where I'll store all my man toys."

Haley bubbled over again with a laugh. "Man toys? What are those?"

"My outdoor gear. Skis, snowshoes, backpacking and hiking stuff. Just my personal gear. Everything for the clients is kept up at the lodge. Come on," he said, opening his door and getting out of the truck. He was excited to see her reaction to it up close. "You can see what's built so far."

Haley got out of the truck and hurried ahead of him. It reminded him of how she raced ahead to see the view the other day at lunch. He liked showing her stuff. She seemed really interested, plus he just liked to share things with her. He wanted to share things that meant so much to him with this woman. Damn, she made his insides squeeze up and flip over all funny in a way that felt damn good.

Haley stopped and pointed to the left side of the structure. "What's that little thing? Some sort of shed? But it's all fancy, with a window and a real door."

Cortez came up beside her. "It's my temporary small man cave until the big man cave gets built. I built the shed about five years ago, way before I could start building the actual cabin. It's insulated, has a little wood stove, and a bed and stuff. Sometimes I stay in there when I want to get away from things. When I just need a break."

She nodded, a tendril of hair fluttering against her

cheek. He couldn't help reaching out to gently brush it aside. Her face dimpled as a smile flashed over it so quick he almost missed it. She curved her head toward him, into his light touch. Pressed gently against his hand, like she liked feeling it there. "I understand that. Sometimes I need a safe space to run to, too."

She cut herself off as if she'd said too much, nervously shifting on her feet, and leaned slightly away from him. He frowned but forced himself not to press. Yet. If she wanted him to know her history, she'd tell him.

"There's nothing special in there, just a cot with an air mattress on it. I'd show you the inside of the actual cabin but there's not much in there either." He laughed and Haley laughed with him, the mingled sound of it gently bouncing around the little glade. Since the cabin was just basically the basement floor and the bare bones of the sides, there wasn't even an inside to look at.

"I want to see it anyway," she said. Her smile dazzled brighter than the sun. Whoa, she was so pretty.

Cortez made a grand gesture toward the non-front door, starting to say, "After you, then—"

A horrifying scream burst out from the woods, not immediately nearby but not too far away, shattering the still air. An unearthly screeching, sounding like a possessed ghost being murdered. A mountain lion. It was followed almost immediately by another shriek, this one laced with warning snarls. Haley started so violently she almost tripped over her feet, her breath whooshing out of her in a gasp. She grabbed at Cortez's arm instinctively, her eyes wildly searching the forest surrounding them. Another call from the forest, loud and mocking, vicious in its intent.

A strange shifter screamed out there, threatening him. Threatening Haley. Cortez's response was instant and completely uncontrolled. His bear clawed to the surface. Cortez swung his head to look at Haley, desperation bubbling through his voice. "Haley."

She swung her head to look at him, the whites of her eyes showing. His bear's protective rage shimmered through his voice. "I can't stop the change. Don't be scared. I won't ever hurt you. The door's unlocked," he managed to growl out, jerking his head at the door to the small shed/man cave just before his feral side took over.

His bear burst out of him, flinging him into his enormous grizzly shape. Instantly, Cortez charged toward the woods on his four powerful paws, seeking the danger that called. He roared back into the trees, defending his place. His home. Defending Haley. His huge, heavy legs thundered over the ground as he charged up the hill, blasting through huge drifts of snow as he bellowed his defiance and anger at some strange shifter getting much too close.

Skidding to a stop, his heavy body sliding through the snow, Cortez managed to halt halfway up the hill. His breathing harsh, he swung his head around, scenting as hard as he could. There. Just a whiff, but it definitely was a big cat shifter. Bastard. The roar had been far enough off that he knew whoever it was wasn't coming closer. He bellowed out his own last enraged roar, claiming this section of the woods, claiming this spot in Deep Hollow, home of the Silvertip bear clan, as his. This was *his* home. Threatening intruders weren't welcome. His roar dropped down into echoes, ringing through the tense silence until they faded.

There was no answer. Sniffing again long and hard, Cortez could no longer scent the other one. He must've left. Smart cat. Shaking himself to dislodge some snow that had scattered down from pine branches above as he thundered by the trees and shook them, Cortez turned and headed back to the cabin. He moved quickly, but not so fast that he would come bursting into the clearing and scare Haley anymore that she probably already was. But when he pulled up to the shell of his cabin, he stopped short and stared.

Haley stood right in front of his little man cave door, but it wasn't open. She hadn't gone in. She stood there, in the open, braving the terrifying noises as she waited for him. He could tell she was scared, sure, but she hadn't hidden. That crazy pride swelled in him again as he saw how brave she was. Very slowly, he moved toward her, huffing gently, trying to let her know that she was safe. That it was him.

"Cortez?" Her voice was faint, but steady. He

bobbed his head once at her, keeping his distance. But then she moved, walking toward him. He stood perfectly still, keeping himself as quiet as he could as she approached.

She was about three feet away when her feet slowed, bringing her to a stop when she was maybe a foot away. Very carefully, her eyes locked on his, she reached her hand out. "Is it okay if I—touch you?" Her voice was softer, but still steady.

In answer, Cortez dipped his head down and tilted it toward her. Haley's hand, her soft, gentle hand, reach forward to touch the side of Cortez's face. Her fingers pushed into his thick brown fur, reaching up to very tentatively touch him on his forehead just above his eyes. "Oh," she said, her voice now a delighted whisper. "You're so soft. I didn't know your fur would be this soft. And even though you're so big"—again, he couldn't help the swell of pride that rushed through him—"I'm not afraid of you, Cortez. I can trust you. It's really you." She gently stoked the fur on his face. "I saw Jessie touch Shane, when he was in his bear form, and I wondered what it would be like. They seemed so happy and easy together. Now I know." The pure wonder and happiness in her voice soothed over him, rippling into his hide, his bones, his soul, with sweet satisfaction.

They stayed like that for a few moments longer, Haley's hand buried in Cortez's pelt as she stood beside him. Tiny little woman beside his enormous grizzly bear. Tiny, brave, powerful. Finally, he softly whoofed at her and moved away. Pacing around to the back of the shed where she couldn't see him, he shifted back into his human form. The change crackled over him fast and hard, making him stumble and grimace.

"Haley," he called out. His voice still sounded hoarse, low. "I keep a spare set of clothes in the shed. Uh, do you mind turning your back for a second while I come around the corner and go in there?"

Her laugh pealed out. "You're asking me that because you're, ah, naked, right?" Laughter and something he was pretty sure sounded like interest stirred beneath her words.

"As buck naked as the day I was born."

"Okay." She giggled again. "My back is turned."

Cortez checked around the corner of the building just to be sure. Hell if he didn't want this gorgeous woman to see him naked, but he didn't think either one of them was quite ready for that. It wasn't really the time or the place. She indeed stood with her back to him, her golden curls escaping beneath her hat and floating down the back of the heavy navy blue jacket she wore. God, she was so pretty just standing here, at his place, surrounded by the thick piles of snow and sheltering trees.

Quickly, Cortez ducked inside his shed, pulled on the spare set of clothes he kept in there, shoved his feet into a pair of boots sitting by the door, and came back out. "The coast is clear."

She turned instantly, the amazed smile still in her

face. Her eyes widened when she saw him. "Your eyes. They're still—they're still different."

Cortez nodded, walking to her. "My bear is still riled, so you can see it in my eyes. He'll simmer down."

She swallowed and looked up at the wooded steep hillside rising up behind his cabin. "Was that another shifter? What happened? Whoever it was, it didn't sound very friendly."

Cortez's mouth set into a line as he too peered up the slope. "No, he wasn't. That was a mountain lion shifter. A strange one, not from around here. We have a lot of strange shifters in town all the time, just being tourists or visiting friends, but that was an angry, challenging call. The guests up at the lodge have some pretty strict rules to abide by while they're here. Brawling and challenging are not allowed."

"Challenging," she echoed softly, her eyes still troubled as she looked into the snowy forest. "But why?"

Cortez shrugged. He'd have to tell the rest of the clan about this. Shifters just coming into town to check out the lodge or go on a tour or hell, just coming for a cup of coffee, was one thing. Shifters coming in and getting all territorial was another. "I don't know. Sometimes they're just out looking for trouble, especially if their animal is too aggressive and they don't have good control." He could hear the unyielding tone in his own voice as he added, "But we'll definitely find out."

Silence pocketed them for a few minutes as they both looked into the woods. Haley shivered suddenly.

Cortez automatically reached forward, put his arm around her shoulders, pulled her close to him. He was half shocked at the unplanned action, but Haley didn't stiffen or pull away. Instead, she leaned into him. "I do know there are bad shifters in the world," she said in a soft voice. "I've heard about them from my friend. But you."

She tilted her head up to look at him. She looked so damn cute, tucked under his arm like that. He just wanted to pull her close to him and hug her. Damn, he wanted to kiss her. Holding fast to some shred of willpower, he restrained himself and waited for her to go on.

"You, Cortez, are good." Her voice was soft but firm as she spoke. "I tend to be very guided by my heart, I always have been. It's part of being a creative person, I guess. I don't know. Listening to my heart tells me that you are good person. Bear. Man." She looked slightly more confused with each word she tried.

Cortez laughed. "Yeah, I'm all those things. Whatever you want." Reluctantly, he glanced at the time. Damn. "I kept you for about an hour now. You probably have to get back to work. Even though it's a Saturday. Right?" He tried desperately not to sound judgmental or needy as he said that.

Haley sucked her bottom lip into her mouth, pulling it gently between her teeth. He almost groaned at how sexy that little move was. Damn, he was about to get a boner out here in the middle of the forest, with pretty little Haley tucked up under his arm looking at him with the sweetest little mouth he'd ever seen.

Then she surprised the heck out of him. "Cortez, you're right. Life isn't only about working. I want to have some fun. Please show me how?"

8

*T*he storm rolled dark and quiet over downtown Deep Hollow as Haley and Cortez strolled along Main Street.

Haley had gone into town quite a few times by now, since pretty much every day she went to the Mountain Muffin. She thought she was familiar with it. But right now, walking beside Cortez, feeling momentarily free of deadlines and obligations and stress over her future, it looked different. Cozy, charming, bright with possibility. Even though the dark skies and impending snow seemed to have cleared the sidewalks, welcoming lights beckoned from the cute businesses along the street. Everything here felt so content and safe.

It also felt safe because of Cortez. She glanced over at him as they walked. After she'd out of the blue told him that she wanted to go have fun, he'd said it was too late in the day go on an outdoor adventure, but there was some fun stuff to do in town that he could show her. They drove into town and parked both their cars at the Walker residence, then headed on foot into the downtown area from there. She'd startled herself, pushing aside work, asking specifically for him to take her to have fun, but it felt like the right thing to do.

Every moment she spent with Cortez felt like the right thing to do.

As they walked under the old-fashioned streetlamps that graced Main Street, which were slowly flickering to life in response to what seemed like an early dark from the heavy, low clouds above, Cortez's hand brushed the back of hers. He looked over at her and gently caught her hand in his. She smiled at him, squeezed his hand, and looked ahead of them. "Okay, fun-meister. What do we do first?"

"Fun-meister?"

"That's your title for right now."

"Hmm. I like it." He smiled down at her, the low light catching the sheen of dark gold brown stubble on his cheeks. Ooh, she liked that. "I think to start off, we both deserve a little treat. How do you feel about chocolate?"

"How do I feel about chocolate? I feel very good about chocolate. Exceptionally good. Do you mean hot chocolate?"

"Nope. I mean the best damn little chocolate distillery west of the Rockies."

"Chocolate distillery?" She sounded as puzzled as she felt.

He chuckled and pulled her forward. "You've definitely spent way too much time working and not enough time exploring Deep Hollow. I'm going to introduce you to the Silvertip Chocolate Company. Can't believe you haven't been there yet, woman." He gave his head a disbelieving shake. "The Mountain Muffin is great, but they don't do chocolates like the chocolate store. This way."

He was right. She hadn't yet made it to the chocolate distillery—and who knew such a thing existed? Clearly, she'd been missing out—because it was on one of the side streets off the main drag. She'd been so stressed about producing, so focused on writing so she'd be able to pay her bills, get her life back on track, that she really had been single-mindedly marching from the house to the bakery every afternoon, then back to the house again. She really hadn't explored town. Glancing almost shyly at Cortez again as he propelled her into the little store, she remembered his comment when they had first met. Life wasn't all about working. Okay, fine. He was right.

In the store, her eyes widened and her grip on his hand tightened. "Oh, heaven," she murmured, eyes darting around to take in the chocolatey joys of the little store. They were surrounded by chocolate truffles, bars, clusters, ganache, pralines, all sorts of fancy little concoctions. Oh, she'd died and gone to yummy chocolate paradise. But... "Distillery? I still don't understand that part."

Cortez took her shoulders and gently turned her around to the left. "Oh, wow! Okay. Wow." It was an actual distillery. Tall, gleaming pillars connected by a little network of metal tubes hunched above squatting copper pots. A man peered into the one of the pots, adjusted a knob on the side of it, then returned to a pan filled with little chocolates set onto a silver counter.

"So what you're telling me is that there's alcohol in some of these chocolates. What you're telling me is that I've entered culinary paradise?" She thought she might drool at all the delicious-looking little confections on display behind the glass cases of the sales counter.

Cortez nodded, raising his hand at the guy working in little distillery room, who waved back. "Damn right. They've got whiskey, rum, absinthe, liqueurs, brandy, vodka, and they put them into the chocolates through a distillation process. It's all made right here, and it's all really good. What's your pleasure, beautiful?" He grinned down at her. A bone melting smile.

Haley was ready to swoon from the deliciousness of the chocolate spirits in the room and the sexy big man next to her. "Anything. Everything. It's all my pleasure." She laughed. "You're right, Cortez. I admit it. Having fun is good."

"Damn straight it is, woman. Okay. We'll get a sampler. You'll like that."

Two minutes later, Haley was biting into her first

ever pear brandy chocolate truffle. One teeny little bite, and she was having a delicious party in her mouth. "Oh," she moaned after the decadent taste that had her closing her eyes in rapture. "This is definitely the best chocolate I've ever had in my entire life. This is one of the best things, period, that I've ever had my entire life," she added, opening her eyes. "Why, it's—"

Cortez's expression stopped her short. He stared at her, his eyes transfixed on her mouth before moving back up to her eyes. He was close to her, so close to her. His scent surrounded her, all big wild man scent, so electrifying. She saw the bright flash of his bear in his eyes. Caught that wild and free streak she had witnessed earlier when he changed into that enormous bruin right in front of her, then gone charging up the mountain like he was an entire goddamned army on his own. Ready to protect her from whatever danger growled out there. They stared at each other for a long moment, the rest of the luscious truffle in her hand momentarily forgotten, sensuous energy whispering and twining around them. A slow shiver of anticipation rolled through her, dancing on her skin. Was he going to kiss her?

No, dang it. The moment abruptly passed when from behind the counter the clerk called out in a chirpy voice, "Your sampler box is ready. I'll ring you up."

Cortez blinked and took a deep breath. He gave Haley a searching look, then turned and went up to the counter, paid for the box, and brought it back to her. It was small, but she knew it contained five more delicious truffles, all different flavors. He pressed it into her hands, a smile tugging up one side of his mouth. "For you, pretty Haley. Come on. I'm too restless to sit. Let's keep walking in town, okay?"

"Sure," she said in a dazed voice. He picked up her hand again, his own large and warm and solid around hers. Back out the door into the late afternoon chill, the skies overhead now even more leaden with the promise of the incoming storm. She could almost smell the snow in the air.

They walked down the side street in silence, a comfortable sort of silence like they'd had before. Haley liked it a lot. She glanced at him again, his massive, comforting, arousing presence beside her. What was it about him? She didn't know. He just felt *right*. He felt so much more right than Justin ever had. She'd never before known how at ease she could feel around a man until she'd met Cortez.

"Down here," he said, steering them left onto another little street. "There's a path that goes by the river, and a bridge that goes over it. There are lights along the path and the bridge. We can walk back up the river on the other side. It'll bring us out at the top of town." He glanced up at the sky. "I'll get you back to the house before it starts dumping snow."

Haley looked around at the postcard perfect little mountain town, the snow on the trees, listened to the burble of the stream she could hear ahead of them. "This is perfect, Cortez," she said softly. "I didn't know what we were going to do when I told you I wanted to have fun, but this is perfect."

"This is pretty quiet and casual. You sure you're enjoying it?" A grin played around his lips.

She smiled back, the taste of pear brandy truffle still in her mouth and a lightness in her heart. "Yeah. Believe me, I'm really enjoying it."

They got to the river path and walked down it to the small pedestrian bridge that crossed over the water. Haley stopped in the middle of the bridge, looking down at the partially frozen creek running just below. "Silvertip Creek, right? It's so pretty." A content smile curved her lips. "It's so peaceful here."

She watched the water for a few minutes, listening to it run beneath the ice that covered almost the entire creek. The sky felt heavy and still, Cortez felt strong and solid beside her, she felt safe and secure and quietly, simply happy. This moment was precious, and she wanted to hold onto it for as long as she could.

"Haley," he said after another minute. She turned her head to look at him where he leaned against the bridge railing beside her. His eyes studied hers, his face serious. "Why are you here? In Deep Hollow? You've seen me change into my bear. I told you the worst thing about me, and you listened to it and accepted it. But I know there's a reason you're here that you haven't told me. I think you probably haven't told anyone." His voice got quieter. "I don't want to push you. I just want to know your story. I want to know you, Haley."

She stared at him for a long moment, hearing the river gurgle along in the quiet air around them. "No one has ever done that before," she finally murmured. "No one has ever wanted to actually hear my story. Not a guy, I mean." *Not a guy I really, really like,* she added in her head.

"I do." His voice rumbled in deep certainty. "Your story is important to me."

The hushed promise of safety, the gentle invitation in his voice, made her decide. Taking a deep breath first, she plunged right in. "I was married for five years before I came here." She said the words softly, carefully watching Cortez's face. His lips tightened, but he just nodded.

"Justin and I met in high school. Got married right after we graduated, even though my parents didn't like him and disproved." She shook her head, remembering. "I should've listened to them. I was only eighteen and so naive. But I thought I was in love. It wasn't actual love, though. It was infatuation, and I was too young and inexperienced to know the difference. I thought he was so smart, so worldly, and I let him control everything about my life. Because I didn't know that's what it was at the time. I didn't understand that he was directing everything."

She looked at Cortez, gauging his reaction. He just listened, giving her space to talk. She went on.

"I had always been a writer, a storyteller, and he found out we might be able to make some money online doing that. He wasn't a big reader, but he loved watching movies and had a lot of good ideas. So it ended up that he created all the stories, he came up with the plots, the characters and everything, and then I wrote them. We published under his name, because it was science fiction and he said most of the authors were guys. I didn't mind because I wasn't the biggest science fiction fan, and it was also easy for me to write once he told me what to do. I thought I was just writing down *his* stories and that I didn't deserve credit anyway."

The sky lowered more, deepening the dark around them. The creek gently bubbled beneath the bridge as Haley talked. Cortez hadn't said a word or even moved. A single glance at his face told her he was working hard to keep his tension in. "We did really well," she went on. "Really, really well. People thought we were wunderkinds, but it's just that we got really lucky. For two years, we made really good money." Her voice got softer as she talked. It was hard to tell the story, to share how naive and dumb she'd been, but she wanted Cortez to know everything. "We talked about the house we would buy, fancy cars we would get, just how amazing it was to finally have some money. I could help my parents, we could save for college for the kids we planned to have one day"—Cortez's face twitched at that, but he still stayed silent—"and we'd be just fine. I was working crazy hard, but he was too. He not only came up with all the ideas, he did all the marketing and advertising, and of course he was the face because it was his name. In social media and everything, he was the one talking about the books like he was the sole author. No one knew we were a team. No one knew that I was the one who actually wrote them. He's really not a very good writer—he just has creative ideas. And I just didn't realize at the time that being the writer, the one who brought life to those ideas, was a very important part of the process. The most important part, really. Without my words, there would be no books."

She caught Cortez slowly curling and and uncurling his fingers, as if fists were ready to punch out of him but he was trying so hard not to. She looked at the dark ribbon of icy water below them as she went on. This part, she had to force out. It still hurt. Not because she missed Justin. Never. What hurt was the realization of how badly she had been played and betrayed.

"To make a long, ugly story short, about a year ago I found out the hard way that Justin was not the person I had made him out to be since I was fifteen years old. I finally saw him for who he really was. He and another writer online had started collaborating, without me knowing. Then he met a woman in real life and they were having an affair. By that point he knew the other writer would be able to write books for him as well as me, or so he said. And he was in love with this other woman he'd met, or so he said. One day when I came home, he had divorce papers ready for me to sign. He was done with me, ready to move on. It totally blind-sided me."

Cortez still didn't say a word. She didn't look at him in case steam was coming out of his ears.

"He said he was really sorry, but it just wasn't fair to me that he couldn't give me the life I'd always thought we would have together. He said he didn't want to hurt me that way. I was sobbing, just completely hysterical with shock. I'd been with this guy since I was a kid." She huffed out a short, sharp laugh. "But eventually I signed the divorce papers because he wore me down, and frankly, he was just so damned nice about it. So *considerate.*" The word came out of her mouth in a sarcastic way. "The way he made it seem was like he was just being so kind to me. That he was only thinking of me, not wanting to hurt me anymore. Divorcing me was the kindest, most compassionate option, he said. And I totally bought it."

Shaking her head for the millionth time at how dumb she'd been, she chanced a quick glance at Cortez. His face was like solid granite in the faint light from the lamps on the bridge.

"I figured I'd be okay financially speaking, because I had my share of the money from the books, right?" Another snort of laughter, again short and pained. "No. I was so, so stupid. As it turned out, everything was in his name. Everything. He copyrighted the books under his name, bank accounts that I thought were joint were only in his name, the one car we owned was in his name. Every damn little thing was in his name." She swallowed. Naked, frightened vulnerability smothered her as she told this part of the story. Such a dumb little girl she had been back then. "I had been so blindly in love that I just didn't realize it. I didn't realize he was an utter monster who'd calculated everything. It took me a long time to understand that he had emotionally abused me for years, so that I thought I deserved nothing and he deserved it all. He left me with nothing. Literally nothing." She shifted on her feet, half wishing she could just run away, half wanting to finish the story fast so she could see what Cortez would think of her now. "Maybe worst of all, I didn't realize that when I signed the divorce papers that I was signing away my rights. They said I'd never contest him for anything, and I stupidly signed. Probably because I was in shock and I didn't even read them, but that was no excuse. I had to move back in with my parents for six months. Honestly, I was basically comatose during that time."

These days, she could finally find some compassion for the little idiot she'd been, but it was still hard to expose that foolishness about her. "It was such an enormous shock to realize that not only was he a monster, I had been such a gullible little fool ever since I first met him. But eventually my parents and my best friend, Pix, managed to help pull me out of my own moping so I could try to start living again. I had to take a job waiting tables in the meantime, and it actually wasn't all that awful. It was reasonably good money, and I got to do a ton of people watching. So I was able to save some money, and it reminded me that I still loved to write, and all those people gave me ideas for stories and characters. Especially," she smiled faintly, knowing it was bittersweet, "romances. It was a romantic little restaurant, so there were always people there on dates or celebrating anniversaries, stuff like that. I realized that I always loved reading romance novels, and I am a good writer. My family and my best friend convinced me that even if my own romance had been shot all to hell, I could still write one. Then I found out about this housesitting gig and it was perfect. So," she concluded with a small shrug, "here I am. And that's my story."

She didn't mention Justin's email from earlier. She didn't want Cortez to look at her like she had a stalker or something. Which she didn't. She just had a grade A asshole for an ex.

A very long silence descended. It was so quiet without her voice now. Just the sound of the stream running beneath the ice. Finally, she looked over at Cortez. His fists were definitely clenched by his sides and his face...Oh, his face. Ooh, yeah. He was mad. Furious. He looked as mad as she'd felt when she had finally, finally woken up and realized how badly Justin had tried to ruin her life. What a sick monster he was.

In a dark, heavy voice, Cortez snarled, "If I ever meet that ex of yours, there's gonna be a problem. A really big problem, and he's not gonna come out on the good side of it."

Before she could respond, his voice punched out again, ragged and harsh. "Haley, my bear is crazy right now. He's raging inside me." Cortez looked at her. His eyes roiled with the anger of his bear. "I don't know if I can manage him right now. I don't want you to see me completely out of control. Fuuuck," he gritted out, clearly fighting himself. He took a step backward, like he might leave.

Wait. *He* was going to run away from *her?* She caught her breath at the gut punch of that thought. No. Absolutely not. She reached out her hands and grabbed his hard fists, gently caressing her fingers over them, trying to loosen them. "Cortez, don't you dare run from me. I trust you, I want to see all of you. I need to see all of you. Justin hid everything from me so I wouldn't know who he really was. I want to see everything about you. I want to know every single thing about you. Please," she whispered, trying to will him into stillness with her voice, her gaze. "Please don't hide from me."

Her hands moved up his arms, feeling the corded muscles there. Up past his elbows, over his forearms, smoothing in over his chest. Feeling him through his jacket, and pushing one hand up to caress his neck, his cheek.

His body went from tense to pliable beneath her touch in an instant. With a groan, he caught her hand where she rubbed it against the soft stubble on his face, pushed his face into her touch, his eyes not leaving hers. With his other hand, he reached forward, behind her waist, pulled her unresisting body into his. "Haley," he murmured, his piercing eyes, so bright like they were glowing, searching hers in the dim light. "I'll never run from you. I just don't want to hurt you."

She wound both her hands behind his neck now as he pulled her into him. "You can't hurt me," she whispered, feeling the truth of those words, then she couldn't speak anymore. He feathered his lips across hers. Soft, oh, he was so soft and tender with her. She opened to him, tasting him with her lips, then her tongue. He groaned again, his mouth moving more strongly over hers, seeking and tasting as if he wanted to swallow her into him whole, meld them together.

With a soft kitten mewling sound, she let him possess her. Open her. Taste her, stroke her until she was a giant bundle of quivering nerve endings, so lit up that she just wanted to shuck his clothes off, then tear her own off too. She wanted to fling herself onto him right here on this bridge over the gurgling creek in this sweet little town that felt like home. She wanted to feel him slide inside her, filling her, claiming her as his. She gasped at how strong her longing was. She never felt this crazy heated up like this, ever. Cortez made her want to do bad things with him. Very bad, sweet, beautiful, sexy wild things with him.

He seemed to have similar thoughts, because he

pushed her back against the railing of the bridge until her ass hit it, then reached down to lift her legs up so she had to wrap them around him. She squeaked with surprise. Gentle but rough at the same time, like sandpaper covered in a stroke of velvet, he growled, "Kissing you right now feels like the best thing I've ever done. I need to have you leaned up against this railing, have you hang on me so tight, because otherwise I might fall down from this feeling so damn good, Haley. *Haley,*" he groaned, her name like a prayer on his lips.

She went breathless at that. So turned on, in a topsy-turvy, dizzy and excited thrill of sensation all at once. They kissed more, more. He reached his hands under her jacket and up her back, stroked his thumbs up and down her spine. The simple caress about drove her wild. Her hips pressed into his, and she felt him big and hard against her. His tongue was in her mouth, she was wrapped up with him, and nothing else existed in the world, nothing else.

He moved against her, with her, led the dance. Set the pace. Stroked her back, dipped his tongue in and out of her mouth, bit her lower lip with gentle teeth, turned her limbs to fire and her thoughts to one sweetly pounding cadence: Cortez. He was hers. He was who she wanted. She wanted him, all of him. Not just his body, even though ooh, yes, this kiss was setting her on fire like a roaring volcano. She wanted every single bit of him: body, soul, fierce warrior heart, kind and considerate man, huge savage bear

405

shifter. Beautiful, big, stunning man. She wanted all of him.

As his lips nipped at hers, as she moaned into his mouth, she knew it felt real. Right. But at the same time, she knew she was still broken and sad, scared and hurt. And she knew he was too. She wanted to hold onto him forever, but at the same time she was afraid. Afraid they were both too broken to be able to patch themselves up and make one another whole.

Instead, they might rip each other up even more until there was nothing left.

9

_____

*H*aley stood in the beautiful little sunroom in the Walker residence where she had started to take her breaks during morning writing sessions. She clutched a steaming hot mug of coffee in her hands, taking sips as she enjoyed the morning sunshine bathing her through the window. Last night's storm had broken away today to reveal fresh new snow piled up everywhere, dazzling in the bright light and the bluebird skies.

Aside from the beauty of the day and a deep appreciation for whoever had invented coffee and hazelnut creamer, all she could think about was Cortez. Oh, that man. That sexy, sexy man. They'd kissed one another to within an inch of their lives last night, huddled so tight together on that bridge she was sure a thin sheet of paper couldn't have fit between them. Finally, they'd slowly walked all the way back to the house, where he kissed her again on the front porch. He said it kind of weirded him out to kiss her on the doorstep of his parents' house even though they were half a world away, which made her laugh. But then he said he wasn't weirded out enough to stop kissing her, so they'd kissed some more right on the porch, with the softly falling snow just behind them.

Oh, it had been such a hot make out session. She wanted to do wild, crazy things with him. Bad, delicious, naughty, incredible things. But then he lifted her hand to his lips, grazed the back of it with his mouth, trailed little kisses all over it. His eyes still bright with his bear, he murmured, "Good night, pretty Haley. I'm really glad you shared your afternoon with me. Really glad you saw where my cabin's gonna be one day when I finish it. I'm glad you wanted me to show you some fun. Most of all, I'm glad you let me kiss you. I think I wanted to kiss you the first second I saw you dressed in your crazy jammies and that orange bathrobe."

She'd been caught between laughter at his words and a soft gasp as he kissed the back of her hand like a total gentleman. A gentleman like her ex had never been. He let go, softly said, "Talk to you soon, beautiful," and went to his truck. But he wouldn't drive away until she closed the door behind her. It was another gentlemanly thing that just made her feel warm from head to toe. Cared for. He cared for her. Such a brute of a man, an enormous grizzly bear shifter, so strong and powerful yet so tender and kind with her.

The part that was totally screwed up, she thought with a frown, was that even though she knew it was real, and she loved that he touched her and cared for her so much this way, she couldn't help but wonder deep inside if she was really worth it. That she wasn't worthy of something deep, true, real.

She shook her head, hard. No. That was the old, cruel shit that Justin had managed to worm into her head. She had to refuse to believe it.

Her phone jingled in the living room. She went right to it, half terrified it would be Justin, mostly hoping it was Cortez. When she got her phone and saw the name flashing there, she yelped with delight and swiped it on immediately. "Pix!"

Her best friend's voice bubbled with laughter over line. "Haley, girl! Guess what?"

"What?"

"I'm heading your way. You ready for a houseguest?"

Haley shrieked with excitement. "Yes! I've missed you so much. Deep Hollow is so cute, I can't wait for you to see everything. When will you get here?"

"Is a few days from now okay?" Pix's voice was just as excited.

Haley shrieked again. "Definitely!"

"But I don't want to ruin your writing schedule," her friend added in a more serious tone. Aside from Haley's family, Pix knew more about Haley's hard journey and her current goals than anyone else in the world.

And now Cortez knew too. Oh, she liked that. A lot.

"You won't wreck my schedule, Pixie girl. I've been learning that it's really important to take breaks and have fun."

Pix's teasing, interested voice said, "Ohhh, really?"

They both laughed.

"Does this is mean my hard-working friend Haley has perhaps met someone who is showing her that life can be fun?"

Haley grinned. She and Pix had known each other since they were little girls. Pix could read right between the lines.

"Yes," she said through a smile she couldn't get rid of. "Oh, Pix, he's amazing. And he sees me. He really sees me for who I am." Her skin shivered at that truth.

"Sweet girl, that's it." Pix sounded relieved and sympathetic at once. "That's the tone in your voice I've missed hearing for way too long now. You deserve this so much. I'm so excited for you. Tell me about him?"

"He's a bear shifter, he's so big and strong. But he's gentle and kind too, even though I think he could rip the head off anyone if he needed to. But he'd never do that unless he was forced to defend himself. He's the absolute opposite of Justin, and he just feels so good. Pix, I'm terrified. Terrified I'll screw this up. But it just feels so *right* with him." The wonder in her voice was real.

"Hooray! I can't wait to meet him. He sounds like a

keeper, Haley. And you deserve that more than anyone I know."

He sounds like a keeper. Just the thought of it made Haley glow after she and Pix hung up. Yes. Cortez was a keeper. A keeper in a way her ex had never been. A keeper in a way she had never truly imagined before. Their kisses, the ones that set her soul on fire and allowed her imagination to fly up and be brilliant, filled her memory again. Cortez had opened himself to her, and she had opened herself to him. She could trust him. Sure, he said he still didn't feel like he could trust himself. But when she had watched him shift into his bear so fast, had seen how he instantly was driven to protect her, charging off into the unknown to challenge back the intruder mountain lion, she'd known then that he was ready to keep her safe.

Realization hit her so suddenly that she went stock still in the middle of the living room, eyes wide.

She believed she wasn't worthy, but Cortez didn't believe that and he didn't see that about her. He thought she was worthy of everything good there was.

And while he believed he wasn't fit to keep those he cared about safe, she knew that was wrong. He would have died to protect her from that strange shifter yesterday.

They each thought they both were screwed up, but that wasn't the truth. No, what was true was that they were both still scared. Just scared. And while fear might suck, it wasn't real.

She vowed to herself on the spot that whatever this incredible thing flaming between them was, they would make it true and whole. She had to see him again. Soon. She had to tell him, no, *show* him, how much she cared. That she was with him all the way. That her past might be shitastic, and his past might be filled with tragedy and pain, but just maybe, Haley and Cortez could make a future together that would be something that looked more like completely awesome.

10

*C*ortez stepped out of the shower, the day's grit thankfully washed off, but he still felt tired as hell. He'd taken some clients out that morning, and they'd had an awesome time snowshoeing up above Silvertip Ridge and then enjoying the gourmet lunch provided by the lodge that he'd packed along. They tipped him really well at the end, telling him he was a damn good guide and that they would be back again soon, this time with friends. That had been great, and he felt somewhat cocky as he returned to the lodge to find Quentin so he could help his older brother make some repairs on one of the maintenance buildings.

That went downhill quick, because Quentin was pissed at him again. Those damn panther shifters from the other day apparently had been going around to every social media site, saying that Tooth 'n Claw Tours was terrible and no one who stayed at the

Silvertip Lodge should ever book a trip with them. He and Quentin had an argument that quickly got so loud, it was a good thing they were way out by the back buildings where guests couldn't hear them. Then he still had to spend the next two hours in his brother's terrible company, each of them banging and hammering so hard it was lucky they didn't split the damn wood.

By that point Cortez was pretty fucking pissed off himself. Even the fresh memory of sweet, beautiful Haley kissing him and touching him and looking at him like he hung the damn moon was just barely enough to keep him from completely losing his shit. His next fuckup? He'd forgotten yet again that he asked Beckett to meet him at the cabin that afternoon to do some work, so he was treated to a text that said, *Are you fucking kidding me man? Get your head out of your fucking ass before I come find you and kick it farther up there. Don't ask me to waste my time again until you figure shit out. I wanna help you but you have to fucking show up.*

Fucking awesome.

By the time Cortez got back to his little place in town, he'd been a tightly wound storm cloud that threatened to explode at the smallest provocation. So right now, still wet from the shower, he was in no damn fucking mood to be nice when someone knocked on his door.

"Fucking hell," he growled. He wrapped a towel tight around his waist and stormed toward the front door, not giving a shit who'd be treated to a sight when he yanked it open. The second he did, the enraged greeting he planned to roar out died on his lips.

Haley. Haley, wearing a green winter hat on her head that made her green eyes seem even brighter, her jacket pulled tight around her, the tentative smile and softness in her gaze as she looked at him from the doorstep. Then her eyes dropped down to his naked chest, which still had water droplets from the shower on it. Then down to the gray towel he'd tied tight around his waist. Then down to somewhere below the spot where the towel snugged against him. Her mouth rounded into the prettiest little *oh* shape, her eyes widening.

"Uh—come in." The way her eyes were trained on his towel was enough to stir his dick into life. He had to kind of shift his feet and lean back from the hips so he wouldn't tent up the front of the towel. Damn, she was gorgeous. Pretty Haley, such an intriguing woman who wasn't afraid of him.

When she swept her eyes back up to his, he saw something in them that completely stalled out his brain and made his boner even harder. Dark, sweet desire. She swallowed, and his gaze traced the delicate movement of her throat. "I'm sorry. I should've called you first. I just wanted to come over here and see you."

They stared at each other for a long minute. "Come inside," he said again, a dark murmur full of promise and need. He stepped aside to let her slip past him, her pretty scent sweeping through him, threatening to drown him in its intoxicating allure. Whoa, damn.

After she came in and he shut the door, he turned around to see the desire in her eyes tripped toward hesitation and nervousness. "I really should have called. I'm barging in on you. I shouldn't have come—"

He strode toward her, closing the distance between them with the desperation of a drowning man reaching for a life ring. "No *should have* or *could have* or *would have* with me, Haley. Everything you do is good by me. Don't you ever question yourself."

She shyly nodded. "Deal," she whispered, a smile brushing her lips.

"Oh, wait." Suddenly remembering the one other good part of his day, he turned and headed for the little kitchen table that served as a catch-all for papers, keys, and other random shit he couldn't find a good place for. "I have something for you." Wiping his hand on the towel to be sure it was dry, he grabbed up the sole book on the table and turned around to offer it to Haley. "I figured you must like to read, since you're a writer. This book is the history of the Silvertip Lodge as written by a guest years ago. Uh, I thought you might like to read it. It's for you," he added. "I mean, your own copy. From me."

He suddenly felt kind of dumb saying that. And just handing it to her like this. He'd seen it in the lodge's gift shop earlier today when he'd stopped in there with his clients, who were looking for gifts to take home with them, and immediately thought of Haley. It wasn't very long, but it had pictures and was a pretty good read. It was probably the only book he'd read in about five years, and he'd only read it because his parents had given a copy of it to each Walker son. Damn, he hadn't even wrapped it.

Before he could apologize for that, Haley reached for it. She gazed at the cover, which was a photo of the lodge on a beautiful summer day, then turned it over to read the information on the back. When she looked up at him, her eyes seemed extra shiny. "You got this for me? A gift? From you?"

He nodded, still feeling somewhat abashed. But it seemed she liked it. "Yeah. I just figured you might be interested."

Her hand trembled as she put it back on the table, then said quietly, "That's one of the best gifts anyone's ever gotten me, Cortez. You—I—Thank you," she ended simply, looking at him like he'd just offered her the gift of life itself.

Looking so fucking sweet and sexy at once, so damned kissable, that his dick roared back to life and probably tented the hell out of his towel. He didn't care, because neither did she. With a single stride he went to her, pulled her into his arms, held her hard and close. She made a little sound in her throat, so sexy and needy, and he was undone.

"Cortez," she murmured, reaching for him with just as much need and passion. He crashed his lips over

417

hers, tasting her, sucking her luscious lower lip into his mouth. Damn, she tasted better than anything he'd ever known he wanted. Damn, he wanted this more than anything he'd ever had before. He wanted Haley. All of her.

Though he was half afraid he would hurt her with the force of his need, Haley was strong. So much stronger than she thought she was. She wanted him, he could feel it in how eagerly she kissed him back, how she pressed against him, how she rolled her fingers up and down his bare back, slicking them over his skin, racing fire through his body everywhere her fingers touched him.

He growled, gripping the nape of her neck, his fingers digging into her skin as he kissed her deep and strong and wild. Powerful, beautiful little Haley wanted him. She wanted to have him like this, to not be afraid of him. She wanted him as badly as he wanted her. Hell fucking yes. Cortez needed to touch her. To feel her. To see her naked before him, the look on her face full of sharp desire for him. Only him.

Pulling back from her, he growled, "Haley. I need to hold you and love you and fuck you right now. I need to feel your body against mine, while I taste you and touch you all night. All night, woman. That okay with you?"

HALEY THOUGHT her heart might explode from the force with which it beat. Cortez was looking at her with such deep intensity, his eyes bright with hunger. Hunger for her. "Yes. Yes, all of it, yes."

He reached forward and kissed her again, so hard it was almost painful, which she wanted. She pulled the pain into herself, gave some back to him, shared it so they could both let it go. He reached down, nibbled his way along her cheek, down her neck. "Mine," she thought she heard him growl there. She moaned in response, her entire body shivering with sweet chills of arousal.

"Clothes. Off. Now." The desire roughened his voice so much that she almost couldn't understand him, but she knew what he was saying. Yes. Yes. A thousand, million times *yes.* His voice was a command, one she was more than happy to obey. She yanked at her jacket with trembling fingers, managed to get it off. Pulled her sweater over her head, then went for her shirt. Dammit, buttons. She couldn't deal with them. Swept up in the feverish need in Cortez's eyes, she heedlessly ripped her shirt off, throwing it aside and barely hearing as the buttons scattered all over the floor.

This amazing man, setting her body on fire from her toes to her hair. He'd gotten her a *book.* The history of the place that was so important to his clan, his family, him. She was awed again by the sweetness of the gift. He thought he couldn't save anyone? He didn't know it, but that's what he was doing by giving her the gift of something that was a piece of his own heart and heritage, in the form of something that was so important to her.

This man, this bear, was a warrior with a huge heart. He might be gravelly and angry and raging at himself under the surface, but that wasn't the real him, the only him, the true him. Deeper inside, in the part of Cortez that was most honest and genuine, he was peaceful and kind and wanted nothing more than to help others. She could see that about him as clearly as anything.

She fumbled with her bra, but he said, "Let me." His voice went quiet, so quiet in the room. He reached forward, put his hands around her back, undid the clasp. Gently slid the powder blue straps of her bra off her arms, letting the whole thing fall to the floor, leaving her bare in front of him. Exposed.

But it wasn't scary, having Cortez look at her. Oh god, no. It was sexier than anything. His gaze was utterly worshipful. "Damn, woman. Damn." It was all he said, and all he needed to. His eyes went back up to hers as he reached down and undid the front of her pants, shimmying them down off her hips. She stepped out of them, kicked them aside, her breath hitching in her throat. He hooked his big thumbs on the other side of her underwear and slid it down as well, kissing her along the way. His lips on her neck, down to her breasts, first one, then the other, his tongue swirling and dragging across her nipples. A ragged gasp exploded out of her as his touch flamed across her body. Down he kept going, his mouth tracing kisses across her rib cage, over her belly, brushing one hip bone, then the other. He was on his knees now, at her feet, grasping one ankle and gently encouraging her to step up so he could slide the underwear off her foot, then off her other one. He tossed them aside, and she was completely naked before him.

"Cortez." Just his name, saying his name, ending it on a rattling gasp that pushed out of her throat as the room seemed to spin around her when he blew a hot breath right against her sex. She cried out from the exquisite pressure.

His hands reached up to hold her hips. "Steady, beautiful," he murmured, the word another sweet breath that tickled across her heated center. "I want to taste you here, Haley. Hold onto me."

Yes, she had to hold onto him, had to grip his shoulders hard with her hands. She would fall over otherwise. He gently breathed against her again, then followed it with his tongue. Haley half gasped, half shrieked as he tasted her, slid his tongue through her wetness, licked the sensitive little nub there, gently explored her and kissed her there as he swirled his tongue around. She never wanted anyone like she wanted Cortez. She was so turned on, every nerve in her body exploding and singing, shaking and unsteady and filled with delirious joy at his touch.

He held tight to her hips, his fingers pressing into

the soft roundness of her behind, his face pressed right up into her sex as he licked and tasted and circled his tongue on her. Haley lost it, lost all sense of place and time and self. She only knew right here, right now, Cortez with his tongue buried inside her, stroking her with a strong, steady rhythm that would drive her over the edge. Soon.

"Cortez," she panted, her fingers gripping his shoulders so brutally hard she knew there would be marks later. "Cortez, please." Her voice was a soft rattle in her throat, desperate with need.

"Yes," he murmured, the vibration of the word against her clit threatening to toss her right over the gorgeous edge of ecstasy. "Yes, my sweet beautiful Haley. Yes. Come for me, beautiful."

That did it, his lips vibrating against her, his tongue thrusting back in to stroke and taste. Her orgasm swept over her like a roaring firestorm as her voice screamed out into the room, a wordless cry as he buried his tongue into her again and again. She held his shoulders and he gripped her hips, holding her up while she shook and shook from the sweet, delirious force of it. The spasms spread out to every inch of her body, splintering through her with the ecstatic rush. Her ears banged, her eyes rolled to the back of her head, and everything was light and stunning and good.

Slowly, slowly, the spasms ebbed away, leaving her to fall limp against him, still gasping. Cortez held her, gently caught her in his powerful arms. Then he swung her up into them, accompanied by her small exclamation. Turning, he strode across the room toward a partially open door, which he kicked open to reveal a bedroom. "Need you now," he growled into her ear, his teeth nibbling it after he said that, drawing another small moan from her. He went straight to the bed, gently set her down on it. Yanking his towel off, barely giving her time to widen her eyes at the sight of his hard body and that thick, long cock he'd been hiding under the towel, he pushed her back, slid his large hand between her legs, pushed them open. She spread herself open for him, willing, wanting. He pressed against her, his hips pushing into hers, his erection against her still slightly pulsing lips.

Then he slid himself in, sweet glorious inch by inch, and she was in heaven again. "Hard," she demanded, panting. "I can take you, Cortez," she whispered as he paused, looking at her. "You won't hurt me."

To prove her point, she reached forward and nipped his neck, catching flesh with her teeth, gently tugging. Biting down, harder. Hers.

He groaned, pulled back, then slammed into her with a guttural cry that she matched as he took her with all the strength she knew he possessed. In, back out, slamming back in. She was so wet he slid in easily, but he was still so big that she gasped from the pleasurable pain of having him fill her so deep. She slid her hand up behind his neck, holding tight. He found her other hand, laced his fingers into hers, held her tight back. Stroking in, he held her gaze as well. His eyes were wild, tender, craving. Bright with his bear, bright with his fierce desire. He held her down, pushed onto her and into her, guided this sexy ancient dance. Controlling with strength and protectiveness in a way she adored.

Wild in his embrace, she arched against him, meeting him as he pushed himself into her again, the sound of their joining a rhythmic beat in the room. He would protect her and open doors for her and give her precious gifts, but here, now, he commanded, he ruled. He was in charge of her, dominating her with his entire glorious body.

And she loved it so damned much. His control gave her a sweet, magnificent freedom to safely lose herself in this moment.

Slamming into her, bucking them both against the bed so hard the headboard started smacking into the wall in time with his thrusts, his breathing intensified, getting more ragged. He was heavy, heavy and hard against her, holding her, riding her to his own explosion. She saw it coming, saw the feral look ripple across his face, felt it as he swelled inside her even more. Suddenly, he reached down and lightly bit one of her nipples, then harder as she gasped her encouragement. He moved his head up, licked and bit her neck, her ear, her cheek, her lips. Locking his eyes on hers, holding her with him. Sexy, sexy man, with her all the way.

He never stopped sliding back and forth, in and out of her, and she was coming again. He was making her come again, the white-hot freight train of it slamming over her as she shattered again. Her second cry echoed through the room. His dick suddenly throbbed inside her, huge, and he spurted into her, his roar joining hers, their cries slamming around the room as Haley's head about came apart from the frenzied ecstasy of it all, the wildness of it all.

Cortez pumped into her again, again, his movements eventually slowing as his orgasm faded off, each of them gasping so hard she thought their hearts might up and gallop out of both their chests. Finally, his pace completely stopped, and he laid his head against her still heaving chest, his fingers squeezing her hard and his breath hot against her breast. Even while his breath still came fast, he became gentle with her again, his touch tender, holding her as if she was precious. As if she was the most amazing thing he'd ever been near.

She reached out her free hand to stroke his cheek, to feel that stubble against her palm. He still held her other one, their fingers still entwined, slick with sweat like the rest of their bodies. He made a deep "Mmm" sound of satisfaction as her fingers touched his face, smiled against her hand. His eyes were soft now, half unfocused, but present. He was with her. Right here.

Carefully, he slid out of her, making her protest, but he immediately turned her, gently, so that he was spooning her, pulling her tight into his chest. Holding her close, his arms big and strong around her, his legs tangled in hers, his sheltering body molded into hers like they belonged that way.

Inside, she knew. She smiled hard, so hard, even as an emotional sweetness prickled at her eyes. They did belong together. Both of them hurting, messed up or not, Cortez was hers, and she was his. That was something she knew without a doubt was the pure truth.

They belonged to one another.

11

*C*ortez grunted as he heaved heavy bags of sand, lumber, and a smaller assortment of random supplies he'd picked up earlier at the do-it-yourself shop in town. Setting them down beside the bare framework of his cabin, he gave everything a once over, then nodded. He'd managed to pick up everything he needed. These were the items he had to have to keep working on the cabin. Not only had he blown off Beckett earlier this week, but even if his friend had shown up to help his lame ass, they wouldn't have been able to do much because Cortez also had forgotten to get new supplies. But he had them now, and he was ready to get working again.

It sounded cheesy even in his own head when he said it, but he felt like a new man. All because of a beautiful, soft, funny, sweet woman who was now deep in his soul. He liked having her there. He felt renewed and refreshed just by realizing what he'd been missing all his life. Haley. He'd been missing her, and now she was here. She was here, and she was his. It was that simple, and that stunning.

He grunted again as he turned away to head back to his truck, but a grin pulled at his mouth. Yeah, he sounded like some sort of self-help guru now. So what. It was all the truth. The right woman really did change everything, as Quentin and Shane had often told him.

As he reached for the handle on the truck, he caught a sudden whiff of something that stopped him in his tracks. Lifting his head, he carefully scented the area. Everything seemed like it should, but something bothered him. He slowly took his hand off the truck door and walked around the clearing, his steps very quiet despite his size. His eyes scanned the forest, his jaw tight, as he used his shifter senses to figure out what had alerted him. His senses in his human form were far weaker than his bear form, but still stronger than any regular human's. He didn't smell that strange cat again, or any other intruders, but something seemed off.

Frowning, he wondered if maybe Beckett had stopped by after all to drop something off as some sort of peace offering. He quickly dismissed that thought. Sure, even if he was pissed at him, Beckett would die for Cortez if it came to it, just like any of the members of the bear clan here. But that sure as hell didn't mean Beckett was a considerate individual who would go out of his way to run supplies up to Cortez's cabin without Cortez asking him first. No, Beckett hadn't been here.

Who, then?

Finally, Cortez shrugged, but he pulled his phone out of his pocket as he still scanned the surrounding snow-covered trees. Pulling up Quentin's number, he shot off a quick text.

Think someone might've been to my cabin again. Not positive.

He started to put his phone away, knowing Quentin was probably busy, but a response came immediately.

I was just about to call you. Abby scented rogue wolf shifters nearby. Remember how much trouble all the wolf packs have been having with rogues lately? Seems like some are nearby. She caught scent of some other shifters too, cats and bears, but we can't say if they're guests or not after that big reunion.

Cortez swore. A huge reunion this past week had been why he'd half killed himself with work and barely gotten to see Haley after their incredible evening together. The lodge had filled with shifters from all over the country who booked it for the entire week. There were tons of them running around, which made it hard to differentiate between them and other shifters who might have come into the area with intentions of starting some shit or generally being assholes.

His phone jangled again. *You know we wouldn't normally care too much, but some guy just called the lodge about five minutes ago and asked for you. Male, sounded aggressive. We told him you weren't working today, and he said he'd find you. Then he hung up. Wouldn't say who he was even though we asked. I don't like it.*

Cortez felt the hairs on his neck prickle even though he knew no one else was here right now. Even so, he turned in a slow circle, letting his baleful gaze pierce the woods around his property.

Don't know who would be calling me up there, he sent back to Quentin.

Neither do I. Stay alert. We're keeping our eyes open up here.

He inhaled deeply through his nose, pulling in all the scents around him once more as he also strove to calm his bear, which was riled again. No matter what shit went down between him and Quentin, his brother had his back just as much as Beckett did. If Quentin was wary, Cortez needed to be, too.

An image of Haley flashed into his mind, her beautiful face opening in ecstasy beneath him. His bear prowled watchfully inside him, rattling along Cortez's nerve endings. Hmm. Maybe that was all it was. He went back to his truck and slid in. Now that Haley was in his life, Cortez's bear would be feeling a hell of a lot more possessive and protective than usual. Any random thing would set him off, even though it had nothing to do with her. He threw his truck into gear and headed down the dirt road that led into town.

Shaking it off, he instead focused on the night ahead. He'd managed to snatch one night with Haley since their first incredible night, but mostly he'd been working hard at the lodge, and she had a new burst of self-confidence and enthusiasm for her book and had been writing like a fiend. But they'd both agreed to take a break and have fun tonight.

It was Deep Hollow's annual tree lighting cere-mony, dubbed the midwinter doldrums pick-me-up fest, and everyone in town always went to it. Haley's best friend, Pix, had been here visiting for several days, so of course Haley wanted her to come to the festival. Cortez had met Pix and instantly liked both her forth-right nature and her sheer zest for living, which was something he wanted Haley to gain more of as well.

During their last phone call, Haley also mentioned that she and Pix had met Beckett in town the other night, and there had been huge sparks between his best friend and her best friend. She'd added that maybe this town was filled with some sort of epic freaking magic and every girl coming through was going to fall for a bear shifter. That conversation had turned into an amazing episode of phone sex, which Cortez had never done before and neither had Haley. But damn, was it ever something they both enjoyed a hell of a lot.

Damn, he liked this woman. A hell of a lot.

When he got to his place, he showered in record time, dressed, and headed into the crowded bustle of downtown Deep Hollow to the tree lighting ceremony area. The event was not only fun for locals, but was hyped up at the lodge as well as several of the other small communities scattered within the remote county. Despite the sizable crowd here tonight, Cortez had no problem spotting Haley almost instantly. She was a beacon to his senses. Probably to his dick too, but that was okay. Haley had told him a few days earlier that she was now basically a walking hormone. That just thinking about him got her so turned on it made her wet. After she'd said that she hadn't blushed, but instead seemed tongue-tied as she looked away and then laughed. He loved that about her. She wasn't like a cutesy girl who turned red, but instead she got so turned on by him that she couldn't find the right words to say. He had to admit it gave him a puff of manly pride.

He went straight to her and pulled her in for a kiss, not caring who was watching. She returned it with just as much vigor, enough that when he gently pulled back to look at her, he said, "Feeling a little frisky, huh?" Her sweet peal of laughter said *yes.*

Only then did he say hello to Pix, who stood nearby and wore a delighted grin. He sensed that Pix approved of him. He also figured she must hate Haley's ex as much as he did. But in the next second Pix's eyes went past him, an enormous smile breaking out on her face. He turned to see Beckett striding up to them. His buddy had eyes only for Haley's friend, though he greeted her without a kiss. Even so, Cortez knew full well when Beckett was interested in a woman. He hoped for Pix's sake that she knew the score with Beckett. He didn't have a good track record with women since his bear was so unruly. In fact, Cortez was half surprised to see Beckett willingly out and about in the large gaggle of people, especially one that included humans from outside of town who didn't know about shifters.

Beckett finally looked at Cortez. No need to beat around the bush. Cortez looked him straight in the eye and said, "Sorry I've been an asshole. That's changing." He didn't look at Haley as he said that, but Beckett briefly glanced at her before looking back Cortez. Clearly he knew why Cortez planned on shaping up. "I picked up some more stuff I needed to work on the cabin. You in for some hard labor maybe tomorrow or so? I'll be there. For damned sure."

Although one eyebrow raised, Beckett just nodded. "Yeah. I gotta make sure you don't do anything dumb like drop a beam on your foot or something."

"Uh-huh," was all Cortez said back. Cool. Things were good with him and Beckett again. He knew everything would've been fine eventually, but he had a sneaking suspicion that Beckett's magnanimous mood had a lot to do with Pix standing beside him. She looked like not only could she take him on, she might actually be more than a match for him. Tiny thing that she was, she seemed weirdly powerful. She'd sure need all the strength she had to handle a guy like Beckett. Cortez shrugged, then grinned as he squeezed Haley close to him. He had enough to think about with her sweet, sexy presence right beside him. No need to worry about his friend's extracurricular activities.

A gaggle of kids ran by, shrieking and giggling with excitement. Cortez had told Haley earlier that the event was most fun for the kids in town, because after the tree was lit up, all the kids were allowed to run up and grab one of the pile of presents tucked under the tree. They were just little things that all the locals offered up. Everyone made sure there was plenty since there were always a lot of visitors in town for this.

As the four of them stood there, talking and sharing a thermos of hot cocoa for which Beckett had supplied marshmallow vodka for the girls to spike it up with, Cortez enjoyed watching Haley's pleasure at the simple, homey little town event. He had to admit he enjoyed it too. This was his hometown, with friends and family scattered all throughout the crowd of people. He knew Jessie and Shane were around some-where with Grant, and all sorts of others, humans and shifters, that he'd known since he was little.

This was his home, even though it was hard some-times when everyone around knew everything about everyone else. Like everyone here knowing about the guys from his SAR team he'd been unable to save in time to prevent them from lives that would be forever challenging. As Quentin liked to say now and then, which often got him popped by one of his brothers, it was what it was. There wasn't a damn thing Cortez could do about the past. The only thing he could worry about now, he thought, looking at the gorgeous woman pressed close to his side, her eyes shining as she laughed and enjoyed herself, was the future.

He was damn well certain that future included Haley Adams.

"Hey, you," she said, squeezing his hand and running her fingers over his thigh.

Naturally, his dick sat up at attention when she did that. He cleared his throat and squeezed her hand back. "You tryin' to get me to throw you over my shoulder and march out of here so I can have my way with you?" His voice was low, for her ears only, though with all the noise of the happy, excited crowd, no one would have heard him anyway.

She grinned up at him in a positively devilish manner. "Nope," she said in a flippant tone. "Just touching you because I can."

Oh, hell yeah. That was something he could live with. "Don't stop," he suggested. "While you're at it, imagine my tongue on you." He liked the way her eyes got all soft and unfocused and how her breathing suddenly changed when he said that.

She smiled dreamily at him, looking half-drunk just on his words. His bear rumbled with satisfaction. Leaning even closer, he murmured, "How about we cut out of here as soon as the kids run up and grab all their toys?"

"Okay." She sounded breathless.

There was a commotion up front as the festivities

began, but Cortez couldn't focus on them. All he was aware of was Haley next to him, pressed in close against him, the heat of her body causing his own body to stay even hotter than usual. He watched her watch the tree get lit up when the town's mayor gave the signal to the lighting guys. He grinned at her grin of excitement and small gasp of appreciation when the enormous pine tree, which Cortez and Beckett had hauled down off the mountain in December to stay in the town square through the holidays until now, was brilliantly dazzled by the numerous strands of lights strung all over it.

Mostly, he felt a sharp stir of happiness in this moment. With Haley, with Beckett, with the whole damn town. For just this moment, he felt good. Content. His bear calm and quiet, his own sense of self rooted solidly to the ground here.

Even if it lasted for just a moment, he'd take it.

When Pix got called up to the little stage under the tree to drop the race flag that was the signal for all the kids to run up and dive for the presents, Cortez watched as his best friend and his—his Haley, he stumbled in his head, because he wasn't sure how to define her just yet—both hollered and whooped with excitement for Pix's shining moment in the town's festivities. Then when the crowds began to disperse, the atmosphere both relaxed and excited at once, he tugged at Haley's hand. She looked at him, her eyes regarding him with a steady gaze over the smile on her lips.

"Think those two can handle it if we leave?" Cortez shrugged a shoulder toward Beckett and Pix up by the tree, Pix cooing over the kids unwrapping their presents and Beckett ogling her ass with a big grin on his face. Haley followed Cortez's gesture and burst out laughing.

"I think they won't even notice we're gone."

"Then come on, woman. I've got plans for you."

The look she gave him said she not only liked hearing that, but she probably had similar plans in mind. He took her hand and hustled them out of there, pushing through the crowds until they got back to the main street and headed for the house. The second he got them both through the doorway and into the living room, Haley surprised him by being the one to make the first move. She just reached for him and started kissing him, before they even took their jackets off. No dummy, he pulled her close to him, pressing her against him while she kissed and nibbled his lips, soft little pecks that quickly had him breathing faster.

"I sure hope you're not weirded out this time by being in your parents' house again." Her voice was husky, with a quiver of laughter beneath it.

Cortez shrugged out of his jacket and just barely managed to hang it on the coat hook in the hallway. "Nah, it's actually not that bad. We didn't grow up here. They bought it when we were all out on our own already."

"I thought you grew up in Deep Hollow?"

"I did, but our place was teeny tiny, way out in the woods. Basically a shack, though we always had food and stuff. They took care of us, loved the shit out of us, made sure we had the really important things in life like schooling and attention and good values. We had good cubhoods." He shrugged. "They didn't have money then, though they saved every dime they could because they had plans to make a better life. After they managed to scrape together enough cash to buy the land up at Silvertip Ridge, we lived there with them in a cabin we all helped build. That's how I learned to do construction. Luckily, by that point we were all almost old enough to get out on our own, so we weren't under their feet for too long. It was a small place."

Haley gave him a curious look, her cheeks still a pretty pink from the walk in the frozen air. "Here all along I thought you were some sort of poor little rich boy. But your parents are self-made and you grew up kind of like me. My parents were wonderful and also made sure I never wanted for anything, but they were nowhere near rich."

Cortez nodded. "My parents always were extremely hard workers, and they passed that on to all of us. Now then," he said in a low voice. "Enough family talk, woman. Let's get upstairs into your room and see if I can find new ways to make you come, pretty Haley."

Haley's eyes widened and she made a faint noise. He could smell her sweet, sweet arousal. Oh, hell yeah. He liked that.

But just as she removed her jacket and pulled off her boots, the front door abruptly opened and Pix stormed in. Oh, shit. Cortez knew from one quick glance that she was very upset. He immediately looked past her to see if danger followed, but she shut the door behind her firmly. When she turned to them, he could see the tears swimming in her eyes and already streaked down her face.

Fucking hell. Beckett. Somehow, he knew his friend had blown his chance with Haley's best friend.

"Pix! What's wrong?" The way Haley rushed to her friend immediately also told Cortez that his evening with her was completely off.

Pix shook her head, her lips quivering.

Cortez shook his own head. "That dumb ox Beckett did something stupid, didn't he? I know him."

But she shook her head again. "It's my fault," she pushed out in a thick voice. But she didn't elaborate. Instead, she turned and went upstairs, her shoulders rigid.

Haley glanced at Cortez, warring emotions on her face. He instantly shook his head and reached for his jacket. "You take care of your friend," he told her firmly, liking the way she wasn't about to abandon a girlfriend just in favor of having some personal time with him. Haley knew how to stick up for her friends. Growing up in a tight-knit bear clan like he had, Cortez instinctively admired her response. "You're a good friend, Haley," he added softly. A smile crossed her face. "We still on for tomorrow? I understand if you feel like you need to take care of her instead."

To his relief, she shook her head. "Whatever happened, I know she's a big girl and she'll be fine tomorrow. Tonight maybe not, but she'll be okay in the morning." That beautiful smile spread over her face. "Besides, she really approves of you and wants me to spend more time with you." Her voice was teasing but firm.

He couldn't hold back his own smile. "Well then, it's a date."

"A date." The smile bloomed even bigger over her face, lighting it up and making his chest squeeze. "I like that, Cortez. I like that a lot."

He answered her with a long, slow kiss goodbye, which had them both panting again. But he finally broke it off, murmuring, "Go take care of your friend. I'll come by in the morning to pick you up."

He could feel Haley's smile warming his back as he turned and left, carefully closing the door behind him.

As he walked away from the house, leaving Haley behind, he was struck by something that made him pause for a moment. He didn't actually want to leave Haley, ever. He never wanted to walk away from this woman, not for real. He wanted her, he wanted to be around her, he wanted to share his damn life with her. She was his. He knew it, his bear knew it, both of their best friends knew it. If he ever saw her crying the way Pix had just been crying, he would cheerfully kill whoever caused it. He would fight for Haley as long and hard as was ever needed.

His only real fear, the one tucked deep inside him in the form of the bear that was calmer but still uncertain, was that maybe he couldn't actually be the strength and honor that she deserved. That maybe he was still too fucked up by the way in which he had failed his friends on the mountain to be the man that she needed.

Fuck. No. She deserved more, and he would have to find a way to give that to her. He squared his shoulders and threw off the feeling of lack. Fuck that.

As he got into his truck and headed across town to his own place, he set his jaw and vowed one thing. He was done letting his old shit rule him. He'd fight to be worthy of Haley's love, and he wouldn't allow himself to get in his own damned way.

They were both worth it.

*H*aley watched, wide-eyed, as Cortez whacked the sink pipe one last time with his hand. "Take that, asshole," he muttered, clearly at the end of his rope.

She couldn't help the little burst of laughter that just snorted out of her. When Cortez turned and gave her a mock glare, she covered her mouth, but more laughter spluttered through her fingertips until she was help- lessly consumed by it, clutching her stomach and trying to stop it without success.

Cortez sighed and looked back at the sink. "Round two. Sink pipe: one. Cortez: zero. Shit, you'd think I could figure this out. But I'm better at building the actual house than playing plumber. I should ask Beckett if he'll take a look at it," he added in a grum- bling voice. "He knows how to sweet talk stubborn old things."

Haley laughed again from her seat leaning against the hallway across from the upstairs bathroom in the house. Cortez had taken it as a challenge to do battle with the leaking pipe that had acted up again. "I think he's busy sweet talking Pix tonight. Don't think he'll come over here anytime soon." She was so pleased for her friend that things might be working out with Beckett after all. She'd found out from Cortez that he was actually a pretty cool guy.

Cortez looked at her speculatively for another moment. "Why didn't you tell me about her? That she's a dragon shifter." He didn't sound annoyed, just genuinely curious. Beckett had told him about Pix's secret, which had been behind her tears the other night. Haley had actually felt relieved that she didn't have to keep that secret from Cortez any longer. She didn't want to keep anything from him.

She shrugged back, still smiling. He looked so good holding the wrench, being all sexy mister fix-it. So hot and rugged, clad in jeans and a white T-shirt, his muscles bulging everywhere. She enjoyed that he liked to work with his hands. The thought made her shiver in anticipation before she answered. "It was her story. She's always asked me not to tell people that she's a dragon, so I never have. Not even my family, not even my ex. I'm glad she and Beckett got things figured out. Pix really loves being her dragon. She just doesn't love the dragon shifter society part of things." Haley frowned, knowing how restrictive that upbringing had been for carefree Pix. The she smiled. "It's so amazing when she flies. I always love watching it."

Cortez sat back on his bare heels, balancing his arms on his knees. "I thought dragon flight was invisible to humans. That's how dragon shifters managed to survive without detection. But you can really see her in that form?"

Haley nodded. "Yes, because certain humans can see them. Pix and I became friends at such a young age that we developed a close bond. She explained to me when she got older and she could understand it that the barriers that shield most dragon shifters from human eyes don't exist when there's a special connection between a human and a dragon shifter. So I can see all dragons now." She laughed at a sudden memory. "When we were kids, I always used to ask if she'd turn me into a dragon."

Cortez gave her another speculative look. "What did she say?"

"That dragon shifters are only born. They can't be made, like other shifter types can." *Like bears,* she thought, looking at the bear she could see somewhere deep in his golden-brown eyes.

"Huh. Never thought much about it. I don't know many dragon shifters. We've got one guy who lives here in town, but he really keeps to himself. And of course some of them come stay at the lodge, but that's about it. They're pretty different than most other shifter types. They have their own rules."

Haley nodded. "Those kind of differences are exactly why Pix distanced herself from the dragon shifter world. She loves being a dragon, but she never liked to live by all their rules." She flicked up an eyebrow at Cortez. "So is it just a fun thing for Beckett, with her? Or is it more?"

Cortez shrugged again, but a smile ticked up his mouth. "Beckett's reputation with women in town is not for being long-term. But when I ran into him at the store earlier today, I have to tell you he's never behaved like that before. Going back in there to buy a girl flowers." Cortez made a tsk-ing sound. "He's gone and lost his damn mind." But he still grinned. Aha. He was messing with her.

Haley grinned back and threw the closest thing she had at him, which happened to be a sock. He held up his hands in defense, ducking. "Don't you pitch your nasty socks at me, woman. That's some dirty pool."

She laughed with him. God, how she loved this. Just a simple, totally unromantic moment. Sitting on the floor and watching a man fix a sink. But they'd just had the best day together. This morning, Beckett had come by, apologized to Pix, and invited her out to dinner. Assured by her strong, level-headed friend that she would be just fine, Haley had left her to spend the day with Cortez as planned. He took her snowshoeing, and they had snowball fights, and he showed her all the cool little trails around the lodge. They had a picnic lunch. And with each moment she spent with him, she

445

fell more head over heels with what an honorable, genuinely decent human being he was. Uh, shifter. Most of all though, she just liked him. A lot. Totally a lot.

Standing up, mock defensively kicking her sock back at her, Cortez washed his hands at the sink, dried them carefully on a towel, and looked at her. "Well, woman. We spent all day today together. Then you made me a damn good dinner. Then I fixed this damn sink. Again. Got anything in your bedroom that needs fixing?" Slowly, with purpose, he padded toward her.

All her laughter left as quickly as it had arrived. Haley stared, her breath caught in her throat and delicious tingles spreading through her, as her sexy mountain man came toward her. He reached a hand down to her, which she grabbed. He hauled her up so easily, like she was lighter than a feather. So damn big, so damn strong, so damn protective and gentle. She felt safer than anything with him. "There might be," she whispered, watching as his eyes brightened. "This way."

Her fingers still wrapped in his, she turned and led him down the hallway to her room. The second they entered it, he turned back around and pulled her into his arms, and abruptly hoisted her up just like he had the other day on the bridge. She squealed like a girl, not even caring, since it felt so dang good because suddenly her pelvis was pressed right into his. He had a huge, rock-hard erection. Her breathing immediately hitched and got uneven as he strode toward her bed. Then he stopped, looking into her eyes as a devilish little grin came onto his face.

"What are you planning?" she asked, as all the blood in her body seemed to rush to her clit. It got deliciously heavy just from his hungry expression.

"That I need to slide my dick into that sweet, soft pussy of yours right this second, Haley. That I want to see you come hard and fast for me."

Holy. Shit. Now mute, her voice strangling in her throat, chest heaving as her breath gasped, she just nodded. He turned and walked them right over to the wall, pressing her back against it and reaching down to urgently unsnap her jeans. He set her down for mere seconds so he could push both the jeans and her panties off her, then hoisted her back up again, totally naked from the waist down.

Her fingers shaking, she reached down to pull up the back of his shirt, trying to push down his jeans at the same time.

"Undo them first, woman," he muttered, his hands going down to unbutton them and yank them off. He kicked them aside. Carefully, he slipped a finger into her. She gasped, hard, as his fingers found the slick wetness that had begun the second he looked at her in the hall and she knew what he was planning. "Ah, babe." His voice sounded half strangled, too.

Without warning, without preamble, he slid into

her, his mouth urgently seeking and finding hers at the same time. She gasped against his lips as he slid in, then back out, then in a few more inches. Back out, and back in all the way, stretching her, filling her.

"Hard and fast," she gasped against him. She'd been aching for him since they'd been interrupted last night and had felt turned on all day. Clearly, so had he. He nodded against her, slamming into her. She grabbed for the back of his neck, his shoulders, and held on, her entire body sizzling with heat at their frantic, wild movements. Deep and long, he thrust into her, bringing her already primed body closer to the edge. She grabbed onto the back of his hair, digging her fingernails in, her legs wrapped tight around him as he bucked into her again and again.

Harder and faster, her head even smacked the wall behind her but she didn't care, their tongues tangling and teeth scraping as he fucked her with a savage intensity she matched stroke for stroke. The denial of the night before, the all day long foreplay of simply being in one another's presence, tipped her right at the edge of the sweet abyss in just a few moments. She trembled as he slid into her again, then the orgasm exploded around her, taking her by surprise as it roared in with blistering hot white heat. Her mouth opened in a soundless cry as the waves shattered through her over and over, in time with Cortez pounding against her and the sound of his own deep groan beginning to break out of his throat. He slammed into her again, so deep, so hard, then cried out with her as he released deep inside her, his hard shaft throbbing and spurting wet heat into her. So good, so good, she couldn't think. Didn't want to. Just enjoyed the blaze of sensation, knowing that he shared it with her at the same time. Together. This man, this amazing man. Hers.

Heartbeat thudding inside her, little black pinpoints around the edges of her vision, her hips slick and sweaty from where she and Cortez slid against each other, Haley slowly relaxed. Cortez gently slowed, a softness in his eyes and around his mouth telling her how good it had been for him. How happy he was right now. She knew her own wide grin matched his. They spent a moment just looking at each other, smiling like fools, until she giggled again. He kissed her on the tail end of it, slow and long and scorching with passion still.

This time, when he pulled back from her, his eyes were serious. His voice was quiet but clear when he said, "Haley. I want to be a better man for you." He snorted out a laugh, rolled his eyes up to the ceiling for a second. But when he looked back at her again, she saw tentative hope there. "It sounds so stupid and cheesy. Like it's just from some movie."

"Hey," she whispered. He looked back at her. "I'll out-cheese you. You're the best man I've ever met in my life." Her voice shook with the emotion, the prickling in her eyes stronger. The next words just popped out of her, easy and natural and true. "I love you, Cortez."

He froze, and for a second her heart plummeted. Then he said very cautiously, "You mean that?" More soft hope stole through his words. Her heart ached for the caution in him, even as it exploded with joy that he wanted her to say *yes.*

She nodded so hard she almost slipped right off of him. "Yes. The same thing happened to my parents. They knew, literally from the very first date they ever had, that they were meant for each other. So I grew up knowing that love at first sight does actually exist. It's real. I thought I had it with Justin—"

"Woman, don't ever say his name again. Especially not when I'm still inside you." Though his words were deadly serious, half his mouth was a lopsided grin.

She laughed through the happy tears and nodded. "That is definitely something I can easily do. What I was going to say was, I didn't understand what love could really be like until right now. With you."

The words floated between them. He looked at her, stroked her cheek with one thumb, his expression the most awestruck one she'd ever seen, especially on a man as big and bold as him. It was like she had just given him the most important gift in the entire world, and he was bowled right over.

Quietly, yet filled with emotion, he said the words right back to her, each one of them ringing with a strength of certainty that shook her to her toes. "I love you too, Haley. This is real."

Then he kissed her again, and again, until the passion rose once more and they rocked back into it, together.

13

*H*aley rolled over and blinked open her eyes when the smell of coffee hit her. Reaching up to scrub at her face, she squinted to focus in front of her. Cortez gently set down a steaming hot mug of the delicious stuff on the little stand beside the bed, smiling when he saw her open eyes.

"Good morning. Thought I'd bring you some coffee in bed to kickstart your day off right before I have to head up to the lodge."

Her heart melted and then seemed to expand, filling her chest with a good, happy feeling. She struggled to sit up in the bed. "You made me coffee first thing in the morning? You're the best bear shifter I've ever met." He huffed out a light chuckle, sitting on the bed next to her and stretching his arm out to stroke from her shoulder down to her hip. But the smile on his mouth didn't reach his eyes. She frowned. "Is something wrong?"

He paused long enough that she became alarmed. Finally he said in a clipped voice, "Quentin texted me this morning. There've been complaints. He wants to see me right now to talk about it."

She stared at him blankly. "Complaints? About what?" Another short pause, then it hit her. "Wait. You mean complaints about *you?* From guests?"

He gave a curt nod. His fingers were still gently stroking over her hip, solid and warm, but she sensed he wasn't completely present. "That's ridiculous." Her voice barked out in disbelief. "How can anyone complain about you?"

He shook his head, jaw tight. "I honestly don't know. All the guests from the reunion last week thought I did great. They said they had a wonderful time on each trip we did." He took a breath before he added, "And…"

He broke off again, his jaw so tight now it must be painful. Haley could see how hard it was for him to admit all this to her. To admit he was imperfect. It softened her and broke her at the same time. She knew imperfect pretty damn well herself. She firmly put her hand over his, squeezing hard, not letting go. He looked at her, squeezed back. "And?" she prompted quietly but encouragingly.

Deep inhale. "And I also got a text from one of the guys on the search and rescue team. He told me that

Tim—Tim's one of the guys who was in the avalanche. He's been in a coma in a hospital in Denver ever since." Cortez's tone was flat. "Anyway, Tim is probably being taken off life support later today. The doctors say all the signs indicate there's no coming back for him."

As he spoke, Cortez restlessly began tapping his fingers on Haley's hip beneath her hand, not even seeming to notice he was doing it. She instantly recognized it for what it was. It was hard, so hard for him to express how upset he must be about this, so while saying something he really didn't want to say, he got the trapped emotions out through some sort of movement. She knew because she did the exact same thing herself. Sometimes, things were just really hard to express.

"Hey." She reached out her other hand to turn his face to her, while also trying to scoot her body down to get close enough to give him a hug. But he stopped her. Gently, he wrapped his arms around her shoulders and leaned in to give her a kiss.

It was a soft, warm, lingering kiss, but she still could sense the distance in him. She knew it wasn't because of her, but she ached inside anyway. They'd had such a beautiful high last night. For it to come crashing down like this must be killing him. She kissed him back with all she had, wishing she could just bag everything and go with him up to the lodge. But he wouldn't want that anyway. He wouldn't want her there hearing from Quentin about how he'd screwed something up. Again.

She kissed him with all the soft strength she could, holding onto him until he pulled away to stand up. She held his hand as long as she could, not wanting to let him go, until he gently pulled it out of her grasp and went to the door. "I believe in you," slipped out of her mouth before she knew what she would say.

His shoulders stiffened, but he immediately swung back around to look at her. His jaw was still tight but his eyes were soft. So soft, and wondering as he looked at her. "Thank you," he said, his voice just as quiet as hers. "I'll call you later. Kick some ass on your book today, okay?"

She nodded and managed to smile, though she didn't dare open her mouth again. She was afraid she'd just start crying. Seeing such a strong, powerful man hurting so badly was painful enough. Seeing it when it was *her* man was almost devastating. Dammit, she wanted to save him from this.

After he left, she sat in the bed for a long time, her thoughts going every which direction in a maddening whirl. Finally she reached over and grabbed the coffee, which was now just warm instead of piping hot. It was still yummy, though. Sweet, amazing man, doing such a simple yet thoughtful thing for her. Naturally, her ex had never done any such thing for her. But Cortez? He would hitch a star and pull it down to earth for her, without her even asking for something crazy like that. She knew in her bones he'd do anything for her. They'd opened up to one another, let one another in, and said yes to love. Haley was completely and absolutely excited about life, her book was going well, she had faith in herself, and everything felt wonderful.

But right now it was impossible to enjoy any of it when the man she loved was hurting so badly, and there was not a single thing she could do about it.

---

*H*aley stared at her computer, her mind as blank as the screen. The words would barely come today. She was a professional writer, she knew how to write through crappy days, illness, a thousand interruptions. So she had gotten some writing done. But it wasn't nearly as much as she'd planned, and it sure wasn't as good.

Cortez had texted her earlier in the day just to ask what she was doing. Hearing from him made her heart pitter pat. But when she'd asked how he was doing, his answer had been vague. *Okay. Call you when I'm on my way back into town tonight.*

She answered him with smile, heart, and kiss emojis, feeling silly as she did. Then she simply said, *Yes.*

Jessie, who was clearing tables near her, caught her

unfocused gazing at her computer. "Nickel for your thoughts?"

Haley smiled halfheartedly and leaned back to stretch. "My thoughts aren't worth that much today, to be honest. Where's Grant?"

A proud smile blazed over Jessie's face. "He went to work with Shane today. Which means Shane is letting him ride in front of him on the tractor while he clears some snow."

Haley sighed at the sweet image. "It sounds more productive than my day's been. Jessie," she asked, hesitantly. "Do you know anything about guest complaints at the lodge?" She kept her voice low, mindful of out-of-towners who might be seated at some of the tables nearby. Everyone in the place was probably too busy enjoying baked goods and coffee as they chatted amongst themselves to pay any attention to what she was saying, but she wanted to be careful.

Jessie finished wiping down the chair seat and then came and stood by Haley's table. "Not much. I think Quentin and Abby are in charge of that kind of thing. Shane does behind the scenes stuff, like maintenance, so he never knows anything about the guests. Since I work here, I don't hear much scuttlebutt about the lodge. Why do you ask?"

"I was just wondering," Haley hedged. But Jessie was sharp.

"Ah. Something go on with a tour?" She framed her words carefully, probably also mindful not to be talking about lodge business in a public place. But Haley knew that Jessie understood why she had asked.

Clinking her often-gnawed fingernails against her laptop, Haley nodded.

Jessie sighed. "Poor Cortez. That sucks. He's had such a tough time these past several months since the accident. But you've made an enormous change in him, Haley. I can see it. Everyone else can, too."

Haley looked up at Jessie's kind expression. "A big enough change that can help him when he keeps getting knocked back down?"

Jessie made a face. "That's a good question. I don't know, but I will say this. He has a much better chance now that you're in his corner. Hey, before I forget, we're thinking of having drinks in town tonight. Me, Shane, Quentin and Abby. I bet Beckett and your friend Pix would come, too," she added with a knowing grin.

"Probably," Haley agreed. She had barely seen Pix for days now, since her friend was ensconced in some sort of love nest at Beckett's place outside of town. She was thrilled Pix had met her mate, knowing what a big deal that was for shifters.

So was Cortez her mate now too? She wasn't sure. She wasn't even sure she was ready for that. After Justin, being anyone's mate seemed like an undertaking that might be fraught with peril.

As soon as she thought that, though, she knew the difference. She'd never really wanted to be with Justin, not deep down. Not in the way she should have. But Cortez? Oh, yeah. He was hers. Down to her toes, she knew that.

As Jessie headed back behind the counter, Haley thought about what she had said. After several more minutes, she realized she wasn't getting get any more work done at the Mountain Muffin this afternoon. She might as well head back to the house and do something useful, like clean for a while. She packed up her stuff and headed out the door, waving at Jessie. As she went out into the dull, gray day, she passed more people heading in to grab a treat. Their casual cheer irrationally bugged her. Had any of them been guests at the lodge and taken a tour? Maybe complained about Cortez? She frowned at people on the street, recognizing how ridiculous she was being.

It just sucked so much not being able to help him. She might as well take it out on innocent strangers while she walked back to the house.

On an impulse, she veered off onto a side street to head down to Silvertip Creek where it gurgled in frozen passage through town. She liked to walk this way, even though it was out of the way and would take her twice as long to get to the house. But it usually wasn't crowded, and on a day like this one, in which gray skies and flat light made everything seem dull and uninspiring, she might even have it to herself.

As she walked, she tried to organize her thoughts

into something that made more sense and thus would give her something to hold onto. An anchor.

1. She really liked Deep Hollow. The community was tight-knit but welcoming, and she felt comfortable here. Like she belonged.

2. She was making some real friends here, like Jessie and Abby. A girl needed strong girlfriends that were fun and would have her back. She instinctively knew that both of them fit the bill. And she would be the same right back for them.

3. Although she hadn't seen Pix in almost three days, they talked and texted. It was clear that what Pix had with Beckett was real. Pix always had been a wanderer, but it sounded like she was going to settle into Deep Hollow, which was awesome. Having her bestie here would make Haley feel even more grounded, not to mention just completely thrilled.

4. This was a fantastic place to be a writer. She could go hiking in the mountains to clear her head, hang out at the Mountain Muffin to get a boost of energy by being surrounded by others, and even if she didn't actually make it as a writer on her own, she could probably get a job at the bakery or maybe even up at the lodge cleaning rooms or something.

5. No, screw that negative shit. She had to stop being so anxious about her writing. She had to shove aside the nasty old voice that her ex had stuck inside her head that said she couldn't do it without him. She'd been getting good feedback from her beta readers about this

book, and she could just feel how strong it was. She only had one chapter to go, and it was going to be good. So basically, she was a kickass writer for sure, and she just needed to stomp on all the ugly bullshit from the past until it was squished into nothing. Stomp stomp stomp.

6. Cortez. He knew how to kiss. Ooh, did he know how to kiss. And he knew how to be nice. He also knew how to be wild, in a super sexy way. Most important of all, he knew how to look right into her and see all the best parts, and then hold up a mirror to her so she could see them too.

7. Cortez again. She for real, truly deeply madly, loved him. Enough said.

8. He was battling inner demons of doubting himself and being unsure about his future, just like she was, but she could see so clearly that he was strong and powerful and would be able to get past anything. Especially with her around to help him see that, just like he was helping her see the same about herself.

9. But right now, she wasn't quite sure how to help him see that, since she was doubting herself again too. So that sucked.

10. Biggest of all: She'd already decided, deep in her heart and on every level of her soul, that this was her new home and that Cortez was her man, forever. Definite truth.

Just listing everything out in her head like that made her feel calmer. Better. More on top of the situation. When Cortez got back later today, she would throw him down on the bed and have her dirty way with him, even though it made her laugh to think that she would ever remotely be able to throw him down considering he was about twice the size of her. Then they would kiss the doubt and fears out of one another, and everything would be okay.

Satisfied with her thoughts, Haley blinked and took note of her surroundings. She was at the river, almost to the bridge. As she'd suspected, no one else was around. She sighed at how pretty it was, despite the grayness of the day. Oh yeah, maybe that was number eleven. Okay then:

11. The natural beauty around here soothed her soul as much all the other good parts. That was super important.

Just before she reached the bridge, her phone jingled in her pocket. Fishing it out, she saw Pix's name flashing on the screen. Hurriedly tugging off her mitten, she swiped to answer with a delighted, "What's up in the love nest, Pixie girl?"

But Pix's tight, worried voice stopped her dead in the middle of the bridge. "Haley, I just saw Justin in town. Where are you?"

A coldness that had nothing to do with the day seemed to creep through Haley. She stood rooted to the spot on the bridge, listening to the icy chuckle of the creek below. "What? That's impossible." Her voice croaked on the words. "He doesn't know where I am. Maybe it was someone who just looked like him?"

Pix shut down her grasping at straws. "No, it was definitely him. I'd recognize that shitweasel anywhere. I don't know what he's doing here, but I don't like it. Where are you?"

Haley shivered, peering at the dimly lit trees on the other side of the creek with trepidation. "I'm on the creek bridge. I'm heading back to the house."

"Beckett and I will meet you at the house. He texted Cortez and told him to call right away, but hasn't heard back yet. He might be working somewhere in a part of the lodge that doesn't have any cell service. How worried do you think we should be? Justin's probably just being an asshole, but I don't understand why he's actually here." Pix sounded concerned. Really concerned. She knew as well as Haley what a monstrous asshole Justin had turned out to be.

"I don't get it either—" Haley barely began when a familiar voice behind her suddenly cut her off.

"Hello, Haley. Imagine running into you out here in the middle of nowhere. Or should I say, in the middle of shifter territory?"

Haley whirled around in shock, her body completely icing over at the voice—and the words.

Her ex-husband, Justin, stood right behind her. The brutally cold look in his eyes and the bizarre, unhinged smile on his face froze her in sheer terror.

"Hey, baby. Miss me?"

15

*H*aley stared back at Justin with the usual stupid reaction that happened when she was really knocked off her axis: she couldn't speak. Words died in her throat, jumbled up in her mind, and she didn't know what to say. Stunned like a deer in the headlights, about to be run over.

In her ear, Pix was saying with increasing urgency, "Haley? Haley, what's going on? Is he there? Haley!"

Justin suddenly lunged forward. Haley squeaked and jerked back, dropping the phone to the ground. With a glacial smile, he shot his leg forward and neatly kicked it off the bridge. Her phone was swallowed into the icy creek below.

She stared at him in horror, her heart beating inside her like that of a tiny little creature that had suddenly encountered a deadly predator. Finally, she managed to shove words past her constricted throat. "What—what are you doing here? My phone," she added disjointedly, looking at the creek before she looked wildly back at him. She took half a step backward. "How did you find me? And how do you know about shifters?" The words came faster, spilling heedlessly out of her as her shocked brain caught up and tried to find some coherence.

Justin smiled at her. A calculating, still utterly creepy smile that went nowhere near his eyes. "Because I'm smart, Haley. I tracked your IP address through that last email you sent me. I also had a very good source of information here that told me you were around."

He tracked her IP address? The insidious lengths to which he would go became crystal clear and even more terrifying. Staring at him, this man who once had been her husband, someone she so foolishly had thought she loved, and really seeing the truth of how genuinely screwed up he was, made something else even more clear.

Cortez wasn't fucked up, nor was he a fuckup. Haley wasn't fucked up, either. No, Justin had just proved to her what true ugliness really was. He was beyond repair. He was a monster. She blinked, stunned at the clarity she'd never before truly recognized.

She'd never been the broken one.

Instead, Justin had been the messed up one all along. He'd just made her feel like she was the one who could never be healthy and whole again. She'd bought it, but it wasn't the truth. It never had been.

"How do you know about shifters?" she asked again, her voice still ragged, trying to buy herself time. She literally had no idea what he was capable of right now, but she knew if he tried anything really scary, she couldn't defend herself. Justin was a pretty big guy. Nowhere near as big as Cortez, but bigger and much stronger than Haley.

His eyes never left hers as he spoke. It was unnerving. "Remember Marisa? The woman I left you for?"

The blunt, perfunctory way he said it took her breath away. How had she ever thought he was a good person?

She moved her head in a jerky nod.

"As it turns out, she was special in more ways in one. She's a panther shifter. She explained everything about shifters to me." A brash grin lined his face, though his eyes were still dead pools of black.

Panther shifters? Like the ones who'd given Cortez such a hard time? Suddenly, despite her fear, she just wanted to reach forward and slap that ugly grin off of him. Narrowing her eyes, she shot back, "There's no such thing as panther shifters. That's just a highfalutin' name for mountain lions. She sounds like a snob." Haley was half delighted and half shocked at her boldness, but Justin's face instantly became so angry, so ruthless, her heart almost stopped.

"What the fuck do you know, you stupid little cunt. All you were ever good for was working for me."

His menacing voice rattled her entire body. Her mind now beginning to gibber with fear even though she tried to hold onto her anger, she steadily replied, "I never worked for you, Justin. I was working for us, you and me both, but you never appreciated it. You lost out on a good thing when you screwed me over."

He sneered, curling his lip. Haley caught a glimpse of something horrifying in his mouth.

Long, sharp canine teeth.

"Oh, my god," she breathed as a deep, instinctive terror clawed its way through her. "What are you? Did she turn you?"

She didn't know it was possible for shifters to show part of their animal while still in human form. But Justin had sharp teeth in his mouth. Teeth like a big cat's.

"Yes. Everything is more amazing now that she turned me, Haley." Something strange lurched in his eyes then. A flash of something more than the cold darkness. A flash of something distinctly not human. She took another step backward.

Had Pix heard her say where she was? Would she know? Haley was alone with someone who clearly was a madman, a madman who now was very lethal. Haley was just a human. Vulnerable. Now, she understood why Shane wanted Jessie to turn. Haley couldn't protect herself against a shifter. Especially not one who seemed insane.

Justin started to laugh, revealing those sharp teeth. Haley could hear her own terrified breathing, ragged and loud in the oppressive silence of the day. She could see it in his eyes now. True, literal madness. Had getting turned into a shifter made him insane? Were mountain lions insane? Or...maybe Justin always had been insane and she'd just never seen it.

"Being turned made me realize what I had been missing. It also made me realize our story isn't over yet, Haley."

He stalked toward her. Hissing. *Hissing*, like a fucking cat. Holy shit. Kitty, kitty, big fucking kitty. Big, dangerous, menacing kitty.

Her heart was catapulting out of her chest, her limbs liquified by fear. Once again, she couldn't move.

"Our story is that you can come with me, Haley." He grinned in a way that raised the hair on her neck. "Not with that stupid bear you've been hanging out with. Your place is with me."

Her blood curdled. What? She stared at him in shock.

He laughed. "Oh yes, I know all about that fucking bear. I've been around here for a while now. Watching you. Watching you with him."

Her stomach lurched. The cat scream in the woods at Cortez's place that day. Justin.

"I'm with a group of shifters who are much better

than any of the ones here, Haley. You can join us. You *will* join us. It's a completely new world." He laughed suddenly, an ugly, definitely crazy sound that scratched the air, making her recoil. "Just think of all the new stories I'll have for you to write down and sell so we can make even more money than we did before. We need that money." His lip curled up in a snarl. A very animal-like snarl. Holy fuck, that was terrifying.

Haley shook her head. *Focus.* She had to stay calm and focus, or else she would die. She tried desperately to make her voice nonthreatening, though it shook so hard she almost couldn't speak. "W-what happened to the new writer you found. C-can't he write down stories for you?"

She was close to the other side of the bridge. It was completely insane and stupid, but maybe if she ran for it, she'd be able to hide in the trees. No. That was totally dumb. As a shifter now, he'd be able to smell her no matter where she headed. Besides, she wasn't sure she could get her legs to work, she was so scared. Cortez. Where was he?

I can't rescue anyone anymore, Haley.

No. He would find her. She believed in her man. Her bear. She had to believe in him.

"The new writer was okay but then he got greedy. He wanted credit and more money. I had to cut him loose. You, Haley." Justin's eyes bored into hers, gleaming in an eerie way. They were freaking her out.

"You'll come back to me. Especially after I bite you and make you mine."

Wait, what? She stared at him in deeper horror. No. No, no, no. Why hadn't she asked Cortez to turn her already? She could defend herself if she was a bear. She could—

"I'm ready, Haley. Are you?" Justin's eyes suddenly glowed a bright copper.

She opened her mouth to scream.

Too late. He changed into an enormous mountain lion and leapt at her like a snarling, clawed wall of doom.

16

*A*n earthshaking roar shattered the silence as Haley turned to run. She slipped on some ice and went down, hard. Screaming, she tried to scramble back to her feet, but Justin grabbed her foot and yanked at her.

Then suddenly, he let go.

A chorus of horrifying growls and snarls ripped through the air, coming from everywhere. All around them. She staggered up and turned around, holding onto the bridge railing, and stared. An enormous, stunning chocolate-cinnamon bear grabbed the mountain lion, his dinner plate-sized paw raking with huge, lethal claws down the cat's back, eliciting a yowling shriek of rage and pain.

Cortez. He was here! He'd come for her, like she knew he would. Hope blossomed in her.

Behind him, another bear charged forward. Shane?

She wasn't sure, but she thought he looked like the bear she'd met during her first day at the lodge. Whoever he was, he was on their side. Following closely after were Abby and Quentin. As she watched, mouth open, Quentin abruptly burst out of his clothes into a huge grizzly bear, Abby erupting into a beautiful but deadly-looking wolf mere seconds after.

In the sky above her, a dragon screamed. Haley wildly looked up. Pix flew up there, her beautiful, powerful friend, a gigantic silver dragon, circling the air and shrieking with rage. Pinpointing Haley's location. Calling for help.

From the woods behind her, more roars and growls ripped out. She whipped her head around and saw a flood of bears, wolves, and huge cats. Holy shit. Friends? Foes?

One of them bared its teeth and dove straight for her, growling, jaws opened wide.

Foe! Definitely foe. She screamed again, sheer panic making her hold tight to the railing and kick her legs out at the oncoming mountain lion in a futile move born of a desperate desire to live. Cortez roared, but she could hear that he was fighting with Justin. He couldn't get to her. Wouldn't be able to help her. There was too much action, too many snarling, leaping animals everywhere. All she could do was hang onto the railing like a useless weakling and wait to be killed.

I can't rescue anyone anymore, Haley.

Suddenly, another bear was there, big, with a black

coat but still clearly a grizzly to judge from the silver-tipped fur and huge hump of his shoulders. He thundered over the bridge past her, meeting the oncoming cat in an explosion of sound as the enormous bodies slammed into one another at full speed. The bear growled with rage, shaking the cat by the scruff of its neck, retreating back when the screeching feline twisted around to sink its claws into the bear. Then the bear rose to his hind legs and simply dove at the cat, meeting it in a terrifying embrace of snapping jaws, hideous snarls, enormous claws that raked at one another. He managed to slice the cat open with his jaws, right on the hindquarters. The cat shrieked, then rolled over, flopping as it tried to get away. Its hind legs were half dragging as it scuttled off, badly limping and bleeding.

The bear roared after the cat, then turned and looked briefly at Haley. Shocked, she recognized the haunted eyes. Riley. It was Riley, Cortez's angry, grief-stricken brother. He nodded sharply at her, then went tearing off to engage another enemy in battle.

Even if he didn't fully trust her, she was part of his family, his bear clan, and that meant something to him. He had just saved Haley's life without even thinking about his own safety.

Overhead, Pix shrieked again, then went into a torpedoing dive towards the earth. She grabbed one of the cats, which snarled in rage and tried to claw her exposed belly. But Pix simply tossed the cat into the woods, where it slammed against a tree and slid limply to the bottom.

Another huge bear roared from behind her, the same side Cortez had come from. Haley whipped her gaze that way. He came charging up, trying to help Cortez. Maybe that was Beckett? Whoever it was, he was a friend. Okay. Friends were here.

Her mind tripped and crashed over itself, trying to make sense of everything, trying to figure out how she could help too. She had to help them! She had to help Cortez.

On the other side of her, the fiercely brawling Shane and one of the enemy cats rolled and flipped and roared, so close to her she could feel their hot breath as their lethal jaws snapped at one another. She shied away in instinctive terror. Help them? Hardly. She, the weak link here, could too easily get killed. Swinging her head around, she looked wildly for an escape route. But there was nowhere to go. She was trapped.

Quickly, she climbed over the side of the bridge and hung onto it over the creek, her arms wrapped tightly around the top railing as her feet tried to find purchase. If she slipped, she'd fall into the icy river and maybe drown or get sucked under the ice. Oh, that sounded bad. Very bad. Terror made her arms grip like steel to the bridge. She started shivering from both fear and cold.

"Haley!" came a shriek from the good side of the

creek. It was Jessie, jumping up and down and waving at her. "Hold on! We'll get you!"

How? Another bear loomed menacingly near Jessie, clearly meant to defend her while also clearly wanting to jump into the fray on the bridge.

Well, it was great that they wanted to help her, but unless they planned to leap into the river and have her ride one of them out of there, she didn't see how that would happen. Clearly the same thing was going through Jessie's mind, because she looked both helpless and freaked out as she stood there, watching the attack. Just as human as Haley, just as helpless against them. And with one bear guarding her, that was one less who could help fight the intruders. Who were they, anyway?

Somehow, Haley knew it all hinged on Justin. Justin, the fucking psycho bastard who'd already ruined her life. And now he was trying to ruin not only her new life, but the lives of her friends, both new and old. Damn it, she couldn't let that happen.

She *wouldn't* let it happen.

Overhead, Pix bellowed again, the sound echoed by the enraged screech of what sounded like a hawk. Haley looked up. Yes, a hawk flew up there, much larger than any regular one. It dove toward one of the cats, a whistling scream tearing out of it, raising goose-bumps on Haley's skin. Definitely a friend, and someone good to have on their side, even if she didn't know who it was. It seemed that the local bear clan had a lot of allies here.

Looking back at Jessie, Haley gasped and shouted. "Jessie! Behind you!"

An enormous mountain lion was running behind them, straight for Jessie and the bear with her. Jessie whirled around, but instantly relaxed. She looked back at Haley and yelled, "It's okay! He's a friend!"

Haley gave up trying to figure out who was friend and who was foe. Clearly not all cats were bad. And clearly, she thought grimly as she looked to the side where the cats mostly were, there were bad bears and wolves as well.

Beside her, Justin and Cortez battled closer, Justin trying to get past Cortez to reach Haley. Cortez attacked him ferociously, roaring and yelling. His head whipped once to look at Haley, a frustrated bellow shaking out of him as he turned back to Justin. Her heart swelled immensely. Cortez was here for her. Trying to save her. Trying to rescue her. She'd sworn to herself that she would protect him too, though she didn't know how. Unless...

Unless she chose to join as one of them and fight alongside her mate and his bear clan.

Unless she chose to become a bear.

She made up her mind before she even stopped thinking the thought.

"Cortez!" She pitched her yell loud enough to be heard above the battle of all these incredible, huge creatures around her. "Turn me. Turn me!"

Cortez's huge head swiveled toward her, his bright

golden eyes catching hers. She nodded firmly, frantically. Then she said it again in a whisper, enunciating the words one at a time. "I want this. Turn. Me."

A soft noise left his throat. He had heard her and understood.

Unfortunately, so had Justin. With the eerie mountain lion scream that sent Haley's stomach into knots, Justin yanked himself away from Cortez and launched for her, his mouth ripped back in a snarl, those giant teeth coming for her. Haley gasped, reflexively yanking herself backward, almost losing her grip on the bridge railing. Cortez bellowed with rage. He moved quickly, so very quickly for such a huge, magnificent creature. One bound and he was on Justin, bringing the cat to the ground, both of them snapping, snarling.

Suddenly, a dragon scream tore through the sky above them again, this time so close the blast of it made every shifter fighting on the bridge startle. Pix swooped low over the bridge, one leg with its razor-sharp claws on the end extended. Haley held her breath. The trees were close to the bank here, too close for a dragon the size of Pix, who was enormous compared to her tiny human self. Her wings were pinioned back along her sides as she swooped through, her eyes a glaring, brilliant green. As she raced over the center of the bridge, she reached out her foot and neatly whacked Justin's chest and shoulder, sending him spinning and toppling out of the way. Instantly, another bear leapt on him, fighting and hanging on with desperate fury to keep Justin from getting up again to stop Cortez. Haley thought it might be Quentin but she honestly didn't know.

In half a heartbeat, Cortez was in front of her, his enormous golden brown face and huge snout inches from her. Even in this form, she could see the question in his eyes. She nodded again, awkwardly clambering over the bridge and stumble-falling into him. "Turn me! It's the only way I can help. And I want this, Cortez. I've always wanted to be a shifter ever since I was a little girl. I thought I wanted to be a dragon, but no. That's not it for me. I trust you, Cortez." She caught his big, fuzzy face between her hands, simultaneously aware of how soft his fur was and how enormous his body was, whispering now. "You're my mate, aren't you? Turn me into a grizzly bear. Just like you."

Her strong, powerful mate didn't wait another second. His mouth opened, exposing his big, alarming teeth. Haley couldn't help her instinctive nervous gasp, but she tilted her head and exposed her neck for him. Squeezing her eyes shut, she hoped that being turned into a bear didn't involve severing an artery at the same time.

There was the faint scrape of something hard and rough against her neck. A tooth, running down the side of it. His touch was gentle, though it stung against her skin. Was he actually piercing it? He stayed there for a few seconds, blowing hot breath on her, then moved his mouth down until the tooth gently bounced over her collarbone. Then he pulled back.

Haley opened her eyes, looking at him. He looked back at her, blinking, huffing softly at her. With shaking fingers, she reached up to her neck. It felt wet. When she pulled her hand away to look at it, blood was streaked on it, but not a lot. He'd just barely grazed her.

Cortez was so damn gentle with her, even in his big huge bear self.

She opened her mouth to say something, though she didn't even know what. Maybe thank you.

Before she could, Cortez was abruptly yanked backward, bellowing as he went.

"No!" she shrieked. Justin again, that fucking bastard. He somehow had gotten away from the other bear holding him and leaped onto Cortez's back, his claws buried into her mate's hide, his teeth bearing down on Cortez's neck. Cortez gave a mighty shake, again and again, trying desperately to dislodge the enemy from his back. But Justin held on tight.

Haley saw red.

She.

Saw.

Red.

That was her man. Her mate. Her Cortez. Being attacked by the insane, sick bastard who had tried to ruin her life. In trying to save Haley, Cortez might die from the effort. No way. No damned way would she let that happen.

Now it was her turn to rescue him.

"Cortez!" she cried out, but her breath was stolen.

Excruciating pain crackled through her entire body as it suddenly seemed possessed. She shrieked and flung her head backward as bolts of pain and agony flashed over her. Bones cracked, broke, lengthened, shortened. Her entire body seemed to collapse and expand at once, sending white-hot shards of agony pulsing throughout her. Haley cracked and ripped open, and

She.

Became.

A.

Bear.

Her bear, a beautiful, huge golden-brown beast. Strong, enormous, powerful. Ready to defend what was hers from the enemy. Ready and more than able to stand up for herself and claim her place here, with her friends. Her new clan.

Her home.

Haley opened her mouth and bellowed out her call, roaring out the amazing truth of her existence to the wild battle going on around her. In almost instant response, other wild throats answered her, bellowing, roaring, howling in excited response. Her family.

She swung her huge head around, searching. Where was her mate?

There. Locked in battle with a monster.

She lunged toward Cortez and Justin, almost immediately falling on her face as limbs she didn't know how to use wouldn't obey her still halfway human thoughts.

Bear, she ordered herself in a fury of anxiety. *You are bear!*

She tried again, relaxing into this body and letting instinct take over. Yes! There it was. She could control her limbs now.

Charging forward, she managed to grab Justin's long, skinny tail with her mouth. She sank her enormous teeth into it. He ripped his fangs out of Cortez's neck and shrieked. Reaching one huge paw up over him, she gashed him across his ass, which seemed as scrawny in this form as it ever had been in his human form. He yowled in pain, his scream echoing over the woods. With a savage kick out at her, he dislodged another point of contact with Cortez's back.

It was all Cortez needed. He roared and bucked upward again, managing to get onto his hind legs and fling Justin off him, even though Justin's fierce claws left enormous gouges, tearing out chunks of fur and flesh on the way. In a flash, Cortez rounded on Justin, tremendous snarls rattling his entire body. Haley instinctively knew what he was telling Justin.

She has chosen me. I have chosen her. My mate. You will never have her.

Justin rolled after he hit the base of the bridge, immediately launching himself back, his teeth and claws extended to kill. Haley rushed toward him at the same time as Cortez did, although her mate reached him first.

Swiftly, much too quickly and more mercifully than the insane bastard deserved, Cortez broke Justin's neck.

At the other end of the bridge, by the woods, a female lion screamed, a keening yowl of grief.

It was over.

Pix's circling and calling out overhead had attracted the attention of every shifter in town, even if visiting humans couldn't see or hear her. But everyone who could, all the local shifters, had come flooding in to help. Haley, still half dazed with shock and excitement and adrenaline, looked around.

More grizzlies. More mountain lions, friends. Wolves, coyotes, foxes. Huge birds of prey, including giant golden eagles and bald eagles. Lynx, bobcats. She watched, stunned and thrilled, as a wave of shifters came to help subdue the remaining enemies.

None of the attacking others were killed, but simply held down and forced to shift back to human shapes, in which they were essentially powerless against those still in their animal form. Although several got away, the twenty or so of them who were captured quickly gave up, including the female mountain lion who had screamed when Cortez killed Justin. Haley realized she must be the woman Justin had left her for. Marisa. Now in her human form, huddled on the ground, sobbing, the woman seemed innocuous and harmless.

Haley honestly felt sorry for her. She probably had been taken in by Justin's shit as well. He had used her just like he used everyone. Haley had no quarrel with her.

One of the bears shifted back into human. Shane, buck naked, who strode over to Jessie on the bank and grabbed her up in a giant hug. Haley harumphed a bear-sized snort at his nakedness. Seeing naked humans from her bear form was pretty funny, actually.

"Babe," Shane said to Jessie, turning to gesture at Haley. "What do you think? You ready to get turned into a bear too?"

Jessie didn't pause even for a moment. "Uh-huh. I'm in. Because that was seriously the most badass thing I've ever seen. I'm ready. Haley!" she called out, her voice shaking yet overjoyed. "You kicked some serious ass. You're amazing!"

Haley whoofed back at her friend, still pumped up by the crazy rush of the battle. By the crazy rush of being a freaking *bear*. Hell yeah, it was amazing.

Overhead, Pix screamed, a long, triumphant cry that rang through the dull sky, somehow making it seem vibrant and bright. She dipped her silver wings at Haley, who lifted her mighty snout and roared back a booming cry of acknowledgement, a heartfelt *thank you.*

Her friends. They were all her friends, her fellow shifters, her community. And they were welcoming her into theirs.

Something big and warm and strong bumped up against her, firmly pressing into her side. She swung around to sniff. It was Cortez, bloody but alive. She whuffled with joy. He checked her everywhere, snuffling over her, assuring himself she wasn't hurt. She rumbled a funny huffing noise from her chest, rubbing her head against his, shoving her face into his huge shoulder.

She wasn't hurt. He wasn't hurt. She was here, with him, her friends, her family, her clan. She was just completely fine.

Just like her sexy, stunning, protective mate. Cortez.

17

*C*ortez looked into Haley's eyes, their beautiful green now shot through with the bright gleam of the magnificent bear she had inside her. She blinked sleepily at him. Damn, she was so beautiful. Even when wearing her favorite purple T-shirt that she liked to sleep in. The one that said in big white letters, *I wish I was a unicorn (so I could stab idiots with my head)*, with a simple drawing of a unicorn charging, head down, sharp horn pointed out apparently to stab all the idiots. Yeah, that was his woman. For sure. Haley was a keeper, wild hair, ratty orange bathrobe, crazy huge work ethic, and all.

His glorious, strong woman. Yeah, he liked that. A lot.

She blinked at him again, then rubbed her eyes and yawned. "You're staring at me."

"Because I still can hardly believe I get to wake up

with you every day for the rest of my life. Here's your coffee," he added, gesturing toward where he'd put her mug on the bedside table. She sat up and kissed him as a thank you. He'd been doing it for her every morning that he could, even though the woman got up at dark o'clock every day to write. Except today, because she hadn't needed to.

She'd finally finished her book, sent it to the people who read it early and let her know whether or not it was good, and they'd gotten back to her last night. It was amazing, they'd gushed. A tearjerker that made them laugh and cry and wish they could be the characters in it. She'd been so ecstatic he thought she'd bounce right off the walls and float off into space.

He'd known she could do it. He didn't know shit about writing himself, and he barely ever read a book, but he knew she would knock it out of the park, because it was what she was born to do. Seeing her shine with elation when she finally really got it, finally understood, that she was good at it even without that fucking asshole ex-psycho of hers, that she was able to handle it all on her own, had made him so damned proud of her. His kickass bear shifter mate. God, how he loved her.

She sat up and cuddled the hot mug between her hands like it was the elixir of life. After a long sip, she sighed with pleasure. Then her face got serious. "So. How are they doing?"

Cortez knew who she meant. The enemy shifters

who'd attacked. The outcasts. He took a deep breath before going into it. She didn't know the half of the realities of the shifter world yet. This was quite an introduction. "Some of them took off before we could get them. They're outcasts, they have no legitimate clan or pack, so they just join up in these really messed up groups and basically make trouble. They're the criminals and thieves of our society, usually. They run drugs, operate the worst of the illegal underground fight rings, traffic women—"

She gasped at that, sloshing some of her coffee. He stroked her arm, soothing, and nodded grimly. "I know. It's despicable. Some of them are actually decent, end up finding a clan that will take them in, and they straighten out their lives. Some of them never belonged in that life, but they were born to parents who lived that way so they never had a chance to know how things could be different. Better. But the ones who are decent, who just got caught up in it, sometimes find their way out. They join clans like ours, if they can prove they'll pull their weight and be loyal. Or at least just live in a town like Deep Hollow, even if they don't affiliate with a bear clan or wolf pack, and just be good residents and not cause trouble. But I'm betting," he added grimly, "the ones who got away will never be good citizens anywhere."

Her eyes troubled, Haley slowly said, "And the ones that were caught? What happens to them?"

He shrugged. "Unless they can prove they just got

mixed up with a bad crowd and they don't want to run that way anymore, they're banned from Silvertip territory. The wolves with them, they call them rogue wolves, are also banned from the wolf pack territories near us. Mountain lions don't have tight bonds the way bears and wolves do, they tend to be more solitary, but we welcome them in town if they want to be here and won't cause trouble."

"Unlike the ones who turned and took in *him*." She didn't have to say the name of her ex for Cortez to know who she meant.

Cortez sighed. "That lion shifter, Marisa or whatever, it sounds like she was just following the leader's orders. He's an asshat, according to her. He got away. But she might end up staying here. Abby got all mother hen with her when she realized the girl's pretty messed up and basically was a pawn for the leader and his cronies. As for your ex," Cortez's lip curled again in anger, "he was already nuts. But he went totally ballistic because of how he was turned."

Haley stared at him. He hadn't told her this part yet, since she'd had enough to deal with just being a new bear shifter along with everything else. He'd spent the last week with her since the battle just showing her how to control her bear.

He sighed. "They weren't mates. She was forced to turn him, even though she thought she loved him. But he was just using her too."

His beautiful, kind mate made such a sound of

compassion that his heart thumped. She was merciful, and sweet. He probably had a lot to learn from her in that department. "Humans that aren't turned by a shifter who's their mate," he went on, "can have really bad reactions. He had no constraints on him, no inhibitions, and no ties to a mate to keep him grounded while he got used to having an animal side. It's very easy for someone turned like that to go totally mad, eventually becoming completely feral. They can be extremely dangerous. Sounds like the outcast leader wanted that. He's got some sort of group of crazy shifters who do a ton of really bad shit."

Haley shuddered. "That's so awful," she whispered. "I had no idea the shifter world could be this brutal. Pix never mentioned this kind of stuff."

He shrugged. "Dragons are really different. They've got their own shit, but not like most other shifters. Anyway." He kissed the top of her head. "That slave driver, Quentin, called me into the lodge. I gotta head up there and see what bee is in his bonnet now. You sleep in more. You deserve it."

As if to punctuate his point, another huge yawn gripped her. He laughed, then so did she. "Love you, babe," he whispered, leaning in for a proper kiss. "I'll be back soon."

"Mm-kay," she murmured, already settling back into the pillows. "Love you too."

He held the image of her sleeping securely in his bed as he left and drove up to the lodge. Once he got there, Cortez strode into Quentin's office like he was storming the castle. Despite his casual face about it to Haley, he wasn't sure why the hell his brother had called him up here early in the morning. He hadn't been back at work since the attack, spending his time with Haley. He was scheduled to go back to work tomorrow. But whatever this was about, he'd face it.

His brother sat at his desk, frowning at a computer screen. He stood up when Cortez came in, walking around to the front of his desk and leaning on it. A long moment passed in silence as each sized the other up.

Finally, Quentin tossed something at Cortez. He reached out by reflex and caught it. Huh. One of the lodge's cell phones. He gave his brother a questioning look.

"I know yours got destroyed in the snow during the fight," Quentin said. "This one's temporary until you can get a new one."

That was weird. Cortez often had lost or trashed phones by being careless with them. Quentin sure as hell had never offered him a loaner before. But he nodded anyway. It had been a pain in the ass the last few days since the fight without a phone.

"People have been texting your old phone, you know," Quentin added. "When they couldn't reach you, some of them finally got ahold of me instead and asked me to pass information on to you."

"What kind of information?"

"The kind," his brother said in an even tone, "that you want to hear. The kind you *need* to hear."

Cortez narrowed his eyes. That didn't sound good. But Quentin's next words rocked him.

"Tim woke up." Quentin looked at him with a steady gaze as he spoke. "He came out of his coma, and he's going to be okay. Still has a really long road to recovery, but he will actually recover. And Scott is going triple-time on his exercises with his prosthetic leg. Says he's moving back here as soon as he has a better handle on it, and he might even try to join up with the SAR team again. They're going to be fine, Cortez." Quentin's voice was firm. "They're going to be fine."

Another silence. Cortez wrestled with the enormous feelings surging inside him. Shock. Joy. Relief. Then, resolve. His vulnerable human friends might have survived his carelessness, but he still had to face his own shortcomings.

He looked his brother right in the eye. "Okay. That's good. It's fucking fantastic. But right now, you need to let me have it. I fucked up here at work. I know I did, and I own it. This is a business, not a charity program for family. Discipline me like you would any employee. That's why I'm here, right?"

Quentin looked at him for a long moment, hands shoved in his back pockets, his mouth twisted one way and his eyebrows twisted the other. Skeptical. Finally, he shook his head. "Cortez. Tell me why you think you fucked up. Why you think you need disciplinary action."

Cortez stood straight, unmoving. "Because some of those reviews and complaints were legitimate. I did have an attitude sometimes, even though I tried to cover it up. Sometimes I was a little short with some of the guests. I didn't give the tours my all. I was," he paused for a moment. Shit, he hated having to go deep like this with his own brother. Then again, this was his own brother. If he didn't go deep with his family, who else? "I was stuck in my head ever since the avalanche. I was letting what happened hold me back. I didn't really take the guests out to have more than easy-peasy casual fun, because I was afraid I'd lead them into danger and they'd get hurt. I was distant with them because I didn't want to really get to know anyone else ever since the accident."

Then he admitted the hardest thing. "I was scared. I was scared of hurting someone else, then getting hurt myself. Okay. There you have it. That's it."

He punched out the last words fast, folding his arms over his chest. He knew he was assuming a defensive pose, but dammit, he'd just given as much as he could. He could share things like this with Haley, but she was also the most precious, incredible, and overall best thing that had ever happened to him. Getting emotional with another guy, even family, went against the man code or something.

To his surprise, a slow smile rolled over Quentin's

face. His brother nodded. He seemed satisfied. "Yeah, I know all that. And I knew you knew it too. But some of the complaints were total bullshit, Cortez. They admitted to it, those shitbag outcasts. Haley's ex and the leader of the outcasts were behind it. Haley's ex figured out she was here and that she was with you. So he got some of the cats to go on tours with you, then make fake complaints." Quentin's eyes were dark with anger. "You know how outcasts are. They like to fuck with the rest of us if they can, because they're just like that. Rejects, angry, hopeless. Probably jealous that we have real clan, real family, when they don't."

Cortez felt hot anger seep through him again. If he hadn't already killed that psycho prick ex of Haley's, he'd happily kill him all over again right now.

Quentin shook his head. "We forced them to remove their complaints from all the online sites. That's done. So. Moving on." He cleared his throat, his eyes suddenly gleaming. "I didn't call you up here for disciplinary action, you big lug."

Now it was Cortez's turn to give his brother the raised eyebrow look. "No? Then what the hell was so important that you made me come all the way up here early in the morning, dragging me out of bed with my girl?"

Quentin smiled again. "She is that, isn't she. Your girl?"

Cortez nodded instantly. "Hell yeah. My girl, and

my mate. Also the most fucking badass newly turned bear shifter I've ever seen."

"She is that too. Glad to have her. I watched her help you figure out your stuff and change, Cortez. She brought you back from that dark. And," Quentin eyed him with a shrewd look, "she helped you calm your bear just when you were starting to really struggle."

Cortez stared. "I didn't think anyone knew."

His brother snorted. "We knew. We were keeping an eye on you. And because I knew you were struggling, I was pushing you so much to do a better job." He paused. "I was wrong about that."

Cortez unfolded his arms. "Wait a minute. Run that by me again? Let me turn on the record button on my new phone so I can have proof that you just said you were wrong about something."

"Ah, shut it." But Quentin was still smiling. "The reason I dragged you out of bed with your new mate is because the Silvertip Lodge has a formal offer for you."

"A say what now?" The way his brother said the Silvertip Lodge, Cortez immediately knew it was something cleared with the owners of the lodge: Their vacationing parents.

"A formal offer." Quentin's voice became businesslike. "We want you to be the director of activities. You'll keep your Tooth 'n Claw tours. Money that comes in from it is yours. But we want you to set things up specifically for lodge clients. Multi-day trips, specialty outings, whatever they want. The plan is to expand on what the lodge is offering, while still keeping the down-home feel that everyone likes so much. You're the best man for the job, Cortez." Quentin blew a breath out of the side of his mouth. "You would've been offered a position a long time ago, but you're always so damn independent. You didn't really want to be involved full-time. But this is your business too, brother. It's family. So." Quentin gave him a querying look. "Full-time, benefits, salary. Everyone really wants you to be a bigger part of it. If that's what you want."

Cortez stayed still for a long time, working his jaw as he digested what Quentin had said. Full-time. He'd be busy. Really busy. He'd be working a lot. Long, hard hours. But he'd be working while having fun, taking other people out to have fun. He'd have enough money to finish the cabin in style. To treat Haley like she deserved. Not that she needed his help, of course. He knew her book was gonna kick ass and she was gonna make good money. But he wanted to bring something real to the table. And now he could.

This offer wasn't an afterthought or a condolence gift. No, it was the real deal. The only people ever hired at the lodge were those who could really pull their weight. Family was involved only if they really wanted to *and* if they really proved they would work hard.

Was he really ready for this? Was this what he wanted?

Softly, as if he could sense the battle going on in his

brother's mind, Quentin said, "Cortez. You're a fighter, not a fuckup. You've never been a fuckup. You just weren't sure what you wanted. But you always come out on the right side. You're a decent person. You're the real deal, Cortez Walker, and I'm fucking proud to call you my brother."

Quentin reached over and pulled him into a hug, holding him tight for a long minute. Cortez furiously blinked his eyes against the prickling there. Dammit. He mumbled against his brother's shoulder, "Thank you." Then he stepped back and cleared his throat. "Yes, I'll take that job. I'll be the best activities director the lodge has ever had."

Quentin tried to shove down a grin but didn't quite manage. "We've never had an activities director at the lodge."

"See? Then I'll definitely be the best one ever."

First Quentin, then Cortez busted up laughing. They laughed for a long time, and it felt pretty damned good.

Okay. This was his home, and now this was his new role in it. It felt awesome. It'd be a new chapter in his life, but with his sexy, sweet mate at his side and his clan at his back, it was going to be a good one.

He was damn well going to make sure of it, every kickass day of the rest of his life.

EPILOGUE

*H*aley thought her face might break from smiling so much, but she couldn't help it. Aside from sex with Cortez (super awesome), knowing that he was the most phenomenal man in the world (totally, definitely phenomenal), the fact that he was hers (freaking amazing), and after being turned into a bear shifter so she now was completely strong and badass and fearless (holy wow amazeballs amazing), this moment right now was by far the most magical thing that had ever happened to her in her life.

A nighttime sleigh ride under the big starry sky with her mate.

The bells softly jingled in the night air, the sleigh runners making a soft swishing noise as they slipped through the snow. Cortez gently clucked to the horses, lifting one of the long leather reins and gently slapping it. Overhead, the dark sky dazzled with a bazillion bright stars on this moonless, totally clear night. She snuggled down deeper under the blanket and into Cortez's side.

"It's so dark. Can they see well enough? Do they know where they're going?"

He chuckled. "We run this track often enough. They know exactly where they are. Plus we've got just enough light so they can see what they need to, and me too." Pretty lights were attached on either side of the sleigh, beaming ahead in front of the horses and down to the sides.

"This is the most magical thing in the world." Haley whispered the words, knowing Cortez could hear them no matter how low her voice, not wanting to break the enchanting quiet more than she had to.

He leaned over to brush a kiss on top of her bare head. Another awesome thing about being a bear shifter was that she didn't get as cold anymore. She didn't have to wear a hat in this weather if she didn't want to. While it wasn't exactly like she could wear a bikini out here, she wasn't as completely bundled up as she would've been back when she was human.

"Gee up there, King Lear. Let's go now, Paxton." Cortez clucked to the horses. They smoothly picked up the pace, their hooves trotting quietly on the snow, occasional snorts decorating the air. Haley felt so happy she thought she might burst. This night was perfect, this place was perfect, this man was perfect, and everything in her life had turned around a hundred and eighty degrees like a beautiful miracle. "Would you pinch me?"

Cortez gave her a startled look, his face half visible in the sleigh's lights and the starlight. "Come again? Is this some kind of foreplay that you haven't told me about yet? Cuz I'm in if it is, but tell me more." He grinned.

She laughed and shook her head. "No. I just want to make sure I'm not dreaming. That this is really real."

"Haley, beautiful woman. This is as real as it gets." His voice wrapped around her, as warm and cozy as the blanket. She sighed in contentment, snuggling in closer to him.

"Are you going to tell me where you're taking me this time?" Cortez had been showing her all his favorite spots on the mountain since they first met. But this was the first time they'd managed to go on a sleigh ride. She'd had no idea it could be done at night. He said it was a very special trip, reserved only for the most special people. Which meant he was probably cheese-balling her, but she liked the thought of it anyway.

"Almost there. I promise you'll like it."

"I believe you," she said softly.

He was right. In just a few more minutes, they passed around the edge of the trees. The horses trotted up a gentle hill. Cortez pulled them up at the top, which was flattened. Spread out in front of them was the most stunning view of Deep Hollow at night. Haley gasped. It was so beautiful, the little town tucked down there in the darkness, lights twinkling cheerfully, surrounded by these big mountains. "Home," she murmured, overwhelmed by that certain truth.

"Yeah. Our home." Pride rang through his voice.

Haley was officially still housesitting, and still would be until the elder Walkers returned later this year, but Cortez spent most nights with her. Sometimes she stayed at his little place in town, but she knew his cabin would be done sooner than later. He'd started working feverishly on it, with a renewed vigor that she knew came from everything. From his friends in the accident being able to move on with their lives, from her being turned into a bear shifter, from the entire community pulling together even more closely after the trauma of her insane ex and the dangerous, misguided shifters he'd gotten himself involved with and brought to their peaceful town.

Most of all, Cortez was fulfilled with his new job at the lodge. She'd known that he could do anything he put his mind to, even if he didn't believe it. But seeing him absolutely shine in his new position took her breath away with how proud she was of him.

"Oh yeah," he added, very casually. "I think I'll join the search and rescue team again. They told me they'd kept a spot open for me, but I knew I wasn't ready. Now, though," he squeezed her hand, raised it to his mouth for a soft kiss, "I am."

Her heart pounding with pride and joy, she held his hand tightly while they looked down at the lights below. "I told you that you were worth rescuing, Cortez."

"You can't rescue me, Haley." His voice was so low it was more like vibration than sound. "No one can."

Haley's heart squeezed, exploded into beating, squeezed again. Breathless, aching, she choked out, "What? I refuse to believe that! You're not beyond saving."

He shook his head and reached his other hand out to catch up both of hers. Holding them close, his palms against hers, his fingers gently stroked her hands. "That's not what I meant. I mean that I'm the only one who can rescue me. I can't rescue you either, Haley. No matter how much I want to. Because I know that you're the only one who can rescue yourself. And you have the strength to do it," he added firmly, smiling gently at her.

Haley couldn't get any words out as she stared at him, the serious expression on his face at odds with the surge of hope in his eyes. "Then I don't completely understand what you mean," she said cautiously.

His teeth gleamed softly in the low light as he smiled. "I can only save myself, and you can only save yourself." Another tight, loving press on her hands. "What I'm hoping is that we can do that together. Side by side. I give you strength, and you give me strength. We'll battle our respective shit together, anything else that comes up." He took a breath, still smiling at her. "I'm with you every step of the way as you rescue yourself, just like you're with me every step of the way as I rescue myself."

He leaned over to brush his lips over hers, then murmured against her mouth. "You and me together, Haley. I believe in the power of us. Mates."

Tears welled in her eyes, spilled over. Her throat was so tight, her chest full, her body overwhelmed by the astonishing joy that ripped through her. She managed to choke out, "So do I," before the tears just flowed out of her eyes like someone had turned on a tap.

He swallowed and muttered, "Ah, hell, woman, you're gonna make me get all mushy too." But his face shone with that sexy smile, the sort of pure joy that was once-in-a-lifetime brilliant. "I love you, Haley."

"I love you too, Cortez," she whispered back, tears running freely down her smiling face. Then she laughed and flung her arms around him, kissing him with all her strength as he kissed her back with all of his strength.

Mates. Joyful and together always with their once-in-a-lifetime, forever love.

The End

Thank you so much for reading *Rescue Bear*! I adored

writing about Cortez & Haley's journey to love and self-acceptance.

What's next for the Silvertip Shifters? Riley & Marisa's story in ***RANGER BEAR: RILEY***. Turn the page for an excerpt.

EXCERPT FROM RANGER BEAR: RILEY

CHAPTER 1

The sickening crack of a rifle shot split open the night, its echo booming through the sky.

"Mama!" The agonized little shriek sliced through Riley's head.

"No!" He sat bolt upright in bed. Leaping out of it in one move, heart walloping in his chest, he landed on his feet with a heavy thud.

Gasping for breath, coated in sweat, he looked around wild-eyed. His bear slammed around inside his head, snarling, fully alert and ready to defend his home.

Silence greeted him. Soft, peaceful quiet.

Riley blinked as awareness slowly surfaced. He was safe in his room, surrounded by the pre-dawn dim. The stillness. The calm. Through the slightly open window, a cold winter breeze whispered. For several long seconds, he stayed motionless, listening for any sounds of danger. He heard only his own harsh breathing.

Finally, he swiped his hand over his eyes, hard, clenching his teeth over a groan.

A nightmare.

A nightmare about something he had never actually heard or seen. A nightmare he hadn't had for a long time. For many years, it had haunted him daily before it faded to a less insistent horror. But the past few months had brought it back with alarming frequency and intensity.

After another long moment in which he thoroughly steadied his breathing, he turned to a chest of drawers against the far wall and yanked one open with unnecessary force. Shoving his hand in and coming out with a pair of loose black workout pants, he pulled them on.

Feet still bare, he padded quietly out into the hallway, heading down to Finn and Laney's rooms. His ears still rang with both the gunshot and the growled cry of his own voice. Afraid he'd actually yelled out loud, he wanted to be sure he hadn't woken his children.

Carefully opening the door to Finn's room and tucking his head around it to look in, relief instantly blanketed him as he saw his son. Finn had kicked off most of his covers, as usual. He was sprawled on the bed, facedown with his head turned to one side, looking like some sort of giant starfish. His quiet, even breathing filled the room in the cadence of peaceful sleep. Smiling faintly, Riley gently closed the door and went to Laney's room.

His daughter was securely snuggled under her comforter, sleeping on her side with one arm flung out, both legs scissored forward at the hips as if she were sleeping mid-stretch. Her face in the early morning light, peaceful as she very gently snored, looked so much like her mother's that Riley's jaw tightened. His heart exploded with love for both his children as it did each time he saw them like this: vulnerable. Targeted for death by some people in this world simply for being different.

Merely because they were shifters, just like their murdered mother.

Soundlessly shutting his daughter's door, Riley exhaled a slow breath as he went downstairs, shoving away the ancient fears. He needed to focus on the here and now. Right now, he needed to work out. Right now, he needed to break a sweat. Right now, he needed to get himself back into balance.

The workout room at the back of the cabin he and his children called home, the small but impressive place he had built by hand years ago, wasn't a gym in the traditional sense. It held only a large mat and was bordered by the floor-to-ceiling window on the east end that looked out over the San Juan Mountains into which the cabin nestled deeply.

Not bothering to turn on the light since the sun would be fully up not too long from now, and also because Riley's eyesight was much sharper than any pure human's, he walked to the center of the mat and stood for many seconds with his head bowed, his arms down along his sides, his bare feet firmly planted. He took a long, deep breath, trying to inhale peace and balance and certainty. Then, he exhaled a long breath out, expelling the rage and unsettled feeling the nightmare had left him with. Again and again he practiced his breathing, focusing solely on his body, on this moment.

His bear whispered inside him, just as present and just as soothed by Riley's actions. It was a serenity Riley had worked on for years now. It was a tentative one, held together only by relentless practice and grasping at hope.

"If you don't do something, your bear's going to rip you apart, Ri." The long-ago wisdom of his best friend, Joe, whispered in his mind. "Find something before that happens."

He had. It had taken a long time and a lot of painful figuring out, but finally he'd settled on something that seemed to help. He'd taken up aikido in the hopes it would help settle the seemingly endless rage and grief over his mate, the mother of his cubs, the only woman he had ever loved, having been ripped from their lives. It took the edge off the restlessness, the rage, so he kept it up for years. Not only for his sake, but for that of his children. They deserved to have a father who wasn't completely driven by grief.

They deserved to have a father who wouldn't also be ripped away from them simply because he couldn't hold it together.

For his bear's sake, he kept his job as a backcountry ranger in the mountains. It gave him a lot of alone time roaming through the wild lands, often in his animal form. That time was pure necessity for his soundness of mind, and it grew more essential with each passing day.

His practice, his job, and the daily needs of his two children often seemed to be the only things keeping Riley Walker on this side of sanity, and he damn well knew it.

"Good job, boss," he murmured to himself. "Good job, bear."

Quietly, he snorted. Good thing no one was around to hear him talking to himself. It was a kind of dumb little mantra, but he liked to say it to himself, out loud, every day.

He needed the reminder he was doing okay.

The past haunted him still, to the point he privately was afraid he'd never truly shake it. Secretly, he hated it —the constant belief no one except his immediate clan could really be trusted. He wanted to trust more than just his family, more than just those in town he knew well. Yet his instinctive suspicion of strangers remained a deep-rooted uneasiness he couldn't dispel no matter how hard he tried. He'd finally given up, accepting he would always be suspicious of those he didn't know.

Keeping his bear on this side of sanity, though—that was harder. Much harder. The giant creature he shared his body and soul with got more aggressive with each passing year, no matter what Riley did to keep a leash on that side of himself. The aikido helped, the meditation helped, the long runs in the mountains helped. But his bear was a hairsbreadth away from being totally uncontrolled. Every day, he had to work to not lose that last bit of lucid connection with his animal.

One of these days, that control would finally sever.

Riley didn't know what the fuck he would do then. Shifters with out-of-control animals had to be put down. They were far too dangerous to the human world. To the shifter world. But he could never allow that. Not when he was a father. Not while he had two children who were like his own heart walking around outside his body.

They'd lost one parent. He'd vowed on that terrible day they would never lose another.

Not today, bear, he thought grimly to himself. *Not today.*

His bear simply rumbled inside him, content at the moment with Riley's deep breathing practice and centered mind. Riley shoved away all thoughts and focused on the moment. The physical here and now.

After he finished long minutes of deep, deliberate breathing, he opened his eyes. The sound of the nightmare gunshot had finally faded away from his head, thank fuck. With relentless intensity, he began his daily aikido practice, moving from stance to stance, he and his bear flowing together through the moves. In this way, they were completely connected. Briefly, but it was there.

Thirty minutes later, covered in a sheen of sweat, he finished. Walking over to a set of cupboards against the wall, he pulled out a towel and wiped his face and neck with it. The sun had just risen, pretty orange and pink dawn colors gently flooding in through the east-facing window. Riley walked over to it, absently rubbing the towel over his sweaty head. He cocked his ears for any noise, but the house was still peacefully silent.

Being a Saturday morning, his children would easily sleep for at least another hour and a half. Since the mountains were still in the depths of winter, Finn and Laney were soundly caught by the instinctive hibernation habits that made bear shifter children exceptionally deep sleepers in the long, cold months. He snorted quietly. His kids also were like any others their age on the teetering cusp between childhood and teenagerhood. They were big fans of sleep in general.

Next to the window, he watched the sunrise with sincere appreciation for its beauty. It slowly illuminated the woods outside the window, which were still patched with snow. The landscape showed few signs of life, which tended to come late here at this high mountain altitude.

As he mentally went through his plans for the coming day, Riley suddenly froze.

In a corner of the woods visible through the window, his eyes tracked deliberate movement.

Automatically stiffening, he quickly relaxed when he recognized his brother Quentin's mate, Abby. In her wolf form, she trotted by on her morning run.

Movement behind her froze him again. When he realized what it was, he felt his face go blank as his mind suddenly churned. His bear snorted and growled deep inside him, the balance he'd gained through practice sloughing off at Riley's newly ruffled thoughts.

A female mountain lion followed like a whispered shadow behind Abby, her huge paws probably moving soundlessly over the forest floor, her movements controlled and wary. Riley sucked in a breath.

Marisa. The shifter who had dragged all the trouble here a few weeks ago. The sexy, broken, bizarrely intriguing woman he'd been unable to stop thinking about despite his utter confusion at *why.*

He watched her, his body utterly still. Humans tended to be number one on Riley's hate list, but some shifters ended up there too. He didn't know Marisa well enough to hate her, but he knew she came from bad, broken stock. That alone was enough to put her on his suspicious to-be-watched list.

Outcast shifters weren't to be trusted any more than unknown humans were.

He didn't care that she was here at the Silvertip

Lodge, protected by the Silvertip clan, which was Riley's family, and particularly mothered over by Abby. None of that meant he had to trust her.

She supposedly had been an innocent pawn in everything that had gone down less than two weeks ago, had been used and abused by the shifters she'd fallen in with merely due to the circumstances of her birth. Outcast shifters sometimes had children and raised them in the lawless life they knew. But that didn't mean she wasn't possibly faking her plight somewhat or that there wasn't actually some sort of secret plan for her to worm her way in here and pave the way for another attack. She came from the sort of shifters who were always looking for a way to grift or outright threaten anyone they came across. Upstanding citizens of the shifter world they were not.

Even so, Riley couldn't help it. The woman was flat out fascinating to him, both as her mountain lion and as a woman. As a human, she was really pretty, although she never smiled and generally looked both troubled and wary. Her prettiness could be a cover for damaged and duplicitous or cruel and evil. Riley had absolutely nothing to base it on, nothing logical anyway, as Abby had tartly pointed out to him several times.

"Seriously, Riley," his brother's mate would say, her eyes narrowed at him in warning, "you need to be nicer to her. She doesn't deserve to have you glaring at her all the time."

Softly, he humphed to himself. He shouldn't have to have a reason to doubt and distrust. He knew better than many here that this was a world of exceptional danger. Sticking to their own was the safest course.

Marisa was definitely not part of Riley's clan. She didn't belong here. She was an outsider.

Then why, damn it, did he find her so damned interesting?

His jaw tightened as he recalled how he first met her: in the massive fight to help save his brother Cortez's mate Haley during what everyone now called the bridge battle. Marisa had howled in a lion's hair-raising screech of despair when the man she'd loved had been killed. Riley had been ready to fight her, to meet the challenge he was sure she would offer in the face of her lover's death.

Instead, she just gave up then and there, collapsing into her human form and breaking down into terrible sobs that wrenched at his heart despite the bloodlust that had come with the fight to protect his family, his clan, and all the residents of the town.

Then, she had looked up at him. Her desperate whisper still haunted him. "Kill me. Please, just kill me."

Shocked, he'd refused. What the hell had happened to her, living with crazy outcast shifters, that she wanted to die? He couldn't tell if her animal was out of control, but if it was, she'd likely hide it from everyone as much as she could. Just as he did.

He still sometimes thought of how small and

broken, how vulnerable, she'd looked when Abby and a few others had gathered her up and led her away, her stumbling bare feet leaving bright red bloody tracks on the snow. He couldn't imagine ever killing someone so haunted. So clearly in need of protection. So damned beautiful despite the anguish marking her features.

As if she could hear his distrustful thoughts, could sense his memories, Marisa abruptly turned her tawny gold head toward his cabin as she padded by.

She looked right at him where he stood in the window. Her gait faltered slightly, but she didn't slow as she trotted after Abby, who hadn't noticed him. He stared, caught by the beautiful lion's smooth, if guarded, stride. Marisa gazed back at him with her golden eyes, keeping him in her sights until just before she disappeared into the woods. At the last moment, she raised her lip in a snarl at him. A warning.

Don't watch me. Don't look at me. Leave me alone.

Riley snorted to himself after she disappeared, then turned his back to stride out of the room with newly angry steps. Fine by him. He didn't want anything to do with her. Broken, fucked up outcast. Submissive lion girl, wanting to die, chickening out of everything.

He snarled. All she'd done in the week or so she'd been here was ask every strong shifter she came across to put her down. Beg them, even. She was giving up. Giving up on life.

That was something Riley couldn't accept, wouldn't ever accept. His mate had died fighting for her life.

Fighting for their cubs' lives. Fierce to the end. She *never* would have given up.

Angered to his bones about Marisa just wanting to die, and even more angry that he gave a shit about it, Riley avoided her as much as he could. Yeah, he had no problem leaving her alone. She was damaged. Hell, she was fucking defective.

His neck immediately prickled at those thoughts. *Bullshit.* He growled under his breath, earlier relaxation completely evaporated. *Fuuuck.* It was a false thought, thinking he could easily leave her alone. Worse, trying to believe she was broken so badly she was beyond any fixing. Something told him she wasn't really that far gone. Not yet.

His jaw clenched even harder as the incessant question, the one he'd been doing his best to ignore since the moment he'd first seen her, roiled through his mind yet again with explosive force.

If he didn't give a damn about the outcast Marisa, why was he utterly fascinated by the defensive, snarling lion girl who wanted only to be put down?

CHAPTER 2

*M*arisa sat where she could see everybody. She quietly observed the high-spirited activity around her, taking in every detail with a hard-won practice she'd birthed long ago from plain necessity. Every doorway, every window was within her line of sight as the bustle of shifters in here decorated the barn for some sort of event coming up. What was it again? She frowned and forced herself to focus on the right here, right now. Oh, right. Valentine's Day.

She huffed quietly to herself. Valentine's Day seemed like a clever way for businesses such as this fancy lodge just for shifters to entice money made up of hope and starry eyes from people desperate for something they thought was love.

Love didn't exist. Love was a bullshit concept made

up by those who just wanted something they could use to control others.

"Marisa!"

Without moving her head, she shifted her gaze to the tentatively smiling woman who called her name. Abby. Wolf shifter, friendly, protective. Just as watchful as Marisa, but Marisa suspected Abby's watchfulness didn't come from the same reasons hers did. Abby was happy. She had a good life. She'd probably always had a good life. Marisa didn't understand it, but she also found she didn't care because it didn't matter. Abby had the sort of life Marisa never would. *Not worth the ripped bedsheets you were born on,* the old taunt jeered at her.

Breathe. She listened to herself and took a deep breath, then another. Then she laughed, so deep inside herself only bad kitty could hear it. It was pretty damned ironic that the one simple mantra she'd used to survive her whole life was the one thing she wanted to stop forever: breathing.

Too bad none of the shifters here would answer her plea to end it. They all must be cowards.

Abby beckoned at her hopefully. "We could use an extra hand setting up. But only if you want to." Her voice was inviting but not pushy.

Even so, Marisa shook her head immediately. *No way.*

Abby's expression was understanding, if slightly disappointed. "Okay. If you change your mind, everything's over there." She gestured at the not-insignificant number of boxes and bags filled with decorations that the others were putting up around the inside of the barn.

Marisa huffed again to herself as she let her gaze sweep the building. They were decorating the place to look like candy hearts had thrown up all over it. It seemed a shame to embarrass a really nice barn this way. Well. Not just a really nice barn, but one she would bet was the fanciest in the entire state of Colorado. The stalls didn't house horses, but chairs and tables and lights and a whole lot more decorations. The floor was swept clean with no signs any equine had ever stepped a single hoof in here. Heated with fancy glowing lamps affixed to the ceilings, built from large granite blocks and heavy, carefully constructed wood, the barn screamed elegance and money.

It intimidated the shit out of her.

Not that she'd let any of them know it. But it made her feel...small. Really small, and really poor. The whole place did. She'd never in her whole life imagined something as fancy as the Silvertip Lodge could exist outside some glossy magazine in the supermarket checkout aisle. And the grocery stores she'd always shopped at never carried those kinds of magazines, anyway. Marisa Tully didn't shop at nice places and never had.

In fact, not only was this the fanciest barn she'd ever seen, this was the third fanciest place she had ever seen in her life, period. The first two fanciest she'd only seen a few weeks ago. Number one was the lodge itself, a beautiful retreat open only to shifters who came from all over the country and even the world. They came here to vacation where they could safely let their animals roam around on the private, guarded property without fear of being glimpsed by humans. The sight of the stunning main lodge building had stopped her short when Abby had gently helped her to it after the bridge battle. She'd instantly felt outclassed by the shifters who lived and worked there, the powerful Silvertip grizzly bear shifter clan that had taken her in.

Taken her prisoner was more like it, but she'd sure never thought a prison could be this nice. Or, she grudgingly admitted to herself, that prison guards could be this nice too. Even if they did refuse to put her down.

The second most beautiful, deluxe place she'd ever seen was the cabin the clan was letting her stay in while she was here. She had shyly said something to Abby about how elegant it was. Abby, bustling around getting it sorted for her the day they'd tucked her into it, had laughingly said it was a decent enough cabin, but she wished they could have put her up someplace even better. She hadn't said it unkindly or rudely. It was just matter of fact to her.

Marisa hadn't answered. There was no point in letting these shifters know she was trailer trash who'd never been anywhere better than a Denny's in her entire lifetime. If she did, they would judge her. Being judged sucked. No thanks.

But still. They were nice to her. A little wary, but nice.

She looked at Abby again, at the others so cheerfully putting up ridiculous red hearts and pink and silver streamers all over this beautiful, stupid-rich barn. Wrinkling her brow, she tried to remember their names.

Pix, the small woman who improbably enough was a dragon shifter. The tall, huge, stern-faced man who was her mate, a bear shifter. His name was...Barrett? No. Beckett. There was also Jessie, a pretty blonde with a really adorable little boy named Grant. Jessie's mate, Shane, wasn't here. He worked weekends at the lodge and was out fixing the lights in a building or something like that.

Marisa's face softened as she gazed at their little boy, who toddled all over the barn on his sturdy little bear shifter legs, covered head to toe in rainbow glitter from a bag he'd gleefully explored before any of the adults had thought to check what was inside. Children, she always liked.

The lines in her forehead intensified as she watched them all. They were just so damned freaking nice. Each one of them, even though they didn't have to be. Not to someone like her. As an outcast shifter with no clan to call her own, no group of shifters having her back anymore since the screwed-up bunch she'd been involved with had been either killed, captured, or fled after the bridge battle, she had no right to be treated well by the shifters here. The same shifters who'd been attacked by the outcasts. But that didn't seem to matter. Every single one of them had just been plain kind to her so far, with varying degrees of friendliness. Some of them looked at her oddly now and then. Occasionally worse.

She knew it was because they all thought she was insane. That she was from bad blood. They also all knew by now she wanted to be put down. She'd been asking anyone who seemed strong enough to do it. No one would. Nefarious, that stupid name the leader of the outcast group had called himself, had told her she was worthless. But even he wouldn't put her down. He'd had a use for her. Using her, like everyone else in her life ever had except Derek.

No. At the thought of her brother, she shied away. She couldn't think about him. He was going crazy just as surely as she was. He'd escaped from the bridge battle, but the same madness he fought might have taken him by now. *Dead and gone, dead and gone.*

She closed her eyes for a second and dragged in a harsh breath. Nothing good ever happened. And if it did, it never lasted.

Inside, she felt dead and broken and knew it would never end. Beautiful lodge or not, spacious little beautiful cabin of her own or not, it wasn't real for her and never would be. She wasn't the kind of person who got to have nice things and never had been.

A faint growl vibrated the back of her throat. She swallowed it down hard and opened her eyes. Her cat, the big tawny beast living inside her, was getting restless. She needed to go out soon for another run to settle the creature. Abby had taken her on a run just this morning, like she'd done every day since Marisa had been here, but it hadn't been calming. No, it had been unsettling. Nerve-ruffling.

All because of *him.*

Riley Walker. Enormous grizzly bear shifter, his coat a startling black with a silvery hump, he was also a really attractive guy in his human form. Okay, fine. A really sexy guy. But she didn't trust any guys, especially not the sexy ones. They were usually the worst of all.

He'd stared at her from the upstairs window of what must be his house as they'd jogged past just after dawn. She had felt his gaze on her, tickling at her skin. The faint sensation of something riffling through her fur, like a breeze that blew her sideways, had turned her head toward the sleek, clearly hand-built log cabin tucked into the trees up by the lodge.

Looking down at her from the window, his face was unreadable. But his eyes—oh, his eyes. Dark, flat, and cold just like they'd been that day on the bridge, they'd stared back at her. Like they were bullets and she was the target. Something in him *wanted* something from her, though hell if she knew what.

She'd automatically curled up her lip at him as she passed, warning him away. *I'm a big, bad mountain lion, boy. Don't you mess with me.*

Yeah, right. Like a huge grizzly bear would ever be scared of a kitty. But maybe he should be. Marisa's mountain lion was a crazy wildcat, a terrible beast, a brute of a killer on huge silent paws.

He'd kept staring at her until she and Abby jogged out of sight, his expression impassive. Like he had secrets as dark as hers. What secrets could he have? He was just a huge grizzly shifter with glacially cold eyes who had refused to kill her on the bridge when Justin had been killed. Justin, that stomach-curdling piece of garbage who'd tried to ruin her life in so many awful ways. She knew they all thought she'd screamed with agony when he was killed because she loved him.

They were wrong.

She'd screamed because she thought his death might release her. It didn't. She'd still been there, still trapped, still broken. It had hurt so badly, knowing the horrible truth that her nightmare would never end, that she'd just stayed crumpled on the ground in shocked despair until Abby and the others took her here to the lodge. Trying to save her.

But they couldn't save her. No one could.

So Riley also thought she was broken. Fine. She didn't care—except that with him, she did care. Dammit. Big jerk, big giant sexy shifter. It *did* matter what he thought of her. Her cat grew even more restless inside. Why? Why did she care? She didn't know him at all, and she didn't want him thinking he knew her.

As if her idiot mouth was disconnected from her rational side, Marisa suddenly called out to Abby, turning her head to look at the wolf shifter. "What's the matter with Riley? Why is he so…dark?"

The room went abruptly, awkwardly silent.

Oh, crap. Every single adult shifter in there, the five or six who'd been chattering and laughing as they worked, just froze for a minute, though at least none of them turned around to stare at her. Marisa kicked herself. Freaking great. Now they would think she was even more crazy, even more fucked up.

Suddenly, she panicked. Maybe they would think she had designs on Riley, that she was some sort of danger to him. She knew some of them *had* to think she was bad, no matter how nice they were to her face. She'd been running with a pack of outcast shifters, after all.

Outcast shifter, outcast pack, crazy girl who wanted to die. That had to be a recipe for disaster to such a freaking good clan like this one.

Abby, also frozen in the midst of taping a giant pink heart with the words WILL U BE MINE emblazoned on it to the metal bars over the side of one of the stalls, her back still to Marisa, answered in a casual if somewhat tight voice. "He lost someone important to him a long time ago. It was very hard."

Without thinking, Marisa blurted, "And he still hasn't gotten over it?" God, that wasn't fair. She'd had to get over so much, so many things, almost right as they happened. She'd never had a choice not to.

With a sudden fierceness that startled her, she deeply, desperately envied Riley's luxury in still being able to live in whatever hurt he had, to know his people loved him, that they let him live in pain and they understood it. That they still supported him, even if his eyes were scary black and dead. No one had ever given a shit about her. She could tell everyone here gave a lot of shits about Riley and his pain, whatever it was.

Riley's dark, angry voice shot out like a whip crack right behind her, startling her so badly she almost fell off the chair. "None of your damned business, lion girl. You don't get to judge me. You don't even know me. But I know you, and you're pretty fucking broken. So broken you don't even want to live anymore. So who are you to be asking questions about other people's lives?"

Marisa stumbled to her feet, nearly tangling with the chair as she whirled around to look at him. Shock warred over her skin, which goosebumped up with the suddenness of his appearance. She'd been so deep in her thoughts, so mad about the crap deal she'd been handed in this life, that for a second she'd stopped keeping an eye on all the doors into the barn and missed Riley's quiet entrance.

And oh, daaamn. Damn it, damn it. Like a kid

eyeing a favorite piece of candy, Marisa just gaped at him, as usual. She couldn't help it.

Damned sexy man. Sexy, sexy man. Even bad kitty got quiet when she saw him, watching him out of Marisa's eyes with a stillness she never seemed to have otherwise.

Riley was huge. Muscles draped over more muscles, his entire body like a honed machine ready to attack at any moment if needed. His golden-brown hair couldn't cover the darkness inside him, which bled out of him like a fury. His face, even hard with anger as it was now, was strong and drop-dead gorgeous, and she was unable to take her eyes off him. Oh, he was hot. So stupid man hot, the kind of hot that had women falling over their feet when they looked at him. Women like her, being an idiot. She wasn't an idiot. Her cat wasn't an idiot.

A growl rumbled deep inside her chest, threatening to work its way loose. Bad kitty trying to get out. Struggling, Marisa pushed her down. *No.* Not now. She ground her teeth and turned her stare at Riley into a glare to match her rising growl, to deflect the mountain lion trying to scramble out of her.

Now she was angry too. Good. Anger was good. It kept her alert and wary. He was so freaking gorgeous, and her hormones wouldn't let her forget it. Even clad in jeans and a long-sleeved button-up work shirt, very rugged hiking boots on his feet, she could tell he was ripped. His biceps pushed hard at his sleeves, and his thigh muscles strained against his jeans.

But what really got her was the heaviness in his voice. The darkness. Worse yet, she heard something that made a shiver rise along her spine, that made her cat yowl with sympathy—*sympathy?*—somewhere in the back of her head.

Broken.

It hit her so hard the breath almost whooshed out of her in a gasp. That was it. *That* was what she'd been sensing about him this past week, the thing she hadn't been able to understand. The reason she was so stupidly fascinated by him, sexy man muscles or no.

Riley Walker was broken and desperate, and his bear was barely in control.

He was hiding it under cold rage, the blank eyes that didn't share anything about him with anyone who cared to look. Marisa cast a wild glance over at Abby, who was staring at them both with alarm, and the others, who'd now turned around too. Couldn't they sense his animal was in trouble? Riley's bear was not only a beast but a savage one barely leashed.

Her cat was clawing at her to get out, to get at him.

Marisa blinked. Wait.

No. Not to get *at* him. Not to attack him or guard herself against him. But to—to run up and rub herself against him?

She couldn't stop the confusion rippling over her face.

What the hell? Bad kitty never wanted to rub up against anyone like she was a trained house cat. Never. Especially not big, dominant male shifters. She just wanted to brawl with them and show them what she was made of. She was made of vicious claws and deadly swipes and fire and brimstone spitting out of her howling mouth.

Marisa's mountain lion was just as out of control as Riley's bear. That was why she had to be put down. That, and other things Marisa didn't want to think about anymore.

"What are you glaring at, kitty cat?" Riley's voice was a challenge, the seesawing battle under it to keep his bear in check apparent to Marisa's ears. But she caught something else in there as well.

Curiosity and surprise.

Well, that made two of them.

She opened her mouth to make a retort, something, anything. Before she could say a word, the barn doors smacked open in a flurry of noise. Two kids tumbled in, laughing and shrieking with delight as they tossed snowballs at one another.

"Hey, now!" Abby said, but her tone was light. Not stern at all. "Shut the door, you wild hooligans. Don't get snow on any of the decorations." A smile busted through her voice, pure love radiating through it.

Marisa felt sudden tightness in her throat as an old memory ricocheted through her mind like a really unwelcome cannonball. *Shut the fucking door, you stupid little girl. You'd better not let any of that rain get inside here and ruin the floor. Worthless bitch.*

The room started to haze out.

Breathe.

She breathed, blinked hard, made herself focus. Focus on what? Ah. She pounced, latching her attention onto the two children. Finn and Laney. Despite herself, she softened, caught by them, feeling suddenly wistful. Kids were cute. Fun. She liked kids, always had.

The minute she'd met these two, a pair of nearly twelve-year-old twins, she'd naturally loved them like they were part of her own family, like they were a niece and nephew she adored. They'd gravitated toward her too, instantly liking her back. They showed her all around the Silvertip Lodge that was their home. Oh, they were so sweet. Silly, playful, and they didn't worry she might be a danger. She was no danger. Not to them. Never. Even bad kitty seemed to like them.

But that didn't matter. Grabbing the inside of her lip with her teeth, she worried at it. Marisa would never have children. There was a hundred percent chance she'd screw them up beyond repair. Being raised by bad seeds meant children came out as bad seeds too. She'd never inflict that sort of terrible future on a child. Especially not now.

"Dad!" Finn's voice launched across the barn, pure childlike joy in it. "Catch it if you can!"

He lobbed a snowball directly at Riley. Turning swiftly so she wouldn't miss it, Marisa witnessed the thing wash over Riley's face that always startled her, coming from the man with dead, cold eyes: softness. As he raised up a fast hand to deflect the snowball, a genuine smile suddenly crinkled up his expression, making him look less monster-like than she could have imagined. In fact, he looked positively *pleasant.*

Riley Walker, the shifter with the uncontrolled bear and some sort of dark anger everyone knew about and allowed to exist, was a loving father. It never failed to surprise her. Did his clan know he harbored a raging, angry, violent beast inside him? Did his children?

Before her perplexed mind could follow those strands, Laney caught sight of her and made a beeline straight over, a giant smile lighting up her cute little face. Oh, that girl would be a knockout when she was older. She needed someone to make sure she knew how to handle it.

"Marisa! We made tornados in a bottle at school yesterday! It was so cool! I know how to do them now. Finn and me will show you." She raced over, sliding to a stop just before Marisa. She stood there and beamed, keeping herself maybe a foot away. They'd learned unasked-for hugs were something Marisa couldn't tolerate. Not even from them, much as she wanted to.

"Finn and I," Riley automatically corrected. His face also automatically turned into a frown as he looked at Marisa. With a powerful will, she ignored it.

"What's a tornado in—" Marisa managed before

Finn turned and also bounced over, his happy grin as big as his sister's.

"Marisa, we have to show you, it's so cool! Dad, can we show her? Please?" Finn used his best begging voice, as did Laney, both of them giving their father pleading looks.

Marisa felt her cat balance quietly inside her, watching with the calm she never had except around these two children, as she waited for Riley's answer.

I hope you enjoyed this excerpt of Ranger Bear: Riley.

SILVERTIP SHIFTERS SERIES

Hunter's Moon: Quentin (*Black Mesa Wolves crossover*)
(Quentin & Abby)

Mountain Bear's Baby: Shane (Shane & Jessie)

Taming Her Bear: Beckett (Beckett & Pix)

Rescue Bear: Cortez (Cortez & Haley)

Ranger Bear: Riley (Riley & Marisa)

Firefighter Bear: Slade (Slade & Everly)

Superstar Bear: Bodhi (Bodhi & McKenna)

Christmas Night Bear: Wyatt (Wyatt & Brynna)

ABOUT J.K.

J.K. Harper lives in the rugged, gorgeous canyon country of the southwest, which is a great place to let her imagination run wild.

For more information about her books, please visit her website: www.jkharper.com.

ALSO BY J.K. HARPER

Silvertip Shifters
Hunter's Moon: Quentin (*Black Mesa Wolves crossover*)
Mountain Bear's Baby: Shane
Taming Her Bear: Beckett
Rescue Bear: Cortez
Ranger Bear: Riley
Firefighter Bear: Slade
Superstar Bear: Bodhi
Christmas Night Bear: Wyatt

Black Mesa Wolves
Guardian Wolf
Alpha Wolf
Hunting Wolf
Wild Wolf
Solstice Wolf
Christmas Wolf

New Year Wolf

Protector Wolf

Fire Wolf

Rogue Wolf

Dragon Mates

Dazzled

Thrilled

Burned

Wicked Wolf Shifters

Surrendered to the Pack: Volume 1, Episode 1

Claimed by the Pack: Volume 1, Episode 2

Taken by the Pack: Volume 1, Episode 3

Mated to the Pack: Volume 1, Episode 4

Wicked Wolf Shifters: Complete Volume 1

Ruled by the Pack: Volume 2, Episode 1

Hunted by the Pack: Volume 2, Episode 2

Destined for the Pack: Volume 2, Episode 3

Wicked Wolf Shifters: Complete Volume 2

Printed in Great Britain
by Amazon

85009060R00310